A Change
Had to Come

Also by Gwynne Forster

When Twilight Comes

Blues from Down Deep

If You Walked in My Shoes

Whatever It Takes

When You Dance with the Devil

Getting Some of Her Own

A Different Kind of Blues

A Change Had To Come

When the Sun Goes Down

Breaking the Ties that Bind

Destiny's Daughters (with Donna Hill and
Parry "EbonySatin" Brown)

Published by Kensington Publishing Corp.

A Change
Had to Come

Gwynne Forster

Kensington Publishing Corp.
http://www.kensingtonbooks.com

DAFINA BOOKS are published by

Kensington Publishing Corp.
119 West 40th Street
New York, NY 10018

All Kensington Titles, Imprints, and Distributed Lines are available at special quantity discounts for bulk purchases for sales promotion, premiums, fund-raising, educational, or institutional use. Special book excerpts or customized printings can also be created to fit specific needs. For details, write or phone the office of the Kensington special sales manager: Kensington Publishing Corp., 119 West 40th Street, New York, NY 10018, attn: Special Sales Department. Phone: 1-800-221-2647.

Dafina and the Dafina logo Reg. U.S. Pat. & TM Off.

ISBN-13: 978-0-7582-2563-4
ISBN-10: 0-7582-2563-6
First trade paperback printing: October 2009
First mass market printing: May 2016

eISBN-13: 978-0-7582-8558-4
eISBN-10: 0-7582-8558-2
Kensington Electronic Edition: May 2016

10 9 8 7 6 5 4 3 2 1

Printed in the United States of America

ACKNOWLEDGMENTS

Writing is a lonely profession. To succeed, we writers must shut out friends and family and concentrate upon the characters we are creating and the lives we are building for them. In all of this, my family and my friends are understanding, sympathetic and supportive. I cannot imagine what I would do without the love and deep caring of my family: Dr. George T. F. Acsádi, my beloved husband, and Peter F. Acsádi, my beloved stepson. And it is with deep love and affection for my dear friends, Dr. Melissa M. Freeman, Jeannetta Harris, Ingrid Kasper, Carole A. Kennedy, and Carol Joy Smith, that I acknowledge their unwavering support. Finally, I thank my fellow writers Audrey Braver, Francine Lange and Gavin Grace for their friendship and for sharing their awesome talent that always amazes me.

Chapter One

"Just let somebody try to stop me now," Leticia Langley said to herself as she read her brand new contract with First D.C. Media, Inc, the parent company of *The Journal.* "Nobody can say I got this job on my back or because I make a gorgeous cocktail-hour date. It's not exactly what I wanted, but it's a stepping stone to what I'll get. I'll show Miss High-Behind Thomas what it means to have a brain."

One month after her college graduation, nine years late, Leticia landed a job as food columnist for *The Journal,* a newspaper in Washington, D.C. Leticia's degree qualified her to write for a newspaper, but not to give advice on food. For the latter, she'd gotten her credentials working as a short order cook in third-class restaurants, waiting tables, and cooking for herself and her late father from adolescence until he passed on after an eight-year illness. However, lack of familiarity with gourmet food wouldn't hinder Leticia; she bet on her sharp mind to get her through most any problem she encountered.

One thing Leticia could not boast about was her appearance. With work and study demanding so much of her, she hadn't had time to worry about the way she looked. Indeed, she had accepted that as her lot in life. But when she went to be interviewed for employment at *The Journal,* she couldn't help noticing the fashionable women, not to speak of the smooth-looking men.

"In that group, I looked as if I were applying for a job as a scrub woman," she said to herself as she left the building that housed *The Journal.* As usual, her quick mind and her knowledge of a wide variety of topics had served her well, and she got the job. But at her graduation from Howard U, she had vowed never again to be a wallflower or the odd woman out, and she didn't like the differences between herself and the women she saw at *The Journal. Never again was anybody going to look down on her.*

She had been so proud when the dean handed her the degree and called her name, Leticia Langley, Summa Cum Laude, best in the class. But as she returned to her seat, Geraldine Thomas, a fair-skinned African American with straight hair, stuck her foot out, tripping Leticia.

"I wish I was black and had short nappy hair," Geraldine had hissed. "Maybe I'd get some of what's coming to me."

Leticia had turned to Geraldine, the classmate who she had helped with exams and term papers, and said, "You expect to get the best, don't you, Geraldine? From student representative to homecoming queen. Well, babe, you got a pretty café au lait face and silky hair, but like the straw man, you didn't get a brain. Look me up in five years, and I'll *really* make you sick."

After that day, every time she answered an ad, she thought of Geraldine, stiffened her back and kept plugging. Now she had a job, a good one, and she was on her way. At home, she looked through her closet and sucked her teeth in disgust. She couldn't say which looked worse, her clothes or her hair. After brooding for a second, she snapped her fingers.

"Nobody's going to tell me that every black woman working at that newspaper has naturally silky long hair. Nobody," she said. She looked at hers, almost too short to curl—though she'd never cut it—and shrugged. In her experience, the brothers tended to freak out over women who had hair more than eight inches long, and those females at *The Journal* knew that. "I'll give the fellows something to sweat about."

She bought a copy of the *Washington Afro-American* and, sure enough, about half of the ads had to do with hair, and most of those were for weaves. She chose a shop on Connecticut Avenue, reasoning that only a successful hairdresser could afford the address and, two days later, she sported a weave with hair below her shoulders. Staring at herself in the hairdresser's mirror, she said aloud, "What a difference a full head of hair makes. Thank God for Korean and Indonesian women."

"You sure look like a different woman," one of the hairdresser's clients said. "You look real good."

"Thanks. I hardly recognize myself, but that's exactly why I got this weave."

"Everybody's wearing them," the hairdresser said.

"Yeah," the client said, "shorten your skirt and put on some high heels, and you'll knock 'em dead going and coming."

She left the hairdresser's shop with the woman's words ringing in her ears. She needed something to wear to work, but she didn't know where to start. Browsing along Connecticut Avenue, she saw many styles and choices and realized that she didn't know what to buy.

Leticia hated to admit to her cousin, Kenyetta, that she didn't know how to dress, because even with her considerable girth, Kenyetta always managed to look great. And another thing: her cousin liked to think that she was steps ahead of Leticia. She had her own apartment, well furnished with the use of her several credit cards, and she'd had Leticia understand that she didn't like the idea of an apartment mate, and that she had to be by herself. Since Kenyetta was the only relative with whom Leticia maintained close contact, she accepted the snub and throughout her college years lived in a one-room apartment on the fourth floor of a building that had no elevator.

After Leticia got home, she called her cousin. "Hey, girl. It's a quarter to twelve. How about meeting for lunch and then going shopping? I just got a job, and I need some clothes."

"Hi. It can't be that urgent. Today's Saturday, and I haven't even done my Monday assignments."

"Use the ones you did for Monday before last, Kenyetta. I'm supposed to start at *The Journal* Monday morning, and I don't have a thing to wear."

"*The Journal*? Why didn't you say so? Let's meet at City Lights at about one o'clock. We can shop right around there. Lots of great stores near Dupont Circle and on Connecticut Avenue. And if you're gonna do some serious shopping, bring your credit cards."

Leticia agreed. As usual, Kenyetta had managed to let her know that, between the two of them, Kenyetta was the one with the smarts. She'd swallow it for now, but it wouldn't always be that way. She waited outside the restaurant to avoid the embarrassment of sitting alone at a table waiting for her cousin, who never kept appointments on time.

To her amazement, Kenyetta walked right past her, went inside and sat at a table for two. "Where are your eyes?" Leticia asked her cousin, taking her seat. "You walked right past me, and I could swear you looked me right in the eye. What's with you?"

"Leticia? Well, I'll be damned! Girl, what did you . . . oops! Is that a weave or a wig? Whatever it is, you should've been born with it."

"It's different," Leticia said, refusing to thank Kenyetta for the backhanded compliment. "I want something to eat that isn't loaded with garlic."

Kenyetta shrugged and looked toward the ceiling as if asking for help. "Then we shouldn't have come to a Chinese restaurant. Try some shrimp."

Leticia ordered the crab balls and shrimp fried rice. "I think I ought to dress more stylishly, Ken, and especially in that office. It's like a house of style."

"Not just that office. Every office is like that. You're just noticing. Let's get this straight. If you're going to buy pants that don't fit and skirts that stop halfway up your legs, I'm going back home as soon as I finish eating this pork satay."

"I must not be so bad now," Leticia said to herself, glancing at the handsome blond man seated diagonally across from her who seemed unable or unwilling to remove his gaze from her. Kenyetta turned to see who or what had Leticia's attention.

"No way, girl. You just leave that alone."

She wasn't used to having strange men admire her, and she felt like bathing herself in it. "If he was a bum, he wouldn't make me preen," Leticia said, "but that guy's rocking. Look, I love to eat dark chocolate, but I'll cook with any kind that's handy. You get my drift?" she said, looked toward the stranger and smiled. He returned the smile, and, embarrassed at her forwardness, she said to Kenyetta, "Let's get out of here."

"You remember where you came from," Kenyetta said. "This isn't Atlanta, but it's not Sweden either."

The waiter brought the check and told them to pay on the way out. When they stood to leave, Leticia's admirer stood, smiled and sat down. She smiled in return and, as she glanced to her left, her gaze landed on a handsome brother who sat alone with his gaze fixed on her. Hmm. If hair did that for a woman, what would happen if she had some decent clothes? She said as much to Kenyetta.

"Don't get carried away. They'll cool off when they find it's not real."

Leticia stopped walking and looked at her cousin. "Sometimes I think you could shoot a poor little bird."

"Why not? Some people live off 'em," Kenyetta said. "Let's go in here. If it's a Mick Burgge, it's in fashion."

Leticia bristled with annoyance, but she didn't let on. "I said I wanted something suitable for business wear. I don't want to look like a movie star on Oscar night. Those pants look nice."

"Low-slung pants are on their way out."

"Thanks," Leticia said. "I don't like them anyway. When we get through dressing me, we're going to start on you."

Kenyetta stared at her. "What's wrong with me?"

"About six dress sizes. Come on. It's getting late."

Leticia had never bought more than two items at a time, and that only rarely, but after seeing herself in a softly tailored avocado-green linen suit with a silk blouse of matching color, she warmed up to her task.

"Who would have thought you had decent legs?" Kenyetta asked, observing her cousin in a knee-length red voile dress. "Girl, you got some catching up to do."

"And believe me, I can't wait."

* * *

Kenyetta Jackson took the bus home to her apartment in a condo on Rittenhouse Street in the northwest section of Washington. It was a neat, attractive block, and the quality and condition of the building in which she lived gave notice that she was making it. She hadn't driven her blue Taurus downtown, because parking—even in garages—was at a premium on Saturdays, and she didn't feel like spending half an hour or more trying to park. She got home as darkness settled in, checked her answering machine, and realized that she wouldn't finish her lesson plans that night.

She dialed the number. "Hi."

"Hi. Where were you?" She told him. "I'll be over in half an hour."

"Uh . . . I didn't think I was seeing you tonight," she said.

At the long silence, her fingers began to shake. "You had some other plans?" he asked.

She calmed herself. "I haven't done my lesson plans for next week, and I have to turn them in Monday morning."

"Oh, that. You can get it done tomorrow when I won't be able to get away. See you shortly."

She freshened up as quickly as she could, changed her underwear, combed her hair and went to the kitchen hoping to make a few sandwiches before he arrived. However, when the intercom sounded she gave up that idea. Minutes later, she opened the door and looked up at him.

"Hi. You're right on the minute," she said, reached up and offered her lips. He grasped her shoulders, plunged his tongue into her mouth and let her feel the pressure of his need.

"Come on in, before my neighbors catch me making

out in my doorway. I'd only been home a minute before I called you," she told him, "and I'm not sure what I can give you to eat."

"Why don't you call out for something? Chinese would be good." He sat in the big leather chair that he favored.

She was about to tell him that she ate Chinese food for lunch when she remembered that he always expected her to pay when she ordered food delivered, and that at least Chinese food wasn't too expensive. "Okay. Anything you especially want?" she asked him.

"Whatever you choose, baby."

She set the table. "Gosh, I don't have any beer."

He slumped in the chair. "Oh, for goodness sake. Can you call them back and ask them to send a carton?"

"I'll try, but we could have some wine."

"All right, I'll take the wine. My throat's dry as all get out."

She poured two glasses of white wine. "How'd I get so lucky?" she asked him.

He threw up his hands. "Oh, she's been acting out all week. Her brother called and said her mother isn't feeling well, and that was all the excuse she needed. She put a few things in a suitcase, got in her car and took off. For all I know, her brother didn't tell her any such thing. She may not even have gone to Richmond."

Kenyetta didn't tell him how easily he could verify it, because she suspected that he merely wanted something to gripe about. Instead, she pushed a big Moroccan-leather pouf to his chair, sat at his feet and looked up at him. "Let's not talk about that." She rested her head on his thigh. "Can you spend the night?"

"I'd better not. No telling what time she'll call me." He reached down and ran his hands over her breasts. "If that delivery man doesn't get here soon, he may have to leave the food with the doorman." When she didn't respond, he nudged her with his knee. "Did you hear what I said?"

"Uh-huh, but it's against house rules to leave food with the doorman. Besides, who'd pay the delivery man?"

He leaned back and rested his head against the chair. "I can see it's not going to be my night. I've been getting a blast of cold air all day, and I guess it continues here."

"Oh, don't say that, honey. After we eat, everything will be fine."

"So you say." He jumped up, leaving her head to bounce against the chair. "I'd better be going."

She sat up straight. "Reggie! For goodness sake, you don't mean that. What did I do?"

"Nothing. And that's the problem. This was just another crap shoot." Before she could get to her feet, she heard the door slam. Simultaneously, the intercom buzzed, and she went to answer it.

"Thanks," she said to the doorman. "I need about five minutes. Then would you send him up?" She didn't want Reggie to encounter the man getting off the elevator. Now, maybe she'd get her lesson plan done. She wouldn't have been able to get in the mood for sex, no matter how she'd tried.

"Why do I do it, when he never takes time to let me enjoy it? Oh, hell! Now I have to eat twenty-seven dollars' worth of Chinese food."

After paying and tipping the delivery man, she put the food in the oven, turned on the warmer and sat down to work on her lesson plans. Junior high school students were trouble enough with their early adolescent behavior. Without engaging studies and assignments, they became a problem.

Reggie was always impatient and had the nerve to appear virtuous to boot. He swore that his wife tricked him into marrying her, claiming that he had impregnated her. But as soon as he married her, her period arrived. His wife wouldn't consider an annulment or a divorce, because according to her, it was against her religion. Sometimes Kenyetta wondered about Reggie's honesty. Nobody put a gun in his back and made him stay with the woman. He could be great fun when things were going his way, but at other times, he was like an ill-tempered child.

She had asked herself dozens of times why she didn't break off her relationship with him, but at least he wanted her, and he said he needed her. Oh, well, she had to get her work done; she'd deal with the matter of Reggie some other time.

She put her work aside and turned on the television. If she could get a man of her own, she'd leave Reggie alone.

Leticia walked into *The Journal* building at Fourteenth Street Northwest off Thomas Circle and headed for the elevator. "Just a minute, miss," the guard said. "You have to sign in and out."

"Thanks, but I work here—beginning this morning."

He showed his white teeth in a wide grin. "Congratulations. Even the man who owns this building signs in and out. What floor you on?" She told him. "They'll get you a badge sometime today, and you have to wear it at all times." He pulled off his braided cap and ran his hands over his short, tight curls. "I hate to see you hang an ID tag on that suit and spoil perfection. Elevator's on the left."

His studied appreciation gave her just the bounce she needed to know that she measured up to the women who walked through that lobby every morning. "Thank you," she said, and headed for the ninth floor.

A woman much younger than she showed her to her office, handed her an office telephone directory and told her, "Mr. Warren calls a budget meeting at nine every morning. He's in room 1010, to the left when you get off the elevator. I'm Dee, your secretary."

"Thanks, Dee. I'm glad to meet you. What goes on in a budget meeting?"

The girl's left eyebrow shot up. "They plan the next edition of the paper, the most important of which is what goes left and right on the front page and what's considered the hottest news. Your copy has to be in by four o'clock. I'll give you a policy sheet. And I'd better warn you. Mr. Warren doesn't like for anybody to say anything or ask any questions until he's had his say."

"Thanks, Dee. I'd like to see that policy sheet."

"Yes, ma'am. The pantry is down the hall to the right, and you can get coffee and buns or whatever. And, ma'am . . . Never be late to Mr. Warren's budget meetings."

So Mr. Warren was a terrorist, was he? She thanked Dee again, went into her office and closed the door. The office suited her, though she wouldn't have minded if it had been larger. She walked over to the window, looked down on Thomas Circle and gave silent thanks. She was only one floor beneath the boss, and from her window, she didn't look down on an alley. She'd get a few pictures and a pair of draperies and give the place a feminine touch.

She hadn't had any coffee, and she'd bet you couldn't take a cup of it to Mr. Warren's meeting. Too bad. She put her purse in the desk drawer, locked the desk, got a writing pad and headed for room 1010. She looked around at the two dozen people sitting there and chose a seat in the back.

A rosy cheeked, slightly overweight man rushed in and took a seat at the table in front of the room. "Sorry, Mr. Warren had to go to New York. We have one new colleague today. Leticia Langley has replaced Roy Bridges, and she has his office. Ms. Langley, would you stand, please?"

She stood, and as soon as all necks had turned, she sat down. A man who seemed to distance himself from both the group and the proceedings sat in the same row as she, his right ankle draped over his left knee. She wondered about him, but tried not to glance his way. The meeting ended after about forty minutes, and Mr. Warren's substitute intercepted her as she reached the door.

"You report to Joel Raymond, senior editor," he told her. "If you have any questions, you may call him. Welcome aboard."

Leticia returned to her office and within minutes, her telephone rang. She waited for her secretary to answer it. Minutes later, Dee cracked open the door and said, "Oh, I forgot to tell you. Everybody answers his own phone."

Leticia fixed the girl with a stern gaze. "What are you planning to do from eight-thirty to four-thirty? I write at my computer, and I can get my own coffee. Perhaps I don't need a secretary."

The girl's eyes widened. "Oh, it's all right. I can answer the phone and take dictation, too, if you like. For goodness sake, don't let Mr. Warren hear that you don't need a secretary."

"I have yet to meet anyone who could get ahead of me, Dee. Close the door, please."

She looked at the library of books on cooking and related matters that lined a wall in her office, noted that there were several on nutrition and decided to make that the topic of her first column. She was deep in the subject of proteins when her phone light blinked. Dee had evidently turned off the ringer.

"Ms. Langley, someone with a question about garden parties."

"Thanks, Dee." She lifted the receiver. "This is Leticia Langley. How may I help you?"

"I'm having a formal garden party weekend after next," the woman said, "and I haven't a clue about what to serve."

Leticia bit her lip as she was about to say, "You're joking." What she said wasn't any better. "Why on earth would you have a garden party if you don't know how to plan one? And why wait until now to learn how to do it?"

"What kind of answer is that? You're supposed to be an expert on this. You're the paper's food columnist, for Pete's sake," the woman said, and hung up. Leticia hadn't thought that her duties included giving advice via telephone, and especially not advice about a garden party.

Ten minutes later, she met Joel Raymond for the first time when he barged into her office without knocking. "What the hell do you mean by telling a person who calls here for help that she's stupid?"

"I didn't say she was stupid. I asked her why she'd have a garden party if she didn't know how to plan one."

"That's why we have people like you," he said, his voice booming.

She leaned back and looked him in the eye. "Not me, Mr. . . . You're not Mr. Warren, are you?"

"Of course not. I'm Joel Raymond, and—"

"And you're my boss." She stood and extended her hand, effectively taking the wind out of him. "Doesn't it seem odd to you that a woman would do that? Besides, aren't garden parties sort of like outdoors happy hours where people just drink and eat chicken wings?"

His scowl was so ferocious that it nearly caused her to laugh. "This is not funny, Ms. Langley. My baby sister has sent out at least fifty invitations to that party, and she has no idea how the hell to pull it off."

"Oops! That was your sister?"

"You bet, and she's furious."

"Look. I'm sorry she didn't ask the man who just vacated this job," Leticia said, making herself sound as contrite as possible. "I don't belong to the garden party set, and I've never been to one. I don't even know what they're like. I have a degree in English with a minor in journalism. As far as food is concerned, I can set a table, but that about covers it." He didn't have to know that she once worked as a short order cook in a restaurant. She had buried her lackluster past.

When an expression of horror covered his face, she hastened to reassure him. "Not to worry. I'm a quick study. I read Plato's *Republic* when I was eleven."

He covered his ears with his hands. "Plato. She's telling me about some Greek philosopher who lived three hundred and sixty years before Christ." He removed his hands and stared at her. "What did Plato say about garden parties?"

Laughter tumbled out of her, and when she could calm herself and look at him, she began laughing again. "I . . . I'll see if I can find a book on garden parties for your sister."

"Yeah, you do that," he said, and left.

She looked through the library in her office, found a

book on outdoor parties from weddings to barbeques, put it in an envelope with a note that read, "Give this to your sister," and sent it to Joel Raymond via interoffice mail.

"If that doesn't work," she said to herself, "baby sister can hike to the library."

As she began once more to tackle her first column, the red light on her phone blinked. When Dee buzzed her, Leticia swung around to answer, and nothing had ever seemed as precious as the feel of her hair swinging from one side of her head to the other. She jerked her head from side to side a few times for the pure enjoyment of feeling the hair hit her face.

"Do you want to speak with the producer of the annual Death by Chocolate Festival at the Mayflower?" Dee asked her.

"You bet I do. . . . Hello. This is Leticia Langley. How may I help you?"

"Whew," a male voice said. "The food desk has gotten some class. I'm Dick Corona, director of the chocolate fest, and I'd like you to review the event for *The Journal*. You're not allergic to chocolate, are you?"

"No, I'm not. You want me to cover the chocolate fest?" she asked, as if he hadn't just said precisely that. She looked up and saw Joel leaning against the half-open door of her office. He winked and gave her the thumbs-up sign. "I'll be delighted to do it," she told the man, and wrote the information on a scratch pad.

"You'll have to eat a lot of chocolate," Joel said when she hung up. "And I'd better tell you that you may regret taking this assignment."

"Why? I should think it would naturally be assigned to this desk."

"Yeah, but your predecessor hated chocolate so Max Baldwin, one of the reporters, got the job. And believe me, Max is going to be incensed, but the director of the chocolate fest claimed that Max was unfair and didn't want him back."

She didn't like to hear that. "Was he unfair?"

"I didn't think so, but he did lay it on rather thick. Max is candid, and he does not mince words. He's also a first-class reporter."

Trying for levity in what she regarded as a sticky situation, she said, "Is he especially fond of chocolate?"

"That's a part of the problem. He's a chocolaholic."

"Oh dear. Do you think that book will satisfy your sister?"

"It advises having waiters pass hot hors d'oeuvres and cocktails among the guests and a three-piece string ensemble. Seems to me she could have thought of that herself. But thanks.

"I'd better introduce you to Max. He dislikes surprises as much as he loves chocolate." They walked to Max's office, but he wasn't there. "We'll do it another time," Joel said. "Thanks again for your help with the garden party."

Leticia completed her first day on the new job with the conviction that she needed to move from food columnist to feature writer, and she began thinking of ways in which to accomplish it. She'd give herself a year as a food writer, less time if she could manage it, but definitely no longer. Writing about chocolate would not support the goal she'd set for herself.

Fired up with enthusiasm for her work as a reporter, she phoned Kenyetta. "How about a movie this evening, Ken? I need to unwind."

"Uh . . . sorry, but I have a date."

"You have? You're going out with a guy this evening? Girl, it's Monday. He must be real anxious if he can't wait till the weekend. Who is he?"

"I'm not talking, 'cause I . . . uh, I don't want to jinx it."

"Well, you go, girl. Maybe another time." She hung up, thinking secrecy about a man seemed out of character for Kenyetta. It would have been more like her to parade the man in front of Leticia, who didn't have a boyfriend. Hmm. She hadn't thought of Kenyetta as devious. But . . . some women could behave strangely when it came to men. It bore watching, and as loose as Kenyetta's tongue could be, the matter wouldn't be a secret much longer.

Leticia couldn't know then that her cousin harbored an embarrassing secret. Half an hour before Leticia called her, Kenyetta began work on a drama script that she hoped her seventh grade pupils would perform at the end of the summer makeup classes. She hated teaching summer school, but at the end of the following year she would have a sabbatical, so she had accepted the assignment, although grudgingly. But she'd hardly written half a page of dialogue when Reggie called her.

"I'm on my way over, and I'm starved. So if you don't have anything in the house, send out for something. See you shortly."

She bristled. The man was beginning to get on her nerves. "Reggie, I don't happen to have any money in the house. Half of the Chinese food I ordered for you Saturday is still in the refrigerator. Stop at a take-out shop somewhere and bring something."

He always treated her to a lengthy silence when she annoyed him, but this time, he let her wait longer than

usual. She was on the verge of telling him that she was
sorry when he said, "All right. I'll stop by Sam's and get
a roasted chicken and something to go with it."

She hung up, feeling triumphant. Why hadn't she
done that before? Nobody had to tell her that Reggie
was feeling unusually needy. She knew he could go only
so long without sex, and Veronica was probably still in
Richmond.

"I'm the one with the trump card," she said to herself, "and one of these days when he's on his high horse,
I'll use it." She didn't quite believe it, but entertaining
the possibility made her feel good.

Leticia settled into her new job and began her campaign to show her editor that she could do better than
write a food column. Not that writing about food was in
any way demeaning, but she knew that food wouldn't
retain her interest, because she didn't enjoy cooking and
didn't consider eating a proper recreational pursuit.
Immediately after she finished her first column on nutrition, and was sitting back to savor her personal ac-
complishment, she received a call from Kenyetta.

"I'm looking at an invitation to the annual family
gathering. Did you get one?" Kenyetta asked.

"What family gathering? Never heard of it."

"It's kinda fun. I've been a number of times. It's more
like an announcement than a real invitation. Why don't
you come, too, and we can room together."

"I don't know. I don't get invited because they disowned my mother. If you ask me, they're a bunch of
hypocrites."

"You're a big-shot reporter. What do you care? There'll
be over a hundred people there. We'll have a good time,"

Kenyetta said. "Uh . . . I never knew what they had against your mother."

"My mother was born and raised down there in New Orleans. Her holier than thou parents sent her to a Catholic girls' high school, and she became pregnant with me. She got tired of hearing that she was a disgrace and that she was going to hell and ran away with my father. They got married in Atlanta and sent a copy of the marriage certificate to my grandfather. My parents didn't contact my relatives again. Daddy sent them a notice when Mama died, but they didn't respond. I say the hell with them."

"I've heard half a dozen variations on that story. Girl, you're missing a chance to show 'em how silly they are. It's three weeks from now. Doll up and let's go down there and rock."

She thought for a minute. From childhood, her life had consisted of work and study, and she had always looked askance at frivolity, but in this case, it could be gratifying. "Right. I'm already in the mood to go. Where will all these people meet?"

"At the Riverside Hilton in New Orleans. That's right in the middle of everything. You can walk to the French Quarter."

"Okay. I'll speak with my editor and see if I can go." In truth, she wasn't as anxious to attend the family reunion as she let Kenyetta believe. Those people judged her mother harshly and mistreated her to the end, not even acknowledging her death, and she didn't believe they would receive her with warmth.

"I promised myself that I wasn't going to let anyone else look down his nose at me," she said to herself. "I'll be there, and I'll show them that I don't care what they think."

* * *

Three weeks later, Leticia and Kenyetta arrived in the torrid, wet heat of New Orleans.

"You're in time for the last of the Essence Festival," the driver of the shuttle bus told them. "And, man, do we have a crowd here this year. You can't see nothin' in this whole town but the *folks*. Where y'all from?" He closed the passenger door, got in and had started off when banging was heard on the back of the minibus. The driver stopped, got out and yelled at the anxious man he'd nearly left behind. "Chill out, buddy. If you'd missed this one, another one would have been here in two or three minutes. Ain't no point in getting excited in this ninety-something degree heat."

The newcomer got into the bus. "Thank God for air-conditioning. I was wondering if this thing would be a furnace." He looked at Leticia. "Where're you from?"

"Washington, D.C.," Kenyetta said, "and we're staying at the Riverside Hilton. Where're you staying?"

Leticia stared at her cousin. If she'd had a wad of paper she would have stuffed it in the woman's mouth. The man ignored Kenyetta and asked Leticia whether she, too, was staying at the Hilton.

"Yes," she said, and in a tone suggesting that she'd rather not give him that information.

Kenyetta added, "But we're leaving Sunday evening."

"Enjoy your stay," the stranger said to a crestfallen Kenyetta.

"I wish I knew why you're always so eager to please men. Today was not the first time I noticed it," Leticia said to Kenyetta after they checked in and were unpacking in their room.

"I was just being nice."

"But he was talking to me, so you didn't have to answer him. How did you feel when he let you know that he wasn't interested?"

Kenyetta fastened her hands to her hips and laid her head to the side. "Who said so? He was talking to me, but you let him have a splash of cold water, and he backed off. If we're going to have any fun, you're going to have to forget that you graduated *summa cum laude*. That doesn't mean peanuts to a man."

"I guess you'd know," she said, refusing to get into an argument. "What time is the reception this evening?"

"Six o'clock. We don't dress tonight, we dress tomorrow night."

Why had she put herself in a situation where she had to ask her cousin for crucial information? She didn't need Kenyetta's attitude of superiority. "I'm going down and register so family members will recognize me as one of them."

"You're not going to wait for me?"

"You'll catch up with me."

In view of her experience at the registration, she was glad she hadn't waited for her cousin. "Langley, you say?" The woman at the registration desk pronounced the name as if it were as foreign as Sanskrit. "Uh . . . what branch of the family?"

"I'm the granddaughter of Bryce Crawford, the great-granddaughter of Aaron Crawford and, let's see. Do I have to go beyond that?"

"I didn't know Bryce had any children," the woman said through pursed lips.

Leticia braced the ball of both palms on the table in front of the woman, leaned forward and said, "Bryce Crawford had one daughter, Lydia Crawford. She married my father, Herbert Langley. Would you like me to draw you a genealogical chart?"

"Well, I never! Here's your badge."

Both outraged and curious, Leticia didn't move. "You wouldn't be related to Bryce Crawford, would you?"

"Why . . . I'm his youngest sister."

Oh, how sweet it was! Leticia looked at the woman and grinned. "It has never occurred to me that I might have an aunt, great or otherwise." She pinned on the badge, picked up a program and left the table.

"Wait a minute," Kenyetta said, just arriving. "I had to make a phone call."

"I didn't know you had any friends in New Orleans."

"I don't," Kenyetta said, and stepped over to the table. "Cousin Anna! I was hoping you'd be here this year."

"Kenyetta! Lord bless your soul. You're as beautiful as ever. Sit here with me awhile."

Leticia went to the bar, bought a large cup of lemonade over crushed ice and started back to their room. However, before she reached the elevator, a man who she judged to be near her age stopped her. "I see you're one of the clan," he said. "Where do you live?"

"I live in Washington, D.C. What about you?"

"I live here in good old New Orleans. I haven't seen you at a previous clan gathering."

"This is my first. My cousin brought me. My mother belonged, but she disgraced our elders and—"

"I can guess the rest. They disowned her, and they're going to drop a lot of crap on you. Are you going to the reception?" She nodded. "It's in ballroom A. I'll meet you at the door at six-fifteen. We can stay awhile and then I'll show you New Orleans. By the way, I'm Mark DuPree, Bryce Crawford's grandson."

She extended her hand for a handshake. "I'm Leticia Langley. That makes you and me first cousins."

"So it seems. I'm glad to meet you, cuz."

"Is Bryce Crawford your maternal or paternal grand-father?" she asked him.

"Maternal. My mother died several years ago. From the gossip I've heard, our mothers were sisters." A grin spread over his face. "I really am going to enjoy that reception. It's time these people started acting civil. My sister married a Protestant, and you can't mention her name around the old man."

"He couldn't be worse than that creature at the registration desk."

Laughter roared out of him. "Aunt Anna? The last living saint. Trash that. One of the last living saints; you'll find a dozen more of 'em in this clan."

A sense of calm stole over her. She'd met at least one person to whom she could relate. "It's wonderful meeting you, Mark. You may save my sanity this weekend. I had a long trip down here, so I'd better get some rest. I'll meet you at six-fifteen. Say . . . what do the women wear to this reception?" She had asked Kenyetta, but she'd rather have a second opinion. Kenyetta enjoyed one-upmanship, and Leticia didn't want to be the victim of it.

Mark looked at her with what appeared to be a quizzical expression. "You could wear jeans and look better than most of the women who'll attend, but it's best to be conservative and wear a dressy street dress. Half of the women are over fifty, and they set the style."

She suppressed the anger she felt at Kenyetta. "Thanks. I'm glad I asked you. My roommate said we don't dress tonight. She's so competitive that she'll do anything to make me look bad."

"Hey. Cut that out!" he said. "You don't have to look up to any woman. And if you don't have a man to help you fatten your ego, get one." He leaned down and brushed her cheek with a quick kiss. "You should've had a brother." She thanked him, and as she turned toward the elevator, he said, "That's a cousin you don't need."

She stepped into the elevator, pressed the button for her floor and leaned against the wall. "I know I'm behind socially, but I'll get there. I'm going to turn myself into a woman that I'm proud of."

Chapter Two

"Where you going so fast?" Kenyetta asked Leticia as she was about to leave the room. "You're overdressed, too."

"I have a date, and I'm not overdressed. It's not my fault that you didn't bring a dressy street dress. You said it was casual, so wear something casual. See you later."

"What do you mean you have a date? You just got here. Besides, you can't date your relatives."

"Elevate your mind, Ken. I'll see you later."

As promised, Mark met her at the door of the ball-room. "You look perfect," he told her. "Come on, let's get this over with . . . unless you want to leave it till we're ready to leave."

She wasn't accustomed to feeling queasy, but the thought of meeting her grandfather had that effect. "You're talking about my grandfather?"

"The old man himself. He barks and, sister, he can bite. Most of the time, I avoid him."

She recognized him before she and Mark reached him. Bryce Crawford stood with his back to the wall, dressed in a dark pin-striped suit, white dress shirt and blue tie, listening to a man who gesticulated wildly as he spoke. Bryce noticed her approach, and when he did a double take, she knew that she reminded him of her mother. The stranger lost Bryce's attention, and he didn't release her from his gaze until she and Mark stopped in front of him.

"Good evening, sir," Mark said. "I've just met Leticia, and I thought you'd like to meet her. Leticia Langley, this is our grandfather, Bryce Crawford."

The scowl on the old man's face did not perturb her, because she had spent the afternoon steeling herself against it. "How old are you?" Bryce asked her without preliminaries.

Dead set on getting ahead of him, she said. "I'm thirty-one. I'm a journalist, and I live in Washington, D.C." When he narrowed his left eye, she said, "I studied journalism at Howard University and was graduated *summa cum laude.*" Let him digest that.

"Oh, Cousin Bryce, there you are," Kenyetta could be heard saying as she approached. "I've been looking everywhere for you." She paused when she saw Mark. "Is he your date?" she asked Leticia, effectively ruining her first meeting with her grandfather.

"I'm glad to have met you, Grandfather," Leticia said to Bryce Crawford. "I have to leave now." She didn't dare glance at Kenyetta for fear that she might throttle her.

"Seems like you should stay for the program and get to know people," the old man said with what she perceived as a grudge. Leticia was tempted to ask him if he received the telegram her father sent him advising him of her mother's death, but decided not to match his rudeness.

"I'll be around all day tomorrow, sir," she said.

He turned from her and focused on Kenyetta. "I see

you're still eating pecans and pralines. Keep it up and you won't be able to get through that door." He motioned to the double doors at the ballroom's entrance.

Considering herself dismissed, Leticia walked away and heard Mark say, "Good to see you, sir."

"Don't let it get to you," Mark said. "He was about as civil to you as I've ever seen him be to anybody."

Her shoulder lifted in a quick shrug. "I didn't realize that people like him existed. Where are we going?"

"You can see the Essence musical acts in Washington. How about going jazz club hopping? It's a good night for it, because most of the tourists will probably be at the Superdome. What do you say?"

"Works for me," she said. "This modern-day black music drives me up the wall." She liked his laughter, and he gave her a healthy sample of it.

"Don't get stuffy on me, now. I like a lot of our singers. You've been listening to too much rap and hip-hop."

"Maybe so, but I love jazz, especially traditional jazz and Dixieland."

He hailed a taxi. "Then let's go to Palm Court first."

She didn't think she had ever enjoyed an evening as much as she did that one. The air throbbed with gaiety and the camaraderie of the crowds in the jazz clubs and on the streets. Years seemed to fall away from her, and though she'd never been a good dancer, with Mark as her teacher, she caught on quickly and let herself go as teenagers are wont to. They returned to the hotel shortly after midnight, and Mark introduced her to some of their other relatives. She hadn't learned how to engage in witty small talk, but it seemed as if the relatives she met that evening thought her sufficiently interesting to give her an hour of their time.

When she began to tire, Mark suggested that they call it a night. "There's a breakfast meeting at eight this morning," he reminded her, "so I'd better turn in. You're a breath of fresh air, Leticia. I'm glad we met," he told her when he left her at her room door. "See you at breakfast."

"Next time you need somebody to teach you how to dress, don't call me," Kenyetta said when Leticia walked into the room. A glance told Leticia that her cousin had propped herself up in one of the beds, waiting to attack. "I wouldn't have run off and left you with those old fuddy-duds," Kenyetta went on, her voice rising. "And what's with you and your *own* cousin?"

Leticia was learning things about her cousin that she'd rather not know. Jealousy was a trait she disliked, because she thought it brought out the idiocy in people. "Hi, Ken. I'm exhausted, and we have to attend a breakfast program at eight. I need a shower." She undressed, took a shower, dried off and got into her bed.

"Well, if you ain't some shit," she heard Kenyetta say.

Refusing to acknowledge the insult, she replied, "Good night, Ken," and turned out the light beside her bed. Suddenly, she sat up. Kenyetta reminded her of Geraldine Thomas, the homecoming queen who thought she deserved all the accolades, the prizes and the subservience of her inferiors. Leticia didn't laugh, because that would have required an explanation. Mark DuPree was tall, handsome and distinguished looking, but he was their cousin and off limits, so it seemed ridiculous for Kenyetta to get sore because he'd been friendly with Leticia and not with her. She eased herself down beneath the covers.

"I can't sleep in the dark," Kenyetta said.

"Then turn on your light. I'm not going to stay awake with this light shining in my eyes just so you can sleep. Don't even dream it. Good night."

"What's happened to you? You didn't used to be like this," Kenyetta said.

"You could say I got tired of being your doormat and elevated myself to your level. Good night."

"Aren't you going to introduce me to your friend?" Kenyetta asked Leticia the next morning when they encountered Mark at breakfast.

"He's not my friend; he's our cousin, and I'll introduce him to you if he walks over here. I'm not going to his table to introduce you." For the next fifteen minutes, Kenyetta kept an eye on the table diagonally across from them.

"Hi, mind if I join you, Leticia?" Mark said, after finishing his breakfast. He took a seat and looked at Kenyetta. "Have you been to one of our previous clan gatherings?"

"I come every year, but this is the first time I've seen you here," Kenyetta said.

His face creased into a grin. "Not to worry, cousin. Sometimes I make myself invisible, and what better time than during one of these clan gatherings?"

Kenyetta leaned toward him. "You're pulling my leg."

Mark looked toward the ceiling and furrowed his brow. "Trust me, cousin, I wouldn't even think of it."

"Kenyetta Jackson, this is Mark DuPree."

"Glad to meet you," they said in unison.

Mark stood. "See you later. I'm discussing genealogy this morning, and I need to look over my notes."

After they told him good-bye, Kenyetta's fork clattered against her plate. "What a looker, and the brother has to be a cousin!"

Leticia didn't think herself evil, but she couldn't help enjoying Kenyetta's discomfort. "Yeah," she said. "Them's the breaks."

For the evening gala, Leticia chose a short evening dress of silver lamé that had a deep décolleté, stopped midway down her thighs and fitted her flawless figure. Silver accessories that included three-and-a-half-inch heels completed her outfit. But minutes after she walked into the ballroom, she heard a buzz, and no one moved. She didn't associate the charged atmosphere with herself until Mark nudged her arm.

"Hi," he said. "I think you're in for it. You look stunningly beautiful, but your local relatives are ready to hang you. Hold your temper, Leticia, here comes Grandfather."

"But—"

"Don't let it bother you. He's back in colonial times, when women hid their figures and wore their dresses to their ankles."

"He'll be mad with you for standing here with me," she whispered.

"So what? I'm sovereign, don't owe a soul, and my income last year was in six figures. Besides, it'll do him good to see what a woman is supposed to look like." He stood straighter and laid back his shoulders. "Good evening, Grandfather."

Bryce Crawford barely glanced at Mark when he said, "You should be ashamed to stand beside her." Then, his narrow-eyed stare focused on Leticia. "They say the apple doesn't fall far from the tree. You're a disgrace, just like your mother. You don't belong here among decent people."

Crestfallen and shaking with mortification and rage, she said, "You forget that I'm an apple from your own tree." He sputtered, speechless, but she walked away from him, content with her minor victory.

"By the way," Mark said, trailing her, "he probably wouldn't have noticed you in this crowd of three hundred if your Washington friend hadn't pointed you out to him."

"That certainly doesn't surprise me. But I'm learning a lot of things this weekend."

"Want to do some more club hopping?" he asked, offering her an escape from the hostility surrounding her.

"Thanks, but I'm staying right here even if nobody talks to me. You go on. I'll be all right."

Mark handed her his card, and she gave him hers. He looked at it and raised an eyebrow. "I'll have my car outside tomorrow morning at eight-twenty. Tell Kenyetta to be on time. The traffic from this hotel to Louis Armstrong Airport can be horrendous, even on Sundays. How about going to the lounge? I need something to eat. These little pieces of meat on sticks and sandwiches the size of my thumbnail are just making me hungry."

"Okay, but then you go back to the gala. You live here with half of these people, but I may never see any of them again. I appreciate your support, and I won't forget it."

She decided not to confront Kenyetta about her treacherous act; though she didn't doubt that Kenyetta expected Bryce Crawford to act as he did. *Have my eyes been closed to Kenyetta's antics these past four years?* she asked herself.

When she arrived from Atlanta to attend Howard University, Kenyetta had greeted her warmly, helped her find a place to stay—though she didn't offer accommodations in her large apartment—and helped

her in other ways. Leticia detected cracks in her cousin's character right away, but ignored them. However,
since her college graduation, Leticia had noticed an aggressiveness in her cousin as well as occasional acts of
jealousy, and although she would hate to lose the friendship, she meant to groom herself to do precisely that.

Back at her office on Monday morning, Leticia got a
taste of male competition in a newspaper office. Her
door burst open at exactly eight thirty-one, and in strode
the man she saw sitting alone at the rear of the conference room on her first day at work.

"What the devil do you mean by undermining me
and grabbing my assignment?" he asked, by this time
his face inches from hers.

It took her a few seconds to recover, but she rolled
her chair back, looked him in the eye and said, "I suppose this is the way you always act, but I'm not used to
such behavior in an office. Come back when you get
yourself together."

"Why, of all the . . . I'd like to know how you managed it. I've had that assignment five years, for the life
of that event. You've been here a couple of weeks, and
you have my assignment?"

She didn't want to vex him further, but she wanted to
cool him off and, at the same time, let him know that
he couldn't push her around. "I'm Leticia Langley," she
said, extending her right hand to him. "I don't think
we've met."

"I'm Max Baldwin, and you know it."

Since he didn't seem inclined to shake, she withdrew
her hand. "That's right. Joel took me to your office the
morning I arrived. He wanted me to meet you, but I
think you were in the coffee room or some such place."

Max stared at her. "My dear lady, I love chocolate, and you have deprived me of the opportunity to gorge myself on the best chocolate there is anywhere and not pay a penny for it. You owe me one, and believe me, I collect my debts."

"You're welcome to go instead of me, Max."

"Instead of *you*? I don't play second fiddle to you, lady. It's my assignment and you're going to do me a favor and let me carry it out."

"Stop calling me *lady*. I have a name and it's Leticia. If you hadn't been so mean and posted that negative review, the director of the chocolate fest wouldn't have called me." She thought for a second. "Look, Max, if the stuff's so bad, why do you want to eat it again this year?"

He pushed his hands into his trouser pockets and kicked at the carpet. "I have to tell the truth to my readers, but for me personally, it only matters that the chocolate is sweet. Last year, those chocolate truffles were dreadful, and I said so. Whoever makes that stuff should go to Brussels and attend some chocolate-making classes."

Wondering how to put an end to a problem that the two of them could not solve, she said, "I'm sorry that I've gotten off on the wrong track with you, but if I don't do what Joel says, I may ruin my chances on my new job. What do you suggest?"

The way he looked at her told her that he wasn't a man to give in easily, in spite of what she perceived to be a soft center. "Do whatever in the hell you want to," he said, and walked out.

When she'd asked him what to do about it, she'd robbed him of his righteous mien and of his stridency. "That's a lesson, girl," she told herself. "The way to deal with that man is to turn the tables on him." Leticia unlocked her desk and took out her notes on obesity in African Americans, looked them over and decided that she had enough information for a good, informative column. But as she began to write, it occurred to her that she may have just broken one of her father's cardinal rules: be careful not to make an enemy, for he may one day be your boss. She was low man on the totem pole, and she could walk into that office any day and discover that Max Baldwin was her supervisor. *I'd better see what I can do to make amends, though groveling is out of the question.*

The next morning, she went to Max Baldwin's office for the purpose of smoothing their relationship, and immediately wished she hadn't done so. Her gaze caught a man slouched against the wall in a lazy, I-don't-care fashion. Shock reverberated throughout her system, and she barely remembered why she went to Max Baldwin's office.

"Sorry," she murmured to Max. "I didn't know you had a guest. Please excuse me."

She rushed back to her office, turned the air conditioner to maximum cooling, picked up a tablet and began to fan herself. "What in the name of kings happened back there, and where did that brother come from?" She didn't know how long she sat in a semicatatonic state wondering what had hit her.

"Oh, damn," she said when she realized how much time she'd wasted. That guy is probably a stud, just the kind I can't stand. I'm not wasting another second on him. Whew! But, Lord, does he ever have *man* written all over him!

She answered the phone. "Can you have a column for me by Thursday?" Joel asked her. "If you can, I'll put a short footer at the bottom right corner of the front page, announcing your column and introducing you."

"Sure, I can have it ready by Thursday," she said.

"Don't forget that it must be on my desk not later than four o'clock."

"I won't forget."

Well, that's enough to shake me out of my silly mood. I'll work now, unless I want to lay an egg, and a big one at that.

She glanced up as the man passed her open door, and wished she hadn't. He saw her, came back and tapped lightly on her door. She knew it was he before she looked up again and saw him standing there, filling up the doorway.

"Yes?" she said, letting her voice suggest that he was trespassing.

His smile complemented the rest of him. "I hope I'm not intruding. Do you have time for a cup of coffee?"

A benign enough question, but his audacity told her that he had observed her reaction to him. "I'm sorry, but I have to meet a deadline. I hope you won't mind closing the door."

His bow had an air of mockery, but he left and closed the door. She slumped in her chair. "That's all I needed," she said aloud. "I could kick myself for going into Max's office."

She completed an outline for her story and called Dee, her secretary. "I hate to interrupt your reading, but I need some supplies. Please get me a couple of USB drives and some ink cartridges. Then would you change the cartridges, please."

"Yes, ma'am, I'll get it. But I thought one of the guys would change the cartridges."

"I expect one can, but if you can't do that, why do I need you?"

"Yes, ma'am."

If Dee thought her incompetent because she hadn't previously worked in a newspaper office and figured she'd be willing to truck down to the supply room herself instead of asking her secretary to do it, she'd better wise up. Leticia was capable of changing the ink cartridges, but she'd seen at least four secretaries do that for their male bosses. Maybe she'd better have a little talk with Dee.

I don't swagger like some of the men around here, but I deserve as much consideration and respect. I can see that this place is no different from the restaurants I've worked in; I'll have to fight for my rights.

Leticia figured that her darkened mood had a lot to do with her reaction to the man she saw in Max Baldwin's office. She couldn't put her finger on the reason, but as much as he attracted her, she got negative vibes from him. Vowing not to let him take up so much space in her head, on the way home she stopped at a book store and bought a cookbook encyclopedia that was guaranteed to occupy her thoughts until she went to bed.

However, that evening she found in her mailbox a letter from a relative who claimed that he met her the previous weekend. She didn't remember the man, and of the many people at the gathering, she had met very few, and she remembered all of them. She read: " 'My twelve-year-old daughter has pains everywhere, and nobody in this little town can tell us why this is. I want to send her to a hospital in Washington where you can look after her. My wife and I have to work, but you're right there in Washington, so it shouldn't inconvenience you. Since you're family, we know you won't mind.' "

Dumbfounded, she telephoned Kenyetta, with whom she hadn't spoken since returning from New Orleans. "Hi, Ken. You won't believe the letter I just got from some cousin or other. Listen." She read the letter to Kenyetta. "I sympathize with this child, but this guy is off the wall. I don't remember meeting anybody named Carl Montague. Do you?"

"Yeah. I know him. That's something he'd do. I haven't met his daughter, but even if I had, I definitely would not assume that responsibility. I always thought he was overbearing. He wouldn't drop that in *my* lap."

"But I feel sorry for the child. Suppose it's something serious."

"What would he have done if you hadn't been at that reunion? In fifty years, he wouldn't lay that on me. No indeed, I wouldn't do it. But you do whatever you want to."

After musing over the problem for most of the evening, Leticia wrote the man, explaining that she also worked full-time and couldn't be responsible for his daughter. However, she told him that she would visit the girl at every opportunity. She also told herself that she had attended her last family gathering, and that if being a relative—however distant—entitled you to impose on someone to such an extent, she was better off without them.

Frustrated and undecided, she postponed mailing the letter. The man's audacity alternately angered her and gained her admiration. At her office the following morning, without research or making any of her usual preparation, she suddenly began to write an essay expressing her views about individuals who decide how other people should spend their time and manage their lives. So great was her passion about the topic that she finished the piece around two that afternoon, took it to Joel and asked him to publish it.

With that out of her system, Leticia sat back, reflecting on her life. She recalled her vow to stand up for herself and never to let anyone take advantage of her without a fight. On her way home, she mailed the letter to Carl.

Two days had passed since she gave her editor in chief

an essay on obesity instead of a column about food, the work he'd hired her to do. She sat at her desk with both elbows on it, cupping her chin. Should she ask him about it? Maybe she'd been presumptuous in writing that essay and asking him to publish it. He hadn't said a word, and . . . maybe he hadn't had time to read it. She logged on to the computer and began searching for information about obesity among people of African descent in other countries. Her door swung open, and she swung around.

Joel strode in and dropped some papers on her desk. "You're in the wrong job."

Shivers streaked through her. He didn't like the essay, and he was going to tell her that she didn't know how to write.

"Wh-what do you mean?" she asked.

He marched to the window and stood there looking out. Not a good sign. "I mean you don't need to write stuff like this in order to tell people how to make corn bread. This is first-class writing, and so was that short on meddlesome people that you sent me a few days ago. I'll publish that after I publish this one."

After those words, she tried to relax, but did his praise mean she was overqualified? "Do I . . . still have a job?" she asked him in barely audible tones.

"Damn right you got a job, but I'm gonna put you on features. Any kid with a degree in home economics can handle this desk."

"Thanks, Joel. I'm glad I won't have to cover that chocolate fest. I hardly leave this office for fear I'll run into Max. He's furious with me."

Joel rested his two-hundred-pound frame against the wall beside the door and shoved his hands into his pockets, opening his jacket and exposing his trim physique. "He shouldn't have written a review that made it look as if he wanted to put that candy company out of business. Even if you write a negative report, don't blast the company."

She stared at him. "I thought you said . . . You mean I still have to cover that fest?"

"Afraid so. But don't worry about Max. His bark is worse than his bite. Inside, he's a real pussycat."

"If you say so, but he didn't sound that way to me."

Joel's brow furrowed deeply. "Maybe he doesn't want you to know. Working on features, you'll have to give up this cozy sanctuary and move into the newsroom."

She sat forward, her temper gathering steam. "In that madhouse?"

His shoulders bunched in a quick shrug. "It's only like that between three and five in the afternoon."

"That's when you hear it," she grumbled. "That place is as noisy as Yankee Stadium was when the Yankees won their last World Series."

Joel walked over to her desk, looked down at her and, as if she hadn't uttered a word, said, "You won't have any privacy in that cubicle, but you'll get a lot more money in your checks." He picked up the essay that he'd dropped on her desk. "This is good. It'll be in the next issue. I want a series on it." Without giving her a chance to respond, he opened the door and left.

The day finally arrived and, for the first time, she walked into the famous hotel. *I'm a reporter,* she reminded herself, then stopped a doorman and said, "I'm a reporter here to cover the chocolate fest. Would you please show me to the press room?"

The man's blue eyes widened. "Yes, miss. Right this way." Score one for her. He'd thought she was there to pay ten dollars and stuff herself with all the chocolate she could eat. In the press room, she helped herself to coffee and a hot-cross bun, scrutinized the place, made a few notes, and then headed for the ballroom, where the smell of chocolate greeted her with the force of an eighteen-wheeler slamming into concrete.

"Oh, my Lord," she said aloud as she entered the room. "What's he doing here?"

She hoped he wouldn't see her, and if he did, that he would ignore her. She turned her back and headed for a far corner of the room, but a girl dressed like a cocktail waitress waylaid her.

"Would you care for a truffle? Bricknell makes the best chocolate on this planet," the girl, who appeared to be no more than seventeen, said as she stuck a toothpick in one and offered it to Leticia. Leticia thanked her and looked for a container in which to discard it. She'd choose what to taste, and she guessed that there were more than two thousand different candies to sample. Just as she stopped at the stall of a European company whose chocolates she liked, she felt something touch her elbow. Instinct warned her that when she turned, she'd look into his face.

"I'm not stalking you," he said, his face lighting up with an engaging smile, "but I confess that I considered doing precisely that. Are you a chocolate freak, or are you substituting for Max?"

"Neither. I'm doing what my editor assigned me to do."

"Touché. We haven't met, not that I didn't try. My name is Wilson Gallagher. Max told me that you're Leticia Langley." He held out his right hand, and she had the choice of shaking it or being rude for no reason. She reached out to take his hand and, at the touch, electric sparks seemed to shoot up her arm all the way to her shoulder. She could see that the contact had had the same disconcerting effect on him as it did on her.

She gathered her wits as quickly as she could. "How do you do, Mr. Gallagher? Don't tell me that you're here to indulge in a passion for chocolate?" She was at once on guard. Maybe Max sent him.

"No way," he said. "I like chocolate, but I'm not crazy about it. I'm writing a book on obesity, and I'm observing the reactions of different people as they eat high-calorie foods—in this case, chocolate. It's amazing. Some people eat it as if it's no more delightful than dry bread, but for some others, it appears to be a taste of heaven."

Her antennae shot up. She was writing a series of articles on obesity, and she made a note to research that angle as she collected information for her review of the chocolate fest. "I'm writing a series on obesity in African Americans," she told him. "My first installment will be in the next issue of *The Journal*. My next one will be about the food and exercise habits of people of African descent who are not Americans. I hope you won't be put out."

She could see that she'd piqued his interest, which had shifted from tomcatting to his profession. "Definitely not," he said. "I can use information from your column as documentation for my book. It's one thing to get information from successive editions of a paper and another to have it in book form, so we're not in competition. I hope we can collaborate in some way."

Professionally, she welcomed that, but she needed to stay as far from that man as possible, and the longer he stood there the more certain of it she became. "Of course," she said, but that lame voice didn't sound one bit like hers.

"I've discovered that obesity slips up on most people, although some are victims of their mother's cooking and of television and are already overweight as small children. People tell themselves that they will go on a diet or exercise or change their daily routine, but they procrastinate about it, and the condition worsens with the passing of time. Bingo, they're obese."

She wanted to tell him about Kenyetta, who was overweight, didn't pay attention to what she ate and bought a size larger each time she got a new garment. But she didn't, because she didn't want to expose her cousin to a stranger.

Wilson looked at his watch, appeared to study her for a moment, and then said, "Could we . . . uh, have lunch one day soon and talk about this?"

His question made sense, but she didn't want to spend time in his company. Did she? Oh, heck! What was she afraid of? She remembered the big guys on campus at Howard University, football heroes who thought they had paid their debt to society when they smiled at you, men who only danced with the homecoming queen. She had disliked them intensely. Maybe she was being unfair to Wilson, but remembering that helped her to maintain an intelligent perspective.

She held out through his third call. "All right," she said, after he literally begged, "we can have lunch, Wilson, but I can't spare more than an hour."

"In that case, have dinner with me. You won't have to worry about the time."

She walked right into that one. "How about lunch Sunday?" she said. Lunch with a man wasn't really a date, was it? They made a date for brunch the following Sunday at noon.

"It'll be the longest five days I've ever spent," he said. "I can hardly wait."

She managed to terminate the conversation and tell him good-bye, but she wanted to kick herself. Hadn't she vowed not to do anything she didn't want to do? She stopped walking and leaned against a pole that someone had decorated with pictures of assorted chocolates. Why was she beating on herself? She hadn't said no because down deep she wanted to be with him. The problem was that he knew it. Feeling guilty of having let herself down and as if to punish herself for it, she stepped over to the counter and bought a bag of truffles and other assorted chocolates. Even without tasting them, they served as the distraction she needed after twenty minutes in the company of Wilson Gallagher. Besides, maybe Max would accept them as a peace offering.

Leticia was not attracted to Max Baldwin, but she didn't feel right about taking his cherished assignment, although she believed he deserved to lose it. She wanted smooth working relations with her colleagues, and that meant she had to be on good terms with them.

Back in her office that afternoon, she telephoned Max. "Hello, Max. This is Leticia. Do you mind if I come to your office? I won't stay but a minute."

"Are you coming to gloat? You can do that right where you are."

"Please, Max. I'm not mean spirited. Is it all right if I come over there?"

"Sure. Far be it from me to turn down a good-looking woman."

She ran a comb through her hair, refreshed her lipstick, locked her desk and walked down the narrow aisle toward Max's cubicle wondering why she'd combed her hair and replaced her lipstick. *One of these days I'll know who I am.*

To her surprise, Max stood and welcomed her with a wide smile. "You sure you phoned the right Max?"

"You're the only one I know," she said, glad to see him in a jovial mood. "I brought you something."

His eyebrows shot up. "Me? You're kidding. How'd it go today?"

"Fair. I didn't taste too much of it, because I don't want to burst out of my clothes." She handed him the bag.

He gazed at the logo on the bag, and a smile formed at the corners of his mouth and slowly spread over his face. He picked out a truffle, moistened his lips, bit off a tiny piece and let it slide down his throat. "Woman, you've just reduced me to putty. Since that little piece didn't kill me, have a seat. Why did you do this? I told you how much I love this stuff." He put another piece in his mouth and relished it. "Nothing is better than this."

Good Lord. The man was so sensual. She could almost taste the chocolate as he subdued it with his teeth and tongue. Joel had said Max possessed a soft center, and she was ready to believe it.

"I don't know how to thank you for this. I'm really bowled over that you actually thought of me."

"You don't deserve it, Max," she said in a playful tone, "but it made me feel good to bring it to you."

Laughter poured out of him. "I wouldn't dare question your motives; I'm too happy with the deed. You want a piece?" He fished around in the bag, picked up a piece of milk chocolate and handed it to her. "Sorry, I can't share my truffles." He put the bag on his desk, gazed directly at her, and she knew he was serious. "I don't forget things like this, Leticia. You made my day."

That Friday, Leticia looked at her paycheck and gasped. As a features writer, her salary had doubled.

She could actually afford a decent apartment. Wasting no time, she spent Saturday looking for one and by five that afternoon had found what she wanted.

"Where you moving to?" Kenyetta asked her. "What's wrong with the one you have now?"

"It's a slum apartment compared to yours. That's one thing that's wrong with it," Leticia said, not bothering to hide her vexation. "And I want to get to work more easily. I'm going to move to a place where getting to work will be less of a hassle. Up in the third alphabet."

"You up to something, girl, but you go on. You made up your mind already."

"Don't worry, Kenyetta. I am not going near your street, so you won't run into me."

"Whatta you mean by that?"

"Relax. I'm not going to interfere with your privacy. I mind my own business."

"Whatta you talking about?"

Leticia heard the panic in her cousin's voice, and knew she'd touched a tender spot. "You want to come with me to check it out?" she asked Kenyetta.

"You mean you already found one? Okay. When you want to go?"

"Monday after work."

"Monday? Look, I . . . uh . . . I have an appointment Monday evening. It'll have to be some other time."

It was on the tip of Leticia's tongue to ask who the mysterious man was, but she quelled the impulse. "Okay. Let me know when you'll be free," she said. But an ugly thought crossed her mind. It couldn't be. Kenyetta was too smart to get involved with a married man.

If Kenyetta didn't go with her, so much the better, Leticia decided after thinking about it. Her cousin would use the occasion to be a superior know-it-all, and she didn't intend to accept any more of Kenyetta's high handedness. She made a list of things she'd need for the two-bedroom, living room, dining room, kitchen and den apartment, and measured some areas to see if her furniture would fit. At last, she would be able to live comfortably. With a month-to-month lease for her current apartment, she would be able to move into the new apartment ten days later.

"How many keys will you have made?" Wilson asked at their brunch date.

"Two. I'll keep one in my pocket and one at the office. Why?"

"Then you'll need another one, won't you?"

She didn't get it. "Why? The building superintendent has a master key."

He reached across the table and pressed his hand to hers. "Won't I need one?"

She nearly spilled her drink in her lap. "Let's not move so fast, Wilson. I'd be a fool to give a man I don't know the key to my apartment. Even if I knew him, I wouldn't do it. Listen, friend, even angels have to earn their wings."

A grin spread over his face. "Touché. Just testing the water."

She wasn't so sure about that. "Really? How many house or apartment keys do you carry?"

"Oh, three," he said, and shrugged at her gasp.

"And you want to add another trophy to your belt, right?"

"Naturally I have a key to my own apartment and one to my summer place on the North Carolina Outer Banks. The other key fits my parents' home. I want to work with you on obesity, Leticia, but I also want more than that with you, and I think you understand that."

She also wanted more, but she didn't have the right

feeling about it. "I get mixed vibes from you, Wilson. You're so sure of yourself, and I have this notion that your needs and what you want are all that matter."

"You wound me. We're attracted to each other, and we owe it to ourselves to see where this could lead. Let's give it a shot, okay?"

She didn't answer, because she knew it wouldn't matter. This bumblebee made her stamen tingle, and she wasn't fool enough to deny it.

Chapter Three

Kenyetta became more deeply involved with Reggie with each passing day, and she couldn't explain the reason to herself. At times, she even resented him. She had given up trying to get him to be fair. He short changed her in bed, and he no longer lied about his relations with his wife. So she had accepted that he didn't intend to leave her, at least not for Kenyetta Jackson. But she continued to rationalize that having him was better than having no man at all and that, with so many men preferring other men, married women had to share. And as long as they didn't know they were sharing, it didn't hurt them.

If she got a shot at a single brother with something to offer, though, she'd be on him like a cheetah on a jackrabbit, and two-timing Reggie could find another toy. She filled the bath tub with warm water, dropped in a handful of crystals that transformed themselves into bubbles and perfumed the bathroom. She stripped, stepped into the tub and congratulated herself on being able to afford such luxury. She wondered how much

Leticia made in her new job and whether her new apartment would have a doorman and a concierge. Kenyetta pulled air through her front teeth. If Leticia got to be president of the country, she told herself, her cousin would still have that red Georgia dirt between her toes.

Kenyetta dressed in a red bra and bikini panties, slipped into a red silk jumpsuit, dabbed expensive perfume in strategic places and prayed that, for once, Reggie would remember that he had a partner and wouldn't leave her high and frustrated. The doorbell rang, and she raced to it.

She opened the door, reached up and kissed him on the mouth. He glanced first to his right and then to his left, making sure, she understood, that he wasn't followed, and stepped across her threshold. "Hi," she said. "It's so nice out. Could we sit out in the back garden? None of the neighbors ever sits out there, so it'll be private."

"Look, babe, I didn't get where I am by being reckless. What do you have to drink? The office was a real bastard today. Not one thing went right. Worse still, the boss was there all day asking dumb questions and making stupid suggestions. If I'd had his opportunities, I'd have been rich years ago."

By the time he reached the end of his sentence, her mind had wandered to another topic. "When did she get back?" Kenyetta never called Reggie's wife by her name.

"A couple of days ago, and man, is she in a snit. She doesn't even grunt when I say something to her. Keeping house is not something I do. I'm a software designer. At least I put the dishes in the dishwasher. Where's the drink, baby? I didn't come here to talk about Veronica."

Kenyetta went to the bar—she'd bought it because Reggie said a single woman ought to have one—poured vodka over ice, squeezed a slice of lime over it and handed him a vodka comet.

He sipped it for a minute. "This is just the ticket to get me in the mood, baby. Come over here and sit on my lap." He finished the drink, took the liberties that he granted himself and got his relief quickly. He leaned against the back of the big chair, stretched out both arms and said, "You're the best, baby."

Too stunned to speak, Kenyetta closed her eyes, because she didn't want him to see what she felt.

She moved off him and said, "Excuse me a minute."

"Oh no, don't go off. I gotta be going. I told her I was going out to buy some cigarettes. By the time I get back there, she'll be ready to eat nails." He zipped up his pants, got up, headed for the door and told her he'd see her in a couple of days. "Sooner than that if I get needy," he said.

She still hadn't been able to utter a word, and when he walked out the door, she let it slam behind him, picked up the glass that had contained his vodka comet and slammed it against the door, sending slivers of glass in all directions. Then, zombielike, she got a broom and dustpan, swept up the particles of glass, emptied them into a wastebasket, dropped herself on the living room sofa and cried for an hour.

Finally, she got up, washed her face, pulled off her clothes and took a shower, but that didn't help. She felt used, and as she thought back over the four years she'd been involved with Reggie, she couldn't remember a single occasion on which he had made her feel precious or even desirable. Either he didn't know what lovemaking was supposed to be or he didn't think she deserved it. If he treated his wife the same way, no wonder she acted out.

"One of these days, he'll wake up and it will be too late," she said, pulling on a pair of short pajamas. "I ought to teach him what he's missing and then dump him."

The next morning, she telephoned Leticia, but her cousin had left for the office and, as a rule, they didn't call each other at work. She sent Leticia an e-mail letting her know that she'd like to see the apartment. As she closed her computer, she wondered if Leticia made more money than she did.

"Everybody makes more money than we teachers make," she spat out bitterly.

Ten years had passed since she'd graduated from the university, and she could measure her progress in inches and cents. Almost nothing had changed. Somewhere, somehow, she'd made a wrong turn, and she was still going in the wrong direction. Damn Reggie!

Leticia opened her e-mail and let her gaze run down the list. Nothing from Wilson, though she didn't realize she'd been expecting a note from him. If he was waiting to hear from her, she hoped he wouldn't hold his breath. He wanted them to be better friends, so he'd have to be the one to work on it. Years ago, she'd dug a hole for herself and managed, with a lot of pain, to get out of it. In the process, she learned to avoid such pitfalls.

Kenyetta's address popped up, and she clicked on it and read that her cousin wanted to see her new apartment. She sent an e-mail suggesting the following evening and got an agreement in reply. Her phone rang, and she observed that she'd been at her desk nearly an hour and hadn't done any work.

"Yes, this is Leticia Langley."

"Cousin Leticia?" She was immediately on guard. "Did you hear me, Cousin Leticia? This is your cousin Carl Montague. I brought my daughter—your cousin Delitha— to George Washington University Hospital yesterday. You said you'd look in on her and see if she needs anything, and I'll be obliged." He gave Leticia his telephone number. "I'll expect a call from you if Delitha has any problems."

She wasn't about to call him "cousin" or pretend that she knew him or had ever seen him. "I wrote you that I could not and would not take responsibility for your daughter. I will visit her, but if she has a problem, it's the doctor's job to get in touch with you. What room is she in?" He told her. "How did you find my office phone number?"

"Cousin Bryce told me you work for a newspaper. This is the fourth one I called. I'll be in touch." He hung up before she could respond further. Her first inclination was to phone Kenyetta, but her cousin was a crutch that she planned to stop using. She got up, stepped out of her cubicle and walked down the aisle, turned and walked back to her cubicle.

"You must really be engrossed in your work." She looked up and saw Joel in her path. "Come on," he said. "What's the problem?"

She stopped. "Do you have any relatives?"

A deep frown altered the contours of his face, and he ran his hand over his short curls. "Relatives? Sometimes I think they'll be the death of me. I spend half of my time trying to ignore them, all except my parents. They always have their hand out for something. Don't let 'em use you."

She went back into her cubicle and sat down. She heard the ring of a telephone. "Line three for Langley," someone yelled. Leticia lifted the receiver. "Wilson here. Have you finished that column of non-American women of African descent? I was wondering if I could come over to your place tonight, and we could see what we have so far."

Her antennae shot up immediately. "My work doesn't follow me home, Wilson."

He didn't pause long, and she knew he'd second-guessed her and had his answer ready. "Then why don't I come over anyway?"

Her breathing deepened and she began a rhythmic tapping of her left fist on her desk. What did this man think she was? "What did you have in mind, Wilson? I can watch TV by myself."

"I thought we agreed that we wanted to get to know each other."

"Then meet me after work and let's go to Starbucks or some place like that where we can have a cup of coffee and talk. Or we could walk down by the Tidal Basin. The weather's nice."

"You don't want me to come to your place?"

"For what you want, no. I'm not ready for that, Wilson. Easy come, easy go."

"Leticia, my dear. You're a genius at misunderstanding me. I only want to be in a quiet place where we could talk and enjoy each other's company. I'll check things out, see what I can find for us to do and call you back. Okay?"

She told him that it was okay, but she had begun to lose faith in the possibility of a relationship with him. He was so sure of himself, and maybe he deserved to be, but she'd had it with that type, and once was enough. She managed to proofread her copy by quarter of four and take it to Joel.

"You sure about these statistics?" Joel asked her, his voice carrying a note of uncertainty.

"Yes. According to the World Health Organization, one third of black South African women and a quarter of men are markedly overweight. That's less than the level here. But the interesting parallel is that in Africa and here, relatively more black women than men are obese."

"But I thought food was scarce in Africa," Joel said

"They eat a lot of starchy food, especially yams. In addition, fat on a woman is thought to mean good health, though I suspect that varies with education and tribe; in some tribes, it is said to indicate that her husband is prosperous. And nowadays, no one wants to be skinny for fear of being accused of having AIDS."

He glanced over the report. "Is all that in here?"

She nodded.

"Great. You're doing good."

A writing pad flew over her head. "Don't worry about that. This time of day, nobody has time to walk a few feet in order to deliver what they can throw," he said. "Pretty soon, you'll be doing it, too. Drop this by Max's desk, will you?"

She pushed open the door to Max's room. "Hi, Max. Joel asked me to give you this. How do you stand this noise? The place is a zoo."

He looked up and smiled. "Thanks, Leticia. You'll get used to the noise. It's the most consistent thing about this place."

"I'll let you get back to work," she said. "Good night."

She packed up her things, locked her desk and took the elevator down to the lobby. When she stepped out of the elevator, she nearly tripped. Wilson Gallagher was leaning against the information desk. When she remembered his friendship with Max and considered that Wilson was probably waiting for him, she relaxed. But he came to meet her and the flower he carried was certainly not intended for Max.

He leaned down to kiss her cheek, but she shifted her stance and avoided his touch. "Max is still in his office," she said without preliminaries. *If only the man didn't get to her!*

"I don't want to see Max. I'm waiting for you."

Stopping by her office could be as troublesome as if he rang her doorbell when she didn't expect him. "I'm sorry, Wilson, but I have an appointment." She went to the information desk and asked the officer to phone for a taxi. A few minutes later she got into the taxi, waved at Wilson and settled back in the seat.

"Where to, miss?"

She hadn't thought about where she was going. "George Washington University Hospital," she said, because it was the first place she thought of. *There I go again,* she said to herself. She'd had no plans for going to GWU hospital, but because she hadn't had the guts to tell Wilson she didn't want to see him, she lied her way out of it, and now she was headed in the opposite direction of her home. At least she could check on Delitha. *I've got to stop this. I'm grown; I work; and I take care of myself. I've got to learn to defend myself and to stand up for my rights.* She shifted in her seat. She *did* want to see Wilson, and that was the problem, but her head told her that he wasn't the man for her. Well, she had told Delitha's father that she would visit her, and she always tried to keep her word. The taxi stopped in front of the hospital.

"Here we are, miss."

Leticia got a pass and went to Delitha's room.

"I'm Leticia Langley, Delitha. Your dad asked me to look in on you. How do you feel?"

"Rotten," the girl said. "It's the pits."

"Do you mean you're still having pain?"

"It's not that. They say I'm overweight, and all they give me to eat is chicken breast and vegetables. That's rabbit food. I asked for some biscuits, and the woman who delivered the tray asked me if I was joking. Everything's broiled. It's enough to make me sick. I want to get out of here."

Leticia hadn't expected a problem child, but she'd bet that this one, short of a religious epiphany, was headed for some antisocial activity. The girl hadn't had the grace to acknowledge the introduction or thank her for coming. Leticia browsed over the chart at the foot of Delitha's bed and noted that her midafternoon snack consisted of clear broth and Swedish rye crackers. *Glad I won't be here when they give it to her.*

She didn't visit Delitha the next day, but phoned the hospital and spoke with the doctor in charge.

"The puzzle has been solved, Ms. Langley," the doctor said. "Delitha became pubescent and hasn't had a pain all day. I'll discharge her tomorrow morning."

She thanked the doctor. "That's really good news. Have you informed her father that she can go home?"

"Why, no. According to our records at the admittance office, you're the one we should contact."

Sweat beaded on her forehead, and she nearly swallowed her tongue. "Doctor, I have seen Delitha exactly once, and that was last night when I visited her. I work, and I will not leave that bad-mannered little girl alone in my apartment all day. It's out of the question. Whoever signed her in can sign her out."

"But she said she wants to go home with her cousin Leticia."

"Wanting is free, Doctor. It doesn't cost a cent. I suggest you call her father."

"I don't suppose I have a choice," he said.

When Leticia got home later that day, she telephoned Kenyetta and updated her on the Delitha situation. "She's not coming here. That girl has no manners! The crassness of him putting my name down as the person to contact! I'm not even going to call him."

"Oh, for goodness sake, Leticia, don't blow a gasket over something like this. They say Carl Montague got rich doing other people's thinking for them. I don't know, but before you can blink, you're doing what he wants you to do. I'll take Delitha back to Edenton, but I can't do it till Saturday."

"Let Cousin Carl come and get his daughter, or he can send his chauffeur up here to take her home," Leticia said.

"Yeah. You're right. If I took her home, I'll bet he wouldn't even reimburse me."

"You want to come over? I can put a couple of frozen quiches in the microwave. That, a salad and some fruit should be enough."

"No wonder you're so skinny," Kenyetta said. "I'll be over in an hour, and I'm bringing butter-pecan ice cream."

After their supper, Leticia watched her cousin devour the ice cream with the relish of one who hadn't had food in a long time. "You have to stop this, Ken. You're becoming obese. I want you to meet a man I know who's doing some research on this. What he'll tell you is almost frightening. At first you promise yourself you're going on a diet and you'll start exercising, but you're lazy and you don't do it. Time passes and you get used to the way you look. Ken, you don't want that to happen to you."

Kenyetta scraped the container. "I haven't had any complaints yet. Still, I wouldn't mind getting into a sheath again. End of topic. How is Delitha going to get back home?"

"If you and I stay out of it, her father will spend some of his money, and one day soon she'll wake up in her own bed."

"I guess you're right." Kenyetta looked around. "This place is terrific, but it's so big. You'll spend your weekends cleaning up. If I were you, I'd get a cleaning woman. Nobody'd catch me spending all of my free time house cleaning. This place is twice as big as mine."

She hadn't thought about that, but it made sense. She'd check her financial status when she got her next paycheck. Joel had promised that she'd get a lot more money. "I'll look into that, Ken, as soon as I get my next paycheck. My boss switched me from food to features, and writing features pays more. On the down side, I've lost my nice private office. I have a cubicle in the newsroom like the rest of the reporters. It's roomy, but I can't close the door and change my clothes, if you know what I mean."

"If you make more money, who cares where you sit?" She looked at her watch for the second time in five minutes.

"Do you have to be someplace?" Leticia asked her cousin.

"Uh . . . not really. It's just nervousness."

"What are you nervous about? It's just seven forty-five, and it isn't dark."

"This is the last time I'm teaching summer makeup

classes," Kenyetta said, in a deft change of the subject. "Next summer, they can get someone else to do it."

She didn't fool Leticia, who had decided that her cousin's occasionally odd behavior bore watching. Shortly after that, Kenyetta hugged her, swore she was on the verge of going to sleep and left.

Leticia cleaned the kitchen, showered and sat down to watch a movie, *The Autobiography of Miss Jane Pittman*, which was based on Gaines's book. Immediately, the phone rang.

"Hi, this is Wilson. I decided that if you have a date with some other guy, interrupting is the least I could do in my own interest."

She curled up on the sofa. "You wouldn't expect me to be rude to my guest, would you?"

"No, but I wouldn't expect you to be any nicer to him than you are to me. Have you got a guy there? If you haven't, I'm coming over. I want to see you."

"You just saw me a little more than three hours ago, and you can't ever come to my apartment unless I invite you or bring you with me. Is that settled?" Her breathing accelerated while she waited for his answer. At last she'd told a man exactly what she meant, and with her pride a mile high, she wanted to dance.

"So you don't have a man there, and you don't want me to come over. Is that it?"

"Right. That about covers it, Wilson. I told you once that I can watch television by myself. Nothing's changed."

"I couldn't get the tickets I wanted. Will you go with me to Blues Alley this coming Friday night?"

"Okay. What time?"

"I'll come for you around eight-thirty."

"I'll look forward to it, Wilson." She said good night

and began dealing with the sense that she'd stepped into a trap.

"This is good work," Joel told Leticia, "but I'd like to see you dig a little deeper into what causes the differences in obesity between black African women and American women of African descent. You hinted that it's attitude as well as diet, and I think people would like to know more about that. Think about it and let me know if you want to expand on it. You're onto something." She could see that she had pleased him, and she left his office in high spirits.

"What's got you so high?" a voice asked as she passed the water fountain.

"Max! I didn't know that was you bending over the tap. I think of you as someone who towers over me."

"Just another tall guy, eh?" He pressed his right hand to the left side of his chest. "You've wounded me."

She patted his shoulder and walked on. Max could be disconcerting when he stared at her unexpectedly, as if he'd never seen her before. Marie Ong, a soft-news reporter, waited for her beside Leticia's cubicle. She had yet to develop warm feelings for the woman, and when Marie scowled at her, she prepared herself for a confrontation.

"Hi, Marie. You waiting to see me?"

"You bet I am. Until you started writing about obesity, I did the features on minorities. Who gave you permission to take over my work?"

She walked past the woman and went to her desk. "If you have questions about assignments, see Joel. I do what he tells me to do. By the way, have you ever written anything on African-American women?" When Marie didn't reply, Leticia said, "I didn't think so. Settle it with Joel." She knew she was a better writer than Marie, and she also knew that Joel liked her series and wouldn't interfere with it.

Friday evening arrived, and Leticia could hardly control her impatience to see Wilson. They would be alone for the first time, and she wondered how he would behave and how she would respond to him. She was sufficiently familiar with herself to know the folly of deciding in advance how she would react to him. She whispered a prayer that she wouldn't do anything she would regret.

The doorman buzzed her at exactly eight-thirty. Minutes later, her doorbell rang. When she attempted to slip the door chain, her breathing accelerated and her fingers shook. She told herself to calm down. Was it fear or excitement about the unknown, and what would she be like alone with Wilson Gallagher? She lifted her chin and admonished herself to remember her days as a short order cook in a third-rate restaurant.

He filled the doorway, and it seemed to her that he exulted in his bulk. Immediately, she realized that she had overdressed, because he wasn't wearing a tie. Annoyed and unable to contain the evidence of it, she blurted out, "You're not wearing a tie. I thought we were going to Blues Alley."

A grin spread over his face. "What way is that to greet a guy who's so eager to see you that he forgot his tie? Is a tie mandatory at Blues Alley?" His face darkened with apparent concern. "Then I guess we can't go."

Her knotted fists went to her hips. "What are you trying to pull? This is childish, Wilson. I wouldn't expect a grown man to try such a trick. This is beneath a teenager. Would you please leave?"

"Aw, Leticia. Where's your sense of humor? A man has to do whatever he can—short of a crime—to get the woman he wants. Aren't you even going to invite me to come in? After all, we do have a date, and you didn't tell me I had to wear a tie."

"We have a date to go to Blues Alley, and if we're not going there, I want you to leave."

He stepped closer, and she took a step back. *Lord, please don't let him touch me.* But his big hand shot out, pulled her to him and fastened her to his body. Terror streaked through Leticia. If he kissed her, she didn't know how she would resist him. He lowered his mouth onto hers and she stopped thinking. Her lips parted and her heart lunged in her chest as she pulled his tongue into her mouth. She hated herself, but she needed what he gave her. When she felt his passion accelerate into a wildness that seemed beyond his control, she pushed him away and, to her surprise, he released her immediately. She staggered backward until the wall took her weight.

In an effort to deal with her shock both at Wilson's aggressiveness and her own wantonness, she breathed deeply and slowly with her hands pressed to her chest until she could look him in the eye.

"I want you to leave," she said.

"You think I believe you? Woman, you just kissed me like someone starved for months. How long has it been since you had a man?"

He'd said just the thing to make her anger override her desire for him. "That's none of your business. I told you to leave."

"If I thought you meant it, I'd be halfway home by now. I know when a woman wants me."

"Don't be so sure of yourself. I could kiss any of a half

dozen men the same way," she lied, "and feel the same as I did a minute ago. Are you leaving?"

He tipped an imaginary hat. "As you like, babe. But when a woman fires up my engine the way you did a minute ago, I know it's only a question of when. Sleep well."

She was willing to let him have the last word, because she didn't want to prolong his stay. The longer she looked at him, available, eager and tantalizing, the weaker she became.

"I read you right," he said, "and don't tell me I didn't."

"Wilson, no matter how I feel about you or what you think of me, I don't want this." She tried a different tactic. "It isn't personal. You're an attractive and engaging man, but I am not ready for what you want and what you're offering."

"Do you think there's a chance?"

She looked at him then with sharper perceptiveness, seeing his humaneness. His swagger, self-assurance and brittleness were for a moment nowhere apparent. Was success in conquering a female so dominant a need in men? Was everything else in his life relatively less important? She knew that her benevolent smile failed to comfort him, but she was on the road to self-realization and that meant honesty with herself and others, so she leveled with him.

"I won't deny that I'm attracted to you, but I don't have the right feeling about this. It's like we're not waltzing to the same music."

His old demeanor returned and along with it, the certainty of success that he projected. "But is there a chance?" he asked, as if her analogy meant nothing to him.

She opened the door. "I really don't know."

He leaned down and pressed a brief kiss to her lips. "I'll call you tomorrow. Good night."

He had disappointed her, and she knew that, given a chance, he would do it again. She didn't think him capable of giving her what she needed, a feeling of security, of being needed and cherished that she hadn't found in any man.

Leticia's phone rang, and she answered it with reluctance, certain that she was in for more of Wilson's shenanigans. But she heard Kenyetta's voice.

"Guess what, girl?" Kenyetta began. "Our problems are over. Delitha's father came up today and took her home. It seems the doctor called him and told him that she was well and had to leave the hospital."

"Did Carl call you?"

"You kidding? That old deadbeat wouldn't do anything as civil as that. I phoned the hospital to find out how she was getting on, and the doctor told me."

Leticia released a long breath. "I'm glad that's over."

"You can say that again."

"You know, Ken, I want to do something different, something other than work, home, church and an occasional movie."

"Look out now, girl," Kenyetta said, and Leticia realized that she'd given her cousin another opportunity to dole out unsought advice. "That's a recipe for trouble, sure as my name is Kenyetta. Been there and done that . . . a lot of that."

"Keep talking," Leticia said to herself, "and pretty soon you'll tell all." They talked for a short while, long enough for Leticia to recover from her blue funk.

But she apparently hadn't shaken it completely. Monday morning, when Joel met her in the corridor, he asked her, "What's with you? You look as if you lost your last friend."

Wilson had said he'd call her the next day, Saturday, but he didn't, and he didn't call on Sunday either. Maybe she'd been too harsh or too demanding. She didn't know, because she hadn't known a man like Wilson.

"So what's up?" Joel asked, and not out of curiosity, she knew. Joel Raymond was all business.

"Me, I'm fine. A little sleepy," she said, knowing it wasn't true. But she wouldn't consider dumping her problems on her boss. Several hours later, she still hadn't been able to concentrate on her work, and when she saw Joel enter her office cubicle, she nearly panicked. Immediately, he discerned her mood, for he observed her with a narrowed left eye. Then he shrugged.

"Langley, I want you to interview the new mayor, and I want a family story as far back as you can get it— grandparents, parents, kids, his wife's background. You name it. I got you an exclusive." He put a piece of paper on her desk and said, "Here's his private number."

"Thanks. I . . . I appreciate it."

Joel sat down, something he hadn't previously done in her office. "You've got a problem, Leticia. What is it? Can I help?"

She was not going to cry. She hadn't cried when she was alone in the world and had only seventy-three cents for food and lodging. She'd gotten a job as a live-in nanny, and a year later had enough money to register at Howard University.

"Something's wrong with you, and it's not a simple thing. You didn't say a word at the budget meeting this morning, and I gave you an assignment that every one of my reporters would kill for. All you said was, 'Thanks.'"

She hardly heard him. "How do you get a man you're attracted to to see you as a person and not just a—"

He interrupted her. "A sex object? I hope to hell you haven't caved in."

Leticia shook her head. "I haven't, but—"

"No buts, Leticia. If he doesn't meet your needs now, he won't later. I'm telling you what I would have told my oldest daughter if she had given me the chance. Find a man who appreciates you as an individual and as a woman. Good looking as you are, that shouldn't be difficult. And if he doesn't make you feel great, drop him. He won't change."

Her instincts had always told her that, so she knew he spoke the truth, but she also knew that because of her loneliness, she sometimes acted against her better judgment. She didn't feel right with Wilson, not even when he had her on fire, though she couldn't finger the reason. Instinct spoke for her, and she'd sent him away.

Joel leaned forward, his features displaying his agitation. "Leticia, I'm fifty-nine years old. I've seen all kinds of relationships and been in a few. When a man cares for a woman, he can't hide it and usually doesn't try. Don't do anything stupid." He got up, but seemed reluctant to leave. "I'd like you to do the story, but if you think you're not up to it—"

"Of course I'm up to it. Joel, thanks. I don't have a family, and things get a little dark sometimes, but I'll . . . thanks for talking with me." She knew his shrug belied his concern.

"It was nothing. Look around you." She was getting used to Joel's cryptic comments, so she didn't react to that one. After work that day, Joel walked out of the building along with her and, to her chagrin, Wilson Gallagher rushed to meet her. After her conversation with Joel that morning, she would have preferred that he not see her with Wilson.

Feeling trapped and angry at Wilson for treating her so casually, she barely paused when he reached her. "Hi, Max is still upstairs," she said without looking at him.

But she hadn't fooled Joel, for he said, "I hope Wilson Gallagher isn't the person responsible for these dark moods you're having. The guy's a player. He's like a forest fire; if you don't stay out of his way, he'll consume you. He's the type who has to have every good-looking woman he meets."

She didn't feel like lying. "I'm learning, Joel."

"Good. He's not your type. You're too soft for him."

They waited at the edge of Thomas Circle for the traffic light. "If he's such a rascal and a womanizer, why does Max tolerate him? They're close friends."

"Friends, yes, but they're hardly bosom buddies. Besides, a man's requirements in male friends are not the same as yours should be." The light changed, and he stepped off the curb. "See you tomorrow. And, Leticia, don't get too close to that flame. It's fascinating, but it'll burn you beyond recognition."

She said good night to Joel and headed for the bus stop, her steps quick and sure as she recalled her new assignment. But half an hour later, when she entered the lobby of the building in which she lived, Wilson greeted her with what seemed to her a forced smile.

She stopped beside the doorman's station. "What do you want, Wilson? An appointment so you can tell me some more lies?" He flinched visibly, but she didn't care. "You were going to take me to Blues Alley, but that was a ruse to get into my apartment. You said you'd call me Saturday, but today is Monday, and I have yet to receive your call. Please stay away from me. I'm becoming allergic to you."

"I don't believe you."

"Wilson, please find your amusement somewhere else. Good night." She knew he wouldn't follow her, knowing that the doorman overheard their conversation.

When she got to her office the next morning, she telephoned Wilson. "My third and probably last column on obesity will be in our Friday edition. I thought you'd like to know."

"Thanks, Leticia. I appreciate that. I finished the chapter on becoming obese, and I'd like you to read it."

"Of course. I'd like my cousin to read it, too. If you'd e-mail it to me, we could meet at a restaurant and discuss it."

"That works for me," he said, evidently pleased with the idea. "Now, are you ever going to give me a chance?"

"Not on the basis of your past behavior." Laughter poured out of him. "What's funny?" she asked.

"I am, I guess. How the hell did I know I was on trial? Let's meet at Fondelli's tomorrow at seven." She agreed and hoped that Kenyetta wouldn't have one of her mysterious appointments. If only Wilson would prove Joel wrong!

"You mean you're introducing me to a man?" Kenyetta asked Leticia in a voice that purred.

"I am not matchmaking, Ken. In fact, there's something simmering between him and me. I just don't know where it's going."

"Tell me about it," Kenyetta said.

"Be sure and get to the restaurant at seven o'clock, Ken." She didn't want to be alone with Wilson, not even in a public place.

"Will do," Kenyetta said.

Leticia read Wilson's chapter on ways in which people become obese, judged it to be the work of a consummate professional and told Kenyetta as much, hoping that her overweight cousin would heed Wilson's conclusions.

Kenyetta arrived at the restaurant at seven thirty-five, breathless and dressed more suitably for dancing than for dinner with her cousin and a stranger.

"Sorry I'm late, but I had so much to do." She looked at Wilson. "Hi. I've been dying to meet you. Leticia said you're an absolute genius, and I *love*"—she stretched out the word—"smart men. Why on earth are you studying obesity? From where I sit, you're absolutely perfect."

Leticia was certain that her eyes had grown to twice their size. She stared at her cousin, and when her gaze shifted to Wilson, her lower jaw dropped. Like a comet shooting across the sky, the man switched his focus from Leticia to Kenyetta and began his campaign.

"Well, I'll be damned," Leticia said, but neither Kenyetta nor Wilson appeared to notice. Leticia had wanted her relationship with Wilson to play out on her terms, but she had no intention of competing with her cousin for a man she wasn't certain she wanted and whom Joel— a man she respected—considered unworthy of her attention. Still, it hurt.

In a piece of acting worthy of Hepburn or Streep, Leticia ordered her dinner, asked the waiter for a separate check and launched the discussion of Wilson's chapter on obesity. Neither he nor Kenyetta seemed interested, so she cut the discussion short and projected a jovial mood as she finished her dinner.

"You two stay as long as you like," she said. "I have to be going."

"Oh, Leticia, I didn't mean to—"

Leticia waved dismissively at her cousin and kept walking. She paid for her meal at the cashier's desk, hailed a taxi and went home.

In the future, I'll keep plenty of space between myself and both of them.

But as Leticia expected, Kenyetta called her at home before she left for work the next morning. "Hey, girl. Where'd you rush off to last night? I was so embarrassed to be alone with that strange man. You could have warned me."

"Spare me that nonsense, Kenyetta. Why did you call? I have to get ready for work."

"Well, if you're in such a big hurry, I'll talk to you later."

Leticia hung up knowing that Kenyetta had made her weak attempt to apologize and pretend innocence so that her conscience wouldn't bother her. If she wasn't so furious with her cousin, Leticia would thank her for exposing Wilson's true colors. Kenyetta never ceased trying to prove that she was more attractive to men than Leticia was, and this time, she may have bitten off more than she could chew. When Kenyetta came to her crying about Wilson, she'd discover that Leticia's sympathy was in short supply.

But with her ego in high gear, Kenyetta had no such concerns. She and Wilson had left the restaurant holding hands. She was fairly certain that she didn't have to worry about Reggie because she took care of him the night before. Wilson was single, he'd paid for the dinner, and that placed him a cut above Reggie, who always made her pay. If this brother knew how to put it down, maybe she'd finally be able to change her life.

"I'll see you home," Wilson said as if he recognized that as his duty. "I didn't dream that I'd meet someone like you tonight or ever. Lady, when you rushed into that restaurant, you took my breath away."

She was smart enough not to comment on that. If she thanked him, he'd think she wasn't used to compliments on her looks. "What's between you and Leticia?" she asked.

A taxi stopped, and he opened the door for her, walked around to the other side and got in. "Where to?" he asked her, and she gave the address to the driver.

"I consider your question an affront. If I was getting something on with Leticia Langley, I wouldn't be in this taxi with you. She saw how I felt about you and left in order to give me a chance."

Kenyetta didn't know whether to believe him, but what he said made sense. He paid the taxi and walked with her to the door of her apartment. "I think you know that I don't want to leave you." His right hand brushed her cheek, and when his finger trailed over her lips, she parted them and sucked his finger into her mouth. The fire of desire leaped into his eyes, and fear shot through her at the turbulence she saw in them.

Quickly, she kissed his cheek and turned her back to open her door. "Good night. I—" He pulled her around, locked her to him and traced the seam of her lips with his tongue. The odor of his heat sent her blood racing to her loins. She opened her mouth and sucked his tongue into her.

He broke the kiss. "If you're going to send me packing, do it now."

The certainty in his voice that she would let him stay dragged her back to her senses. "I'd like you to stay, but this is not the night for it. We . . . uh . . . we'll see each other again."

"Is that a promise?" he asked, making certain with his

tone and demeanor that she understood what he meant. She nodded.

"What's your phone number, Kenyetta?" She gave it to him. "I'll be in touch," he said.

She went inside, flopped on her living room sofa and kicked up her heels. *Leticia can forget about that brother. He wants me. And I intend to satisfy him so thoroughly that he'll never be tempted to look twice at another woman.*

Chapter Four

With its lingering summer weather, late autumn in Washington, D.C. held in abeyance the threat of winter, which, after almost five years, Georgia-born Leticia could hardly tolerate. She stood on her back balcony shaking out her bedsheets and letting the crisp air renew her thinly clad body. She longed for a swing like the one on her father's front porch, in which as a child she had spent so many hours swinging and dreaming. The midsummer flowers had served their purpose and withered away, but for as far as she could see, marigolds of every height, variety and autumn color—from pale yellow to golden brown—decorated the landscape. Awesome beauty in her favorite colors, and she had never taken the time to let herself enjoy it.

She sat down on a high stool, let the wall support her back, folded her arms and gazed at the beauty surrounding her, a scene so different from the world she left behind when she moved there. She had a rewarding job with excellent prospects for the future, a good salary and, at last, a home in which she took pride. But she continued to live as she had for years—working, going home, reading or watching television, and going back to work the next day. She hadn't made close friends, and her one friend, her cousin Kenyetta, could hardly be called a true friend. Friends don't make a play for your date, or she hadn't thought so.

She had made the mistake of falling for Wilson, though luckily she hadn't fallen all the way. But Lord! She was so lonely for a soul mate, someone who would like her and accept her for herself, for what she was. Be it man or girlfriend, she needed a person with whom she had the basic things in common. She hadn't made a lasting friend in college, either, she recalled. She managed to stand up for herself most of the time now, but she knew that the most popular of her classmates and, later, her co-workers, weren't the best students or the best reporters, but the ones who had the most self-confidence. She vowed to work harder on her belief in herself.

The wind picked up, and she collected the sheets and went inside to make her bed and finish cleaning her apartment. That was another thing: she spent Saturdays housecleaning and grocery shopping, when she wanted to browse in bookstores, loaf around in museums or stroll along the Tidal Basin. She wanted to soak up the music, art and culture that had been a part of her coworkers' lives from the time they were small children, but of which she knew little or nothing. She needed time for activities that would enrich her life. She said as much to one of her colleagues as they stood in the coffee room the following Monday morning.

"I don't know when I last cleaned my apartment," Glenda, one of the reporters, said. "If you're a feature writer, you make enough to hire a housekeeper, or at least a weekly cleaning woman. If you get someone to come in five and a half days a week, it's not a lot more expensive than these twice-weekly cleaners you hire through an agency."

"I'll put an ad in the paper."

"You'd have better luck if you put one on the bulletin board in your church," Glenda told her. "And get an older woman."

Leticia thanked her, went back to her desk and sent an e-mail to the church secretary, stating her requirements for a housekeeper. Four evenings later, she met Willa Evans for the first time. She opened the door, and the tiny woman looked up at her and smiled so brightly that Leticia thought at once of a mid-afternoon summer sun.

"Good evening, ma'am. I'm Willa Evans, and if you want somebody who'll give your home the loving care that you'd give it, I'm your housekeeper."

Leticia smiled because she couldn't help it. "You don't look big enough to lift a broom. Come in, Ms. Evans."

"Don't worry, ma'am. There ain't much of me, but what's here don't take a backseat to no woman. You'll see."

Leticia believed her. "Have a seat," she said after walking into the living room. "May I see your references, Ms. Evans?"

"Yes, ma'am. Every time you say 'Ms. Evans,' I almost look around to see who else is here with my name. Nothing fancy about me. Call me Willa." She handed Leticia a large manila envelope and a CD. "The last man I worked for made the CD. He travels a lot and gave me that in case he's out of the country when I need him."

"Why did you quit working for him?"

"He got married, and he's moving to Augusta, Georgia. He wanted me to go with him, but me and the Deep South don't mix. I was born down there."

As Leticia glanced over the references, the words she saw most often were honesty and loyalty. She liked that. "I'll read these tonight, check a couple of them tomorrow and call you tomorrow night. How's that?"

"Fine, ma'am. I'm not worried, 'cause I know that everybody I ever worked for was more than satisfied with my work. I've never been dismissed."

"I imagine you haven't." She showed Willa the remainder of the apartment and quoted a salary to which Willa agreed. After noting the woman's address, she gave her a twenty-dollar bill for taxi fare home.

Later, she read the letters of recommendation, chose three to call and, noting that it was only eight-thirty, called the writer of one.

"Mrs. McCullen, this is Leticia Langley. I'm considering hiring Willa Evans, and she's given me your name for—"

The woman interrupted. "Is she looking for a job? Good heavens, I lost her phone number, and I need someone myself. I want her back. That woman is priceless, and such a joy to be around. Did she give you her number?"

After an awkward moment, Leticia recovered sufficiently to thank the woman. She added, "I'd be glad to give you her phone number, Mrs. McCullen, if I wasn't considering hiring her myself. Thanks for your help." The next morning, she checked two other references, decided that she'd be fortunate to have Willa Evans work for her and concluded the agreement the following evening.

"I'll see you in the morning, ma'am," Willa said. "I need a weekly budget and a grocery list, and please put the mending on the dining room table."

Shaking her head, Leticia went into her kitchen—the room in which she felt most comfortable—and sat in one of the kitchen chairs. A housekeeper. What on earth did she want with a housekeeper? She thought back to when she'd kept house for a policeman and his family in order to support her sick father and herself. What would her father's neighbors think of the girl who, for the first twenty years of her life, washed her clothes by hand in a metal tub and found privacy in an outhouse? When that became intolerable after her father's death, she'd moved to Atlanta.

Leticia got up and took a Popsicle from the freezer. A freezer, yet! *You've come a long way, baby!*

She went over her budget, added twenty-five percent to the amount she spent for food, deducted the cost of her laundry bill and considered herself fortunate because she would no longer spend her Saturday mornings cleaning and the afternoons in supermarkets.

"You don't have to cook breakfast," she told Willa when the woman arrived the next morning. "I give myself forty-five minutes to dress, eat and get out of here."

Willa frowned, or maybe she scowled. "Skipping breakfast is a bad habit."

"Yes, I know. I listed the things I don't like to eat. Apart from that, cook whatever you like for dinner. The money's in that red box. See you around five." When she got to the office, she went directly to the coffee room, as the reporters called it.

"Say, you're as scarce as hen's teeth," Max said. "You're right down the hall there, and I haven't seen you in two weeks."

"That's because you've been on assignment," she said.

His eyebrow shot up. "How'd you know?"

"You weren't at budget meetings. When you're there, we all know it."

"Right. I'm known for speaking my mind. Your columns on obesity were first-class. Keep it up." He poured a second cup of coffee for himself, picked up three hot-cross buns and went back to his desk.

If they had been friends, she could have asked him about Wilson, but she was glad that the thought hadn't occurred to her. As far as she was concerned, Wilson was history. She wondered, not for the first time, how far the relationship between Wilson and her cousin had progressed. It began with sparks shooting between them like rockets, so she wouldn't be surprised if by now, the fire of it had consumed them. Better Kenyetta than her.

However, Kenyetta was already fighting for her life. Walking the line between Reggie and Wilson was no easy trick, and since she didn't trust the temper of either man, she found it necessary to carry a pad and pen in order to keep track of her own lies. She didn't want Wilson to get away from her without her having discovered whether he was a better lover than Reggie, who had become so demanding that she hadn't found an opportunity to make the comparison.

"If I can't see you tomorrow night," Wilson told her when he called, "I am not going to call you again. No woman strings me along, and that's what you've been doing."

"I have not, and I'll prove it," she said, knowing that Reggie would leave Wednesday morning for California on company business. "I have to write a report for my principal and it's due Wednesday morning, so I can't see you Tuesday, but we can celebrate up a storm Wednesday night."

"I'm holding you to that," he said. "You've been driving me up the wall. I'm ready to explode."

"Wonderful. At least you'll be glad to see me."

"Are you a tease? Remember two can do that. When I get you, I'll show you what teasing is."

"Oh dear. I'm scared to death. I'm shaking all over."

"Keep it up."

"I'm sorry, Wilson. My bark is worse than my bite."

"If you say so, but I don't believe you. Sleep well and get plenty of rest. You're going to need it. See you Wednesday around seven."

Her laughter reverberated through her apartment. "You bad-mannered boy. I can't wait to see you."

By the time she hung up, she had unbuttoned her blouse, kicked off her shoes and loosened her skirt. She went into the kitchen, tore off a piece of paper towel and wiped her forehead. This man was not to be played with, but if she acted too serious, he'd be gone in no time. She knew the type, and she intended to smile at him every morning when she was eighty years old.

She opened a can of vegetable soup, cooked a hot dog, toasted a bagel and sat down to eat her dinner. The doorman buzzed her, and for a minute she considered not answering. "Yes. Who is it?"

"A gentleman to see you. He said you're expecting him."

"Thanks," she said, although she was not expecting a visitor. She put the chain on the door and peeped through the viewer. She wasn't expecting Reggie, and anger boiled up in her when she saw his face. She opened the door.

"You were here last night, Reggie. What's up?"

"She was on the warpath, so I walked out."

"Excuse me while I finish my dinner."

"You got enough for two?" When she said she didn't, he replied, "Send out for something."

"Not tonight, Reggie. I don't have any money."

"I don't believe you. Where's your pocketbook?"

She jumped up and glared at him. "What's come over you? You don't own me. If you touch my pocketbook, I'll call the police."

"And what will I be doing while you're calling the police?"

"Not a damned thing. Why do you think the doorman has three cameras in that lobby?"

"Aw, babe, for Pete's sake, can't you take a joke? I haven't had any dinner."

"And I haven't been to the bank." The longer she looked at him, the madder she got. "Excuse me. My soup's getting cold. And, Reggie, the management said that all tenants have to give the doormen the names, addresses, and telephone numbers of all visitors who come here after six in the evening. If the name isn't on the list, the doorman won't let them in the building."

He lunged forward and stared at her. "What the hell kind of crap is that?"

"People complained that the doormen should ask their permission to allow a guest to come up, but sometimes he's busy."

"They're just nosy. Maybe it's that security guy getting into everybody's business. Find another place to stay."

"Why? I'm happy here."

"Look, babe. Cut me some slack. You can find another place in no time."

"Look, *Reggie!* You have your wife and your nice house up on Connecticut Avenue. This is all I have and all I can afford. So, baby, I'm keeping this, and I know that when you think about it, you'll say I'm right." She finished eating and put the soiled utensils in the dishwasher. He was so used to her catering to his every whim, that he probably didn't believe she was staying, but he'd better. She wasn't leaving her apartment for him or any other man until one of them put a ring on her finger.

"What'll I eat?" he asked, his voice a pouting growl.

"I don't know, sugar. That was my only can of soup."

Suddenly, his demeanor changed, and he narrowed his eyes. "You got your ass on your shoulder tonight, but you'll be crying for me to come over here and cool your tunnel."

She bit her lip. One day she'd tell him that her tunnel never got hot when he was around. And that wasn't half of what she could say that he wouldn't want to hear, but a bird in the hand was worth two in a bush, and she didn't have Wilson yet. So she swallowed the words that she would have loved to say.

"I can't help it if I don't have any food," she said, skirting the issue.

"That ain't what this is about. See you."

He let himself out, but she knew he'd be back. The difference was that now he'd have to make a date with her at least the day before or the doorman wouldn't let him in. At times, like tonight, she didn't really like him. Why couldn't she stand up to him and tell him that he couldn't have both his wife and her? Other than humiliation, what did she get out of the relationship? She sat in the dimly lit living room for a long time. Was it better to have no man at all, to have no one who wanted you? Maybe Wilson would be the answer to her problem with Reggie.

At noon that Wednesday, she telephoned the company for which Reggie worked and asked the operator if she could speak with him. "I'm sorry, miss, but Mr. Parish left this morning for California. He'll be back in the office Monday morning. May I tell him who called?"

She hung up. She didn't have to worry that Reggie

would find a way to surprise her that night when she was with Wilson. But after that, what?

Leticia gasped when she heard Mark DuPree's voice on her phone at *The Journal.* "Mark, this is a wonderful surprise," she said. "Tell me you're here in the nation's capital."

"How are you, cousin? I'm here in the national's capital."

"You're kidding. Can you meet me for lunch? I'm on Fourteenth Street Northwest, just south of Thomas Circle. Just ask the taxi driver to take you to *The Journal.* I'm hungry, but I'll wait for you. There're a couple of good restaurants right down the street."

"Be there as soon as a taxi will get me there."

"I'm on the ninth floor. I'll meet you at the elevator." She'd been deep into her work, which meant chewing her pencil, eating the lipstick off her lips and pulling her hair.

"How's the interview with the mayor and his family going?" Joel asked her when she passed his office.

"Great. The man's wife is downright loquacious. I can hardly ask more than one question per interview. She must be hard-up for company."

"I know. Ned's not a talker. For your sake, it's a good thing she is."

Leticia stopped at her desk, got her bag and headed for the elevator bank, pleased about the possibility of having a good relationship with at least one of her relatives.

When Mark stepped off the elevator, his teeth shone in a brilliant smile, just as she remembered him. He greeted her with open arms as Max and Joel approached them. One of the men cleared his throat, and Mark broke the hug.

"Hi," she said, looking at the two men. "This is my cousin, Mark DuPree, who just stepped off the plane from New Orleans. Mark, this is my supervisor, Joel Raymond, and my colleague, Max Baldwin. We're off to lunch."

"Good to meet you, man," they said, almost in unison. "Enjoy."

"Let's go to the DC Coast, Mark. I could use a good meal. Besides, you treated me in style when I was in New Orleans."

"I'm on an expense account," he said, "so I should take you to lunch."

"Maybe you should, but you are not going to." Leticia rarely ate lunch in style, and she welcomed the change. They were seated immediately and began to study their menus. "I'll have the smoked lobster with crispy fried spinach," she told the waiter, "and some rice noodles."

"Sounds great," Mark said. "I'll have the same and a glass of pinot grigio."

"Now," he said, "tell me why your colleague—Max, I think his name is—why he looked at me as if he wished he'd had a gun."

A frown settled on her face. "Max? Whatever it was, it wasn't personal. He stays to himself, at least as far as I know."

"Don't believe that, Leticia."

"How's Grandfather?"

"No idea," Mark said. "Haven't seen the old buzzard since he was rude to you when you were in New Orleans." Mark shrugged it off. "I can get tickets to the Kennedy Center tonight. I understand there's a jazz competition with classical and modern jazz men blowing at each other." He laughed. "Any fool could predict the winners. How about it?"

"Oh, Mark, I'd love it." She thought for a minute. "Can you get a ticket for Kenyetta, too? I bet she'd like it."

"Sure. Tell her to be there no later than seven forty-five. I don't go late to any concert or play."

After lunch, she phoned Willa to tell her that she would like to eat dinner around six, after which she called her cousin Kenyetta.

"Hi, Ken. Remember Cousin Mark, who we met in New Orleans? He's in town, and he's got tickets to a jazz program at Kennedy Center tonight. You're invited. He said be there at a quarter to eight—on time."

"Girl, I'd love to . . . to see Mark and that program, too, but I've got a date."

"Almost every single time I ask you to go somewhere, you have a date, but nobody ever sees your friggin' date. There's something screwy about you and your dates. Okay. I'll tell Mark you're busy. See you."

Her annoyance wasn't justified, Leticia knew, but she was becoming increasingly certain that her cousin had a secret agenda, one that wouldn't pass muster in broad daylight. That evening, she mentioned her suspicion to Mark. "And all these dates are midweek. She's always free on weekends." Mark listened silently.

"Well, she probably isn't a lesbian," Leticia went on, "because she wants every man she meets, including her relatives, to think she's hot stuff. I think she's got a married man, and that's the dumbest thing a woman can do."

"I think so, too."

Leticia had noticed from the business card he gave her in New Orleans that Mark was a professor of human resources at a university in New Orleans. "Are you attending a conference here?" she asked him.

"No. I'm testifying as an expert before a congressional committee."

"I hope you tell them about these companies sending work overseas."

"Why don't you write a column on that?" he asked her.

"I can't add anything that every other newspaper and television station hasn't already covered."

"Do some research on the way that practice is contributing to the rising costs of living here. Trust me, it is."

She told him she'd give it some thought. The more they talked, the more she wished they had the entire evening in which to do so, although she knew she would enjoy the jazz.

During the concert, she clapped, screamed and stomped her feet along with the other happy patrons and, as they left, she collected fliers on programs scheduled for the next six months. She no longer had to do her housework, grocery shopping and laundry, and she meant to put more effort into enjoying the world around her.

Kenyetta phoned her the next day and asked about the concert. "That concert ranks high on the list of things I've enjoyed in my life," Leticia said.

"Really? It must have been a gas. Sorry I missed it."

"Want to meet me for coffee right after work?" she asked Kenyetta, figuring that it was no use asking her to do anything after six o'clock.

"Okay. Let's meet at Starbucks at five, and you can tell me all about Mark and the jazz concert."

She'd never seen Kenyetta so flushed and distracted. To test her cousin's presence of mind, she said, "What do you think I did this week?"

Kenyetta lifted her shoulder in a quick shrug. "No idea, but you'll tell me."

Clue number one, Leticia thought. *Nobody is more nosy than this woman, but right now, she isn't interested in a thing.* "I hired a full-time housekeeper."

"What's she going to do all day? Knit?"

Leticia nearly laughed. Kenyetta was in another world. Ordinarily she would have been irate at the thought that Leticia had a housekeeper and she didn't. Her cousin would have accused her of all kinds of outrageous things. Leticia didn't need more clues. Something had shaken up the woman, and Leticia was ready to bet it was a man, and not the one she previously suspected. Still, she decided to probe.

Leticia propped her elbows on the table, supported her chin with her thumbs and looked her cousin in the eye. "You know, Ken, when I first came to Washington, I looked up to you." That got Kenyetta's attention. "I thought you had everything that I aspired to. You had your college degree, a good job teaching and a nicer apartment than I would have dreamed of having."

"Don't gimmie no buts," Kenyetta said. "What are you getting at?"

"You're overweight, but you're still young and pretty, so it doesn't make a bit of sense for you to throw your life away on a married man. How could you do such a stupid thing?"

It did not surprise her that Kenyetta spilled her hot coffee on the table and in her lap. "See what you made me do!" she yelled. A man dashed from behind the counter with a damp cloth, wiped her dress and then the table. "It's all right, ma'am," he said. "I'll get you a refill."

"Who told you I was . . . ?" Kenyetta's scowl impaired her looks.

"I suspected it, but you confirmed it for me a minute ago when you spilled that coffee. The fact that I knew shocked and frightened you. I'm disappointed in you, Ken."

"Listen, don't you sound so high and mighty. After you've been here for years and haven't had a single date with an eligible man, you'll take what you can get, too. I learned that Washington has twice as many women as men, and as far as I'm concerned, that means a woman who's got a man, married or single, has to share. It's every woman for herself. Damned if I'm going to be without."

"But what about his wife? That man promised his wife he'd be faithful. How can you believe anything that he promises you?"

"Don't be so righteous! I don't want to marry him. He's using me, and I'm using him. If she was much of a woman, he wouldn't need me."

"That's your excuse? What if she finds out?"

"Won't be no skin off my teeth. He made his vows to her, not to me."

Leticia didn't want to believe what she heard. In recent weeks, her cousin had given her several unwelcome shocks, and she was beginning to conclude that she didn't know Kenyetta as well as she thought she did. Since her cousin was being candid, she had two more questions for her.

"How long have you been involved with that man?"

Kenyetta waved her hand, shrugged and said, "About four years. What difference does it make?"

"In another four years, you'll be thirty-five, and single males at that age are pretty poor pickings. I'm thirty-one, and they're scarce enough now."

"I'll worry about that when I have to," Kenyetta said,

but she had the look of a person rapidly losing her bravado.

"You didn't see him last night, though, did you?" Leticia said, anger boiling up in her at the measure of her cousin's treachery and selfishness. "You were with Wilson Gallagher last night, and you slept with him."

"What the hell is this? Why are you cross-examining me?"

"I'm doing no such thing, Kenyetta. You knew that I was interested in Wilson, because I told you so. But you made a play for him the minute you got to the table, and you had planned to do that before you left home. Otherwise, why would you have dressed like a tart?"

Kenyetta reached for her purse and pushed back her chair. "I'm leaving here."

"If you do, I follow you screaming what I have to say. So don't you move. You did me a favor, because you have proved that what my boss told me about Wilson is one hundred percent true. I hadn't wanted to believe him."

Kenyetta leaned forward, her face bare of her usual look of importance and self-assurance. "What did your boss say?"

"Why should I tell you when I'll have fun watching you discover it for yourself? Don't run to me when he gets tired of you. Oh yes, are you dropping your married boyfriend? I'd love to see you shuffle those decks."

"Don't worry about me, Leticia. If you were as clever as you think, you'd have Wilson for yourself."

"The reason I don't have him is because I wouldn't go to bed with him." Let her chew on that. She put five dollars on the table to cover her latte and pastry, and said, "See you." She left Kenyetta sitting alone at the bistro table.

* * *

Kenyetta stared at Leticia's departing back. She'd been so careful to hide her relationship with Reggie from everyone who knew her. Who else had guessed she was seeing a married man? If Reggie found out that Leticia knew about them, he'd have a fit. She wondered if Leticia was mad enough to tell Wilson about her affair with Reggie. When she made a play for Wilson, she hadn't imagined what she was getting. What a man! Reggie played stick ball to Wilson's Derek Jeter. As she thought back to the evening, her temperature began to rise, and she crossed her thighs in frustration.

She had raced to answer the doorbell, remembered to slow down and play it cool.

"Hi," Wilson had said, when she opened the door. "There doesn't seem to be a restaurant nearby, so if it's all right with you, I'll order us a gourmet meal, and we can eat it here." She had been about to accuse him of a Reggie-like trick when he handed her a bunch of red roses. "I'll call the restaurant I usually patronize."

Don't say one word, girl. See what he'll do next. "Do you like lobster?" he asked her.

She hadn't eaten much of it, but she'd loved what she'd had. She nodded. "It's one of my favorite things to eat."

He took out his cell phone, dialed a number and ordered two lobster dinners. "Tell Jess to send me a bottle of my favorite." He gave her address and apartment number.

She didn't ask him to identify his "favorite," because she knew restaurants could not legally sell alcohol off the premises. He gave his credit card number, so he was paying. She turned on her smile and prepared to please him.

"I'd better set the table, but I don't want to leave you

alone, not for a second. Why didn't you kiss me?" she asked, looking at him from beneath lowered lashes.

He treated her to what she thought was the most dazzling smile she'd ever seen. If she wasn't careful, this man would burn her until she blistered. "Baby, when I get started, I don't plan to stop till I get to heaven."

She swallowed almost loud enough for him to hear it, whirled around and headed for the table. And in her silk jumpsuit, she let her back action promise him plenty.

"What kind of work do you do, Kenyetta?"

She was certain that she answered that question the night they met. Was he checking on her? "I teach sciences in junior high school. I agreed to teach makeup classes this summer, so I can get an early sabbatical, but I don't think I'll do it again. What do you do?"

"I've written a couple of books that did well. My stuff is regularly published in newspapers and magazines. I'm writing a book right now."

"That's right. Leticia told me about that." She could have kicked herself for having mentioned her cousin, so she moved to another subject. "My cousin from New Orleans, Mark DuPree, was here yesterday testifying before the Senate, and he invited me to go with him to the jazz concert at Kennedy Center, but I couldn't make it."

"Too bad. The bands really rocked. Most fun I'd had in ages. The place was crowded, and everybody let it all hang out."

She answered the doorman's buzz. "Yes. That's fine. Send him up."

"Is that our dinner?" Wilson asked her. She watched his sexy gait as he took his time getting to the door. "Thanks, man," he said to the delivery boy. "Buy yourself a drink."

"Yes, sir. Thank you, sir." She assumed from the profuse thank you that Wilson gave the boy a generous tip. She put the food in serving dishes, watched in awe while he opened the wine without spilling a drop, and took her seat at the head of the table. She bit her tongue and kept her mouth shut when he didn't sit opposite her at the other end of the table, as she had envisioned many times since they met, but instead moved his place setting to her right.

"I was too far from you," he explained, at her inquiring look.

She inhaled deeply the tantalizing odor of the food and said to him, "This is fantastic. One look at you told me you were a classy guy."

His chest seemed to protrude a bit more. "I try. I wanted you to enjoy it." He poured a bit of wine into his glass, tasted it, and filled her glass.

"Here's to a woman who's gorgeous from head to foot," he said, looking at her with eyes that promised a long, sweet night.

She sipped her wine and put a seductive smile on her face. For once, a man was doing something for her, and she meant to reward him. One taste of the lobster with bits of spinach in rolled shrimp, and she nearly forgot to converse with Wilson.

"I see you like this," he said.

"I love lobster," she said, "and I've never had any cooked this way or that tastes this good." She didn't try to decipher his wink; the meaning didn't matter. Half an hour after they finished the great food, she'd be rocking to his rhythm, and they both knew it.

French crepes with raspberry sauce completed the meal. She rose to clear the table, but he stilled her. "This is my treat, so I clear the table and clean the kitchen."

She sat alone in her living room listening to Luther

Vandross's recording of "So Amazing." *I hope this isn't going to turn into the biggest flop since I discovered there wasn't any Santa Claus.*

Wilson strolled into the room with the remainder of the wine and two glasses, poured some wine for each of them and said, "What time do you usually get up on a weekday?"

Both of her eyebrows shot up and stayed there. "Six-thirty. Why?"

"Don't get excited, sweetheart. If you want me to go home, I'll go."

"I do, but definitely not right now."

His face creased into a broad grin. "Just making sure we're on the same page." She got up to change the CD. "Don't bother with that. The only music I want you to listen to is mine."

She looked at him from the corner of her eye. "Then you'd better turn up that music, 'cause I can't hear it." She had thought he'd rush her, the way Reggie always did, but the brother was taking his time, and that was making her antsy. She reached up and stroked the side of his face as gently as she could. "That stubble's gonna scratch my face," she said, "but I don't much mind. It's something that says *man.*"

He leaned over her and stared into her face. "Are you seeing another man?"

She didn't like that question, but he had a right to ask it. "Sometimes. Why?"

"I wanted to know." He continued to stare into her face, and she tried not to wilt, but he was getting to her. "Why'd you decide you wanted me?"

"Same reason why you decided you wanted me."

"Woman, you do something to me." He parted his lips over hers and flicked his tongue as if asking for entrance. She let him in, pulled him into her and sucked.

Her breasts began their telltale heave and their nipples tightened until she rubbed them in search of relief.

"Let me do that," he said. "Let me at it."

She lifted her left breast from the confinement of her bra and offered it to him. Within seconds, she wanted to climb the wall. Reggie never sucked her breasts. She held Wilson's head and let him suckle. His hand went from her belly downward until he reached his target, and his double onslaught wrenched a scream from her.

"Stop playing with me, Wilson. Do something to me."

"Where do you sleep?" he asked her, and she jumped up, grabbed his hand and started for her bedroom. A glance told her that he was fully erect. He helped her to finish undressing, and after she stretched out on the bed, he put on a condom. She started to ask why he did it, but controlled the thought.

"Look, baby, if you're a woman who needs to be in control, please stifle the urge. It doesn't work with me. Okay? If you follow my lead, we'll make memories."

"Just show me what you want." He didn't answer. But half an hour later, when she climaxed for the third time, she collapsed beneath him, weak and satiated.

After he left her, a few hours before daybreak, tears streamed down her cheeks. He'd rocked her out of her senses, but during the entire evening into the night, he hadn't said a single endearing word to her. She'd given him everything she knew how to give, but he hadn't said he wanted to see her again.

For once, she'd had the world by the tail; Wilson Gallagher knew how to put it down. She'd have to wait and see.

"Can I get you something else, miss?"

Kenyetta snapped out of her reverie, gathered her belongings, paid the bill and left. She hoped her cousin wouldn't tell Wilson about Reggie. She had plans for

Wilson, but after the night they'd had, shouldn't he have called her by now? She stepped out of the coffee shop and hardly noticed the raindrops.

Leticia, too, thought about Wilson, his charm and charisma, and what she had decided was his lack of character. She stood in her kitchen—the place in her apartment that received the most morning sun—creating from memory a watercolor of the old house in which she grew up outside of Atlanta. Lost in her thoughts, she stopped painting, braced her knuckles on her hips and looked toward the ceiling while gray paint blotched her previously flawless blue tile floor. Thank God she'd been spared the heartache she would have endured if she had gotten closer to Wilson. How could the man have the effrontery to make a play for her cousin in her presence after telling Leticia he wanted a chance with her?

As for her cousin, maybe Kenyetta was a lesson well learned. At least Kenyetta had had the guts to let her know what a treacherous thing she did. But somehow, that side of Kenyetta didn't ring true. On a number of occasions, she'd found her cousin to be compassionate, caring and supportive. Why would such a person stick a sharp knife in you where she knew it would hurt most and then twist it? And why would she enjoy getting another woman's man?

Leticia snapped her fingers as understanding dawned on her. Kenyetta lacked self-esteem, and she got a feeling of superiority by taking another woman's husband and luring a man in whom her own cousin and friend had expressed an interest. As she thought of it, she realized Wilson was no better. He had to have every woman he met in order to prove his manhood. Leticia sucked her teeth in disgust.

She didn't assert herself or defend herself as forcibly and as often as she should, but she could almost measure the progress she'd made since graduating from Howard University. She had a long way to go, but she'd get there, and in fending off Wilson Gallagher, she'd taken a giant step. Next, she had to make some positive moves and stop accepting whatever befell her.

Chapter Five

Not long after her discovery of Kenyetta's treachery, Leticia stood before her bathroom mirror brushing her teeth, stopped in the midst of it and stared at herself. Half the women she met didn't look better than she, didn't have prettier breasts or a more tantalizing behind. So what was wrong with her? With her pricey extensions, she had long hair, and she wore fashionable clothes and spiked heel shoes. But since her makeover, not one man had taken a serious interest in her. She remembered the white guy in the restaurant months earlier, but she wasn't singing that tune. One thing was certain, she had to take a serious look at her life. Something wasn't working. She dressed and went to the kitchen for the breakfast that Willa insisted she should eat.

Willa's out of tune notes greeted her as she sat down at the kitchen table. After several verbal scrimmages, she'd won the battle against eating her breakfast in the dining room. She looked at the scrambled eggs, sage sausage, grits and orange juice and threw up her hands.

"Here, have some of these good old buttermilk biscuits. I just made 'em."

"Willa, I'm a perfect size ten, and if I eat this stuff every morning, I'll soon be a perfect size twenty."

"Nonsense! Men love to hold a little flesh. I won't say they want to hug a hippo, but if they wanted bones, they'd go to the graveyard." She poured two glasses of orange juice, put one of them at her own plate, and the other at Leticia's. "You got a nice figure, but you don't want him to think he's grabbing air when he wants to hold you. I declare these young women don't try to see things from a man's point of view." She held up her fork and pointed to the plate of biscuits. "And you ought to invite a nice young man to dinner one Thursday night. I won't be here, but I'll leave everything nice, and he'll think you prepared it."

Leticia couldn't help laughing, though she knew that to laugh at Willa was like pouring oil on a fire. She needed very little encouragement. "I couldn't mislead a man I thought enough of to invite for a twosome dinner, Willa. That wouldn't be fair."

She rolled her eyes to the ceiling. "You ain't gon' catch them knocking they selves out being fair. Some men are nice people, I guess, but they ain't anxious to show you they niceness."

Leticia looked at her plate and gasped. "Good Lord! Do you realize I ate all the grits, eggs and sausage you put on my plate?"

"You ate two of my buttermilk biscuits, too. And don't worry, ain't no man gonna ask you for no bones."

Leticia stared at the woman. "If one does, he'll see how fast I can run."

"Ma'am, would you please leave the kitchen window cracked open at night so all the . . . uh . . . bad vibes can find they way out?"

"Bad vibes? You mean negative spirits? What the dickens would they be doing in my kitchen?"

Willa let out a long breath and, from her tone and demeanor, one would think she spoke to a small child. "They come in with the grocery bags, the voice of that radio commentator who's always putting people down, the monthly bills and who knows what. You really ought to have your apartment blessed, and put a few dimes in the kitchen cabinets."

Leticia drained her coffee cup and pushed her chair back from the table. "I'm not superstitious, Willa."

"Neither am I, ma'am. I just believe an ounce of prevention is worth a pound of cure, and that means give the bad vibes a chance to get out before they start creating trouble."

"Okay, if it will make you happy, I'll leave the kitchen window cracked open, but it would be just as simple not to tune the radio to that station."

"Oh, ma'am, I couldn't do that. Listening to him makes me feel good. I'm smarter than that man."

To be more intelligent than that man wasn't much of a stretch, Leticia thought, but refrained from saying so.

At the office, she sat through an hour long boring budget meeting. If she ever got the courage, she'd tell the publisher to change the paper's dull and uninteresting front page. She left the meeting along with Joel and Marie.

"Was this meeting a waste of time?" Marie asked.

"No," Joel replied. "We have to emphasize every day that it's important for reporters and columnists to meet their deadlines, and that also goes for the copy editors, sorters, distributors, drivers and me," he said, pointing to his chest.

When they reached Leticia's office cubicle, he followed her in. "I want you to do something, and hear me out first. The boss likes your series, and he wants you to extend it, but that means you've got to go out of the country to gather your material." He sat down beside her desk and strummed his fingers on it. "It means three weeks or a month in Africa. Of course, you'd get a per diem and all expenses paid. Unfortunately, our travel planner doesn't know Africa that well, so you'd have to plan the whole trip yourself. One thing: when you check into a country, call the U.S. consulate immediately, let 'em know you're there, where you are at all times and ask for help with travel, introductions to important people, and so on. Before you go, I want you to go to New York to consult with the UN missions of the countries you plan to visit."

Joel crossed his knees and leaned back. "What do you say?"

"Next time, hit me in the back of the head with a baseball bat."

"When do you want to leave for New York?"

"I have to decide which countries I want to visit. I'll make some phone contacts with African missions to the UN and let you know."

"Langley, this can be pleasant, or it can be as dangerous as hell, so choose some countries where there's currently no violence. Otherwise I won't sign off on it."

"Gosh, Joel, I never dreamed you thought I was anxious to get my neck into a noose. Trust me, safety will be my first consideration."

"It's my job to protect my reporters to the extent that I can," he said in a voice gruff with affection.

It had been years since anyone had expressed genuine concern for her well-being, and she realized for the first time that Joel cared about her. She reached out and patted the back of his hand. "I'm glad you're my supervisor, Joel. I'll do my very best."

As if his chair had suddenly become too warm, he jumped up. "I'm sure you will. Let me know what you need."

What a strange man, she mused after he left. By four o'clock, she'd turned in her column, contacted the Nigerian and Kenyan missions to the United Nations, and made a list of the things she had to do before leaving.

Two weeks later, she had her passport, health shots and certificates, the requisite medicines, toiletries, and clothes she would carry, as well as some important contacts. She had also lost five pounds in spite of Willa's robust meals.

"I'll be away for three weeks, Willa. Consider these three weeks a gift for being such a blessing to me."

Willa shook her head as if perplexed. "I ain't that much of a blessing. This job hardly keeps me busy. Go with the angels and come back safely."

Leticia stepped off the airplane and made her way into the Murtala Muhammed International Airport at Lagos, Nigeria. The huge, modern oversized airport was in itself a problem to maneuver, but add to that the suspicious characters claiming to be government officials who approached only obvious foreigners, and her fear and anxiety overcame her fatigue. The mayhem at customs made the last two minutes of a tight Super Bowl football game look like a friendly family picnic. She'd never encountered so many confident tricksters posing as immigration officers, some of whom threatened her with deportation if she didn't turn over her passport and valuables. She ignored them. One woman attempted to pull her shoulder bag off her shoulder, but when she kicked at her, the woman ran away.

Leticia passed beautiful shops, a restaurant, a bank and a post office, but barely looked at them. The air-conditioning was off inside the airport, her clothing had begun to stick to her body, and breathing was as much as she could manage. She reached the baggage claim area and wanted to cry, certain that she would never see her belongings again. She had no doubt that in a universal competition for chaos, that airport baggage claim area would win the prize.

She decided that since bribery seemed to be the currency of choice here, using some would probably be the one way she'd get safely to her hotel. With a twenty-dollar bill in plain view, she asked a uniformed officer how to get a reputable cab. He left his station and accompanied her to a driver, who she guessed was his cousin or other relative. He put her things into the cab and made himself appear surprised when she handed him the money. She negotiated a fare and got into the old taxi. The airport was heaven compared to the road and the traffic into Lagos.

"Is it always this hot?" she asked the driver.

"Coming to de cool time, de Harmattan bring de cool, but de ting is it bring de dust. Not so bad here like it is in de norte, up near Kano." She later learned that Kano was a large state in northern Nigeria, and that its occupants were mostly Moslems. "You from de States?"

She told him that she was from Washington, D.C. "How long you stay here? You on business, we cut a deal, and I be your driver. You get a driver that take you someplace, take your money and leave you there. I'm Christian like my father and grandfather. I don't do dat."

She'd see how he behaved when they got to the hotel. "I'll think about that. What is your name?"

"Paul, madame. I have brothers named Peter, Matthew, Mark, Luke, John and Joseph, and sisters named Martha and Mary. We are all in de Bible," he said with unmistakable pride.

"What is your father's name?" she asked him, unable to resist.

"My father is Daniel Jimmah, madame. He is a chief. I take you dere to see him. You want something, he get it for you." A few minutes later, he turned into the driveway of a large building and stopped. "De hotel, madame. Very big and very much money. I get your bags."

She walked into the spacious lobby and the first thing she noticed wasn't its decor but its air-conditioning. While she waited at the reservation desk, Paul came in with her bags. "Aren't the porters supposed to do that?" she asked Paul.

"Yes, madame, but dey tink you don't know it. Dey plan to make you pay."

"Have a seat over there, and we'll talk about your driving me while I'm here."

"Yes, madame, but I stay here. Dey tell you you don't have reservation." She stared at him, but he nodded his head. "You'll see."

"Did you want something, madam?" a receptionist asked her. What a strange question!

"I'm Leticia Langley, and I have a reservation."

The man smiled and checked the computer repeatedly. "I'm sorry, madam, but I have no record of it."

"If you have five or ten dollars, hold it in your hand so he can see it, and tell him how grateful you'll be if he finds a nice room for you," Paul whispered to her.

"But—"

"Madam, dat's the only way you'll get de room here or in any other hotel."

She did as Paul said. "I'm tired, and I'd be so grateful if you could find me a nice room."

"I'll do what I can for you, madam."

"I'll take your bags up," Paul said. "Dis is why it's best to have a driver. I know dis country and dese people. I tell you de truff every time."

They agreed on a price during her time in Lagos, and the next morning, he took her to the United States consulate. When she left there, she had most of the information she would need during her stay in Nigeria. That afternoon, she visited the village in which Paul's family lived. It impressed her that, when Paul entered his grandmother's house, he went to her and prostrated himself on the floor before the chair in which she sat. Then he stood.

"Mammy, dis is Miss Langley. I am her driver today, and she wants to talk wit you. Miss Langley, dis is my grandmother."

Leticia put her hands together, bowed briefly to the woman, acknowledged the introduction and requested permission to ask her questions about Nigerian women.

"In de first place, no respectable Nigerian woman of your class would ride around de country wif a man who wasn't her husband or a relative, even if de man was a taxi driver," the woman said. "She would visit friends, and go to market, church and school wif her personal chauffeur, but nothing further. She wouldn't do any work at home and would cook only in emergency. In our tribe, the Yoruba, a man pay de bride price for his wife and, if she want divorce, her family has to pay it back or she has to find a man who will pay it back in exchange for marrying her."

Leticia wanted to ask the woman about the marriage

bed, but didn't have the nerve, so she said, "We don't have standards for relationships between a man and his wife, except those dictated by law. Wife abuse, adultery, failure to support a family and certain crimes are grounds for divorce. Relations between them are by mutual agreement," she said, hoping that the woman would reciprocate, and she did.

The woman's eyes widened, and an expression of surprise settled on her face. "Well, what you call adultery, de man here consider his right. While we nurse de baby, we don't sleep together, and de man do as he pleases. If he stupid, he bring home disease. If you not nursing, and you tell de man no, you have a fight. When we hear de night fights, we know de reason."

"What about that operation girls have that removes the clitoris when they start puberty?"

"A lot of dem die from it. Some men won't marry a girl if she didn't have it. People say women who don't have the operation cheat on de husbands and that some become night women."

"So he can cheat, but she can't?"

"He has a right to sex, but she nurse de baby for two years, what he gon' do?"

"Who gets the children if they divorce?"

"De children belong to the man and his family. The more children de woman has, de more she mean to de man and his family. Now we don't talk anymore. De cook has a chicken on a spit, and we have roasted corn and Coca-Cola. We roast de corn right in de ear. It's very good."

Time seemed to have slipped by while Leticia talked with the old woman. At first, the woman's intelligence surprised her, but she soon realized that the use of *de, dey, dat* and *dem* did not indicate ignorance or lack of education but an inability to pronounce a *th* construction. She hadn't eaten since early morning and, by noon, she had become very hungry, so she ate with relish.

"I've just learned the best way to cook corn," she told the woman. "This was delicious."

The woman nodded. "I'm happy to meet an American woman like you. I have only seen de tourists with de long painted fingernails, shorts and sneakers. You come back to Nigeria, you come to see me."

Leticia thanked her, got into the taxi with Paul and headed back to town. Along the way, she saw women, some of them almost ready to deliver, digging in the fields, their bellies almost dragging on the ground.

"Paul, I haven't seen any men digging in these fields."

"De women do de farming out here, madame."

"Why doesn't somebody make a hoe with a long handle, so the women won't have to bend almost to the ground?"

"I don't know, madame. Dey always do it dis way."

"Tomorrow, I'm going to Ile-Ife. Can you take me?"

"It's forty-five miles, madame, and I don't go dat far. How long you stay?"

"I'll be back day after tomorrow."

"Madame, lock your valuables in de hotel safe in your room, and be careful. De tieves and robbers along de roads and highways."

Back at her hotel, she asked the receptionist for the best way to get to the University of Ife, in Ile-Ife. "Take a Lowery," he said. "They go every couple of hours. Check with the bell captain."

So far, she hadn't seen anyone who looked like a bell captain, so she asked a uniformed young man who carried someone's bags. He told her to ask the bell captain, and when she said she didn't see one, the man replied, "He soon come."

After waiting an hour in the lobby, she saw a green bus drive up, went to the driver and asked if the bus went to Ile-Ife.

"Speak to your bell captain and get a ticket," he said.

By now exasperated and bordering on anger, Leticia took a twenty-dollar bill from her purse and showed it to the driver. "I need to get to the University of Ife at Ile-Ife. Do you go there?"

He eased the bill from her hand and said, "Do you have naira?" She nodded. "Five thousand, please."

She handed him the naira equivalent of fifty U.S. dollars and asked for the ticket. He rolled his eyes in disgust, opened a tin box and handed her one. Half an hour later, the bus began its journey with about thirty passengers, for which she gave thanks since the air-conditioning didn't work. A few miles past Ibadan, the third largest city in Nigeria, the bus—now filled well beyond capacity—stopped, and the driver told everyone to get out.

"I'm not going any further," he said.

"You owe me some money," Leticia told him.

"Yeah? And the sun rises in the west and sets in the east. Don't bother me, woman."

"He don't pay back nothing," a woman, with one child on her back and another at her knee, told Leticia. "Where you headed?"

"The University of Ife."

"Then you go with me. I work on the campus."

Very soon, what looked like a twenty-five-year-old SUV drove up. The woman grabbed Leticia's hand. "Come on, or we won't get in." Leticia followed, stumbling and grabbing at whatever she could, including human flesh, until she found herself jammed into the little mammy wagon, as the locals called them.

She'd never thought of breath as being a precious commodity, but she couldn't seem to get enough of it, and when she did get a good breath, she nearly fainted from the assorted odors of humans, chickens, plants and even a young goat. Equally disturbing was the inability to move even an inch. She wondered about the children around her and the baby on the woman's back and whether such circumstances accounted for Nigeria's high infant mortality rate. After about two hours of that and more potholes than she'd ever bumped over, the mammy wagon came to a halt. At that point, she was willing to walk the remainder of the way.

"Lady, we get off here," she heard a female voice call. "Get off, lady. It's the university stop."

Trusting divine providence, since she couldn't see for the surrounding bodies, she managed to get off. Seeing the woman standing there with the two little children, Leticia let out a long breath. "That was some ride," she said. "Thanks so much."

"I hate the mammy wagons, but when the bus drivers decide they don't want to go any further, they take the money and go back to Lagos. All you have out here are these old cars. At least it didn't break down."

"How am I going to get back to Lagos?"

"Come over to the library where I work. My name is Nettie Adefunya. I'll get one of our drivers to take you back, but it's not official. He'll do it for about five thousand naira. Okay?"

"Thanks, Nettie. My name is Leticia Langley and I'm in Nigeria to get information for a story I'm writing. Would you be willing to talk with me?"

"Sure. Just don't use my name."

"Oh, okay." They walked up the endless road to the campus.

"This is the university guest house," the woman said. "I suppose you have a place to stay. If not, you can stay there. I'll be in the library tomorrow from nine to one if you want to talk then."

"Thank you so much. I don't know what I would have done if I hadn't met you."

"You're welcome. Getting around here without a car isn't easy. See you tomorrow."

Leticia walked into the guest house praying that people working at a university would be different from those working at Lagos hotels and airports. "Hello. I need a room for tonight, please."

"Do you want your meals, too?" When she hesitated, he grinned and said, "There's no place else here to eat, unless you go to the cafeteria where the students eat. They're building a restaurant, but it's not ready."

"Room with meals, please. I plan to leave tomorrow afternoon."

"If you need transportation, I can get you a good driver. It's not official, but he'll take you back to Lagos for six or seven thousand."

"Thanks so much," she said, aware that she shouldn't close any doors. "I'll let you know."

The room was comfortable enough, and the air-conditioning worked, though she had a sense of unease when she saw the mosquito net. After a shower and dinner that included Jamaican patties, she made notes and a list of questions to ask Mrs. Adefunya.

The next morning she walked out to the main road, which seemed like any other deserted highway bordered by trees and bushes, and wondered that she was still on university acreage. At nine-thirty in the morning, the hot sun bore down on her, sapping her energy. Why hadn't she asked someone at the guest house how to get to the library or at least how to get a ride there? She saw a little red Volkswagen Beetle approach and held out her hand, reasoning that if the man wanted to bother her on that isolated road, he could do it anyway.

"Where are you headed, miss?" the man asked.

"I'm going to the university library."

"Hop in. I have a class in about five minutes, and I'll just make it."

She got in and let out a long breath in prayerful thanks. "What do you teach?" she asked the man.

"I teach physics. These students are hungry for information, any kind. So teaching is a joy, especially morning classes. Afternoons are too hot, at least for me."

She didn't ask if he was a Yoruba because she detected the accent. "This campus seems to be enormous," she said.

He stopped at a modern building. "It's twenty-nine square miles. Here we are, miss. Enjoy your stay." She thanked him and found Nettie Adefunya without difficulty.

"You're just in time for some coffee," Nettie said when Leticia arrived at the library. "How was the room?"

She wouldn't have dared to complain. The air conditioner went off during the night, and she'd fought with that mosquito net until she felt like an insect herself. "Not only did I get a room," she said, evading the question, "but I got my meals as well."

She sat at Nettie's desk and sipped the coffee. If she had ever tasted any stronger, she couldn't recall, but she had no intention of putting milk in it and probably getting deathly ill. She told Nettie about the story she hoped to write and took out her list of questions. "How did you meet your husband?"

"My father and his father arranged the marriage,

and my father-in-law paid a huge bride price for me," she said proudly.

"My husband was educated in England," she went on, "and I guess he met some English women, because I get the benefit of it. He treats me as an equal unless he's around his brothers. Women and men don't socialize in groups."

"What if you go with your husband to a party?" she asked.

"He's with the men, and I'm with the women in another room. That's practically a law. Here at the university, the teachers mix, but in other places, they don't."

"The women here tend to be heavier than the men. Do you eat the same food?"

Nettie released a rich, musical laugh. "Sure. You think I give him better than I eat? We don't wear those underclothes that you American and English women wear. We are proud of our bodies, and the man is happy if his wife looks . . . healthy. It means he can afford to take good care of her. American men like the breasts. Here, the breasts are for babies. Men like the behind to be nice and healthy."

She leaned to Leticia and whispered, "I would love just once to be in bed with an American man. I want to know why your women are so crazy about the sex. We women need the men for security. You can't live alone, and you can't go back to your family."

"Suppose your husband should die."

"God forbid. One of his brothers, perhaps the oldest one, would marry me and take the children, but I would have to work like a dog. At least we wouldn't sleep together unless he lost his wife."

Leticia had gotten more than she hoped for and from a woman who knew something of American and

European customs. True to her word, Nettie called a man who agreed to drive Leticia back to Lagos in the university's Peugeot 404, which was relatively new and air-conditioned. Paul sat in the hotel's lobby waiting for her.

"You got back all right, madame. I tell you I didn't sleep." She told him about the trip to the university. He shook his head. "Nobody is dat lucky, madame. What time we leave tomorrow for de plane?"

She gave the registration clerk the flight time. "Give yourself four hours in case the roads are impassable," he said. When she stared at him, he lifted both shoulders in a shrug. "Accidents, you know."

"I'll be here at eleven," Paul told her.

She phoned the U.S. consulate, informed the officer that she would be leaving the next day and gave him the taxi number and flight number. If she had as much luck in Nairobi, Kenya, as she had in Nigeria, she wouldn't bother to go to The Gambia or to Angola, where her French would be sorely tested.

Fortunately, her seat mate on the plane was a Peace Corps worker who had spent the last eleven years in various African countries. "East Africa is a different world from West Africa," the woman, who introduced herself as Phyllis Jacobs, told her. "The English influence is still strong in Kenya, and most Kenyan women dress like Europeans and Americans. Short dresses, slacks, shorts, low-cut blouses, whatever they like, but further south, you'll find some Moslem women in traditional Arabic dress."

"Does that mean the women in Kenya are liberated?"

Phyllis turned to look Leticia in the face. "Liberated from what and to what? The educated ones living in Nairobi are liberated to some extent, especially if their family is very wealthy, but women here can't do as they please. If they're married, they answer to their husbands. If not, to their father or an older male relative. The more children they bear, the better their status within the family. In some tribes, a man demands sex even if the woman is almost ready to deliver . . . if not one way, then another as long as he gets satisfied. That's not considered bad or abusive, but his right. It's the way it is, and she has to tolerate it. Most marriages are arranged by the women's parents, with her family getting as much money or goods as possible out of the deal. Thereafter, she belongs to him and his family."

"Whew! I'm never going to gripe about anything again."

They took a taxi together into town, exchanged addresses, and Phyllis assured Leticia of support should she need it. She checked into the Sheraton Hotel and immediately observed a difference between Kenya and Nigeria. Neither the taxi driver nor the hotel clerks and busboys expected a bribe. She enjoyed an excellent meal of pork chops, rice, string beans and melon, went to her room and phoned the U.S. consular office.

"We'd like you to stop by tomorrow morning," the woman said. "It's a short two-block walk from your hotel to our office."

Leticia agreed, then went to the front desk and collected as much information about Nairobi as the hotel offered. The following morning, she put on her walking shoes and headed for the market, where local traders plied their wares.

"You need an escort, lady?"

She noticed a young boy walking beside her. "You're too young to be out here so early."

"I work every day, miss lady. I have to save money for wife."

She stopped walking. "How old are you?"

"Twelve, miss lady. I protect you like any man. Somebody snatch your pocketbook, I catch them. See this stick?" She hadn't noticed it. "Somebody do something else to you, I hit them across the back of the neck. Good spot. My name is Eslan. I be your friend, guide and protector while you in Nairobi. Five hundred shillings a day."

"Where are your parents, Eslan?"

"My papa is in the straw market buying straw for the baskets my mama and my sisters make. Come. I take you to the big market, and you buy some souvenirs, miss lady."

She walked along with him asking him questions about his life. "Why did you stop school?"

"I can read, write and do numbers. Now I have to work. You from New York?" She told him that she was from Washington, D.C.

"Hey, you," he screamed, yelled some words she didn't understand and flew after a man who she realized had snatched her pocketbook. Stunned, she ran after them, but Eslan caught the man, hit the thief's arm with the stick, causing him to drop the pocketbook, picked it up and ran back to her with it.

"You see?" he said proudly. "Eslan is very useful. Six hundred shillings a day." She stifled a laugh. The rascal knew he had proved his worth. A frown covered his face. "How many hours a day you need? Put the pocketbook across your shoulder, miss lady. The man almost got away."

Thinking fast, she asked him, "Where is your mother now?"

"She in the big market selling baskets. I take you to her?"

She could see that he was anxious to give his mother

an opportunity to sell some baskets, so she said, "I'm writing a story about women in Kenya. Do you think your mother would talk to me?"

"Yes, ma'am, miss lady. She speak good English, too. I tell her you give her five hundred shillings. Okay?"

"You little hustler," she said under her breath. To him, she said, "Great, but not a shilling more."

He looked disgusted, so she said, "What's the matter, Eslan?"

"Miss lady, you have to learn to bargain. If I say ten, I really want five. If I say twenty, all I'm asking for is ten, but you have to bargain."

She liked Eslan's mother at once, and when the woman offered her a stool, she gladly accepted it. She decided to begin with an impersonal question, and ask the woman whether she had ever voted.

"Yes, I voted last time, but the men tell us women how to vote, and if we don't do as they say, there's the devil to pay, so we either obey or lie about it. This year, for the first time, we have seven women in parliament. I can't even discuss this with my husband or my mother-in-law."

"You don't like her?"

"What choice I have? She rules, and everything is for my husband. She searches all my things every day looking for birth control." The woman laughed. "The nosy old woman can't find it. I'm wearing the Mirena IUD, so she can look all she want. I have five children, and that's more than plenty."

"Does your husband know you're wearing an IUD?"

The woman stared at her. "He'd beat me half to death."

They talked for a while, but Leticia had to be at the consulate at ten, so she paid the woman, bought several of her baskets, a pair of wooden salad servers with giraffes on the end of the handles, thanked her and called to Eslan. "I have to be at the U.S. consular office in fifteen minutes."

"No problem, miss lady. We take shortcut."

"I'm planning to go down to Mombasa," Leticia told the consular officer. "Women there are supposed to have a life that's different from women in and around Nairobi."

"Maybe in style, but not in substance. How many ways can men find to make women inferior to them?"

Leticia told the officer what she'd learned from the women she interviewed.

"Well, you'll find in Mombasa that the youth are somewhat freer, and there will be a bit more socializing of men and women in groups, but only in the upper class. These other problems prevail, except in a few individual cases where the man has traveled and studied abroad and decided that he wants to live differently. But research studies find that those are comparatively rare. Why not try a Moslem country like The Gambia?"

In the end, Leticia crossed Mombasa off her itinerary and, instead of going to The Gambia, decided to interview one of the many Moslem women she saw in Nairobi. She got her chance that afternoon when she sat in the Sheraton lounge drinking tea.

"But you come from America," the woman said. "You have many Moslem women in America, and the law for one of us is the same everywhere. We live by the teachings of the Koran. My husband has one wife. He could have four, but he would have to treat us all equally, and my husband says he would rather not risk it."

She thought of a question that she considered inoffensive. "Can a Moslem woman divorce her husband?"

"Of course. The general grounds for divorce, according to the Koran, are failure to carry out marital duties and to live with each other in kindness, peace and compassion. As you may imagine, this covers a broad range of conditions. Either man or wife may seek divorce if the conditions aren't met. Adultery on the part of either is a sin, and it is not tolerated."

"What about the men of the family stoning a woman to death if she is accused of certain things?"

"If she's guilty of consorting with a man to whom she is not married, the stoning may still occur in villages, but I doubt it could happen in any big city. I don't know."

They talked for a while, and Leticia wanted to ask the woman, who, she discovered, had two university degrees, how she could tolerate being in purdah, covered everywhere except her eyes, but she didn't. She knew that culture dictated the way in which the people lived, even what they ate and how they ate it. She wished the woman well, thanked her and told her good-bye.

Leticia went up to her room, organized her notes, decided that she had more than she needed for two good columns, called the airline and reserved a seat on a plane to New York that would leave at noon the following day.

Leticia had thought first-class flight accommodations an unnecessary expense, but when she found herself seated next to the distinguished Washington journalist Broderick Nettleson, she could barely contain her delight. He stood when she arrived at her seat, tall and strikingly handsome with little bits of gray at the temples and a clean-shaven face. From his pictures in newspapers and magazines and appearances on television, she would have recognized him anywhere.

"Let me put that up for you," he said of her luggage.

It wasn't a voice that you would disagree with. She thanked him and slid to the window seat. "I'm Leticia Langley."

His eyebrows shot up, but she couldn't imagine why. She had just combed her hair and refreshed her makeup. She looked down at her blouse, didn't see any foreign matter on it, and tried to relax.

"I'm Broderick Nettleson," he said. "Do you happen to write a column for *The Journal*?"

She blinked several times. How would a man like Broderick Nettleson know what she wrote? "I'm so pleased to meet you, Mr. Nettleson. This is . . . well!" *Compose yourself, girl.* "Yes, I do, but I'm surprised you'd notice my column."

He adjusted his left pant leg and stretched out his long legs. "Oh, I read *The Journal* regularly. It's a good paper, and I can't afford to be ignorant of the competition's style and standard. I like what you've written on obesity, and especially the one comparing women of African descent who live in different cultures. Is this why you were in Nairobi?"

"Yes. Our publisher liked the series and asked for more depth, more information about the differences in the lives of African-American women and other women of African descent. I got plenty of firsthand information, but food habits alone don't account for the differences."

"Of course not. I'll be interested to know how you treat it. You may have to go off topic."

A sigh seeped out of her as she faced facts. "I thought as much when I organized my data, but if I do that, my editor may be annoyed."

"If you start with the wrong premise, this can happen. When it does, be true to your data, and don't try to get blood out of a turnip. Write a good story, and he'll love it."

"Thank you. I appreciate this. I've only been working as a journalist since the end of June."

He turned toward her. "Are you serious?"

"Why, yes. I was late getting out of college. Long story. Taking care of my sick father and then working to save money for college, so I just graduated in June. Around those kids at Howard, I felt like I was ninety years old."

"How did you handle the competition?"

A feeling of complete satisfaction flowed over her. "Mr. Nettleson, I skinned every last one of them. Summa cum laude."

A grin spread over his handsome face. "Hot damn. Way to go! Do you live in Washington?" She told him that she did. "I'd like you to meet my family—my wife, twin sons, daughter and stepson, and my wife's grandfather. We're a big family, and when I'm away from home, even if I'm just around the block, I can't wait to get back to them."

"I guess that's what happiness is," she said.

He reclined his seat and leaned back. "You bet, and you're the one who creates it. Keep that in mind, and you'll always be happy."

"Champagne?" the flight attendant asked. Broderick shook his head. "Never drink alcohol on a long flight. By the time the plane lands, you feel like a crumpled tin can."

The attendant's smile lingered. "Hors d'oeuvres will be along in a minute."

As Leticia watched the woman all but lick her lips as she looked at the man, she thought of Kenyetta and realized that she hadn't seen a woman appear to lust after a man since she'd left the States.

"Where are you from?" she asked the attendant.

"Georgia," she said, returning to her southern drawl. "I'll be right back with some stone crab legs." She looked directly at Broderick. "I want you all to remember this flight."

"I'm sure we will," he said dryly. And turning to Leticia, his eyes twinkling with merriment, he asked, "Won't we?"

"Oh, absolutely," she said, though she could not have imagined the truth of her words.

Chapter Six

Leticia and Nettleson transferred together in New York to another airline for the trip to Washington. "Before long, you ought to get a note from my wife, Carolyn Logan Nettleson, asking you to come to one of our little get togethers. You'll know some of the journalists by name, if not sight. Paul Faison and Robert Weddington of *The Maryland Journal* and their families; J. L. Whitehead of *The Times*; and Allison Wade of *The Herald* are some of the people you'll meet at our place. We'll be glad to have you join us."

She wasn't given to stuttering, but when she opened her mouth, "uh . . . uh" was the only sound she heard.

His grin didn't help. "Take it easy there," he teased. "You've earned your spurs. You're a fine writer." He shook her hand. "Looking forward to seeing you again."

"Thank you. These past nine hours have been some of the most precious of my life. I hope to see you again."

"I'm dreaming. I know I am," she said to herself as she got into a taxi for the ride to her apartment. "Broderick Nettleson called me a fine writer. That man sits on top of the pile. If I told Joel, he wouldn't believe me."

She couldn't wait to begin writing her column. When she arrived at the office on Monday, two days later, Max Baldwin knocked her for a loop when he encountered her in the corridor.

"Good grief, Leticia. What a surprise! You were gone a long time. Would you believe I missed you? I hadn't realized it, but you brighten up this place. Did you have a good trip?"

"Did I ever! I can't wait to finish writing up this stuff. I learned a world full while I was gone."

"When you stepped on African soil, did it seem as if you'd come home at last?"

"No way! But that's another story."

He shoved his hands into his pants pockets and slouched against the wall. "I'm sure it is. Maybe one day, you'll share with me what you can't put in your column, because that'll be the best part."

She stared at him. "How'd you know?"

"Been there. You always get more than you need, and the best data will have nothing to do with your story, so you either change the story, or write a second one using the stuff that *really* fascinates you. Right?"

Hadn't Broderick Nettleson said the same thing? "You're either a veteran at this business or you're clairvoyant."

"I haven't had an indication yet that I have psychic powers."

"Thanks for the nice greeting, Max, but I'd better get to work. Joel will be in my office the minute he hears I'm back."

He shook his head. "Be smart and go to his office and tell him you're back safely. Joel doesn't act it, but he's a worrier."

"Thanks, Max. You're a good buddy." She thought

he seemed crestfallen, but didn't dwell on it. She got a note pad and pen and rushed to Joel's office.

"Come in," Joel said in response to her knock. "Leticia!" He sprang from his chair and rushed to meet her. "Great. The lions didn't eat you, but the sun sure baked you. You're three shades darker. Sit down. I'm glad you're back safely. Did you get anything?"

His eager expression spoke louder than words. He regarded her as one of his reporters, not merely the person who sat in her office, did computer research and put the results in a column. She was a reporter. She extended her hand for a handshake, and his vigorous response seemed to seal her status.

"I'm glad to be back," she said. "It was an experience I'll never forget. But if I'd known what I was going to face beforehand, I might have been a little hesitant about the trip. I got tons of stuff to write about."

"I told you not to take any foolish risks," he said. "Maybe not in those exact words, but you knew what I meant."

She couldn't keep the grin off her face. "Joel, the simple act of getting off the plane in Lagos was to put my life at risk. The place is lawless, a great big expensive and modern airport manned by people who do as they please. The only thing you can count on is that you have to bribe your way into and out of everything."

If she thought he'd be aghast at that, she couldn't have been further from the facts. "Did we give you a big enough advance to see you through it? Put the bribes on your expense account. I'm anxious to see your reports."

As far as she knew, Joel didn't engage in office gossip or discuss relations among his reporters, but Max's behavior that morning perplexed her, so she decided to take a chance.

"Joel, sometimes I can't understand Max. He's so tough, but at other times, like this morning when I met him in the corridor, he's different. Does that tough hide of his cover a soft center?"

Both of his eyebrows shot up, and he braced his palms on his knees. "Gosh, I don't know, Leticia. If he's got a soft center, he's never bothered to show it to me. I wish he would. Max does some powerful reporting, so I respect him, but he'll tell me to go to hell as quickly as he'll look at me."

Her lower lip dropped. "What?"

Joel laughed in a way that she thought was grudging. "He knows he can get a job anywhere. He stays here because he can do as he pleases." He narrowed his right eye. "He's a good man, Leticia. You won't find a more honest, straightforward guy. If he shows you a softness, there's a reason for it. I already told you to look around you."

Leticia left Joel, pondering his last words as she went. Did Max like her as a woman rather than as a colleague? She remembered his crestfallen demeanor when she called him a good buddy. She had never thought of Max as a romantic possibility, though she'd noticed his good looks and commanding presence.

It's not so. Max can have any woman he wants, and there's no reason he should look twice at me. He was only being nice.

It surprised Leticia that she'd been so eager to see Willa, and that the woman had grown on her so easily. She gave Willa one of the baskets with a leather handle that she bought in Kenya.

"Lord, ma'am, this is so nice. You thought of me. Well, I'll have this till I die."

"I'm glad you like it, Willa. I had a long talk with the woman who makes them."

"She sure is clever. I see you took to Africa, or maybe it took to you, 'cause you sure look like you been there. You lost some weight, though. Didn't they feed you?"

"I didn't drink water or milk products, and I didn't eat any raw vegetables. I walked a lot and experienced so much aggravation that it's a miracle I weigh anything. When you buy corn again, would you please roast it on the grill without shucking it?"

"That's the way they cook it?"

"Right. It's delicious."

She remembered that while in Nairobi, she bought some small soap stone Zimbabwean carvings of busts of old men and old women and put a set of them in her briefcase.

The telephone rang, and she was about to run for it when Willa said, "Kenyetta calling for you, ma'am."

Leticia hesitated. Her last conversation with her cousin left her feeling bereft of a friend, and she'd left Kenyetta sitting alone in Starbucks. She picked up the receiver. "Hi, Ken."

"Where you been, girl? I called here several times and nobody answered. I started to think you'd gone to New Orleans or somewhere."

I'm not going to let her irritate me. "Why would I be in New Orleans, Ken?"

"Don't ask me. You and Mark are so tight, I—"

Leticia interrupted her. "I thought you called to make amends, but I see you called to irritate me."

"Oh, girl, don't be so sensitive. What did I do that needs amends, for Pete's sake? Where *were* you?"

"If you don't know what you did, I won't waste my time telling you. I was in Nigeria and Kenya on assignment." Let her digest that.

"What? Girl, you're lying. You ain't been to Africa."

"I brought you a handwoven, straw tote with a leather handle from Kenya, the same kind you buy downtown for forty dollars."

"I didn't know they made 'em in Kenya. Thanks. Uh . . . you seen Wilson lately?"

Leticia nearly swallowed her tongue. As tempted as she was to lie and say she saw him almost every night, since she didn't know the purpose of the question, she hedged. "Why are you asking me that? You and I don't discuss Wilson. Is that clear?"

"Well, you don't have to hike your ass up on your shoulder. I just asked. I'll be by shortly and get my present. I love those bags."

Leticia hung up and walked into the dining room where Willa sat folding the laundry. "Willa, what would you do if your closest relative and best friend walked off with a man she thought you wanted and who she knew you were seeing?"

Willa stopped folding the laundry, propped her elbow on the table and supported her right cheek with the palm of her hand. "By now, I wouldn't know which state either one of 'em lived in. That woman ain't in the least acquainted with common decency, and the man ain't worth a rat's behind. I hope you don't still have anything to do with them."

"No, but she's my only close relative." She paused as she remembered Mark. "I have one more, but he lives in New Orleans."

"Honey, even the Bible tells you in so many words to get rid of the hindrances in your life."

"Oh, I've finished with the man, and I'll be careful never to trust my cousin again."

"Hmph. I don't believe in holding grudges, but she'd be a mote I'd get out of my eye in a hurry. You can get other friends, and they won't double-cross you either. You need a little more self-confidence."

Leticia knew Willa was right, and she decided that it would serve Kenyetta right if she got a good scolding from Willa. Half an hour later, the doorman announced Kenyetta, and when Willa opened the door for her, Kenyetta stopped as if in shock and said, "Well! Well! Where's Miss Langley?"

Leticia heard her and rushed to the foyer. "Hi, Ken. Mrs. Evans, this is my cousin and my best friend, Kenyetta Jackson. Ken, this is Mrs. Evans."

Kenyetta pulled her lips together and cast a sideward glance. "Oh, that's right, you said you'd hired a cleaning woman."

Leticia caught herself as her hand shot out toward her cousin. "I told you no such thing, and you know it. I told you that I had hired a housekeeper. Mrs. Evans is my housekeeper and my friend. And believe me, I needed a friend, because I didn't have one."

Kenyetta strolled past the two women and headed toward the living room. "Well, 'scuse me. Ain't we high-falutin' these days! I came to get my basket. How about some tea or coffee? I think I'd rather have tea. "

Willa walked over to Leticia. "If you want to fire me, ma'am, I'll accept that, but I won't be making no tea for your cousin. Nobody treats me like trash; I'm a housekeeper, but I wouldn't sleep with my best friend's man like Miss High and Mighty here. And I respect anybody who's old enough to be my mother."

Leticia resisted a giggle. "What about a married man? Would you have an affair with one?" she asked Willa, aware of the merriment on her face and in her voice.

Willa used the question to get in a sharp dig. "Do I look like a slut to you, ma'am?"

Leticia clapped her hands, fell back against the chair

and laughed aloud. Kenyetta's comeuppance couldn't have been more perfect if she and Willa had planned and rehearsed it.

"Just give me my bag. I'm leaving," Kenyetta said. "I don't know what's come over you since you got a maid and went to Africa."

When Leticia gave her the bag, she said, "Wow! This is the best one I've seen. If it didn't look like a shopping bag, it would almost be nice enough to wear for dress. Thanks, cuz." She left without saying anything to Willa.

"She acts superior," Leticia said, "but she really has an inferiority complex, and I'm just beginning to realize that."

"Yes, and she went out with your guy to prove that she's better looking than you, but she should live so long," Willa said. "I hope she doesn't come here often."

"Not to worry. I intend to feed her with a long-handled spoon."

"Long enough to extend a couple of blocks, I hope."

Leticia patted Willa on the shoulder and went to her room to begin outlining her first column on the lives of African women. She'd put in a section on obesity, but nothing more. The overweight condition was so profuse among mature African women that it would be easier to discuss the exceptions, and she hadn't collected information on that topic.

She arrived at the office before Max the next day and put the two beautifully sculpted busts unwrapped on his desk. "That ought to erase the hurt I caused him yesterday," she said to herself, went to her office and got busy. A few minutes later, she answered her intercom for the first time. She hadn't thought that anyone used it.

"Langley speaking," she said, using her last name as all the other reporters did.

"Mind if I come down to your office for a minute? This is Max."

"I know who it is, and yes you may." She didn't laugh, because she suspected he might be sensitive, but not doing so cost her some effort.

She looked up as he opened the little swinging door without knocking. "Hi, Leticia. Since you're the only one around here who's been to Africa recently, I assume these are from you. I'm stunned. I don't know what to say."

She leaned back in the chair, smiled at him, and teased, "Well, you could thank me."

"You mean I didn't? I do. It's just that I'm overwhelmed. I love them. They're precisely my taste. And to think that you . . . How come you thought of me?"

She didn't want to take away his pleasure by telling him that she'd only decided to give them to him the previous evening. Instead, she said, "I don't know. I just did."

"It's just about the nicest present I've had in a lot of years. I . . ." The muscles in his face moved repeatedly, as if he were in a state of discomfort, but she knew he was fighting for control. "Thank you, Leticia. These mean a lot to me." Without saying anything more, he whirled around and left.

What a strange and complicated man! *Something tells me that neither I nor anyone else in this office knows Max Baldwin. I wonder if I did the wrong thing.* She picked up her pen, started to write and stopped. "If I made a person happy and didn't hurt anyone in doing it, I did the right thing."

She managed to write a comical piece about the toll that international flight takes on the human body and to deliver it to Joel by a quarter of four. "You'll be getting thin stuff from me until I finish the story on African women."

He glared at her. "*Story* did you say?"

"Just testing. Since you don't mind, I'll write three columns on it."

"Three's good, and three's enough. Thanks for the filler."

She thought the piece she gave him was better than a fill-in, but she didn't say so. His opinion was the only one that counted.

Leticia cleared her desk, locked it and left the building. As she stepped outside into the brisk October air, Wilson Gallagher joined her. She stopped walking. "What do you want, Wilson? Kenyetta isn't enough for you?"

"It isn't just that, Leticia. I made the biggest mistake of my life. She came after me and hit me like a Mack truck. Before I knew it, she'd sucked me into her cocoon, and I couldn't get out."

"Really? You poor baby. What do you want me to do, spin you another cocoon?"

"I made a mistake, and I'm asking you for another chance."

"I'll give you a chance," she said. "A chance to appear in court on the charge of harassment. If you think I want Kenyetta's leavings, you're sick." She couldn't deny that it still hurt and that she felt something for him, but she didn't want him. She deserved better. "If you don't want a scandal, you'll leave me alone." She strutted off leaving him stunned in her wake.

Though she usually used public transportation, she hailed a taxi and got in. Yes, she deserved better. Some man would appreciate her for herself and not for the shape of her behind. She knew she was attractive, because in recent months she'd learned to make the best of her assets, and no one could tell her that she wasn't capable. She'd gotten through the inhospitable airport in Lagos without incident, ridden in a mammy wagon in ninety-five-degree heat with five times the wagon's reasonable capacity for humans; heard a lion roar hardly more than ten yards from her and didn't scream; hitched a ride with a man alone on a deserted road, because she had no alternative; and managed to negotiate her way where bribery was the modus operandi. And half the time, she didn't understand what language was being spoken. Damn the likes of Wilson Gallagher. That night, she ate everything Willa put in front of her, did so with relish, went to bed and slept like a baby.

Leticia had fixed in her mind how she wanted her relationship with her cousin to proceed, but Kenyetta was set on a different course. *No matter how uppity Leticia gets, I'm gonna stick as close to that girl as scales stick to fish, and if she thinks she's getting Wilson back, she's a few bricks short of a full load.* Kenyetta phoned Wilson, as she had done at least three times a day recently, though without results. On this occasion, she called him from a public telephone booth in order to frustrate his caller ID.

"Gallagher speaking."

"Hi, honey. I thought you'd left town," she said in her sweetest voice, and added in low and sultry tones, "Can we get together tonight?" At his silence, her voice rose. "Where've you been hiding?"

"I haven't been hiding, Kenyetta. I've simply moved on."

She knew it was a mistake to sound frantic, but she couldn't restrain herself. "What you mean you moved on? You were so hot after me you scorched the air. Is this what you do? You play with people till you get tired of them?"

"You're being unfair, Kenyetta. You're a grown woman, you've been around, and you know the score."

"All those things you told me were a bunch of lies? Is that what you're saying now?"

"Look, babe, don't get hysterical. Easy come, easy go."

"You've gone back to Leticia. Don't lie. I know you have. Well, we'll see about that. When I tell her I'm pregnant, Miss Perfect Virtue won't give you a second glance."

"Don't make me laugh. Did you think I didn't take extra special precautions with you? Like I didn't know what your game was? If you're pregnant, babe, it is definitely not mine."

She shouldn't have made that threat. Now she'd lost all chance with him. "You're talking like this because you've made up with Leticia," she said, trying to make the conversation less serious.

"Don't I wish! See you around."

She hung up, dispirited because the call had only worsened their relationship. She mused over his comments and realized that he hadn't said he'd gone back to Leticia, but that he wished he had. Hmm. She'd have to find a way to ease back into Leticia's good graces. She'd really made a mess of things when she went to Leticia's house to get that basket. Nice one, too. *I'll think of something*, Kenyetta resolved.

On the way back home, two blocks from the convenience store in which she made the call, she stopped in a Baskin-Robbins and bought half a gallon of butter-pecan ice cream, the one thing guaranteed to get her out of the dumps, at least until she realized what she'd done to her weight.

* * *

Leticia's thoughts did not center on Kenyetta and her treachery but on her story about African women. After a weekend of hard work during which she hardly combed her hair, not to speak of getting dressed, she finished the first segment of her story. On Monday morning, she sent the column to Joel and waited on edge for his assessment of it. An hour later, he pushed open her office door. "You done great. I just sent it to the boss."

Her lower jaw sagged. "You sent my column to Mr. Warren?"

"You bet I did. It's first class, and I wanted him to see that I don't have to rewrite your stuff." She realized that she gaped at him, but who wouldn't after receiving that kind of compliment from a supervisor?

"Thank you, Joel. I appreciate the chance you gave me, and I tried to do my best."

"Your best is as good as I want." He walked off shaking his head, but a few minutes later, he phoned her. "The boss wants your story on the front page. Way to go, Leticia!"

When she got a copy of the issue that carried her story, she went into her office, put the DO NOT DISTURB sign on her door and looked at the front page, evidence that she'd made it. She had succeeded as a journalist. For several minutes, tears blinded her. She dried her eyes, and when she could focus on the paper, she saw Max Baldwin's column opposite hers on the upper right of the front page.

She had thought Max might be a chauvinist, but from his story on jobs thought suitable for men and women, she realized that she had judged him unfairly. She put the paper in her briefcase and went to the coffee room, where Max and Marie stood chatting and drinking coffee.

"Your column in today's paper is a brilliant piece of writing, Leticia. Congratulations," Max said.

Marie tipped an imaginary hat. " 'Scuse me. I don't dare stand here with you two geniuses. I gotta get back to work so I can be like you guys."

"I enjoyed your story," Leticia said to Max. "It's a perfect piece of writing. And it made me realize that you are not the male chauvinist I'd thought you were."

"Me? A chauvinist?" Max asked her, his face a puzzled frown. "You're joking. I was thinking that since I'm now your equal—getting on the front page along with you—maybe you'll find me more interesting." She suspected that her eyes widened to twice their normal size. Very little he could have said would have stunned her more thoroughly. "I guess you meant that as a compliment, Max, but you're the paper's ace, not me. You're the one who gives it its class." She poured a cup of coffee, put a lid on it and went back to her office.

Max slouched against the wall, pensive and mildly irritated. How could any thinking person consider him a chauvinist? Leticia didn't know him and gave no indication that she wanted to. Yet, she'd spend time with a player like Wilson, although he credited her with the good sense to avoid getting involved with the man, at least according to Wilson.

Max hadn't taken an easy road in life, although he knew that few men of his class would choose to live as he did. When his mother was released from the hospital after having suffered a stroke, he didn't put her in a nursing home, but took her to his home and hired an LPN to live with them full time and care for his mother. Knowing that his mother was happy and comfortable gave him peace of mind.

Max didn't share that part of his life with his colleagues and friends. And when the woman he cared for insisted that he put his mother in a nursing home, he cut her out of his life. As an only child, he considered it his duty and privilege to care for his widowed mother, who had worked as a cook, cleaning woman, hotel maid and at other menial jobs to send him through school, including Harvard. The mother who he loved and to whom he owed everything.

What Leticia Langley thought of him mattered a great deal. He hadn't sorted it out, but she had a way of getting to him, first with the chocolates and then with those exquisite little carvings. But there was something else, and though he hadn't figured it out, he would. She was tough. She was smart. And she was as soft as a kitten. Oh, what the hell! He threw the remainder of his coffee into the sink, went back to his office and got to work.

Half an hour later, on an impulse, he dialed Leticia's phone number, thought better of it, hung up and walked down to her office. "Did you really think I was a male chauvinist?" he asked her.

She seemed taken aback. "I . . . I didn't think about it a lot, but you've got this tough, alpha male persona, so I . . . Yes."

"Well, I'm not, and you owe me an apology. In fact, you should start making amends by taking me to dinner tonight and paying for it."

"What! You're joking."

"Am not. Actually, you've wounded me so deeply that even if you take me to dinner every evening this week, you'll still have more to make up for. And I mean it."

She knew he was probably joking about paying for his dinners for the next seven days, but she wasn't sure whether he was serious about the rest. "Be serious, Max.

We can't get involved. Think what an ugly situation we'd create for our colleagues if we started something and then split up." She hadn't given thought to starting any kind of relationship with Max, but she'd promised herself that she'd have better relations with people, and that meant laying it out on the table.

When he leaned against the dull gray wall that she disliked so profoundly, folded his arms, crossed his ankles and gazed steadily at her, she realized he might be serious. She couldn't say whether she felt disappointment or had a sense of awe.

"Let me tell you, lady, that if I ever got you, we definitely would not be splitting up." He laughed, or at least, he emitted a noise that sounded like laughter. "Leticia, the very idea is ludicrous."

"Why would you tease about something like this?" she asked him, thinking that she appeared more serious about it than she should. He said nothing, merely continued staring at her. She was about to ask him how they got to that topic when he whirled around and left.

"My Lord," she exclaimed to herself. "I'm either losing my mind or Max is having a serious breakdown."

At home later that afternoon, still uneasy about her conversation with Max, she received a call from Kenyetta. Fortunately, she answered the phone, for she didn't want a confrontation between Kenyetta and Willa, and she knew that her housekeeper was yearning for a chance to tell Kenyetta precisely what she thought of her.

"Hello."

"Hi, Leticia. You've been awfully quiet lately. Roni Crawford, one of our cousins in New Orleans, is getting married, and we ought to attend the wedding."

Wasn't it like Kenyetta to try making amends without apologizing? I didn't get an invitation and I am not going to New Orleans. "Listen, Kenyetta. If Roni What's-Her-Name wanted me at her wedding, she would have sent me an invitation. Count me out."

"But we ought to go, Leticia. We'll have a lot of fun."

"Not me, Kenyetta. Besides, I don't want to go anywhere with you." She let out a deep sigh. She'd said it. For once, she'd stood up to her cousin.

"Aw, Leticia. That's no way for cousins to act."

"Oh? So you remember that we're cousins? I thought you'd forgotten. Cousins don't have affairs with each other's significant others, or is that merely my imagination? You need to straighten out your values, kiddo."

Leticia hung up, and immediately, her thoughts went to Max Baldwin. Wilson looked and acted like a gentleman, a man cut from very select cloth, and look at what a rake he turned out to be. You couldn't judge a man by his looks, his manners or any of his other outward trappings. Though Max had all the externals going for him, he was also a man. They were as different as night and day.

"It's starting to get dark early, ma'am," Willa called to her. She didn't know where Willa was at the moment; the tiny woman possessed a trumpet for a voice, and she chose to call out rather than walk. Leticia peeped into rooms and crevices until she found Willa looking into a closet beside the door leading to the balcony.

"Do you want to leave earlier?" she asked her.

"No, ma'am. I was thinking we could barbecue out of doors in the evenings. My parents did that when we children were little, and I've kept up the habit. It's not fun doing it in the daytime. Oh, and maybe you'll ask some of your nice gentlemen friends to join us some evenings. Nighttime is very romantic."

"Willa, what the devil are you getting at?"

"Me? Nothing. Besides, me and the devil don't mix. I stay out of his business, and I encourage him to stay out of mine."

"My dad always said you should give the devil his due."

"As far as I'm concerned, he ain't got no due. You trying to talk me out of having some night barbecues? There's a real nice pit in the far corner of that garden out back and some lovely garden furniture, but since I been here, nobody's used it. It's like everything else; if you don't use it, you lose it."

"Okay. We'll have a barbecue."

"Thank you, ma'am. Just please don't invite no relatives."

Leticia hadn't noticed the barbecue pit and garden furniture at the rear of the garden that was supposed to serve the tenants in the building in which she lived, so she went out on her balcony to check. In the short while that she'd lived in that neighborhood, she'd been so engrossed in her work that she had paid little attention to her surroundings. Melancholia overcame her when she saw in the distance a large red disc slowly sinking toward the edge of the earth. To its north, a crescent shaped moon lay on its back waiting for the sun to slip out of sight so that it could take over the business of lighting the world.

The setting brought to her mind her days in rural Georgia when the hour of dusk brought out the fireflies, chirping crickets and the croaking of bass or bull frogs. She had no romantic attachment to those days other than the memories of her beloved dad. She looked toward the heavens.

"Dear God, why can't I have some happiness? I thank you for my intellect, but is that all there is for me?" She shook her head in an effort to cast off the feeling. "I refuse to be miserable," she said to herself, and headed for the kitchen.

"Willa, I'd like to take some pastry to the office tomorrow. Do you have the time and the ingredients to make something nice?"

She'd broached the matter gently in case Willa didn't like the idea, but the woman's face lit up as if someone had switched a light on her.

"How many people?'

"I haven't counted them, but not more than eighteen or twenty. Is that too much?"

"No indeedy! I can knock out a lemon-filled cake and a batch of scones in no time."

"Thanks, Willa. You're growing on me."

"And I aim to be so important to you that you wouldn't even think of getting on without me. This is the best and easiest job I ever had, and you're a lovely person to work for. I'll put 'em in a shopping bag ready for you when you leave home tomorrow morning."

That morning, the weight of the bag impressed Leticia so that she could hardly refrain from peeping. She took a taxi to work, put the bag in her office and got to the budget meeting just in time. Rube Warren sat at the head table looking every bit the boss that he was.

"Glad you got here, Langley," he said. "I thought you'd like to know that AP, Reuters, Huffington Post and Bloomberg picked up your story and Max's story from yesterday's front page. We expect that from Max, and we're pleased to know that you're also frontline."

Embarrassed by her colleagues' applause, she blurted out, "Thanks, Mr. Warren. I brought some homemade goodies for everybody. It'll be in the coffee room at eleven o'clock. Sorry, I didn't bring coffee."

"I furnish the coffee every day," he roared. "God forbid you should have a birthday. What did you bring?"

"Peach and cranberry scones and a lemon-filled cake."

"Well, hell! I'll be by your office and get mine as soon as this meeting adjourns. I have to leave the building in about an hour."

They finished the budgeting a little later than usual, and Rube Warren went directly to her office. "I don't know when I last had any homemade pastries," he said, choosing a peach scone and a slice of cake. "This is a real treat. Now, I'll get my coffee. Thanks."

He could have sent his secretary for both the pastry and the coffee, but he didn't. *A lesson in the true meaning of status,* she thought. Truly important people don't have to flaunt it. She vowed not to forget that. She dialed Max's phone number.

"Hi, Max. This is Leticia. Good morning."

"I know very well who it is. Congratulations."

"Thanks. I called to congratulate you and to ask which pastry you want me to save for you."

Did he always have to ponder his responses to her? "Are you still there, Max?"

"Barely. I'm shocked that you want to be sure I get my preference."

She wanted to kick herself, for she hadn't considered that she was treating him as someone special. "We're both celebrating," she said, covering her tracks. "What do you want me to put aside for you?"

"A huge slice of that cake and two each of the scones."

"Will do." She wrapped his portion in napkins and put it in her desk drawer.

The messenger knocked and entered. "You got mail today, Ms. Langley," he sang out in his adolescent part-tenor, part-baritone voice, and dropped several letters and an internal-office envelope into her in-box.

She shuffled through the mail, glanced at the last letter and shrieked. "It isn't. It can't be." She opened the letter with trembling fingers and read:

> Dear Ms. Langley,
>   Broderick and I would be honored if you would join us and a few friends, some of whom you may know professionally, at our home for drinks and an informal buffet dinner and conversation. I'm looking forward to meeting you Friday next at 7 p.m. Please e-mail me your response and your address (CLN701@LoganNettleson. net), and a car will arrive for you at 6:30.
>   Warm regards,
>   Carolyn Logan Nettleson

A glance at her watch told Leticia that she had twelve minutes in which to set out the pastries in the coffee room. She locked her purse in her drawer, grabbed the bag of goodies and Carolyn Nettleson's letter and rushed down the corridor to the coffee room. Immediately, Joel peeped in, but she didn't have time to stop and talk. Willa had packed a half dozen large serving plates and matching individual cake plates as well as napkins and plastic forks. She'd have to ask her where they came from. At the bottom of the bag, she found a white plastic tablecloth that had a linenlike appearance.

"I'll help you," Joel said. "I see this is going to be real special."

She handed him the letter. "Would you read this? I practically fainted."

"Is she talking about Broderick Nettleson?" he asked, his tone incredulous.

"One and the same. Broderick Nettleson was my seat mate from Nairobi to Washington. He's real nice, but I didn't believe him when he said his wife would send me an invitation."

"Why not? Nettleson's a regular guy, and just about the sharpest in the business. If you tell me you made this stuff, I'm going to camp out at your house."

"Then I won't tell you. I use my guest room for an office."

"You made a hit with the boss when you said you'd brought pastries for morning coffee. Say, this looks great. Everything matches. Nothing like a feminine touch. I hope you're accepting the Nettlesons' invitation."

"You bet, that is if I don't fly away with my personally manufactured helium."

"Now, now. You belong with the top reporters. That piece on African women is as good a job as anybody is going to do."

"Thanks, Joel. Mr. Nettleson said he'd read my series on obesity and he thought it was really good. In fact, when we introduced ourselves, he asked me if I worked for *The Journal*."

"You see?" He bit into a cranberry scone. "I'd better stop telling you how good you are. You'll start to believe me, and you'll be a pain in the behind. Say! This thing is fantastic. You have enough, so I'll get a peach one."

"Don't you want some cake?"

"I'd rather have the scones."

"Hey man, we weren't due here until eleven, and you're already eating," one of the printers said to Joel. "Leticia, I expect you realize that you've spoiled us." He bit into a slice of cake. "Holy Moses! This is da bomb!"

She wondered where Max was and whether he had decided to test her. By now, all of the staff had crowded into the coffee room, which, though adequate for its purposes, couldn't accommodate the entire staff at one time. Hopefully, she'd have enough goodies for all. She couldn't tell Max in the presence of the others that she had left his share in her office.

As if he'd planned to be late, Max's tall frame suddenly blocked the doorway, and he let his gaze sweep the room until it landed on her. "If you guys have put away everything already, there's going to be hell to pay," he said without even the tiniest hint of a smile.

"Not to worry," Marie said. "There're plenty of scones left, but not much cake."

Max picked up a plate and helped himself to the scones and cake. After eating one scone, he walked over to Leticia. "This is pure heaven. If you have any more talents, please say so now. For instance, you don't direct a symphony orchestra, do you?"

The man made her nervous. "You're not the type to drink on the job, Max. So you must be extremely tired if you're associating me with musical talent."

He lifted his left eyebrow. "I'm dead serious. Thanks for bringing this. It's wonderful." That said, he turned and left, taking his plate with him. She shook her head from side to side in bemusement and didn't care who saw her. However, she didn't promise herself to decipher the enigma that was Max; she wasn't certain that, if she did, she could deal with what she found.

Chapter Seven

Leticia hadn't imagined that such a simple gesture as providing pastries for the morning coffee hour would increase her popularity with her colleagues, not to speak of her boss. When hardly a crumb remained and she began cleaning up, they relieved her of the job. She went back to her office and was trying to collect her thoughts before outlining her second installment on African women when her phone rang.

"Langley speaking."

"Hello, Langley. Did you save some cake for me?"

"Did I . . . ? You ate a plate full in the coffee room. Aren't you concerned that you'll gain weight?"

"Absolutely not. My regular exercise takes care of the calories. Did you or didn't you?"

"I did, but you're—"

"I'll be right there."

He walked in wearing a smile of pure joy. "I don't know when I've enjoyed a pastry that much."

"If anyone sees you with these," she said, handing him the scones and cake that she had stored in her drawer, "I'll be accused of favoritism."

He moved his left shoulder in a quick, almost imperceptible shrug. "Big damn deal. If they don't know how to curry favor, that's their problem. Besides, I asked and you promised, so I must deserve it."

She couldn't help being amused at his childish behavior. "I had to apologize for my remark about chauvinism, and if you don't change your ways I may find myself apologizing for having mentioned your ego."

He bit into a scone. "Of course I have an ego. It's part of being human. In fact, it's only the second of three stages of early childhood psychological development. You'd like to see me without an ego? You wound me."

That man was getting to be like a sprig of ivy. If you didn't clip it, in no time at all, it would wrap itself around you. The problem was that she had no desire to clip him. He had become her favorite colleague. "Max, please get out of here so I can get some work done. I can't knock out a piece in ten minutes the way you seem able to do. I have to sweat over it."

He stood and gathered his treasures. "If I hang around you, I'll be an insufferable egotist. Woman, I sweat out every word. Thanks for the goodies. You deserve a kiss for this." She didn't have to reply, because he was on his way out when he said it. She wondered if his habit of leaving suddenly was meant to avoid acknowledging her reaction to what he'd said or done, and whether he did the same to other people.

"The less time I spend trying to figure out that puzzling man, the better," she told herself, and got busy with the story that intrigued her more and more. She was discovering that although ignorance was a curse that could rob a person of numerous pleasures in life, including good health, it could also protect one from emotional misery and distress. She'd heard it said, especially in her youth, that what you didn't know wouldn't hurt you. And as she wrote of the condition in which some African women lived and the treatment that some of them had to tolerate, she could appreciate the truth of that proverb. For if they knew how many women lived in more pleasant circumstances, misery would be rampant among them.

She left early in order to shop for something to wear to an informal buffet dinner. She wore suits to work, and she figured she needed something softer. When she arrived at her apartment, Willa opened the door before she could put her key in the lock.

"The goodies were a rousing success," she told Willa as she entered the apartment. "I mean there wasn't a crumb left. They gave you rave reviews. Thank you so much."

"I knew they'd love it, but did any of those nice men say anything special about them? Men love anything with lemon in it, and they do love scones. Did any of them want to come to dinner?"

"Willa, it wouldn't be in good taste for me to get involved with a man at my office."

Willa's hands went to the bones that were stand-ins for hips. "Bunkum. You spend most of your time at the office. Where you gonna meet a decent man if you don't meet him there? I'd say you could meet one at church, but I wouldn't introduce a daughter of mine to any that I've ever seen at my church. Seems like the real nice ones don't pay much attention to the Lord these days."

"I'm invited to dinner Friday with some big-shot journalists. I bought a new dress, and I want you to tell me what you think," Leticia said to Willa. Then she went to her bedroom and changed into the sleeveless, burnt orange tissue-wool sheath that flared a little around the knee and showed just enough cleavage to give assurance that what was hidden was real. "Well, what do you think?" she asked Willa.

"What I think don't matter. It's what those men will think, and if you ask me, they'll think plenty. It's ladylike enough for your style, but, honey, as my granddaughter says, 'it's really rocking.' You got it all right where you need it and not a bit more. It's perfect. What kind of shoes you wearing?"

"Don't mention shoes to me, Willa. I hate them. I'll wear brown patent leather shoes with heels a lot higher than I'm comfortable wearing, but it's just for a few hours." She hoped that none of her male colleagues would be there to see her looking like a sexpot.

The evening came and the Nettleson Town Car arrived for her promptly at six-thirty. She draped a brown velvet stole around her shoulders and left home with the feeling that, if she made the best of the evening, behaving as if she were one of them, she could be headed for a new and better life. But building relationships between her and other people, especially strangers, was not her forte as much as she strived for it. Once she stepped out of her professional role, she seemed to lack the skills needed to deal with people. She told herself that she could only do her best.

The car stopped inches from the steps of a big brick and stone house on upper Sixteenth Street Northwest in what she supposed was Silver Spring, Maryland, past the District of Columbia line. The house sat well back from the street on a large plot of land that hosted many trees, shrubs and flowers. The driver of the car walked with her to the front door and rang the bell.

"Thanks, Lawrence," a young man of about seventeen said to the driver. "Miss Langley, I'm Drew Hopkins Nettleson. Broderick Nettleson is my stepfather. Come in. We're glad to have you."

"Greetings, Drew. I'm delighted to meet you," she said. "I've been looking forward to this visit." She wanted to spend time talking with the boy, to learn how one so young developed so much polish and self-assurance. Soon a tall, good-looking and elegant woman rushed toward them.

"Miss Langley, I'm so glad to meet you. I'm Carolyn Nettleson, and I'm one of your fans. Your column in yesterday's *The Journal* did a service to women everywhere. Come on in and say hello to everybody. You've met my son. I have twin stepsons and Broderick and I have a daughter. That's just by way of explanation. We consider all four of them *our* children. My grandfather may drop in after a while, or he may not. He can't tolerate small talk, claims it makes him physically ill. That's probably why he and Broderick get on so well."

"Are you also a journalist?" she asked Carolyn.

"Oh, no. I'm a public school teacher and a commercial artist. Art is my first love, but I feel morally obligated to teach, because I have the credentials. Broderick is putting Jill, our daughter, to bed. She won't go to sleep unless he reads something to her. Would you like me to take your stole?"

"Thanks. It's rather cool outside, but very pleasant in here." They took a few steps and encountered Broderick carrying his daughter in his arms.

"Jill says she'll go to sleep without procrastinating if she can meet Ms. Langley. I told her she can hear about Africa some other time. I'm so glad you're able to join us, Ms. Langley."

"Thank you, I've been looking forward to it. I've met two of your children, and I hope I get to meet the twins."

"You will. They don't allow themselves to miss anything or anyone who comes here. I promised to put Jill to bed, so Carolyn will introduce you to our other guests."

As if they'd been friends for years, Carolyn draped an arm around Leticia's waist and walked with her into what seemed to be a great room. Its striking cathedral ceiling, massive stone and marble fireplace and floor-to-ceiling windows made the term *living room* too modest a word for it. A huge original Reardon hung between the paneled windows, and an Elizabeth Catlett sculpture rested on a grand piano.

"Ms. Langley, have you met Paul Faison and his wife, Darlene? Paul writes for—"

"I know," Leticia was happy to say. "You write for *The Maryland Tribune.*"

"I do indeed," he said, and she was beginning to wonder if a man had to have height and stunning good looks in order to be a top level journalist. "Thank you for knowing that. When did you join *The Journal*?"

She smiled because he spoke to her as if she were an equal, though if she ever reached his level, she'd gladly dance on the Washington Monument. "I began work there in the latter part of June this year."

"Where had you worked previously? I'm doing the interviewing," he said with a laugh, "so you'll only have to tell this once. Everybody else is listening."

She let her gaze sweep the group, smiled like a pro and said, "Nowhere. I only graduated from Howard in June. Oh, I'm as old as I look. I postponed entrance, and that accounts for the late graduation. I didn't have to repeat courses. Honest." She spread her palms outward as if in entreaty, bringing a laugh from the group.

"I'm sure of that," Paul said.

"This is Paul's publisher, Robert Weddington."

"Glad to meet you, Ms. Langley," Robert said. "If

Rube doesn't treat you right and Max can't stand the competition, I'll be waiting. I like your work. My son's teething and irritable, so Lynn, my wife, stayed at home with him."

Leticia noticed that an elegant woman around her age squeezed her way to the center of the group. "These guys are so big, Leticia, that I get lost whenever I'm in this group. I'm Allison Wade. Since Robert explained why Lynn isn't here, I grant myself the right to explain that my husband, William N. Covington, Bill to most people, is on a government assignment. I'm glad to meet you. I get lost in this gang. No matter who's here, every man is six four or taller."

She liked Allison at once. "I'm glad to meet you, Allison. Yes. I'd begun to wonder if a man had to be tall in order to be a successful journalist. My male colleagues at *The Journal* are also tall." An appraisal of Carolyn and Allison told her that she'd worn exactly the right thing, dressy but not too revealing. Drew offered her barbecued shrimp on a long toothpick and a maid or housekeeper followed with a dip and napkins.

"You're in high school, I take it," Leticia said to Drew after thanking him for the shrimp

"No, ma'am. I'm in George Washington University."

"You don't look old enough," she said.

"I'm seventeen, ma'am. You can't live in this house with my parents without learning a lot. I graduated early."

"With honors, I'll bet."

"Yes, ma'am. Valedictorian."

"Congratulations. At the expense of monopolizing you, I'm anxious to know how one so young has so much poise."

He seemed pensive. "When you have to deal with . . . things, you learn a lot and you get a lot of self-confidence."

"Any parent who has a son like you is very fortunate."

His eyes widened and a smile lit up his face. "Thanks, ma'am. Thanks a lot."

She accepted the glass of chardonnay that Drew offered her later, took a few sips and decided she better hold it and pretend for the remainder of the evening. She hadn't learned to drink more than one glass with her dinner, and she didn't think it wise to practice in the company of some of the biggest names in print journalism.

"What part of town do you live in?" Allison asked as they were serving themselves dinner.

"Woodley Road," she said proudly, happy that she didn't have to give her old address on Florida Avenue.

"Then we're not so far from each other. Bill travels a lot, and I need someone to see a movie with when he's away. My colleagues are men, and I sure can't go to a movie with them. Would you go with me sometime?"

"I'd like that," Leticia said, careful not to show the exuberance that she felt. "Yes, that is, if it's not about murder, witches, ghosts or vampires."

Allison laughed aloud. "You'll never catch me paying my money to be frightened to death. No indeed."

At the table, the guests sat where they chose, and Leticia had Allison on her right and Robert Weddington on her left.

"What do you think of Max Baldwin?" Allison asked her. "I know he's a fine writer, and he's won some awards. I mean as a man, what do you think of him?"

Leticia was not going to bite that one. "He's becoming my favorite colleague," she said truthfully. "He's very straightforward. I like that in people."

Allison took a sip of wine and pushed her steak

around on her plate. "I'm not prying. I was trying to find an opening, an opportunity to tell you that he's single and a truly great guy. He and Bill are friends."

"Really? Is Bill a journalist? I know he won an award for a book about diplomacy, diplomats or something like that, but—"

"He's a diplomat, but he's happiest when he's playing the guitar with a jazz combo, and he is very, very good at it."

"I love jazz, especially classical jazz where the musicians interpret a melody. You know, like Armstrong, Ellington, Johnny Hodges, and others of that style."

"I'll keep that in mind for the next time Bill and his buddies get together at home. They play for themselves, and that's when the music is best," Allison said.

"Would you mind telling me how you two met?"

"I got an assignment to travel with him and interview him for an article entitled 'A Day in the Life of William Nicholas "Bill" Covington.' At the end of the six weeks, he knew more about me than I did about him, but we made it anyway."

"I hope you have some more to tell us about African women," Robert Weddington said to her. "Otherwise, we'll consider you a tease."

"Thanks," she said. "I'll have two more installments. Joel said three's enough."

"He's probably right. Whose idea was it?"

"I began with the subject of obesity among our women, then the differences in obesity between African and African-American women, and Mr. Warren liked the stories and wanted something of greater depth. But when I got to Africa, the data I found began to talk to me, and this series is the result."

"You're a bright woman, and Joel is to be congratulated for not making you stick to a topic that would be like comparing lemons and oranges. You went with your data, and that's always the smart thing to do." He was the third top-flight journalist to tell her that, and she didn't plan to forget it.

The room darkened and she looked toward the only source of light. Seeing two fiery blazes approaching, she decided that the moment belonged to some pranksters. But the room light returned, and she saw two young boys, obviously twins, of about eight years who were dressed like Robin Hood and who carried desserts. "What a delightful way to serve cherries jubilee and baked Alaska," she said to her table mates.

"Right," Robert said. "Carolyn always has at least one clever gimmick, and she always serves two desserts. Way to go."

By the time she left the Nettleson residence, the others had dispensed with formality and begun to call her Leticia. For her, calling Broderick Nettleson and Paul Faison by their first names was tantamount to calling her late father "Hank," his nickname. But she managed it and got a feeling of belonging from the more intimate atmosphere and the camaraderie that it created.

That weekend, she completed the final installment on the African women and collected as many newspapers as she could find to get ideas for future columns. She wrote a thank-you note to Carolyn Nettleson and, with nothing more planned, sat on her balcony trying to read a short story. However, she didn't want to read or do anything else alone. She missed Kenyetta, for she always called her cousin with she was in a blue funk. But the hurt Kenyetta had meted out to her over the past five years seemed stronger and more piercing and she didn't want to be around her cousin. Still, she hated the loneliness, the raw, empty feeling that she didn't seem able to banish. *The answer to this is to get rid of some of this free time I have every weekend.*

The following Monday afternoon, she received a call from Allison Wade. "I belong to Windmills, a service club," Allison told her after their greeting. "The group consists of men and women who work to raise funds in order to help people who can't help themselves. If I give a party for the group at my house, everybody pays to attend, and that includes me. We support programs for the homeless, soup kitchens, children of incarcerated women and such. Most of the people are interesting. We meet once a month for dinner at Pratt's Clubhouse, and we give each other moral support. In one of our fund-raisers, we women paid twenty dollars to learn to belly dance, and the men paid fifty to watch. It was very successful. Would you like to join? The only criterion is that you dedicate yourself to helping the less fortunate."

"I'd love it, Allison. Just tell me when and where."

Leticia imagined that years would pass before she recovered from her introduction at Windmills as the journalist who rocked Washington with a story on the plight of African women.

"Do you think you could write some comedy skits for our next big fund-raiser?" the president asked her at the first meeting she attended.

"I've never done that, but I can try." The notion suddenly took hold of her, and she couldn't wait to try her hand at it. After she got home that night, she wrote on the back of an envelope,

> *One night, a man said to his wife, "I'm going out. Don't wait up."*

> *"Okay, but how long will you be gone?"*
> *"Long enough to take care of business."*
> *"Good,"* she said. *"That'll give me more than enough time."*
> *"Time for what?"*
> *"To take care of business."*

She considered that one to be fair, but she wasn't sure she'd find it amusing if anyone else had written it. She tried again and liked that one, though she'd cleaned it up from her original idea. Leticia could hardly wait to get an opinion about it.

The next morning, she went directly to Max's office without stopping at her own.

"Hi," he said, but his casual tone belied the startled expression on his face.

"Max, look at this, please. I'm writing comedy skits, and I want to know if these are funny."

He rubbed the back of his neck, half frowning and squinting as he did so. "Okay. Have a seat. This may take a while."

"It's only about a dozen lines altogether," she assured him.

"Yeah, but I have to switch moods."

"You have to . . . gosh, I interrupted you, didn't I?"

"You don't think I was sitting here waiting for a reason to break out laughing, do you?"

"I'm sorry, Max. I shouldn't have barged in like this. Maybe some other time." She sounded dispirited, but she'd been counting on his saying that the pieces were funny.

"Sit back down. You asked me to read it, and I will. I'll give you my honest opinion."

Chills shot through her. *What if he thinks I'm a donkey's ass for writing this?* She'd been in the process of sitting, but cut it short and reached for the sheet of paper. "Thanks, Max, but maybe I don't want your honest opinion."

He leaned back in his chair, gazed at her for a while as if searching for some rare thing, and then he laughed aloud. Laughed and laughed until she thought he might be hysterical. "Max, for goodness sake. Nothing's that funny."

He looked at her with one closed eye. "That's what you think. Since when have you been afraid of me? And for heaven's sake why?" He leaned forward, snatched the paper from her hand and said, "Everybody who knows me knows I'm sweet as sugar, a real pussycat." And with the speed of a NASCAR engine, he sobered. "I'd never intentionally hurt you, Leticia. Don't you know that?"

He could knock the wind out of her faster and more easily than anyone she knew or had ever known. "I . . . I guess so. It's just that . . . when I think I understand you, you turn another page."

Max made a pyramid of his ten fingers, supported his chin with them and searched her with his large, all-seeing eyes. "I see. You're full of surprises, too, lady. It hasn't occurred to me that you want to understand me. Nobody here does. It's assumed that I'm tough, uncaring and concerned only with my next award. So I act the part."

He had effectively jerked the rug from beneath her. She didn't want to feel compassion for him or any other man that she worked with, but she sensed in him a kindred soul. "Oh, Max. Please don't talk this way. Look, I'd . . . I'd better go on to my office while you read that. Thanks so much."

To her amazement, he said nothing, only redirected his gaze to the paper on which she had written the few comic lines. *What kind of life does he have, and why is he so . . . so different?* The question took over her mind as she tried to get back to work, but she could say truthfully that she didn't want the answers.

He phoned her a few minutes later. "Leticia, the first one is funny only if the comedian can deliver it. The second would be hilarious if the preacher called the secretary something stronger than 'old hag.' If I were writing it, he'd call her a bitch. Nobody expects a preacher to say that, and it would be funny."

"You think I have any talent in this sphere?"

"Absolutely, but you can't tie your own hands. You're very ladylike, but comedy rarely is. Let it hang out."

"Thanks, Max. I . . . thanks a lot." She hung up and didn't move for a good ten minutes. Something was going on, and she couldn't put her finger on it. She was developing a friendship with Max, and she would never have believed that she could be on equal terms with a person like him—accomplished, sophisticated, aware of his place in the scheme of things. Maybe she was making progress. Was she more self-assured because she'd held her own with the Nettlesons and their guests? She lowered her head into her hands. Was she ever going to stop feeling inadequate in social situations? While in college, she'd thought that her looks and poor clothes held her back socially. But as she thought back to her college days and compared herself to other girls there, she knew that the problem lay within her.

Renewing her vow to change, she telephoned the president of the service club later that day and told her that she would try to write some funny skits for the fund-raiser. "I've written a couple for a stand-up comic, and I think they're pretty good."

"They don't have to sound as if Woody Allen wrote them. We need about twenty minutes. And, Leticia, we're so glad that you want to be active."

"Thanks, Margo. I promise to do my best." Thereafter, she spent at least two hours each evening writing comedy routines. She wanted to show them to Max, since only he knew she had an interest in writing comedy, but she couldn't gather sufficient courage. If the routines were off the mark, he would say so.

She decided to spend more time watching people as a source of inspiration for her skits, but in three working days, the funniest thing she saw at the office was two of *The Journal* printers walking backward as they observed three very pretty and voluptuous journalism students on a field trip that included watching the production of a newspaper. The two men, coming from opposite directions, plowed into each other and were sent sprawling on the floor.

After a lot of thought, she gave some of the skits to Margo Overstreet, who claimed to have been named after Margo Channing, the role Bette Davis played in the movie *All About Eve.*

"If you don't think they'll work out," she said to Margo, "I have more than enough responsibilities to keep me overworked. Who's going to do the acting?"

"Why, we will, of course. Nobody who comes to see us will be expecting Bill Cosby or Steve Harvey. All we want is money for our projects."

Margo then asked Leticia if she'd like to meet for brunch one Sunday. "I love brunch, because the good ones offer you everything you can think of eating. How about it?"

"Sunday coming is free," Leticia said. "Would that be a good time?"

Margo arrived at the Willard for brunch looking fit for the cover of *Vogue,* but Leticia soon discovered that the woman was anything but stuffy.

Margo chewed on a piece of smoked sturgeon, swallowed it, put her fork down and looked at Leticia. "Your column on African women changed my life."

"How? What do you mean?" Leticia asked her, startled.

"I decided that if I didn't want sex, I was going to say no. Those poor women don't have an alternative, but I have. Recently I told my husband no, for the first time in these six years we've been married. He asked me if I wanted to talk about it. It seems he'd felt all along that something wasn't right, and he tried to correct it, but he needed my cooperation, and I was faking it. He talked to me, telling me what I meant to him, how and what we could have together if I'd let him teach me. So I cut out that puritanical crap and . . . well, we've been on a honeymoon ever since. These days, he doesn't have to ask. I hate to think what I'd have kept on missing if I hadn't read that column." She raised her wineglass. "Here's to you, Leticia."

Leticia patted Margo on her arm and worked hard at not showing how dumbfounded she was. "Margo, I'm flabbergasted. Hearing that makes me feel that enduring those mosquitoes, sand flies, roaring lions and other inconveniences was more than worth it. I feel kinda proud."

"There're lots of women like me, or like I was, and I hope something shakes them up. Have you had a chance to talk with Jeannine? She's a stockbroker. She won't ask you for your patronage, and she probably doesn't need it, but she'll give you some tips on investing, and if you follow them, you'll soon have a good little nest egg. We have lawyers, physicians, professors, public school teachers, musicians, actors, travel agents, and women in several other fields as members of our local branch. Allison Wade was our only writer until you joined us."

"When will you give the members a chance to read my script?"

Margo's face darkened, and she poked her tongue into her right cheek. "Leticia, you do not give thirty women the right or the opportunity to make suggestions on the outcome of *anything*. You'll get thirty different and incompatible responses. I plan to tell them when to come for the rehearsal tryout. That's that. Democracy is for reasonable people."

A grin altered Leticia's face. "Is that Margo or the wine talking?"

"Margo. When the wine talks, you may not want to be there. I believe in being candid, Leticia. So tell me, when I invite you to dinner, should I invite an eligible male, or can you bring your own?"

"I don't have one right now, Margo. He dropped me, dated my cousin and best friend, and now he wants me back."

"I hope you told him to go to hell."

"In so many words, I did."

Margo sipped more wine. "Girl, you should have told him in exactly those words. I'll bet he was a really sharp-looking stud, perfect from head to toe. One of those dumped me and, instead of crying my eyes out, I fell right into the arms of my husband. Thank you, Jesus."

Leticia chuckled.

"When you come to our house, you may bring a guy if you want to, but I don't entertain by gender numbers."

Leticia left Margo with a feeling that she may have found a niche. If even a few of the other women in the service club were like Margo and Allison, women who knew their strengths and were not ridden with envy, women who enjoyed the company and moral support of their sisters, she'd come home.

Still glowing from the first brunch she'd ever eaten, the wine and the kindred soul she discovered in Margo, Leticia hadn't been in her apartment ten minutes when the phone rang. She answered it and heard Kenyetta's voice.

"Hey, girl, you still pouting? You really should have gone to that wedding. A lot of people asked about you, including Mark. I told him you didn't come because you were mad at me. Let's go to the movies tonight. There's an old one that I've heard about for years and never saw. *The Red Shoes.* It's about dancers. You'll learn something about ballet."

"I don't care to learn about ballet from the movies, Kenyetta, and I didn't go to that wedding because I did not get an invitation, so you shouldn't have lied. I just got home, and I'm not going back out today."

"Then why don't I bring some barbecued ribs and potato salad over and we eat supper together?"

"I just finished brunch at the Willard, and food's the last thing I want to think about. I want to get out of these clothes. Bye." She hung up, and for once, she had no guilt feeling about it. She'd felt great when she left Margo. But the more she was in her cousin's company, by phone or otherwise, the more she had to fight for her self-esteem. Kenyetta was a downer.

When the phone rang immediately, she knew that Kenyetta had something more to say. "You're back with Wilson. I know you are."

Leticia took a long deep breath. "You listen to me, Ken. Wilson harassed me, begging to continue with me where he left off when he took up with you, and without so much as telling me good night. I wouldn't have him back if he crawled on his belly like the snake he is. I deserve better and more from a man. I'm not surprised that you think he's what you deserve. At least he's single, and after years of taking what's left from a married man, Wilson must look like heaven to you. Please leave me alone about Wilson Gallagher. I don't give a damn what he does or who he does it with. Good-bye." Leticia hung up and suddenly raised her arms and whooped. She'd told Kenyetta what she thought. How sweet it was!

That Tuesday night at the Windmills monthly meeting, sixteen of the group's thirty members wanted to try out for Leticia's comedy routine, and the chair ruled that the remaining fourteen would determine the final cast with their applause. Shivers raced through Leticia's arms and legs, and her belly seemed headed for her feet as she watched in horror as one person after another butchered her lines. She admitted that the four receiving the loudest and longest applause represented the best of the lot, but what a lot! Rehearsals began immediately, but she knew she wouldn't have the stomach to watch any subsequent practices.

The next morning, for want of other comfort, she knocked on Max's office door. "Come in." It sounded like a growl, so she knew he was busy and didn't want to be disturbed, but she needed to vent.

"I know you're busy, but—"

"But you're going to disturb me anyway. You could at least have brought us some coffee."

"Since you're not going to run me out, I'll get us some. Cream, sugar or both?"

"Neither. Thanks."

She got the coffee, and as she was about to knock on Max's door, Joel passed. "I wouldn't disturb him if I were you. He's in one hell of a foul mood this morning."

When she put her hand on the doorknob, Joel frowned and shoved his hands in his pants pockets. "You're going in there anyway?"

She winked at Joel. "You have to know what makes the cookie crumble. Max loves coffee."

"Well, I'll be damned." He walked on, shaking his head.

"What's eating you?" Max asked her after savoring a long sip of coffee. "This is just what I needed."

She told him about the skit and the characters chosen to perform it. "Max, I worked so hard on that routine, and not one of those people has the slightest knowledge of acting. They read like second graders pointing a finger at every word."

"I can imagine that would be upsetting, but after they memorize the lines and rehearse a few times, it's bound to be better."

"You had to be there. In life, there are some situations so bad that you don't even pray over them. Honest!"

"Yeah, but I don't like to think like that. I take the view that I can fix it, and if I don't cure it, I at least make it better. Every time."

She knew her face reflected her surprise, but his reaction to it didn't warn her to be cautious. "I'm not surprised. Friday night before last, I met some people who said nice things about you. One in particular literally praised you." From his expression, she knew he'd shifted from lighthearted to very serious, but she didn't see a reason to stop.

"I was out of my league, Max, so I mostly listened. One, who you know well, said you're a fine person and a top level writer and asked me what I thought of you as a man." He sat forward, looking more anxious than she would have imagined he could be. She ignored that. "I said you're my favorite colleague, and you're straight-forward. As I think of it now, I might have said that you may be the most honest person I've ever dealt with."

He drained the coffee cup and threw it into his wastebasket. "I already told you that if I take seriously what you say about me, I'd be such an ass nobody could stand me. Go back to your office before I do something stupid. Thanks for the coffee, and for dumping on me. You made my day." She scrutinized him to see if she'd hurt or displeased him, but she couldn't read his emotions.

"Go on," he said, waving toward the door. "Scat. I've got to work, and your presence sure as hell isn't con-ducive to that." After she returned to her office, she re-membered that he hadn't asked her where she was when others spoke of him or who said what she quoted to him. She didn't believe for a second that Max lacked self-confidence, but she had a difficult time believing that he had so little interest in what was said of him. Re-calling his serious expression when she began to relate the conversation at Broderick Nettleson's house, she phoned him.

"Baldwin."

"Max, this is Leticia. You didn't ask me where I was Friday before last or who the conversationalists were. Don't you want to know?"

"I figured that if you thought I should know, you'd tell me. It was enough that nobody said anything bad about me, or at least that you didn't say they did."

"I was at Broderick Nettleson's house, and those sing-ing your praise included Paul Faison, Robert Wedding-ton, and Allison Wade."

"*Get outta here!* I should have known it; that's my gang. I was giving a lecture in Boston, or I'd have been there. How'd you meet the Nettlesons?"

She told him and added, "I've been on cloud nine ever since."

"Don't genuflect to that crowd, Leticia. You were there because you belong. The Nettleson affairs are very small and very select. I'm happy for you. You may run into Joel at one of these things, too." A long pause ensued. "Thanks for the details, Leticia. Your telling that gang I'm your favorite colleague means a lot to me. They think I'm all investigative journalism and no heart, but that's because they only see with their eyes. Talk later."

"They only see with their eyes?" What else were they supposed to see with? She wished he wouldn't drop those cryptic remarks on her and then walk away or hang up. If he could see with something else, she'd like to know about it.

Chapter Eight

Leticia's comedy, *Leftovers,* opened at the YWCA on a rainy Friday night. Leticia deliberately sat in an aisle seat in the fifth row of the big auditorium in case she wanted to get out in a hurry. The curtain rose, and Jeannine Shaw, the club's vice president, walked out on the stage smiling when the script required that she be scared to death, because she'd just ruined the favorite dessert of her husband, whose salivary glands had been anticipating it all day. A spattering of laughter and giggles flittered through the audience, though Leticia's script gave no reason for it. Leticia stopped holding her breath and prayed.

"The best thing about lemon tarts is the *crud,*" Jeannine said in a loud and self-assured voice, and the audience whooped with laughter. Leticia slumped in her seat and would have covered her face if she'd had anything with which to do it. At long last, intermission arrived, and she sneaked out, unnoticed, and went home. Mortified.

"Somebody who says she's Margo is on the phone, ma'am," Willa said to Leticia the next morning, unaware that Leticia had deliberately ignored the phone call.

"Thanks," she called back, and plodded her way to the phone in her bedroom.

"Where'd you go?" Margo asked without preliminaries. "The audience gave you a thunderous, standing ovation. They kept applauding, hoping that you'd come out and take a bow. Where'd you go? They laughed all the way through it. I think we'll put it on again in a few weeks. I hope we got media coverage. It's the best thing we've ever done."

Leticia didn't want to criticize Jeannine to Margo. So she said, "My nerves got the better of me." That much was true, but not for the reason Margo would think. "Thanks for the good word, Margo."

"I guess you're used to success with your writing, but if people enjoyed anything I did as much as that crowd enjoyed your comedy routines last night, I'd be beside myself. Still, modesty is a good thing, and I admire it. You're a treasure, Leticia."

She thanked Margo, and though she knew her work succeeded because the performers butchered it, she admitted to herself that she was glad it hadn't flopped. Nonetheless, she wasn't gratified; the possibility existed that the audience hadn't laughed with her but *at* her.

"How'd it go?" Max asked her at the office the following Monday morning. "I wanted to see it, but since you didn't invite me . . ." He let the thought hang.

"Oh, Max. After the first three or four minutes, I didn't listen. I couldn't. One woman delivered her lines about as smoothly as an eight-wheel flatbed truck lumbers over pot holes on a brick road."

"Hey." He raised both hands, palms out. "You know you're exaggerating. It couldn't have been that bad."

"Yes, it was," she grumbled. "The club's vice president—a dud if there ever was one—said the best thing about lemon tarts was the *crud.*" His eyes widened, and then laughter spilled out of him.

"But, Max, I wrote *curd.* Lemon curd is used in pies and tarts. The audience whooped and screamed with laughter." He fell back against his chair, spread his arms and let the laughter pour out of him.

"Max, please. It was so humiliating. I sneaked out at intermission and went home."

He sobered, straightened up with apparent effort, but she could see him struggling to control the laughter. "Would you please sit back down? Leticia, you can *not* be serious. You wrote a comedy, and people screamed with laughter. What more could you want?"

"I wanted those idiot actors to speak my words and to act according to my directions in the script. That's what I wanted. I did not write *crud,* and I did not tell that stupid woman to smile with joy when the smoke coming from the oven indicated that her pie was burning up."

At the mention of the word *crud* again, he slumped in his chair and shook with the laughter that poured out of him. "If I'd written a comedy and even one person laughed once, I'd have considered myself a success, since I know nothing of the art of writing comedy. You should be happy, Leticia."

"Well, I'm not."

"Next time write *crud.* It's a learning process."

She jumped up to leave, irritated and disappointed because he hadn't given her the sympathy she craved. "You don't understand, and you're not trying," she shot over her shoulder as she reached for the doorknob.

He stood at once and walked toward her. "Come on, sweetheart. That's not fair. Where's your sense of humor?"

"Right now, I don't have any, and you've got too damned much." She flung open the door and marched to her office, wishing she had the nerve to poke him.

Now what had he done? He didn't understand her one bit more than she understood him. A comedy writer succeeded if people laughed at what she wrote. People thought the skits hilarious for the wrong reason, and that gesture of approval humiliated Leticia Langley. He sat down at his desk, dialed her number and hung up. The hell with it! He thought about her too much anyway.

Not much surprised him, but when he saw jokes on the first page of the paper's human interest section with Leticia as the author, he rushed down to Joel's office. "Man, what's this? You expect people to take Langley's column seriously if they read this stuff?"

Joel looked up at him, leaned back in his chair and crossed his knees. "I thought it was funny."

"So what? She's a serious journalist, and she makes the paper look good, but jokes don't do a damned thing either for a journalist or for a first-class urban newspaper. You trying to kill her?"

"Okay. You tell her you think the whole idea is stupid and that you told me not to print any more of it."

"I can't do that. But, Joel, you know I'm right. Three weeks ago, she was a guest at one of Brod Nettleson's dinners, because her column impressed——"

"What? She didn't tell me that. Hell, man, she should have told me. I'll speak to her, but I . . ." He ran his fingers over his tight curls. "She doesn't understand this business, so it's my fault. I'll straighten it out. Thanks. Uh . . . does she know you're speaking to me about this?"

"Definitely not. She'd probably fly off the handle faster than a ball comes out of a cannon. And don't you tell her. You get it?"

He wanted to erase Joel's satisfied grin with the back of his hand.

"I got it. You betcha," Joel said.

Max headed back to his office, and the closer he got to it, the more he fumed. Joel was one of the best editors anywhere, and he should have known better than to print that junk on the front page of the features section. That could undermine everything she'd accomplished. He kicked the door open, slammed it shut and sat down. She should have known better.

He turned to that section and read the routine again. It *was* funny, but you couldn't get any cornier unless you smoked a corncob pipe. He laughed at one line. All right it was good, but just good enough to ruin her career as a journalist. He'd give a lot to know how Joel planned to repair the damage.

A few minutes later, Max heard her voice when he answered the phone. "Hi. Did you see my comedy skit on the features page?"

He gazed heavenly, asking for guidance. "Uh-huh."

"What do you mean, 'uh-huh'? You didn't like it?"

"It made me laugh, but I didn't like where I saw it."

"Max, would you please stop talking in circles."

What the heck! In for a penny, in for a pound. She'd be mad, but pussyfooting around the truth was not his style. "I wouldn't have published it in the paper for which I write serious journalism. If I wanted to write for comedy, I'd do it under an assumed name." There! She'd be mad as hell with him, but he was too old to change, and besides, he didn't want to.

"Max, I . . . Max, I think I hate you."

"I expected that, or worse, but Leticia, you can always

count on my telling you precisely as I see it. This recent comedy writing is not good for your career as a journalist, and I'd lie if I prettied it up and said otherwise. I'm sorry if you hate me." He hung up. For two cents, he'd knock Joel across the District Line. What the devil had the man been thinking?

Leticia got up, walked to the end of the corridor and stared down on Thomas Circle. It wasn't her favorite among the city's circles, because it lacked character, at least when compared to Logan and Dupont. Had she made a mistake? She didn't think that Max would mislead her, because she believed in his honesty and integrity. And she didn't hate him, though she wished he had handed his opinion to her in a more palatable way.

That morning, she'd received requests for material from three comics, and one had asked her to write for him exclusively. No doubt, she had a decision to make, and she had to do it soon. The comic who asked for her exclusive services mentioned a fat sum, but she knew that if he ever lost out, she'd go down with him.

At dinner that night, she mentioned her dilemma to Willa, who as usual, didn't bite her tongue. "I didn't know you went to college to learn how to write jokes for some comics who think the N word is funny. You may get rich, but you ain't gon' be doing your reputation no favor." She helped herself to some more string beans. "These sure are good. I read your columns every time they come out, but I ain't read the funnies since Charles Schulz died."

"But Willa, *Peanuts* is still running, and it's still the best, at least for me."

Willa pointed her fork in Leticia's direction while she swallowed her corn bread. "Not to me. I'm loyal. And as for your column, how'm I supposed to take you seriously if you gonna write stuff for comics who don't do nothing but pollute the air with they language?"

"Not all of them do that. Bill Cosby didn't."

"Yes ma'am. That's like saying African Americans are absolutely equal; look at Condoleezza Rice. But don't listen to me; it's your life. I'm just your housekeeper who loves you and wants the best for you."

Leticia told herself not to laugh, but it didn't register with her brain, and laughter shook her until she began to hiccup.

"I didn't know I was so funny," Willa said. She went to the kitchen and returned with a lemon meringue pie. "I already learned that if I give you a dessert that's got lemon in it, you'll stay happy for a good long while. How does it taste?"

"Willa, I am ashamed to say that you have my number, but you'd better not try manipulating me."

Willa turned her head to the side, and her shoulder almost brushed her chin as she lowered her gaze and said coyly, "Would I do something like that, ma'am?"

"Yes, you would, and I wish you'd read my script at the YWCA the other night. At least you're an actress."

"I do declare, ma'am. That's funnier than any of that stuff you had in the paper today. Honest to goodness."

She'd gotten used to Willa's irreverence. After all, the woman was old enough to be her mother and, indeed, Willa treated her as one would a daughter. Leticia didn't question it, because Willa's kindness and caring filled a hole in her life. What to do about the opportunity to write for a comedian bothered her, but she told herself to focus on her column, that she'd deal with comedy when she had to.

As it happened, Joel took the decision from her the next morning. She answered the intercom knowing it

would be he, for none of her other colleagues used it.
"Could you come to my office, please, Langley?"

"Be right there."

He handed her a printout. "Read that. It'll be in to-morrow's paper."

She read:

> *I'd hoped to find an Art Buchwald for the paper, and I thought that, owing to her witty way with words, Leticia Langley might be that person. So I asked her to produce some samples. I liked what she gave me so much that I printed it on the first page of the features section. But Ms. Langley isn't comfortable writing comedy, so I'm still looking. If anyone knows a good literary funny man or woman, send him or her this way. Joel Raymond, editor in chief.*

"What do you think?"

"I thought you said you liked my comedy writing."

"I did and do, but I hadn't thought about what it might do to your reputation as a respected journalist. I shouldn't have printed it under your byline. If you continue it here or any other place, use a pen name."

"I get the point, Joel," she said, making up her mind quickly. She didn't want him to think that she was an opportunist who'd take on anything for money rather than a professional journalist. "I suppose I should thank you for making up my mind for me. What you say makes sense. Go ahead and print it, and thanks for your thoughtfulness."

Joel clasped his hands behind his head, leaned back and eyed her with half a squint. "Are you being sarcastic?"

She didn't laugh, although she had a sudden urge

to. "Joel, if you think I've got the nerve to serve you up a dish of sarcasm, you don't know me. By the way, a comedian offered me two and a half times my salary here to write routines for him. I turned it down. I don't want my well-being to depend on the fortune of someone who's constantly tempting the legal authorities and who's known for living on the edge. Besides, I have a feeling that I'd dry up in no time and want to write serious topics again."

"I could have told you that, and I don't want you to lose the respect of your peers; you didn't earn it easily. You worked hard." He swung around to his desk as if preparing to go back to work. "So I needn't worry that I'll pick up *The Tribune* one day and find your comedy skits on the front page?" His grin was meant to make light of the matter, but she wasn't fooled. Joel had worried that she might leave him for more money than the paper could or would pay.

Was she being cynical? She looked him in the eye. "I'm a journalist, Joel, and so far I'm happy here."

"You got friends here, Leticia." That said, he cast his gaze on the copy that lay on his desk awaiting his attention.

She went back to her office, walking slowly, deep in thought. Was he telling her that he was her friend? Somehow, she doubted that. Minutes passed, and she couldn't shake the feeling that she'd left something undone or some strings untied. Should she have told Joel that she was capable of making her own decision about her career and her future? He'd never convince her that he would have dared make that choice for Max. She still had a lot to learn. Her job, in fact her life, held problems and pitfalls for which no amount of schooling could have prepared her. And she should have stood up to Joel and told him the truth when he asked if she was being sarcastic. If there was a next time, she wouldn't be caught napping.

A phone call from her cousin Mark surprised her. "The news isn't so good, Leticia, though it could certainly be much worse. Grandfather had a mild stroke, but he's in the hospital, and—"

"But I don't—"

"Whoa. Hear me out. He asked for two things: the Bible and a chance to speak with you. I'm not saying what you should do. I'm only delivering the message. He sent for me, he said, because I introduced him to you. He's old, Leticia."

"But, Mark, that man treated me as if I were some rubble to be swept out of his yard." She couldn't help feeling offended that the old man would ask anything of her and that Mark had the audacity to make her feel guilty.

"I know. I was there. If you decide to come, let me know. I'll take care of you while you're here. And, Leticia, I'm not the judge as to whether you should or shouldn't come, but if you're coming, don't take too long to do it. "

"Are you saying he's terminally ill?"

"Leticia, anybody who's ninety-two years old and has a stroke is terminally ill."

"Yeah. I guess so. I'll call you after I get home. Thanks for letting me know."

At home that evening as she and Willa ate dinner, Willa complained about Leticia's inattentiveness to the wonderful meal she had prepared. "Nobody turns up they nose at my corn bread and smothered chops, ma'am. You sure you're all right?"

Leticia heard herself telling her housekeeper and friend how her grandfather had treated her mother, dismissing her from the family and from his life, and how the man gave her similar treatment on the one occasion that they met. "I don't owe him anything; yet now that he's had a stroke and is probably at death's door, he wants me to go to New Orleans to see him."

"It's getting too cool for iced tea," Willa said. " 'Scuse me a minute." She returned with two mugs and a teapot. "The water didn't boil long enough, so this'll have to set a while. Two wrongs ain't gonna make a right, ma'am. Just because he's a jackass don't mean you gotta be one. Besides, he may have something to tell you that you'll wish you knew someday. If it was me and my granddaddy, I'd be packing if for no reason other than I'd get one last chance to tell him off."

"You wouldn't tell off a sick man, would you?"

"The end of life is a time for truth. I wouldn't be rude, but I sure wouldn't leave him with the wrong impression. How's he gon' pray for his sins if you leave him with the impression that he ain't sinned? He wouldn't get no gift like that from me." She filled the mugs and took a sip from her own. "That sweet enough for ya? How long you think you'll be gone?"

An hour later, she phoned Mark and gave him her flight number and time of arrival. "I don't feel good about it, Mark, but going to see him is probably the right thing to do. I haven't told Kenyetta, because I don't want to travel with her." She gave him Kenyetta's number. "Call her if you like."

"Are you still angry with her?"

"Mark, Kenyetta is unprincipled, and I'm happier not being around her."

"I see. I'll see you at the airport tomorrow."

She packed a red silk suit and high-heeled black boots, remembered that New Orleans was probably too hot for the outfit and replaced it with a red and gray printed voile sundress, red bolero and white sandals. She admitted to herself that she wanted to annoy the old man with her snappy, flirtatious apparel.

"I should either get over his insult or stay home and let him die in peace," she told herself. "There's no point in going there with a grudge."

She had a window seat on the big MD-80 as it sped above the clouds en route to New Orleans. She tried to work on her column, but the bumpy ride made writing all but impossible, and she had elected not to bring her laptop. She sighed in relief when the plane finally touched the ground. As promised, Mark's smile greeted her when she entered the waiting hall.

He hugged her, took her bag and put an arm around her as they walked to his Volvo. "I have an air-conditioned three-bedroom house, a patio and swimming pool to which you are welcome, but if you'd prefer a hotel, I'll take you to a good one."

"I'll stay with you."

It pleased her that he had a housekeeper, and that he assured her Plato, his big German shepherd, would be friendly. "I should have told you to bring a bathing suit," he said, "but we'll stop on the way and get you one."

"I don't swim," she told him.

"Then, I'll teach you . . . provided you'd like to learn, of course."

"I would like to, but I'll only be here this weekend."

"That's plenty of time, and you'll be glad you learned. It's a wonderful way to relax."

He parked at a shopping mall, locked the car and went to a store about three doors away. "You can put the bathing suit on my credit card."

"No way would I do that, Mark." She bought a yellow one that left almost nothing to the imagination, though she didn't see a real choice. As they rode on to his house, talking about the buildings and residential areas that they passed, she marveled at his awareness of his environment.

They entered his home, palatial, or so it seemed to her, and charming and miles from the Mississippi. "I'm surprised you're so far from the river, Mark."

"Building here was a conscious decision. That river holds no romance for me. When I think about it— which isn't too often—I think about all the slaves transported on it. I detest every song that has the word *Mississippi* in it."

"A good thing, too. Katrina left you unimpaired."

"In a way, yes, but I have to give a large portion of my income to those who were affected by it. I don't mind, though. There are no free rides in this life."

"You are an amazing man. How did you get to be so clever at so young an age? You aren't a day over thirty."

"I'm thirty-four, and if you're a black man down here, you'd better be clever and you'd better be discerning. Close your eyes for ten minutes, and you could be dead or worse."

He dropped her bag on the floor in the foyer and called to his housekeeper, "Anybody home?"

The woman who rushed to greet them, her face wreathed in smiles, could have been his mother. Her warmth seemed to envelop them both. "I'm so glad to meet you, Miss Langley. We don't have much company, because Mr. D is gone all the time. This sure is nice. We gon' have dinner in a few minutes."

Leticia looked at Mark. "I forget that you southerners call the noonday meal *dinner.* I was ready to question my sanity."

He looked at his watch. "If we have lunch at twelve-thirty, we can start your swimming lesson at four. Okay?"

"Yep. I promised."

After their dinner, she walked around the house admiring its elegance and beauty. Large magnolia trees with white blossoms that perfumed the air sat on opposite sides of the garden. And monardas huddled near a fresh pond, their purple petals soft and velvety to her touch. She saw them at a distance when she first visited New Orleans for the family gathering in what seemed like ages ago, but they were much more beautiful close up. As she walked toward the patio and the swimming pool, she stopped, almost made breathless by the sight of the Louisiana irises, a profusion of red, yellow, pink, lavender, purple and brown.

"This entire environment is so peaceful, soothing and beautiful. How can you bear to be away from here so much?" she asked Mark when she reached the patio.

"A housekeeper is not somebody a man rushes home to."

"Do you have a girlfriend?"

"I've met someone, but she hit me so hard when I saw her that I'm forcing myself to move slowly. The hot stuff doesn't always last, and it can blind you, too."

"Do you see her often?"

A smile that seemed wistful played around his lips. "That's one of the problems. When I stay away from her, she's all I think about. What happened to that guy you were contemplating?"

She described Wilson. "He's not compatible with my DNA," she said with a laugh. "After his fling with Kenyetta, he came back with his tail between his legs like a little puppy, but I—"

"Told him to go to hell, I hope."

"It amounted to that. Mark, how does a woman know when a man is interested in her or just out for . . . for his fun?"

"Depends on the man. If he shows you that he has

your interest at heart, and if he puts your needs before his own, give him a fighting chance."

"Thanks. I'll remember that."

She changed into the swimsuit and had her first swimming lesson. "How do you feel about it?" he asked. "You did well. Want to try tomorrow after we see Grandfather?"

"Yes. Thanks. I wish we didn't have to go to that hospital, but . . . we'll get through it."

"How are you?" she asked Bryce Crawford, who was sitting in a chair beside the bed when she walked into his hotel room. "Mark said you wanted to see me."

"Thank you for coming. Where is young DuPree?"

"Here I am, sir," Mark said, poking his head through the doorway.

"Thank you for this."

"No problem, sir. You're welcome. I'll be outside, Leticia."

Leticia took a chair across from her grandfather. She still had no idea why she'd been called to his bedside, although she was happy to see he'd acquired some manners.

"After Mark's mother was born, I didn't want any more children, but Lydia came along anyway," Bryce began without prompting. "I was hard on her, and I don't blame her for taking up with your father, because she didn't get the love and attention she needed at home. It wasn't her mother's fault; she did what I permitted. When Lydia got pregnant, I wasn't about to let her destroy my good name, and I put her out. But your father took her to a justice of the peace, married her and left town with her.

"He notified me when she died, but I was still nursing my hurt and anger. When you came to the family re-union, I took it out on you. Mark mailed me copies of the paper you write for, and I read your columns, including that series on African women. I wanted you to come down here so I can tell you how talented I think you are. I'm ashamed of the way I've behaved, and if you can't forgive me, I'll understand. And I'll have to accept it." He lifted his right hand but let it drop in his lap as if he didn't have the strength to hold it up.

"I'd been feuding with Frank Langley, your grand-father, for years, and I hated him because he married the woman I wanted. I took it out on his son, Herbert, your father, and wouldn't let him court your mother. If the two of them hadn't had to sneak around in order to see each other, she might not have gotten pregnant. I messed up plenty. Minnie, your grandmother, was never happy. Oh, she smiled and pretended, but I knew how she felt. I hope you have a happier life."

He tried to lean forward. "Are you married? Do you have any children?"

She reeled from the shock of his confession, so far was it from the proud and condescending man she met months earlier. "I've never been married," she said in a hoarse voice, "so I don't have any children." What else could she say to him? She had vowed to be honest in her dealing with people, but she couldn't tell him that he should have been ashamed to put her mother out of his home.

Thinking fast, she latched on to something imper-sonal. "Thanks for reading my columns. I'm glad you liked them."

"You've got plenty of guts to do some of the things you did in Nigeria. Your mother was like that, too. Nothing frightened her."

She stood and looked down on him. The tall, statuesque man she met only five months earlier now seemed fragile and gaunt. Unable to deny the pain that shot through her at the thought of what might have been, she leaned down and kissed his forehead.

"Thanks for letting me know you weren't well, sir. I think you'll be fine soon."

He shook his head, and a tear rolled down his cheek. "Thank you for coming, and thank you for forgiving me. You didn't say you do, but I feel that you have."

"Yes, sir. I have, though I'm sorry I missed growing up with you and my grandmother. Get well soon."

"I don't think about getting well, Leticia. I've had more than my share. Good-bye." He tried to raise his hand again, but failed. So she took his hand, kissed his cheek again and left him.

When she stepped out of her grandfather's room, Mark rushed to her. "Is . . . everything all right?"

"I think so. At least for him. As for me, I never had him. I know my life would have been fuller and richer if he'd been a part of it, but I don't believe in hanging around in the past. I did the best I could to leave him at peace, and I'm satisfied."

"You're first class, Leticia. Real people. I know it cost you something, because the old man hasn't been much of a grandparent to me, either. But I have to live with myself, so I'd have done what you did. It's enough that he has to deal with God. And pretty soon, too, I imagine."

By dinner time at twelve-thirty, she was doing the breaststroke well enough to enjoy swimming and had decided to join a health club and continue swimming lessons after she returned home. "You're welcome to stay with me when you return to D.C.," she told him when he took her to the airport, "and I hope that will be soon. I feel as if I finally have a brother. Thank you so much for everything."

"It's been my pleasure, cuz. If you need me for anything at all, you know how to reach me. Safe journey."

Sunday afternoon at home, Leticia finished a leisurely lunch, curled up on her living room sofa and opened a copy of the *Washington Post,* but immediately the phone rang, and when she answered, Jeannine's voice grated on her ears.

"Leticia. I know it's Sunday and you probably don't want to be disturbed, but several of our members were interviewed about you, and *The Herald* is putting out a fantastic piece on you and what your presence to the club has meant."

An attack of nervous jitters besieged Leticia. "Please, Jeannine. I'm not writing comedy any longer. My editor convinced me that no one will take me seriously as a columnist if I write jokes."

"Oh, nobody mentioned the funny stuff, since it didn't get a good review. We talked about your African junket. The part you told us about at the meeting."

"But won't that mean *The Herald* is promoting its competition?"

"Good heavens, no. Annie's brother is editor in chief, and he's not crazy. Be sure and get a copy."

Leticia thanked the woman and hung up. If she was worth a story in a rival paper, she had arrived professionally. She went to her computer, looked up Geraldine Thomas, her old nemesis, and located her at once. The next morning at the office, she put a copy of *The Journal* that carried her story and byline and the copy of

The Herald that ran a story of her in an envelope and mailed them to Geraldine. *How sweet it was!* She almost skipped from the mailroom back toward her office.

Impulsively, when she reached Max's office, she stopped and knocked on the door. "Come in," he said in that urgent, it had better be important way of his.

He didn't look up immediately, so she remained silent until he stopped typing. He glanced up a little and then enough to see her face. "Hi. What's up?" he said. "If I hadn't seen your shoes, I wasn't going to say a word in the hopes that whoever it was would leave."

"If I go get some coffee, will I be more welcome?"

His smile jolted her. Was he playing games? Surely not Max. "You're welcome without it, but I sure would love a cup."

She brought coffee for two and cranberry muffins. "Don't start expecting it," she said. "I have a feeling you'd spoil easily."

"I can't confirm or deny that, Leticia, since nobody ever tests the theory."

She sipped her coffee, broke off a piece of muffin and got comfortable. "Max, a man like you ought to be able to get himself spoiled at will." He jumped up, obviously having spilled coffee on his trousers.

"What happened?"

"Woman, you are damned disconcerting."

"I did something a minute ago that made my soul sing."

"That's two of us," he murmured, and though she heard him, she didn't understand the basis for the comment. "What did you do?" he asked.

She told him how Geraldine's comments deflated her moments after she completed her summa cum laude address at their commencement. "I told her she'd hear from me, and I meant to keep my word. Oh, Max, you don't know how much I enjoyed watching the mail clerk cancel that package and drop it into the bag."

Still enjoying his treat, he said, "Why do you let yourself still care, Leticia? Some people are mean, and they get pleasure from making others feel badly. One of my professors once said to the class, 'Those who can, do; those who can't, criticize.' Forget about it. You graduated at the top of the class. She didn't, and it rankled her. Decide who you are and what you're worth as a human being, and don't let any living, breathing person puncture your belief in yourself. If anyone thinks you're arrogant, it's their problem. Try to please everybody, and you'll become a phony. Being true to yourself is not a simple matter, but it's worth the attempt."

She'd stopped eating and her coffee had become lukewarm. When she first came to *The Journal*, she thought him slightly, but not entirely nugacious, but each time they talked, her respect for him increased. "I'll keep that in mind," she said, sounding weaker and less resolute than she would have liked, but he'd given her something worthy of serious thought.

As if to lighten the air, he said, "Thanks for remembering how I like the coffee, and for spoiling me. That's something that's lacking in my life."

"Oh, you're full of it," she said, and laughed to cover her embarrassment.

His hard stare, coming so quickly after his jovial manner, shocked her. "You think so?"

"Oh, Max. I'm sorry."

"Sure. That and ten cents will get me nothing," he said in a voice that was too soft. He swung around to his computer, and she had no choice but to leave.

Why did she have a tendency to upset him when she had no desire to do that? She couldn't believe that he attended Harvard University, joined a fraternity, worked with some of the best journalists extant, most of them men, and couldn't take a little teasing. Something didn't fit. How could he be so sensitive?

After musing over it for a few minutes in her office, she threw up her hands. "If I don't get my work done, I'll be looking for a job, and his highness, Mr. Baldwin, will still be sitting at that kidney-shaped desk—the only one in this building—like Napoleon on the throne of France." She ran her hands ruthlessly through her hair. What a mess! *All I wanted to do was to share my triumph with someone, and he's the only one in the whole of Washington, D.C., who I cared to tell. Why him?*

She pushed back from her desk, jumped up and, with no place to go, sat down. "I will not cry, dammit, because I don't cry over things." She wiped the tear, opened her computer and began to type furiously: *Now is the time for all good men to come to the aid of their country.* She didn't care what she typed. She had to do something to change her mood. Hearing a light knock on her door, she didn't look up but said, "I don't want any company. I'm busy."

Max walked back to his office. He'd upset her, but he couldn't help it; at times, she could be so insensitive. He wanted to know from her what the hell it was about him that gave her the notion he was invincible, hard as a rock and not susceptible to hurt of any kind. Maybe it was a good thing she'd said she was busy. He'd gone there because something drove him, and he had no idea what he would have said to her. They all respected each other's need for privacy, because they were in that building to work. So she knew he wouldn't impose on her. Back in his office, he started dialing her number before he sat down.

"I was rude, Leticia, and I'm sorry."

"Thanks for that, Max. I'm sorry, too. I keep getting on the wrong side of you, and I don't want to. I hope everything is all right between us, because you're still my favorite colleague."

"Thanks. And you're mine." He hung up, because he didn't have more to say. *At least not right now, I don't.*

He worked until after six and got home just in time for dinner. The M Street traffic going toward Georgetown had come close to defeating him, and he told himself that, with the price of gas being what it was, he'd probably save money by taking a taxi and leaving his Town Car at home. But he liked the freedom that driving to and from work afforded him. He parked in the garage beneath the building that the paper occupied and in his own garage at home, so he didn't have parking problems.

His mother's cat greeted him at the door. He scratched the big tom's back and headed for the sunroom beyond the dining room, where his mother sat in her wheelchair among the plants and flowers that she adored. He bent over, kissed her cheek and pulled up a chair beside her.

"How are you feeling?" he asked, holding both of her hands in his.

"Fine. It's been such a beautiful day, and Beryl took me out on the deck for some sunshine this morning. It was wonderful. You're late today. Did you have a special assignment?"

"I was working well, and time seemed to fly by. But I did a decent piece of work this afternoon, and I'm pleased with it. What's Ella having for dinner?"

"She didn't say. I asked, but she said it's a surprise."

"Then we'll let her surprise us. Where's Beryl?"

"I'm the one who's supposed to be forgetful. The nurse is off this afternoon, and Ella looks after me. Remember?"

"Now I do. Let me freshen up. I'm starved. I forgot to eat lunch." He ran up the stair whistling, stripped, showered and changed into jeans, a T-shirt and a pair of sneakers.

Ella met him at the bottom of the stairs. "Your mother was real perky this afternoon, even singing some hymns. So I sat there and sang with her. She forgot some of the words, but I supplied 'em when I could. Lord, she sure is blessed to have you. Some men would have put her in a nursing home. God's gonna be good to you."

"She's my mother, Ella, and when I needed her, there was nothing too difficult, too onerous or inconvenient for her to undertake in order to help me. The least I can do is keep her as comfortable and happy as I can."

"I just wish you could find a nice girl."

"I had one. Remember?"

"Oh, you know I didn't like her, and I didn't try to hide it from you, either. She was too selfish and too interested in silliness like style and fancy things. You're well off without her."

"I know, but it . . ." He patted Ella on the shoulder. She'd been his closest friend since his mother's stroke six years earlier when he closed his mother's house and brought her to live with him. "It's hard sometimes," he said.

"I know, son. I know."

The phone rang just as he, his mother and Ella sat down to eat dinner. "Leave it, Ella."

"It's all right," she said. "May be someone we want to talk with. . . . This is Mr. Baldwin's residence. Yes, he's here, but he just began dinner. Oh, how are you, Mr. Covington? Yes, I'll be glad to tell him. Give my regards to Mrs. Covington. Bye."

"That was Bill, huh?" he asked when she returned to the table.

"Yes, sir. He's having something next weekend and said you shouldn't make any other plans."

Max figured he could use a refreshing change, and Bill Covington always provided just the environment for it.

Chapter Nine

"Did you really go to New Orleans without telling me?" Kenyetta asked Leticia. "This is the third time I called you and you didn't call me back. I said, did you go to New Orleans last week?"

"No, Kenyetta. I went the weekend before last. Mark told me my grandfather wanted to see me, and I went."

"Well, he's my cousin, so you could have taken me with you."

Kenyetta had a way of attempting to make her feel guilty, but she knew that now, and she had no intention of falling for it. "I don't feel guilty about not telling you, Ken, so don't waste your breath trying to work on my conscience."

"My, but we're getting so haughty. Some of the teachers at school said they read your column on African women. A couple said they didn't believe all that stuff, that you must—"

Leticia cut her off. "Save it, Kenyetta. I don't care about those people. If they want to remain ignorant about important issues, I do not give a damn. Did you want something? I mean, did you call for some purpose? If not, I have a few things I need to do. Hang in there."

The more she was the target of Kenyetta's insinuations and vituperative remarks, the less of her cousin's company she wanted. Indeed, she had begun to separate in her mind the close friend Kenyetta had once been from the person her cousin had become in recent weeks. She'd come to realize that Kenyetta's easy smile and quick laugh camouflaged a mean spirit and a delight in stepping on her fellow human beings. Leticia knew that from the first time she stood up to Kenyetta—much to her surprise—her cousin had been more careful about the sharpness of her tongue and the things she said to her. The thought encouraged Leticia.

After considering not answering the telephone, for she wanted to take advantage of the quiet of a Sunday morning and work, she capitulated after five rings and answered.

"Hello."

"Hello. Is Ms. Langley there?"

She didn't recognize the voice. "This is Leticia Langley."

"Oh, I'm so glad I caught you. This is Allison Wade Covington. I'm having some people out to our country home on the eastern shore of Maryland this coming weekend. It's still warm enough to enjoy the Chesapeake—I don't mean swim—and the outdoors, too. If you can join us, I'll send a car for you Friday afternoon, and we'll come back Sunday afternoon. It's about a ninety minute drive."

"Allison, I'd love that. Thank you for asking me. Would you mind telling me how I should dress? I haven't spent much time around the water."

"Not at all. Bring a couple of pairs of pants or jeans, long sleeve shirts, sweaters and something dressy for

Saturday evening. You might want to change into a dress for Friday night. For Saturday, that dress you wore at Brod's place or something similar would be perfect."

"Thank you very much. What time should I expect the car?"

"Would four-thirty be too early? Traffic across the Bay Bridge is extremely heavy around five-thirty."

"I can be ready at four if that would suit you better."

"Wonderful. See you Friday."

Instead of getting to the work she'd brought home, she went to her closet to examine her wardrobe. Social invitations meant spending money, and she wanted to save what she could. Most journalists her age had bank accounts and investments, but she'd started late, and although she considered herself financially solvent, she had very little wealth. After searching her closets for nearly an hour, she threw up her hands, dressed and went shopping. *I refuse to be the odd person in any group. I've had enough of that.* And another thing, she vowed, "I'm not going out socially in the conservative clothes I wear to the office. I'm burying Mother Hubbard as of now."

If I want to make changes in my life, I have to deal with both the inside and the outside. She had learned that people judged you first by what they saw and later—maybe—by what you had to offer.

That Monday morning, she sat down at the table, saw that she didn't have a place setting in front of her and went to the kitchen to find Willa. "I'm late this morning, ma'am. If it ain't one thing, it's another. One of my late sister's kids got in an accident, and the whole family's upset. He was on that motorcycle of his, and well, I tell you, it don't look good."

"Do you want some time off?" she asked Willa. The woman looked up at her with eyes that seemed to hold a desperate appeal. "Willa, do you need any money? How can I help you?" She put her arms around the frail woman, and to her surprise, Willa snuggled close to her.

"Just pray, ma'am. I don't need any money, but I want to go see him. He's my favorite nephew, but he was always so hardheaded. Wouldn't listen to nobody but me, and here lately, he doesn't listen to me either. But if I go, who's going to look after you?"

"I'll manage. And don't worry, I won't get anybody to take your place."

"Thank the Lord. I was worried about that. I'm getting older, and I can't do the heavy work some women ask the housekeeper to do. This job is perfect for me."

"Well, stop worrying. I'll be away next weekend, so shop lightly. Maybe I'll bring us some blue fin crabmeat."

Willa's eyes brightened. "You going to the Chesapeake? Ma'am, I do love those blue crabs, and November is a good time for them."

"I'm spending the weekend with some friends who have a house on or near the bay. I haven't been there."

"Well, ma'am, I sure hope you have a good time and that you meet a real nice man. It ain't good for a woman like you—young, smart, pretty and all—to be alone all the time."

"Thanks. When do you want to leave?"

"Tomorrow night I can get a bus for—"

"A bus from here to Charleston? Don't even think it. I'll get the tickets and I'll give them to you when you come tomorrow. A bus trip from here to Charleston, South Carolina, would kill an elephant."

Willa stared at her. "You gon' pay my train fare there and back?"

"I'm getting you air tickets."

Willa put a bowl of cold cereal, a glass of orange juice and a cup of coffee in front of Leticia. "Well, well. I'm finally gon' see what it's like to fly. I don't have to tell you I thank you. I'll find a way to make it up to you. You'll see. I tell you, I didn't know how I was going to get there, because I sent what little I could to my niece to pay for my nephew's intensive care. What a relief."

"When you come to work tomorrow, bring your suitcase."

Leticia sent Willa off the next day, although she felt badly for having acceded to the woman's argument that she could make her way to the airport and onto the plane alone. Navigating in an airport was an ordeal for seasoned travelers and could terrorize a neophyte.

The Covington car arrived at four o'clock that Friday afternoon, and Leticia wasn't surprised to see a custom-built Cadillac. The cool wine and finger sandwiches available to her in the bar impressed her, and she ate two of them, but skipped the wine. In a comfortable car, with soft music playing and tasty sandwiches, the temptation to drink the wine needled at her, but she needed her wits, and wine wouldn't let her keep them. She laughed at herself.

Every place one went, the first thing offered was an alcoholic drink. She had either to learn how to drink or how to pretend she was drinking, and so far, she'd done neither. If she held a drink in her hand, she sipped it absentmindedly with the result that, not having done it consciously, she didn't enjoy it but still felt the unwanted effects.

"Keep a clear head," her father, a teetotaler, had preached, and she could see the logic in that. The big car eased up to the Chesapeake Bay Bridge, once the world's longest suspension bridge, which spanned the bay. Water was visible as far as she could see, whether to her right or to her left.

"We're in Talbot County now," the driver said, "so we'll be there pretty soon."

She thanked him, for she knew he'd told her so that she could freshen up if she liked. She pulled down what proved to be a large mirror, brushed her hair, and refreshed her lipstick. A rub of her face with a facial tissue sufficed for makeup. Fifteen minutes later, the car stopped at a big white house, and two big brown and white collies ran out to greet the car. Carrying her bag, the driver walked with her the few steps to the door and lifted the knocker. Instead of knocks, however, bells chimed out Duke Ellington's "Satin Doll." She loved jazz, and her blood raced in anticipation of the weekend.

A big man well over six feet tall opened the door and said to the driver, "Thanks, Malachi. I'll take that." He picked up her suitcase. "I'm Bill Covington, Leticia, and I'm happy to meet you. Come on in. Allison got home about three minutes ago, and she's upstairs changing. I hope the ride over was pleasant."

"It was, and I'm glad to meet you. I love jazz, and your door chimes gave me a warm welcome."

His eyes seemed to . . . she wondered if that was a natural twinkle. Surely, he wasn't winking at her. No point in guessing.

"Are you one of those people who has a natural twinkle or wink?" she asked him.

"I sure have, Leticia, and the damned thing has gotten me into more trouble than you could imagine. Please ignore it. I'll show you to your room. We're expecting a couple more people, but only one will be staying with us. The others live over in Trappe, about twenty miles from here. You can stretch out, relax, do whatever you like. The others are due here at six-thirty, so if you'd come down around then—before if you want to—that'll work. Play it loose."

"Thanks, Bill. I'll get down there sooner or later." He reached inside her room door, put her bag down and said, "That's just about my style. I'm against stress. See you eventually."

Leticia looked around her, taking in the soft colors of lavender and rose on the bedspread, wallpaper and draperies, the white furniture and carpeting, and decided that Allison had two guest rooms, one for women and one for men. Nobody would expect a man to be comfortable in that room. The color scheme was repeated in the bathroom, where the scent of lavender, barely evident, teased her nostrils. She loved the scent as well as the colors. She put the soap to her nostrils and sniffed. Wondering what she'd find if she looked out the window, she pushed aside the drape, opened the Venetian blinds and cast her gaze on the wide expanse of the bay. Directly below her she saw a well-tended garden and a huge aluminum grill.

She remembered to call Willa. "I'm on the bay, Willa. Tell me how your nephew is and whether you can come back on your reserved flight, or whether you want me to exchange the date to a later one."

"He ate for the first time this morning, ma'am, so right now, I'm planning to be back on the plane I'm supposed to fly on. Thanks so much for thinking about me." She cared deeply about Willa, for the woman had begun to represent family to her. They ate together and supported each other when things weren't going right. Further, Willa considered it her right and duty to give advice whether or not Leticia wanted it.

Satisfied that her housekeeper didn't need her help, Leticia unpacked her clothing, hung some items up, stripped and got into the pink bathtub that she had filled with warm water and crystals, guaranteed to make pink and lavender bubbles. Or so it stated on the bottle's label. A glance out the bedroom window later told her that the evening meal would not be a barbeque and would not be eaten out of doors in the fifty-five degree weather.

She slipped on a pair of navy blue velvet pants and a lavender pink tunic top that reached a few inches above the knee, had generous side splits, three-quarter sleeves and a bosom-flattering low neckline.

Her eyebrows shot up when she saw herself in the full-length mirror. "Lord, I'm really working it tonight." No one could say she was overdressed, but anyone would applaud her taste. She added a pair of fifty-cent size marcasite hoop earrings that she'd bought the previous Sunday and congratulated herself on having shopped at an upscale store that had knowledgeable saleswomen. She sprayed Chanel perfume in strategic places, saw that it was six thirty-five and headed down the stairs.

Midway down the steps, she stopped. It couldn't be. . . . But that voice was unmistakable. Her first thought was to turn back and change into something simpler. But she hadn't brought anything else to wear. She'd brought her only cocktail dress for Saturday night. Besides, it was certainly more conversation-worthy than what she had on.

"Oh, what the heck! A good shock would serve him well," she said, raised her chin, squared her shoulders and made her way down the stairs.

Seemingly headed up the stairs, Allison met her at the foot of the staircase. "I was just going to call you. Welcome, and don't you look wonderful. I thought you might have fallen asleep."

"That room is exquisite, Allison, and terribly romantic. I've never been in a more feminine room. Thank you for the invitation." She looked at her hostess's royal blue jersey jumpsuit and gave silent thanks that she'd selected the proper thing to wear.

"It's so nice to have you here. Come, I want you to meet our other guest." It *was* him! "You know Max, of course. Max . . ."

Leticia swallowed hard as Max stood, walked toward her and stopped. "This is a metamorphosis if I ever saw one. Hello, Leticia. You look . . . well, breathtaking."

"Hi, Max. I didn't know you were coming." She marveled at her composure. The man was looking at her as if she were something from outer space, as if he hadn't seen a woman in a long, long time and loved what he saw.

Max turned to the two men she hadn't met. "I expect I've embarrassed her, but we work together, and she dresses conservatively for work to match her brilliant mind. This is Leticia Langley." He looked at Leticia and winked. "Deek and Harold Matthews."

"Glad to meet you," they said in unison.

Bill Covington walked in with a tray of drinks, and she noticed that he'd changed into a dark business suit. The doorbell rang, and Allison went to open it. "Come in," Leticia heard her say. "You're just in time."

"It isn't often that twin sisters get attached to twin brothers," Bill said, introducing Deana and Tori Sharp to Leticia and Max. The brothers claimed their women, letting everyone know which twin belonged to which brother. Leticia accepted the introduction and breathed more easily, though for the life of her, she didn't know why.

"We're all here," Allison said.

She wasn't surprised to find Max at her right when they sat down for dinner. "I honestly would not have recognized you if Bill hadn't told me you were upstairs. How can you camouflage yourself so thoroughly? I thought the other Leticia was an attractive, lovely woman but, sweetheart, this one is a knockout."

"Thanks. Now stop telling me that I look like a mouse all week. Surely you're not suggesting that I wear this to work. Are you?"

He rubbed his jaw with his forefinger and thumb. "No, because every guy there would see what I'm seeing."

"What?"

"How'd you get here? Did Bill send Malachi for you?"

She knew he'd changed the subject because he didn't want to repeat what he'd said, and she'd have to think about that comment, too. "Yes, and with a complement of wine and hors d'oeuvres, but I restrained myself."

"You're kidding. Last time Malachi drove me out here, I was feeling no pain when that car pulled up in front of this house."

"And you think I'd have showed up here soused?" She turned sideways to get a good look at him, dapper in a navy blue suit, pale blue shirt, red tie and handkerchief. This brother was hot stuff. Elegant.

"I couldn't possibly think of you and soused at the same time. No, indeed." He looked at her and let a grin float over his face. "But tipsy, now that's a different matter."

"I don't get tipsy."

"Try it at least once before you die, and make sure I'm there to see this flower bloom."

"Max, please don't make us mad with each other here in front of all these people."

"I'm usually the one who gets hurt," he said, "and you're not going to say or do anything tonight that gets to me, because this Leticia I'm looking at wouldn't do that."

A rueful smile crossed her face, and his left eyebrow edged up. "I think we'd better quit talking," she said, "because I almost said something smart."

"My mother sent us these," she heard Bill say. "Nobody beats her crab cakes." A young woman dressed as a waiter passed around a large platter of small crab cakes. "They're not even cool," he said. "Malachi just got here with them. Leticia, my mother lives about a fifteen-minute drive from here."

"He's right. You'll never eat anything like these," Deana Sharp said. Leticia bit into one, looked up and saw that all the others awaited her verdict.

She rested her fork on the side of her plate and looked at Bill. "I want to make friends with your mother. If you fed me nothing but these until I got full, I'd be as happy as a little crab in crustacean heaven."

"Same here," Deek said. "And imagine, she gets a basket, a string and a few slices of bacon, goes down to the bay and pulls them out herself, so they're super fresh."

"You guys talk," Max joked, as he reached for more crab cakes. "While I eat."

Two hours later, they finished a six-course meal and went to the den for coffee and relaxation. The Matthews brothers and Bill picked up their instruments and began to tune them.

"Are they going to play?" Leticia asked Max, who had taken a seat beside her on the sofa.

"They sure are."

"Say, Max, how about playing the piano?" Harold said. "I'd rather stick with the guitar tonight."

"Aw, man, three guitars and a piano will sound as if

something's missing. Two and a piano will work, but Deek should have brought his bass fiddle."

"I brought my bass guitar," Deek said.

"You only want to hear one guitar when Bill is playing," Max said. "He's a jazz master. Play 'Back Home Again in Indiana.' Ever since Lester Young made that piece famous back in the forties," he told Leticia, "every jazz saxophonist takes a shot at it. Guitarists, too. It's Bill's signature piece. And for good reason."

She wanted to ask Max a lot of questions. Where had he met Bill? Were they writer friends or friends through a mutual love for music and, especially, jazz? Did he love the water and the out of doors as she did—although she rarely had time to enjoy nature, and had learned to swim a little only a few weeks earlier. And most important of all, why did he seem so much less formidable here in Bill Covington's house than he did in the office? She stole a side glance at him. Maybe it was the way he'd dressed. Although neat in a sports jacket and slacks at work, at the moment, this man had an aura of elegance that she didn't usually associate with him.

I'm going to keep my mouth shut about it, she told herself, *because Max hurts easily.*

The trio—lead guitar, bass guitar and piano—struck up some classic jazz, and she leaned back, crossed her knees and let the music flow over her. Thinking that she had missed that sort of life, the music and camaraderie that went with it, she leaned forward with her face in her hands and let her entire being drink it in.

She felt his arm around her. "What's the matter, Leticia? Are you okay?"

Shocked that she had given in to her feelings, she sat up, looked at Max and smiled. "I'm fine. I suppose I got carried away."

"But your entire demeanor suggested that you were unhappy."

She patted the hand that still held her. "Thanks, but I'm all right. Really." He released her, but she got the impression that he did it unwillingly.

Bill, Deek and Harold played until after midnight. Bill strummed a few times and then began a dazzling rendition of Fats Waller's "Honeysuckle Rose."

"When he does that," Max said to Leticia, "he's saying he's ready to turn in. And as much as I'm enjoying this music *and* your company, I'm ready to do the same."

"Me, too," she said. "It's really been a long day."

"The real reason," Max said with a grimace, "is that Bill gets up at the crack of dawn, starts cooking breakfast and expects everybody to come and eat it."

"You mean he does the cooking?"

"Bill would never let his precious Allison slave over breakfast for this many people, and he wouldn't ask the housekeeper to come earlier. Bill is a very considerate man, and he demands consideration from his friends."

"Hmm. Whose collies greeted us when I arrived? I haven't seen them since."

"They're in the dog house. They're the Covingtons'." When she frowned, he laughed. "That's where they live, Leticia. In the dog house."

"You think you're funny."

"In this case, I know I am." He stood, extended his hand to help her rise, and when she hesitated, something odd flickered in his eyes.

She took his hand and stood. Something wasn't right, but she had learned to be careful of what she said to him. Max Baldwin was a wordsmith par excellence, and when you said something, he took you at your word. By the same token, he always said exactly what he meant.

"I've enjoyed your company tonight. It's been . . . really nice, Leticia. Good night."

He headed toward the stairs and, without pausing or looking back, said, "Good night, all."

"Well, that's a first," Allison said to Leticia some minutes later.

"What's a first?"

"Max loves a good meal, and he really loves jazz. He usually sits in that chair, leans back with his eyes closed and listens. The only time he says anything is when he requests a piece. Otherwise he doesn't talk. At ten-thirty, he says good night and goes to bed."

Leticia looked at her watch. "It's twenty minutes past one. Figuring that man out would be a full-time job."

Allison's eyebrows shot up. "You really think so? Max isn't complicated. He's too straightforward to be a mystery. You know, he and Bill have been close since their college days when they were roommates. They can almost read each other."

Well, *she* certainly couldn't and didn't plan to try. "It continues to surprise me that Max isn't married," Leticia said.

"Don't arrive at your own conclusions about that, Leticia, because you'll definitely be wrong. I admire Max almost as much as I do my husband. If you need anything at all, let me know. I want this to be a wonderful weekend for you."

Leticia said good night and made her way up the stairs to her room. She wasn't sleepy. However, when she recalled Max's prediction that Bill would be up early cooking breakfast, she hurried to complete her ablutions, set the clock alarm to six-thirty and got into bed. Yet she couldn't sleep. For the second time, Allison had gone to considerable lengths to impress upon her that

Max was an admirable man. Leticia, too, believed that, but . . . She tried to stop thinking about it so that she could sleep. She finally slept, and in her dream, began to drown. Max pulled her out of the water and carried her to shore.

Leticia had barely finished drying her body after her morning shower when she heard what sounded to her like a school bell signaling time for class. She put on a pair of beige slacks and a burnt orange cowl neck sweater, slipped a pair of moccasins on her feet and gold earrings in her ears, brushed out her hair and sped downstairs.

"Good morning, Bill," she said. "Good heavens, am I the first one down?"

"You are, but I expect Max will be down in a minute. The bell wakes him up. He doesn't believe in alarm clocks."

"Why doesn't that surprise me? What can I do to help?"

"You can set the table out there on the sunporch. From there, we can see the bay. Half an hour earlier, you could have seen a fantastic sunrise."

She went back to the glass-enclosed sunporch, found a tablecloth, dishes, napkins and utensils and set the table for four. She remembered that the Matthews men and their women had not stayed for the night.

"I was going to make waffles," Bill told her, "but I don't know where I put the recipe. What a drag!" He had the look of a beaten man, and she figured she should help, since it would take no effort on her part. "I can make them without a recipe, if you'd like," she said. "I need butter or a good butter substitute, self-raising flour, three or four eggs and some milk."

"You're sure?" He seemed very uncertain.

"Trust me, I never use recipes for pancakes, waffles, biscuits, corn bread and things like that."

He ran his hand through his silky hair. "You don't look like you could cook your way out of trouble."

She flexed her right shoulder in a quick shrug. "No? I could make a living doing it if I had to."

He put the ingredients on the counter, gave her a large bowl, heated the waffle iron and stood there to watch. She dumped some flour into the bowl, melted several heaping tablespoons of butter, added that, cracked the eggs and began stirring, adding milk as needed. Then she poured some batter onto the waffle iron.

"It can't possibly be that simple." They both turned around and saw Max lounging against the door frame.

"We'll see," she said. In a few minutes, she opened the waffle iron and divided the waffle among the three of them.

"I need some butter and maple syrup," Max said. "I love waffles almost as much as I love crab cakes."

Bill tasted the waffle and looked toward the ceiling. "Man, this is good stuff. Leticia, you have to give me the recipe."

"You saw the recipe. I couldn't write it down if my life depended on it. I do it by feeling."

Max sat down. "Bill, would you please wake up Allison before this batter spoils? Gosh, Leticia, I had no idea you could do this. You're a bag of surprises. And how do you manage to look like this first thing in the morning?"

"It was easy, Max. I showered, brushed my teeth, dressed, combed my hair and came downstairs."

His stare, long and penetrating, disconcerted her, and she said, "Max, you're making me uncomfortable."

"I'm sorry. You're the last person I'd deliberately hurt. Why don't you wear your hair down all the time?"

"It's not appropriate. I go to the office to work. When I hold my head down for any length of time, this hair gets in my face."

"I like it this way," he said. "You might as well cook us some more waffles, because Bill may not get back down here with Allison for another hour or so. They're still lovers."

"Yeah, but I wouldn't embarrass my guests," Bill said. "Allison will be here in about five minutes, so you can cook the waffles, Leticia, while I scramble the eggs. After breakfast, I'd like to take the boat out. What do you say, Max?"

"Great. We can fish, too, if you like."

"Fine with me, but let's see how the ladies feel about fishing."

Leticia didn't remember ever having fished, but she eagerly embraced it. "Oh, I'd love to try my hand at it. I've never fished, but I'm told that you only have to sit still, be quiet and let the fish do the work. Suits me just fine."

"What'll you do if a fish makes a mistake and grabs your line?" Max asked her.

"You'll pull it in for me." She saw the glances between Bill and Allison, and it dawned on her that they had ideas about Max and her. They couldn't have been farther off base.

After breakfast, Bill drove them to his boat, and by nine o'clock, they were cruising on the bay. As the sun grew hotter, Leticia put on Allison's battered straw hat and remained on deck with Max while Bill and Allison went inside the boat to prepare lunch. "It's getting too hot here," he said. "Let's go to the other side." Having said that, he stood, extended his hand to help her get up. This time, she took it at once and walked with him to the other side of the deck.

"It's hot over here, too," she said. "Let's go inside."

He steered her to the lounge. "Sit here a minute while I get something cool to drink. They probably have lemonade, iced tea or soft drinks. Which would you like?" She told him iced tea or ginger ale. "I'll be back with it in a minute," he said.

When he handed her the glass of iced tea, he sat beside her, and that surprised her, because there were several other seats available. "Leticia, please feel free to say no, but I want to ask you something."

She turned fully to face him. "What is it?"

He looked her in the eye with such directness that she had the feeling he was measuring her in some way. "Would you go with me to my fraternity's annual dance? I don't usually go, but I want to this year. Will you?"

She wanted to pry, to ask why he wanted to go this year, when he wasn't in the habit of attending, but she didn't dare upset their warm and friendly time together.

She could see that he was both anxious and nervous, so she quickly said, "I'd love to go with you, Max, but what would I wear?" At his wide-eyed, surprised countenance, she said, "I've never been to a fraternity dance, Max, and I don't belong to a sorority." She could see that he was set aback, but she was not ashamed of the truth. "I didn't get a bid while I was in college, and I have no idea what they're about. Max, I didn't have one date while I was in college."

"I got a couple of frat bids," he said, "but believe me, I scrambled, scratched and fought to get them, and you should have done the same. Greek letter organizations are useful throughout your life, so you should join either the AKAs or the Deltas. You're well known, so it won't be difficult. You know, Leticia, I don't think I would have asked you for a date if I'd been at Howard along with you. As the best student in class, your status would have intimidated me."

"Why? I'm sure you were an honor student."

"That I was, but the thought of going after the brains of the senior class would have put the fear of hell in me. Fortunately, I have better sense now."

"And a lot more self-confidence," she added.

His sigh surprised her. "Yeah. Nowadays, the most important things to me are not the material things that I see or the status trappings that people tag us with."

"I feel that way, too, but it's hard to keep an eye on what's most important, although some of the outer trappings are important, Max. I hated the way my hair looked, short and unmanageable, and I got a weave. It looks so much better, more of a reflection of who I am."

"The important thing is that you feel better, that you're happier with your hair, and that's a good reason for doing it. I've always had this secret fantasy of playing the Dobro with a jazz trio or quartet. I play the piano, but the Dobro is my real love."

"Why? Because so few people play it?"

"When I fell in love with the Dobro, I didn't know that." Suddenly he stared at her. "Are you still trying to understand me?"

"Uh . . . gee, I don't know. Did I make you uncomfortable?"

He took her left hand, turned it palm up and looked at it. "No. You haven't made me uncomfortable. I wish you did understand me." He murmured the last words beneath his breath, but she heard him and suppressed the urge to put her arms around him and to comfort him.

"Wear your prettiest evening dress when you accompany me to the fraternity dance," he said, stuffed his hands in his pockets, looked down and kicked at the broadloom carpeting on the floor. "You did say you were coming, didn't you?" His tone was casual, but this man who always stared into her eyes until he nearly bruised them was looking at the floor, his posture and demeanor reflecting self-consciousness.

She'd forgotten about the dance. Impulsively, she reached for his hand, and his head jerked up. "I said I'd love to go, Max. When is it?"

"Saturday after next. Will you let me know the color of your dress? I wouldn't like my cummerbund to clash with it."

She thought for a minute. Monday was a good night for shopping. "I'll tell you by Thursday latest. Okay?" His expression bloomed into a smile that, as if by magic, transformed his face, and his large dark eyes sparkled with flashing lights. She stared at the change in him until a cloud covered his face and, to her amazement, he seemed to disappear behind it. No one had to tell her that her reaction to his having allowed her to see what he felt made him feel exposed and gave him a sense that his privacy had been invaded.

Shocked at his sensitiveness and anxious to repair the damage, she squeezed his fingers. "Please don't withdraw. It always upsets me when you close me out, leaving me to try and guess what I did to hurt you. I wouldn't hurt you for anything, Max. I mean it."

He trapped her fingers in his big hand, leaned back on the sofa and began to talk. "Deep inside of me somewhere I realize that. I'm almost always alone, Leticia. I like company, and I like people. Correct that. I like certain kinds of people. But the things I do that please me most—apart from my work as a journalist—are playing a musical instrument, reading, gardening, going to museums, fishing and occasionally playing or watching tennis. Except for tennis, one does these things alone.

"I'm an only child. I don't remember my father, but I do remember my mother working two jobs and depriving herself personally to help me get through school. I had fellowships to Harvard, but maintenance there exceeds most schools' tuition. There is nothing I wouldn't do for her. I worked, too, and I was happy to find work, any kind of work, but she made the sacrifices, not me. In spite of the hard knocks, I've gained probably more than I deserve in life."

She listened carefully, remembering that he'd once said people see him with their eyes and not with their hearts, and they think he's tough and uncaring. He'd told her a lot, but she heard much that he didn't say, and she was acutely aware that he was holding her hand.

"If you'd like to play the Dobro with a jazz group, why don't you do it? You have weekends free, and you could form a group with the Matthews twins and Bill. It would make you happy."

He shifted so that he could see her face fully. "Yes, it would, but I go to bed early, around ten-thirty, and I'd have to struggle to the office Monday mornings feeling as if I had a hangover. Another thing, Deek and Harold are professionals; they earn a living playing jazz, and I don't want such rigid demands."

"Play Friday and Saturday nights with them, or put an ad out somewhere for partners. If you don't think club playing is appropriate for a journalist, play for a charity group. Allison and I belong to a good one." She leaned toward him and gripped his right arm with her free hand. "Do it now, Max, while you're young, energetic and filled with enthusiasm. You don't want to be eighty years old, looking back and saying you wish you'd done it."

"I'm going to give it plenty of thought. The idea of playing for a service club is attractive. I hadn't thought of it. Will you come to hear me play?"

"Of course I will."

"You know, I had already decided that you were much more than a good-looking woman, talented and smart. You're nice. I mean real nice. And I'd better quit right there."

"You guys ready for lunch?" Bill asked. "Allison and I weren't sure we should invite the two of you together. Reporters are famed for competing with each other, and since you two work for the same paper—"

Allison interrupted Bill as she put a platter of deviled shrimp on the coffee table. "Leticia told us over at Brod's place that you were her favorite colleague at *The Journal*, Max, so we decided to risk it."

"If you had asked me, I would have told you that she's my favorite colleague there as well. We upset each other from time to time, but we always straighten it out rather quickly. What's this?"

"We're having the rest of the crab cakes, deviled shrimp, boiled ham slices, cherry tomatoes, roasted corn, and iced tea for lunch. Tonight, we'll have a decent meal."

Max looked at Leticia and shook his head. "Leticia, these people are food freaks. Every meal here surpasses gourmet quality, and I will not permit anybody to suggest that what's here in front of me isn't first-class fare." He put several shrimp on his plate and tasted one. "What did I tell you? Food for the gods."

"After lunch, you may rest, fish or we can dock the boat and go home, whatever you like," Bill said.

Max looked at Leticia, and she realized that he

would leave the decision to her. He had said he liked to fish, and she didn't know of any place around Washington where one could do that, so she said, "Why don't you two rest, if you like, and Max and I can fish."

"Gal after my own heart," Max said. "Fish don't like to bite at noon, but let's try anyway."

"Okay. We'll remain anchored. If we get a strong wind, Max, don't hesitate to wake me up," Bill said.

"Come on," Max said, taking her hand, and it occurred to her that he had a tendency to assume leadership, but she wondered if he behaved that way only with women and whether she liked it. "Let's fish near those rocks and shrubs. If nothing else, we may get catfish, though I'd rather pull in some bass."

He baited her hook, threw out her line and handed it to her. Then he prepared his own line for fishing, pulled two deck chairs together and said, "Let's sit here. If it's too personal, tell me to shut up, but would you mind telling me why you finished college so late? Were you sick?"

"I don't mind at all. My mother died when I was little, and my father raised me alone. There were no relatives around to help him. Shortly before I finished high school, he became ill. I finished high school, and I had a scholarship to Howard, but I couldn't leave him. He had been a wonderful father, creating a home for just the two of us. He didn't even have close male friends, because he said men couldn't be trusted around young girls. So I didn't accept the fellowship. I stayed home, but the money gave out, and I went to work as a waitress, a short order cook in a two-bit restaurant, a laundress, babysitter, you name it and I did it.

"I knew he couldn't get well, but I kept him as comfortable and as happy as I could. A nurse for him was out of the question. He lingered for almost eight years.

Each successive stroke brought him down a little further. I didn't consider it a burden. Neighbors helped me when they could, but I didn't ask for help. When you love someone, you don't count what you do for them, and the cost is immaterial. After he died, I worked for two years and saved enough for my first year at Howard. I knew that after one year, I could get a fellowship, because most colleges won't let a straight A student fall through the cracks. I finished in three years."

He had been silent while she spoke, but long after she stopped talking, he still didn't say a word, and she began to feel that, with her background, he thought her unworthy of his company.

"This is eerie," he said at last. "You won't believe the similarity of our lives. I've been more fortunate than you, but . . . gosh, this is weird. I . . . I wouldn't have missed this weekend with you for anything. You are an exceptional person."

"No, I'm not, Max."

"To me, you are. Say, your line is bobbing. You've got a bite." He reached around her and tugged on her line. "Yep. That's it, and he's big, too." He placed his hand over hers and reeled the fish in. "Would you look at that? I've been fishing in this lake for four years, and I've never landed one half this big." He slipped the basket into the water and brought up a big striped bass.

"What will I do with him?" she asked.

"Eat him, honey. Don't worry, he won't feel it."

She poked him in the midriff with her right index finger and, realizing what she'd done, quickly withdrew it. "Sorry, but you can be very amusing sometimes."

He looked down at her without moving a single facial muscle. "Sometimes? You wound me." Then, as if to reduce the intimacy between them, he shifted his gaze. "We'd better get this baby on ice." He stood, held out his hand, and she took it and followed him below deck as he carried the bass, with drops of water marking their steps.

"Why am I letting myself drift into something that I may regret?" Max asked himself as he stretched out to rest. He hadn't enjoyed his shower nor the few minutes he'd spent doing yoga exercises. He was not accustomed to allowing people or situations to control him, but he'd never been as comfortable with anyone as he was with Leticia. He had opened himself to her, although he wasn't sure she realized to what extent, and even more importantly, he had a feeling of oneness with her. He had to watch it carefully, because he didn't plan to hike down that road again.

He got downstairs that night around seven, shortly before the other guests arrived. Being familiar with Bill and Allison's parties, he figured he could count on small talk—which he hated—with between fifteen and twenty people.

"It's buffet tonight," Allison said.

"It didn't occur to me that you'd sit down twenty people for dinner," Max said.

Her wink was that of a woman well aware of her skill and competence. "I've sat down twenty-two. I did it for my mother-in-law's seventieth birthday."

He followed Allison's gaze to the entrance of the den and felt a twist in his gut. Leticia let her gaze travel over the group until it landed on him, then her face bloomed into a smile and she started toward him, the rhythmic sway of her hips enticing him like syncopated jazz. He moved from his perch against the wall and went to meet her, lest some other man intercept her before she got to him. In all those months, seeing her daily, how could he not have realized how beautiful she was, how softly feminine and downright sexy?

When he reached her, he said of the peach chiffon dinner dress, "You ought to wear this color twenty-four hours every day. You're blinding me."

"I'm sorry. I'd never do that intentionally. You look good in this blue suit, too. Very good."

He smiled, ruefully he knew, for it was what he felt. "Thanks, but I'm not blinding you."

"Say, man, you can't have this woman all to yourself." He looked over his shoulder as Wilson Gallagher approached him.

"Oh, yes he can," Leticia said, slid her arm through Max's and turned her back to Wilson.

Max didn't move. He'd been friends with Wilson since college days, and he wasn't about to have a friendship with any woman on Wilson's list. "What's this about, Leticia?"

"I have told Wilson Gallagher that I don't want anything to do with him. I don't like his style. There is not and never has been anything between us and there never will be. We almost started a friendship, but he slept with my first cousin, and that finished it. I have never even held hands with that man." She said it loudly enough for Wilson to hear her.

Max slid an arm around her waist, turned her to face Wilson, looked his friend in the eye and said, "Back off, Wilson, and stay off. I've never been more serious in my life."

Wilson held up both hands, palms out. "You surprise me, buddy, but I bow to you."

Max would wager that few people knew Wilson as well as he did. "Don't call me on this, Wilson, because you know what the result will be."

"Don't worry, I get it," Wilson said, tipped an imaginary cap and walked away.

"Thanks," Leticia said. "Mind telling me what the result would be if he didn't heed you?"

"Not at all. I'd give him a busted face, and he's well aware of it. I've known him since college, and I know he has very little respect for women. But I don't blame him or any other man for wanting you." He didn't attempt to check her reaction to that. He'd said it, and she could take it or leave it.

Chapter Ten

At home Sunday evening, Leticia reflected upon her weekend with Allison and Bill Covington and with Max, but mostly, she went over in her mind what she'd learned about her colleague. Max had asked if he could drive her back to Washington and, because she would save the Covingtons the cost of a trip—she rationalized—she'd agreed, or at least that was what she told herself. But as they sang raucous and witty songs, laughed and joked all the way home, she had to admit to herself that she accepted his invitation because she enjoyed his company. Max won points with her when he drove her home, walked to her apartment door with her, held out his hand, and said he couldn't remember having had a more pleasant weekend. She didn't question why she later felt bereft, as if he had deserted her.

She thought about the obvious differences between Max and Wilson, how easily she had accepted Wilson's shallow charm and the heavy dose of masculinity that he poured on women, including on her cousin Kenyetta. Wilson hadn't a shred of honesty, she had observed, but Max was the epitome of it. If she had learned nothing else over the weekend, she now had some bases for judging a man.

The next morning, Monday, as she was about to leave for work, Willa handed her a large shopping bag.

"What's in this, Willa?"

"Well, I didn't have anything to do yesterday afternoon, what with you gone and all, no dinner to cook, so I made some raspberry scones, some brownies and some hot-cross buns. It ought to be enough for you and your friends at the office to have several each."

"Ah, Willa. You're going to make me real popular at work. Thank you. Now, I'll have to confess that you made them, and they'll all find excuses to come to my house."

"It wouldn't hurt none for us to have some company sometime, then I could really put on the dog."

"You'll get your chances, Willa. Don't worry." She picked up the bag, tested it for weight and used her cell phone to call a taxi. "I'll be late getting home tonight, Willa. I have to shop for an evening dress."

"Glory be. That means there's a man in the picture. A woman like you wouldn't leave home decked out in an evening gown all by herself." She frowned and was silent for a moment. "Would you?"

A grin settled around Leticia's lips. Just wait until Willa got a look at Max. He could hold his own with any man. "Yes, Willa. I will have a date, and he's a six-foot-four-inch knockout."

Willa braced her knuckles against her slim hips. "Ain't no telling what you gon' tell me next. Can you invite him to dinner?"

"I could, but as of now, I have no plans to do that. See you this evening." She went to the kitchen, put two plastic bread bags into her briefcase and went down to the lobby to wait for her taxi. Later, in her office, she closed the door, put three scones, three brownies and three hot-cross buns in one of the plastic bags, and placed the bag in her desk drawer. After writing a note that the homemade goodies were courtesy of her housekeeper, she set out the pastries in the coffee room, she stapled the note on the bulletin board above the pastries and went back to her office.

About twenty minutes later, Max called her. "Is there some reason why you didn't alert me to the goodies you put in the coffee room? I went in there, and there are only a half dozen scones left. I would have thought that after—"

She didn't let him finish. "Max, before you accuse me, have all the facts. I put some aside for you."

She listened for an indication that her gesture pleased him, but he said nothing. *Someday, I hope to meet a man who can be counted on for consistency,* she said to herself. *Damned if I understand the creatures.* She tried to make light of it, but it hurt. It also made her mad, and she picked up the rubber duck on her desk and threw it with all her strength precisely as Max rushed into her cubicle.

"*What the heck!*" Max exclaimed, rubbing the side of his head.

Leticia slapped her hand over her mouth and stared at him, wide-eyed. "Sorry. I thought you were in your office ignoring my nice gesture."

"Well, you can see that you were wrong. I came to get my stuff."

"You could at least thank me," she said, unashamed that she sounded like a petulant child.

"I couldn't imagine that you'd put some away for me."

"No? I remember your having said that I'm a really nice person, but it seems to me that you don't remember it. And you didn't bring me any coffee, either."

A grin spread over his face. "That was another time and place. I'm not used to people in this office being nice to me. Where are my *goodies*?" As soon as the word left his mouth, his demeanor changed. If he'd pasted his thoughts on his face, they wouldn't have been more obvious. His large eyes flashed with desire, and he looked away from her. She cast her gaze downward, opened the desk drawer and, without lifting her gaze to his, handed him the pastries.

His fingers gripped her hand. "I never forget a kindness, Leticia, and my debts to you are piling up. Thanks."

"You're welcome, Max." But she didn't look at him, and when at last she heard the door close, she let herself breathe. "He's nice. Almost sweet," she said to herself. "Surely I don't want to mother a guy that big, but *something's* going on, and it's not a little thing." A few minutes later, he walked into her office, put a container of coffee along with sugar and cream on her desk and walked out without saying a word.

She left work half an hour early and headed for the Friendship Heights shopping area. A new gown would cost her money, but she wanted to look her best. She'd bet she was the only thirty-one-year-old woman in Washington, D.C., who had never had a formal dance date. It could be her only one, and she meant to enjoy it.

"I know I can't afford that," she said to herself as she passed Versace. "Neiman Marcus ought to have something."

"I'd like a simple but elegant dusty rose or lavender pink evening dress. I don't mind some top cleavage, but I don't want the sides of my breasts exposed," she told the saleswoman.

"I understand. Madam wants something elegant and tasteful," the saleswoman said, and swished away with head high and carriage perfect.

"At least I had sense enough not to go to the racks looking for sales," Leticia said under her breath.

When the woman returned with two evening gowns, one dusty rose and the other lavender pink, Leticia 's pulse increased. Both fit perfectly. "They're both your color, no doubt about that."

Leticia tried the dusty rose after the other and saw that the color made her glow.

"Would you bend forward, please, take a deep breath and then sit down for a minute?" Leticia did as the woman asked. "Now stand up. Is the dress comfortable? I mean can you move easily in it?"

"It's perfect," Leticia said of the dusty rose dress. She immediately decided to buy it, because she had never looked that good in anything.

"I would take it," the woman said, "because it fits your body perfectly. Not a single flaw. We'll deliver it tomorrow between nine and twelve."

She thanked the woman, handed her a twenty-dollar bill and didn't wait for her reaction. She bought silver evening shoes and a silver clutch and headed home. How did that woman know anyone would be at her home in the morning? Another reminder of how the rich lived. She passed a store that served hot dogs and pizzas and turned in to get a hot dog and ginger ale so that she wouldn't have to cook when she got home. As she was about to sit down, she remembered Willa, laughed at herself and headed home.

That evening after her dinner, she searched her sewing basket until she found a piece of ribbon the color of her evening dress. She attached it to a note on which she wrote, "Dear Max, This is the color of my dress. Yours, Leticia." The following day, after doing some research on the Internet, she rented a black velvet evening cape, found a pair of silver, elbow-length, leather evening gloves and considered herself properly prepared for a formal dance with one of the most respected journalists in the business.

"What's this?" Max said aloud when he walked into his office and saw the note. Frowning, he put the scrap into his pocket. He would never have considered wearing a pink cummerbund, but if he did, she'd be pleased. Reluctantly he faced the fact that he wanted to please her. He dialed her office number.

"Hi, Leticia. This is Max. Thanks for this little piece of ribbon. I'll do my best not to clash with you."

He got a cup of coffee, passed on the donuts and went to Joel's office. "You going to the frat dance next week?" Max asked his boss and fraternity brother.

"My wife wants to go. Women don't care whether they enjoy these things; they just want a chance to dress up, show off themselves and their man. If you think guys are competitive, watch it in women. I'd rather stay home, but if I even mention the possibility, I'll be in the dog house indefinitely. This is the big event of the year for Bridget. Bottom line: if I can crawl, I'll be there. You don't usually bother. You thinking about going this year?"

Max sat down and sipped his coffee. "Yeah. I'm going this year."

Joel brought his long body upright and looked Max in the eye. "Is she anybody I know? I mean, you're not with—uh . . . I forget her name—any longer, are you?"

Max drained the coffee cup, stood and tossed it into the wastebasket. "Joel, you've known me long enough to understand that when I finish something, I don't go back to it, and that includes people and especially women. It was over with Meredith eighteen months ago. Period."

"Do I know her?"

"Yes, you do." He nearly laughed at Joel's open mouth and wide eyes. "See you later." Max left the man, thinking that he'd finally gotten the better of Joel, and that he'd cherish the moment indefinitely. He knew that Joel would jump to the wrong conclusion when he saw him with Leticia, but he hoped the man knew how to mind his own business. If he didn't, he would learn, in this case, that their status as supervisor and employee, as well as fraternity brothers, wouldn't matter to Max Baldwin. Nobody meddled in his affairs.

On the way home that afternoon, he stopped at his tailor's shop and showed the man the piece of ribbon. "This is the color of my date's evening gown. I need accessories for my black tux. The occasion is a week from Saturday."

"If you'd like to match her dress, I can make them in this exact color. But if you wear that, you're making a social statement. What about it?"

He thought for a moment. "Make them in precisely that color. Thanks."

"You can have them this coming Saturday."

"You can have the rest of the day off," Leticia told Willa when she arrived home around four the Saturday of the dance. "I won't be home this evening, and I'm too excited to eat a big dinner."

"It's all right, ma'am. I need to get this mending done, and this is a good time." She showed Leticia two of her woolen skirts and a robe. "The hem's coming out of these skirts, and this robe's falling apart in the seams.

Money's too hard to get to be throwing things out when they can be mended good as new."

Leticia listened to Willa's rambling. "It's up to you." Did Willa think she didn't realize that the urgency about the mending was attributable entirely to Willa's determination to see her date? Seven-thirty seemed a bit early for a formal dance, but she didn't doubt that Max knew what he was doing.

"I'm pulling out the stops," she told herself. "If he's honoring me with this invitation, I'll do my best to reciprocate."

Willa answered the doorman's ring at seven o'clock. "Send him up," she said.

Leticia told herself to calm down. It seemed as if a flock of birds had attacked her stomach, and her fingers trembled as she struggled to pull on her gloves. "Willa, would you please button these gloves for me?"

"Yes, ma'am. Coming." Willa stopped at Leticia's bedroom door and stared at her. "Lord, I sure hope this man has the morals of a saint and the will power of a Martin Luther King Jr. You look out of this world." She buttoned the gloves, stood back and smiled.

The doorbell rang, and Leticia never saw Willa move that fast.

"I'm Max Baldwin. Is Ms. Langley here?"

"Yes, sir. Please come with me."

Leticia took a deep breath and strolled into the living room, where Max stood facing her. Tremors of anxiety shot through her when he walked toward her unsmiling and as serious as she had ever seen him. Didn't he like the way she looked? He reached out and took both of her hands.

"You . . . you look like a queen. I never dreamed . . . Leticia, you're exquisite. I'm honored that you agreed to be my date. I—"

She began to smile. It would be all right. "Max, did you look at yourself in the mirror? I'm the one who's honored. All you need is a couple of medals on your jacket and a sword at your side. You look like a prince of royalty." Not knowing what else to do, she reached up and kissed his cheek. His hand gripped her wrist, but she didn't back off.

"I'll be the proudest woman at that dance." She stepped back and gazed at him. "Gosh, we'd better go," she said airily. "As good as you look, I may decide to keep you for myself."

He smiled for the first time. "If you think I'd object, think again."

Willa cleared her throat, and Leticia whirled around.

"Mrs. Evans, this is Max Baldwin. Max, Mrs. Evans is supposed to be my housekeeper, but she's more like a dear friend and sometimes like a mother."

"I'm glad to meet you, Mr. Baldwin. Ms. Langley told me her date was a six-foot-four-inch knockout, but that was an understatement if I ever heard one. I love to cook, so you come over some evening, and I'll show you what gourmet is."

Max walked over to Willa and took her hand. "I can't remember a nicer welcome. See if you can get her to invite me. So far, I'm getting no place with her."

Willa put her hands on what passed for her hips and looked at him from beneath lowered lashes. "If you ain't joking, you oughtta be. She ain't a stupid woman by no means."

"Say, you must be the person who bakes those fabulous scones," Max said to Willa, changing the subject. "I've eaten those things in many places, but yours are the best. I'm delighted to meet you." He handed Leticia a dozen long-stemmed roses the color of her dress.

"We'd better be going. I got a reservation for seven forty-five."

She took the roses. "Max, these are so beautiful. Thank you for being so thoughtful."

"I'll put them in a vase for you, ma'am. Y'all have a good time. Nice to meet you, Mr. Baldwin."

"Won't you be cool?" Max asked her. "We'll be riding, but—"

"I have a cape." She opened the foyer closet, removed the cape and handed it to him. He draped it over her shoulders and waited while she slipped her arms through the straps.

"I thought we'd have a light supper before going to the dance and eat something more substantial later on, provided you want to," he said.

"Sounds like a great idea. I'm in your capable hands." A driver opened the door of a Cadillac, and Max held the tail of her cape as she slipped into the backseat. *This man knows his way around a formal occasion,* she told herself.

"You didn't drive?" she said to Max when he slid in beside her.

"I wouldn't put you in the front seat wearing an evening gown. Gosh, Leticia, you really look lovely."

"I'm glad I found this dress," she said, opting for honesty. "Max, you look so elegant, and I know you had your accessories made to match my dress. I don't know why you did it, but I have to tell you I've never felt so . . . so . . . well, the only word I can think of is *cherished.* Please don't misunderstand. You've made me feel wonderful."

After a light supper of pepperoni omelets, freshly made rolls and fruit tarts, they took the elevator to the hotel's grand ballroom. A grin on Max's face alerted her to the presence of someone he knew, and almost at once, she saw Joel Raymond walking toward them with a good-looking, willowy woman at his side.

"You two look like British royalty," Joel said. "Leticia Langley, this is my wife, Bridget. Well, Max, you've never half-done anything, and brother, tonight you didn't hit the jackpot. You walked away with it."

"Thanks," Max said, his face shining in a winsome smile. "I'm delighted that you recognized us."

"Well, I knew to keep my eye out for the most stunning couple at the ball," Joel responded.

Bridget's laugh was warm and friendly. "You're looking spectacular tonight, Max, but you always do. Maybe we can all stop someplace for a drink together later." She looked at Leticia. "I'll be willing to bet Max won't drink a drop of anything with alcohol in it until he leaves this dance. He's the epitome of good taste and common sense. One of my favorite people."

"Thanks, Bridget. You've embarrassed me. Leticia will think I paid you to say that."

"No I won't. I could have said the same thing . . . and meant it."

Leticia did not see Joel's raised eyebrow when Max slid his arm around her waist. She was in complete shock at spotting her cousin, Kenyetta, headed in their direction.

"We'll meet you here at eleven and take it from there, Max said. "See you later." He steered them in the opposite direction, but she had spent enough time in his company recently to know that he was intentionally avoiding someone. Could it have been Kenyetta?

"Who do you see that you'd rather not waste time with?" she asked him. He stopped walking and stared down at her. She couldn't figure out whether he was pleased or displeased until a rueful smile flittered across his face.

"You're getting to know me, and I like that," he said. "Will you dance with me?" She nodded, listened to the violins and, when he opened his arms, she stepped into them. Before long she had fogotten all about her cousin. Max danced smoothly, his body seeming to float with the music, and she had to resist moving close and letting herself go. The music changed from a simple two-step to a modified samba. He took a few steps, testing to see whether she would follow. She didn't know the samba, but she knew how to move to music, and she gave in to it. At once, she matched him step for step, with every swing of his hips and every twist of his shoulder. The music changed again, this time to Ellington's "Mood Indigo," and he pulled her so close that her breasts nestled against his chest, her thighs brushed his and the print of his hands on her body heated her from head to foot.

"I could get used to this with you," he said, and she missed a step. "Why are you surprised?"

"Stop befuddling me," she said, stalling for time.

He held her closer. "Befuddling you? That's mild compared to what you're doing to me."

The music stopped. She shook her head as if to clear it and moved away from him. Suddenly she heard, "Girl, you didn't tell me you'd be here tonight. Who's this number ten you're hanging out with?"

Leticia stepped away from Max and faced Kenyetta. "I can't think of a reason why I should have told you."

"Aren't you going to introduce me to your . . . uh . . . friend?" She extended her hand to Max. "I'm Kenyetta Jackson. Who on earth are you?"

Leticia would have sworn that Max censored Kenyetta with his gaze. "I know who you are, Miss Jackson."

"Really? I didn't know I was so popular." She stepped closer to him. "I don't know your name."

When his top lip curled, Leticia rejoiced, knowing that her cousin was about to get her comeuppance. "You don't need to know it," he sneered. "Women who hang out with Wilson Gallagher don't interest me. If you'll excuse us . . . " He let Kenyetta fill in the rest.

"How do you know about her and Wilson?" Leticia asked him as they walked away, leaving Kenyetta speechless.

"Because Wilson has a big mouth. He never keeps a conquest a secret."

"Then he's not a gentleman."

"Whoever said he was? Speaking of the devil." His arm slid around her waist and tightened. "What's up, man?" Max asked Wilson, as if they hadn't had words about Leticia two weeks earlier at Bill and Allison Covington's house.

"You've got the most gorgeous woman in the house. I'm wondering if you're feeling more generous than when we three were last together."

A feral grin started around Max's mouth, but eyes of cold steel gazed at Wilson. "I haven't changed one bit since the day we graduated from Harvard, Wilson. So don't push me. Ms. Langley is with me, and I heard her tell you that she wants no part of you. Let this be the last time you try this stunt. By the way, your girlfriend was here a few minutes ago. You two deserve each other. Good night."

"Which girlfriend?"

"Kenyetta Jackson." Max took Leticia's arm and walked away. "I'm sorry about that, but I have a feeling that he won't give up until you indict him for harassment, or I give him the opportunity to swallow his teeth."

"Don't worry, Max. He isn't spoiling my evening. I'm having a wonderful time with you. Aren't Bill and Allison supposed to be here?"

"Bill's a frat brother, but he's on a mission. I see Lucas Hamilton and . . . that must be his wife. Now there's a first-class guy for you." Max walked with her across the ballroom. Shimmers from the crystal chandeliers danced like silver flames across her gloves, and she noted with pride that she was one of the few women in the crowd who wore elbow-length gloves. Most wore none at all. As they approached the Hamiltons, the man waved to them.

"Max, this is my wife, Susan Pettiford Hamilton, interior decorator. Susan, this is my good buddy, Max Baldwin, reporter and columnist for *The Journal.*"

"I'm delighted to meet the woman who brought this guy to heel," Max said. "Susan and Lucas, this is Leticia Langley, reporter and columnist for *The Journal.* Leticia, Lucas is a stellar architect. When I build a house to suit myself, he'll design it."

"We read *The Journal,* so we're familiar with your work, both of you," Susan said. "We don't get up here often, and we have two children, so you two must come down to Woodmore to see us. We have plenty of room, and we'll make it very pleasant for you."

They're all cut from the same cloth, Leticia thought, *but I'm learning that I can hold my own. I have to.* To them she said, "I'm delighted to meet you, and I look forward to seeing you again and to meeting your children."

"I see our friend Wilson is still playing the game," Lucas said.

"Yeah," Max replied. "One day he'll grow up and discover that he's missed out on what matters most in life. It's a pity."

Leticia met many of Max's acquaintances—some

closer than others—that evening, and she noted that
the men had in common success, self-confidence and
good-looking women. As the evening wore on, Max
danced with more abandon, and it seemed to her that,
when they weren't dancing, his arm stayed snugly
around her waist. She hadn't spent a lot of time dancing, but she discovered that she loved it and that, with
practice, she could excel at it.

"It's a few minutes of eleven," Max said, "and I
promised Joel and Bridget we'd meet them about this
time. It'll take us ten minutes to get through this crowd.
Shall we go?" She nodded, and he stood, walked around
to her chair and assisted her in getting up. As they wove
their way across the ballroom, she couldn't help thinking that the dazzling diamonds and other jewels adorn-
ing the women would buy food for a lot of hungry people.

"If I had those diamonds, would I think that way?"
she asked herself, and decided that she was far from an-
gelic; a seven-hundred-dollar dress was no less an example of conspicuous consumption than diamonds. Maybe
more so, since the diamonds could be worn more often
and passed on to someone else after one's demise. Suddenly, she heard her father's words: "As soon as you get
to be perfect, you can start judging and censuring other
people."

"There you are, man." Joel's voice brought her back
to the present. "Bridget's hungry, so we thought we'd
get a late supper. Would you two join us?" Bridget looked
from Leticia to Max, and Leticia knew the woman would
conclude from their response the nature of Max's relationship to her.

Max looked at Leticia, including her in the decision.
"We didn't eat much earlier, so what do you say we join
them?"

Leticia noted his consideration and it made her feel

warm inside. "I'd love to. I must have lost a couple of pounds on that dance floor tonight. I think I'm starved."

"Want to eat downstairs?" Joel asked.

"That would make sense," Max said. "The grill room is open until one o'clock."

She liked Bridget, and seeing Joel with his wife, a university professor, added to her feeling of security about working with Joel. His willingness to marry a smart woman proved he wouldn't see a female with brains as a threat to him.

Bridget and Leticia ordered deviled shrimp and a salad, and both men ordered filet mignon steak and hash-brown potatoes. Max looked at her and commented, "I don't see how a person who's starved could settle for what you're eating. Starved means hungry."

"I know," she said, "but I have to consider what I'm wearing."

"Indeed," Bridget said. "Looking great comes with a price."

"Leave me in my ignorance," Max said. "I don't want to know. Whatever damage I do tonight, I'll work off tomorrow morning."

"I can say this now, and it won't sound official, Max," Joel said. "I'd appreciate it if you'd ask Wilson not to visit you at the office. Violence against another person is a crime. The idiot hit on Bridget tonight, and then swore he didn't remember that she was my wife. Of course he's lying. He's known Bridget for years."

"You should have invited him outside," Max said. "He hasn't changed a bit since he was a freshman in college. He kept two lists on the inside of his room door—the ones he'd had and the ones he planned to get. He didn't even spare his roommate's sister. His roommate was a little guy, so I gave Wilson the shellacking he deserved."

"I don't want him in my sight," Joel said.

"Look, it's only a quarter of twelve and we don't have to get up early. How about dropping by Blues Alley? We'll just catch the last show," Max said.

Both Joel and Bridget registered surprise with raised eyebrows and widened eyes. "I didn't know you liked jazz," Joel said. "Over at Bill's place, you always sit quietly and sleep, and around ten or ten-thirty you say good night."

"I don't talk when I listen to music, and I'm not asleep. I also don't stay up late, because I need a clear head when I'm working."

Joel stared at Max. "Well, I'll be damned. It isn't for nothing that you're the ace."

Max sat with Leticia, Joel and Bridget at the edge of the stage at Blues Alley, wanting with every fiber of his being to take the guitar away from Buck Hayes and give that piece the playing it deserved. The man was a neophyte at best. *Leticia's right,* he thought. *If I don't do it now, I never will.* Oh, how he itched to play that guitar. He felt Leticia's hand on his beneath the tablecloth.

He leaned toward her. He wasn't trying to hide his interest in Leticia from Joel, but neither was he parading it. "What is it?" he whispered.

"I'll bet he isn't half as good as you are. I can't wait to hear you play."

He couldn't believe it. How could she possibly know his feelings at that moment? "Are you clairvoyant? I'd swear you read my mind."

"No, I'm not, but the more I get to know you, the better I—"

She stopped as if afraid to say what would come next. He didn't believe in hedging, so he said it for her, speaking softly. "The better you understand me?" She shifted her gaze away from his and focused on the musicians, but she didn't fool him. He'd pushed her into a corner, and she was not comfortable there.

After an hour of what he considered mediocre playing at best, Max looked from his watch to Joel. "This wasn't the best idea I ever had. I hope you haven't been bored. We're ready to go."

"It wasn't the top, but it wasn't bad. You listened with the ear of a pro, and I just enjoyed myself," Joel said. "Ready to go?" he asked, looking at his wife. She nodded, and they waited until the end of "River Rushing Blues," and left.

In the car for the drive to Leticia's apartment building, Max thought about the evening. Something was going on, but he didn't feel like examining it. She had everything a man wanted—at least according to his eyes, ears and brain—but he was not going to expose himself to another woman's selfishness and chicanery. He'd rather be alone.

She reached over and patted his hand. "I've never had such a wonderful evening, Max. I have enjoyed every second of it. Not even Wilson and Kenyetta could mar it for me. You are a very special man."

"You allow a man to be special, Leticia." He squeezed her fingers, and the emptiness crashed down on him. *Lord, how it hurt!*

As he exited the elevator and walked with Leticia to the door of her apartment, he realized that he hadn't wanted the evening to end. For the first time in a long while, he'd had a date whose company he enjoyed, who hadn't attempted to gain the attention of every man around her, and whose looks, manners and demeanor made him feel ten feet tall. At her door, he held out his hand for her key, and when she handed it to him without hesitation or any display of uncertainty, he knew that she trusted him.

He opened the door, handed her the key, leaned down and shocked her with a kiss on her cheek. "Thank you for your company, Leticia. Tonight, you made me feel like a king." He didn't wait for her response, but turned and headed for the elevator. He believed in moving on while he was ahead.

Leticia watched him for a minute as he strolled down the long hallway, and she couldn't help wondering why he suddenly seemed so solitary, so distant. She had an odd feeling of abandonment, or was it discontent? After an evening like that one, when she knew she had shone as a woman and the man with her fit the role to perfection, should she be standing there alone watching him leave her? And shouldn't the evening end with at least a real kiss? She shook her head and stepped inside. What had come over her? She worked with Max, and the last thing they both needed was daily temptation in the office. Besides, he was just a friend.

She closed the door, undressed, completed her ablutions and sat on the edge of her bed. As late as it was, it seemed too early to go to sleep. She threw on a robe, went to the window and looked out at the clear, moon-lit night. So much had happened in the past six months that she'd missed the end of summer and most of the autumn. Not a tree had one green leaf. The lush, sub-urbanlike neighborhood in which she lived, where trees, flowers, shrubs and all kinds of plant life had flourished seemingly only days earlier, now appeared as if it had al-ways been barren. *Gosh, is my life running away from me? I've just begun to live.* She went back to her bed, saw the red light flashing on her answering machine and ignored it.

But when she checked the machine the following morning, she heard Mark's voice. "Please call me at once, Leticia."

She dialed his number. "Hi, Mark. If you've got bad news for me, I don't want to hear it."

"I'm sorry, cuz, but our grandfather passed last night. It was unexpected, because he was walking around yesterday, jovial and in great spirits. He didn't show any signs of deterioration. The good news is that the doctors think it was sudden, and that he didn't suffer."

She felt as if she'd been hit with a hammer. She'd known that, for a man her grandfather's age, each additional day counted was a miracle, but after her trip to New Orleans to visit him, she hadn't called to ask him how he felt or to let him know she cared. *It's too late for that now,* she told herself.

"I'm sorry. Thank you for calling me."

"Are you coming down?"

"I don't know. I'll call you after I straighten out my thoughts."

"All right. If you need any assistance, let me know, and I'll meet you at the airport. The funeral is set for Tuesday."

She thanked him, told him good-bye and hung up. She didn't know what she felt or whether she felt anything. What was the purpose in going to the old man's funeral? He certainly wouldn't be cheered by her presence, and she didn't much care what any of her relatives other than Mark thought of her going or not going.

She showered, dressed in brown pants and a salmon-colored turtleneck sweater and started down the stairs. The phone rang, and Willa answered. "Well, how are you, Mr. Baldwin? Did y'all have a good time last night? Good. I'm so glad you did. Now, don't you forget to encourage my boss to invite you to dinner." She paused, obviously listening. "Yes indeedy. You do your share, and I'll do mine. Yes, sir. I hear her coming down the stairs. Bye . . . Ma'am, Mr. Baldwin is on the line."

"Hello, Max."

"Hello. Mind telling me why you sound so cool?"

"I'm sorry about that, because I don't feel cool toward you, but I'm going to give Willa a scolding for what she just did."

"What did she do?"

"Don't be naïve. She meddled in my business."

"Not much. I just told her what my favorite foods are. I didn't get nosy with her or anything. At least I don't think I stepped over the line in any way. Now, would you mind greeting me again?"

She didn't want to laugh, but although the voice certainly belonged to Max, the words did not. She could not associate him with the fake innocence and smooth charm. "Who's this? I thought I was speaking with Max, not this smooth-talking charmer." The image of him affronted by her remark brought a gale of laughter pouring from her throat, until he said, "For goodness sake, what's so funny?"

"I didn't know you had it in you, and I enjoyed it. How are you this morning, Max?"

"Considering the amount of sleep I got, I'm feeling great. What about you?"

"Physically and mentally I'm fine, but when I got in last night, I found a message to call my cousin. I called this morning and learned that my grandfather passed away last night."

"My gosh, Leticia, I'm so sorry. Where and when will there be services for him, and when do you leave?"

"The service will be in New Orleans Tuesday, but I don't know whether I'm going. It's a long story, Max. Who am I going for? He won't know I'm there, and except for one person, I don't care what the three hundred attendees think."

"Then go for yourself. Go because you forgive him his failings and because no matter what he did or didn't do, he is your grandfather. I'll take you to the airport."

She could hardly close her mouth. He'd made the decision for her, and . . . But he was right, she knew. "I'll phone the airline and—"

"I can do that for you. Do you want business class or economy? And what day do you want to leave?"

"Economy. I'd like to leave Monday morning." She gave him her credit card numbers. "Thank you. I'm sure I would have procrastinated all day."

A half hour later, he called her again. "You have a ten-forty flight. I'll e-mail the electronic ticket to you."

She stared at the phone. Was he behaving as a friend or as a man who . . . She refused to let the words form themselves in her mind. "Max, thank you for this, for being my friend. You're . . . every day now, I learn something else about you that is admirable and beautiful."

"If you say anything else like that, I'll have to defend myself. I'll be at your place Monday morning at eight o'clock."

"Oh. If you come at seven-thirty, I'll bet Willa would happily give you a nice fattening breakfast."

"I'll be there at seven-thirty. In the meantime, if you need me for anything, here's my cell number." She wrote it down. "See you." She heard the dial tone and got the urge to throttle him. For the next twenty minutes, she sat in the living room going over their recent times together, but she couldn't say he was this or that, or even the kind of friendship he wanted.

"You gon' raise the devil with me 'bout what I said to Mr. Baldwin, but I don't care," Willa said. "Come on and eat your breakfast. He's a real man, just the kind you need, and furthermore, I got a notion that you know it."

"Please don't encourage him, Willa. I won't let anyone plan my life, and that includes you. So don't try it. Incidentally, you'll have a chance to prepare Mr. Baldwin's breakfast for him Monday morning."

Willa nearly dropped the plate of "pan perdue"—a Cajun style French toast—and, with her mouth agape and eyes widened, rushed around the table to face Leticia. "I hope I ain't hearing you right, ma'am. It's . . . it's just not what I'd expect of you, ma'am."

"I don't understand. What are you talking about?"

"Him sleeping . . . Ma'am, this is too much."

Laughter poured out of Leticia. "Willa, if I was going to let a man spend the night, you can bet he'd be gone long before you got here. Anyhow, I don't have that kind of relationship with Max Baldwin."

Willa's hands went to her hips. "Why not? He's the best you're ever gon' find, and he looks good enough to eat. You can see, can't you, ma'am?"

"Make up your mind, Willa. Oh, yes, and I have twenty-twenty vision. May I have the remainder of my breakfast, please, and would you kindly sit down and stop thinking about men?"

"Stop thinking about men? I see you ain't feeling well this morning."

"Trust me, I feel great. After last night, nothing and no one can drag me down."

Chapter Eleven

Leticia battled guilt until she submitted to her conscience and telephoned Kenyetta. "Hi, Ken. Mark called me night before last to tell me that my grandfather died. The funeral is Tuesday."

"What? How come nobody told me?"

"I don't know. Anyhow, I'm telling you now in case you want to go."

Leticia could almost smell her cousin's rising irritation over not having received personal notification from somebody in New Orleans. An announcement from anybody there would have satisfied her.

"How can I go? Today's Sunday, and I don't have time to shop."

Leticia released a long breath and looked toward the ceiling as if asking for patience. "Why do you need to shop, Kenyetta? You won't be going to a grand ball, and all the men at the ceremonies will be your relatives."

"Hmph. I know you don't care how you look, Leticia, but I do."

She didn't see the point in a verbal spar with her

cousin. "Look, I gotta go. Have a great day." She'd done her duty, and she didn't have to listen to her cousin's put-downs and ego trip all the way to New Orleans.

Monday morning, more cheerful than she had a right to be when on her way to her grandfather's funeral, Leticia tripped down the hall a few minutes before seven-thirty and called to Willa.

"What smells so good?"

"I bought some good old sage sausage. Men love it with waffles and with grits and scrambled eggs."

Another one of those women who loved to make men happy, eh? She couldn't help bristling a little. "Really, Willa. Surely, it won't surprise you to know that women like that stuff, too. At least, this woman does."

"Yes, ma'am, but what you eat don't amount to peanuts. If you want me to, I can lay it out every morning, and with pleasure."

"I'll bet."

The doorbell rang, and Leticia delighted in getting to the door before Willa did. She slipped the chain, opened the door and looked up at Max. "Hi," they said simultaneously. What did she say now? "Is it cold out?" she asked him.

She wished he wouldn't grin as if he'd caught her stealing cookies. "May I came in?" he asked her with a signifying wink. Her gaze was locked on his gray suit, white shirt and gray and yellow checkered tie, something he didn't wear at work. In the office, he usually wore slacks and a tweed jacket or, in the summer, light pants and a darker jacket that came close to matching them, but didn't always make it.

"Oh, sure. Yes, of course you can. Willa's expecting you. I mean . . ."

His grin spread over his face, lighting his eyes until

he laughed aloud. "I never thought I'd see you without your famous aplomb, Leticia."

"It's not nice of you to mention it, Max." Feeling freer with him than she had previously, she took his hand and walked with him to the dining room. "Willa cooked this breakfast without thought as to my taste or preference. Have a seat."

This was not the Max she knew at the office. He wasn't stern and aloof or seemingly concerned mainly with his image as an ace reporter. This man was her warm and caring date of two nights earlier, the engaging and understanding man who joined her as a guest of Bill and Allison Covington. The man who surprised her with his attentiveness and his similarity to her in morals and manners.

"We have to say grace first," Willa announced, "so y'all wait a minute." She put the food on the table, joined them and said grace. "And, Lord, would you please take this situation here in your hand?" she added. Willa handed them bowls of fresh pineapple chunks and sweetened raspberries. Leticia looked at the food and then at Max.

"You're welcomed to eat like a little bird," he said, "but I'm going to eat some of everything I see. My cook gives me Rice Krispies for breakfast. I'm sick of 'em, but she says they keep blood pressure down."

Willa smiled at Max. "I opened a fresh can of dark roasted Columbia coffee." She poured a cup and handed it to him.

"I drink coffee, too," Leticia grumbled.

Max hooted and looked at Leticia as if to say, "Sorry. I can't help it if I'm her boy." What he said was, "This waffle is to die for, and it's been years since I ate any sage sausage. Willa, I'm going to give Ella your phone number."

Leticia watched Willa preen. "Who's Ella?" Leticia asked Max, and wanted to bite her tongue.

"Ella cooks and looks after my house. I thought she was perfect, but how can she be when she doesn't give me sage sausage and Belgian waffles?" After he finished eating, he went around the table to where Willa sat and kissed her cheek. "You're wonderful, Willa. I can't tell you how much I enjoyed my breakfast." To Leticia, he said, "Thanks for inviting me. You knew I'd enjoy it. It's really sweet of you."

"But I don't rate a kiss on the cheek," she muttered to herself, and she suspected he heard her, for his eyes twinkled and a grin formed around his lips.

Max glanced at his watch. "We'd better be moving. Traffic to the airport can be heavy at this time." He shook hands with Willa and picked up Leticia's overnight bag. "Ready?"

She nodded. "As I'll ever be."

"You rented a car?" she asked him as they approached the black limousine.

"I want to see you to the gate, and I couldn't do that if I drove my car, because I'd have to park too far away."

At the airline's kiosk in the airport, Max printed out her ticket and handed it to her along with a receipt for her return ticket. "They won't let you go to the gate with me," she told him, and she knew that the tenor of her voice told him of her disappointment.

"I got a general clearance several months back, so I can pass security. You ought to do that."

Considering the crowd ahead of them, she figured it would be a good idea. After removing her shoes, the jacket of her suit, and her cosmetics bag and putting them into the plastic tray for security check, she removed her laptop from her suitcase and placed it in another tray.

On the way to the gate, they passed a newsstand. "Let's stop here a minute," he said, went in, bought a copy of the *Washington Post*, a package each of cookies and Snickers and handed them to her. The man was taking care of her, and she had a right to know why. The words *Why are you doing this?* were on the tip of her tongue when he said, "I don't know what you'll face or how you'll feel there. It's an occasion that can generate feelings you didn't know you were capable of experiencing. So, a little TLC is something for you to fall back on." He looked her in the eye. "There's more where this came from."

As if he considered the thought closed, he took her arm and walked with her to the gate. "They're boarding. Did you bring my cell phone number?"

"Yes, I did. Thanks for—"

Max didn't let her finish. "Don't thank me." He leaned down, kissed her cheek, turned and walked away.

Was that all she could expect in life? A kiss on the cheek? He'd kissed Willa on the cheek. Was he telling her that she wasn't entitled to more from him than her cook received? She had vowed to change, and it was time she did it. "Damn you," she said when he was well out of earshot. "Next time you do that, I'm going to show you what a real kiss is supposed to be like."

A man who had evidently witnessed the chaste kiss and heard her reaction grinned at her and said, "That's it. The guy must be loonie. Damned if *I'd* kiss you on the cheek."

But with his sharp ears, Max heard her. If he was getting to her, fine; that was no more than she was doing to him. He had a mind to kiss her cheek when he met her at the airport Wednesday on her return from New Orleans just to see what she'd do. He didn't question his protectiveness toward her. It had been instinctive almost since he met her. She had an uncanny sense, almost an instinct about his feelings, and particularly when he was down. And for some reason, she disliked his being hurt or unhappy. He needed to sort it out, but he knew himself well enough to appreciate what the consequences would be when he did figure it out. He wasn't quite ready for that.

He got to the office late, shortly after ten, and missed the morning budget meeting. A note from Joel was stuck to his telephone. He didn't jump when teacher clapped, so he ignored the note, but he'd hardly taken his seat when Joel phoned him.

"I get some breaking news, and neither you nor Langley is around to cover it. You two had the entire weekend to celebrate."

"You're not minding your own business, Joel. Didn't Leticia tell you her grandfather died Saturday night?"

Joel's long pause didn't fool Max. Something had registered with the man, and he was gauging how much he could say with impunity. Finally, he said, "Yeah. She left a message on my answering machine. How do you happen to know about it?"

Max leaned back in his chair and prepared to enjoy himself. "Ah, what fools ye mortals be. Temerity is thy middle name."

"She's a nice gal, Max. So watch your step."

He laid the phone on his desk, almost ran to Joel's office and burst in without knocking. "Man, what the hell gives you the idea that I would mistreat Leticia or any other woman? I know she's nice. I probably know it better than you do. So lay off."

"Bridget thinks she's good for you. She said you were a different man with her. I thought so, too."

Max plowed his fingers through his short, not-quite-straight hair. "She's special. Leave it at that, Joel."

"As long as you know it."

Max stared at Joel while he debated with his temper. He didn't allow anybody to give him a tongue lashing. "Be careful, Joel. I think a lot of you, but not enough to let you treat me as if I'm a kid."

"I think a lot of you, too," Joel said. "No offense intended."

Max looked at Joel for a long time. "All right. No offense taken." He knew he was different with Leticia; he had been from the first, but he'd be careful in the future not to show it.

When Leticia reached the baggage claim area in New Orleans's Louis Armstrong Airport, she saw Mark striding toward her. At once, she knew why she'd come. She dropped her bag and reached out to the one person who she knew cared for her. Maybe Max cared for her. She wasn't sure, but she knew that Mark did.

They held each other for a few minutes. "I'm so glad you came, Leticia. I've just learned that Granddad's lawyer is reading the will this afternoon and that you should be there."

"Me? You can't be serious."

"I am. His lawyer is one of my close friends. From the hint I got, the number of relatives and pretenders attending the funeral will be a lot smaller than it would have been if the will had been read after the burial."

She knew so little about her grandfather, but she refused to take responsibility for that. "I didn't realize that he was wealthy," she said to Mark.

A sad expression clouded Mark's face. "I guess he was. And it's a pity, because the old man was known for squeezing a penny until it screamed. He didn't seem to enjoy it. Now he's gone, his wealth is here, and people who didn't earn it will have the benefit of it."

They stopped at Mark's home long enough for her to freshen up and change her clothes. As they rode the elevator to the lawyer's office, Mark chuckled. "Granddad was just mean enough to say that you didn't inherit unless you attended the reading. I sure wouldn't put it past him."

Indeed, Bryce Crawford had made precisely that stipulation. "In other words," Leticia said to Mark after the reading, "if you didn't attend the funeral, it means you were disinherited."

"Right. We all knew he was foxy."

Leticia was in a state of amazement when she left the lawyer's office. The old man had owned three houses, his own dwelling and two that he rented out. He left them, his bank accounts and stocks to his seven grandchildren. Mark and Leticia received his own dwelling and its contents.

"I suggest we sell the house and everything in it and divide what we get," Mark said. "It's easier that way. What do you think?"

"Good idea. Ask your lawyer friend to take care of it."

As Mark predicted, not three hundred, but sixty relatives attended the funeral. *Word certainly gets around,* Leticia thought. She gazed down at her maternal grandfather, marblelike in his stillness and elegant for eternity in his black tuxedo, white-lined pleated shirt, and gray and yellow paisley tie, cummerbund and handker-chief.

"It's what he ordered and paid for," the undertaker explained when questioned.

Mark's eyes glazed with unshed tears. "Look at him. It's the story of his life. Everything for show, even the way he treated his children."

She thought of her mother and her docile accep-tance of banishment from her home and all that she knew because of her father's need to save face in their community. *Have I inherited from my mother a reluctance to plow my way through life, passionately going after what I want and need in my relationships with people? What has changed since the day I got my degree?* Leticia attributed the success she'd had wholly to her mental prowess. She'd met some people, but in six months, she'd made only two friends, Mark and Max. She still didn't have a girl-friend with whom to share her triumphs, failures and fears, to dish the dirt, talk about men and shop.

"What's the matter, Leticia?"

"I need to straighten out my life."

He walked with her back to his car, alternately hold-ing her hand and hugging her shoulders. "Is he the guy who gave me the dirty looks when I met you at your of-fice?"

"He's wonderful to me, but he kisses me on the cheek."

Mark's husky laugh had the ring of a man who un-derstood the problem. "Does he know you want him to kiss you? If he doesn't, why don't you turn your head and show him?"

"Just let him do it again," she said. "He'll get the sur-prise of his life."

* * *

Although she hated to leave Mark, Leticia was glad to have the dreariness of the funeral and burial behind her. She remained stunned by her grandfather's generosity until she realized that it was as much a recompense for her mother as it was a gift to her. She asked the lawyer to send her a picture of her grandfather and grandmother, told Mark good-bye and headed home.

She reached the baggage claim area in the Ronald Reagan Washington National Airport and saw Max. "Hi," she said, both surprised and comforted to see his familiar face. "I didn't realize that you were planning to meet me."

He took her bag in his left hand, put his right arm around her waist and headed out of the terminal. "How did it go in New Orleans?"

"I have a lot to tell you but, Max, you're confusing me."

"Not if you keep your thinking cap on."

She could feel her temper rearing up. She was getting mad and didn't care if he knew it. Men didn't even treat their little sisters as he was behaving with her. She stopped walking and stamped her foot.

With concern etched on his face, he held her closer. "What is it, Leticia? What's wrong?"

"You. You do all these nice things for me and you . . . Oh, nuts to you, Max, and don't kiss me on the cheek when you take me home. I mean it."

At first, his face bore a quizzical expression. Then he shrugged in a nonchalant fashion. "Okay, Leticia."

"Dammit, Max. Is that all you have to say?"

"You told me not to kiss you. If a woman doesn't want me to kiss her, I won't kiss her."

She felt as if she would explode. "I didn't say I don't want . . . Oh, hell! Let's go."

He picked up her bag, put his other arm around her

waist and proceeded with her to the exit and the waiting limousine. Inside the car, he said, "Are you all right? Apart from being mad at me, that is?"

"I'm fine, and I am not mad at you. I'm vexed because you give me mixed signals. My grandfather left me half of one of his dwellings and its contents and, let me tell you, that's quite a lot. I'm stunned."

"You couldn't have given me better news. He cared for you, and he wanted to make amends for his wrong-doings."

"Yes. To my mother as well as to me. He told me he regretted it. His lawyer will supervise the sale of the house and its contents and give half to me and half to Mark, my first cousin."

When the limousine stopped in front of the eight-story white-brick apartment building in which she lived, Max asked her, "Am I allowed to walk with you to the door of your apartment?"

She looked hard at him. He was serious. "What makes you think you have to ask?"

"I don't want to make any mistakes with you."

With great effort, she resisted the urge to pinch him somewhere, and any place would have sufficed. "Please don't look so innocent, Max. I can't stand it."

At her apartment door, he took her key, opened the door, tipped an imaginary hat, smiled and walked away. "I could kill you," she called after him. "And that's not all I could do." He didn't stop walking. She'd give anything at that moment if she could understand him. In some important respects, she knew him, and she could discern his moods, when he was pleased or displeased and when he bordered on anger, but deep down, she had no idea what made him tick.

* * *

Several evenings later, Max called her at home, and that surprised her because, from the time he left her at her apartment door following her return from New Orleans, she'd seen him only at *The Journal* staff's morning budget meetings.

"Are you going home for Christmas?" he asked her.

"No. I don't have anyone in Atlanta, and Mark's the only person I'd want to see in New Orleans, and he's going on a cruise with his girlfriend."

"I see. I usually have dinner Christmas Eve. Would you have dinner with me? You shouldn't be alone, and I'd enjoy your company."

She would have expected him to say most anything but that. It bothered her to have anyone feel sorry for her. It wouldn't be the first time she'd had Christmas dinner alone. Time was when she was glad to have a turkey wing and mashed potatoes for her Christmas meal.

"Thank you, Max, for caring, but I don't want to impose on you. I'll be fine. Honest."

After what seemed like ages, he said, "If it could possibly be an imposition, I wouldn't have asked you. Good night." He hung up.

For a long minute, Max stared at the mobile phone in his hand. He didn't realize that he'd sent it across the dining room until it crashed into a chair. It had taken him a long time to reach out to a woman, any woman, but he'd made himself do it, because she was the one person who could bring joy to his life at Christmas. And she ought to know that he cared for her. He knew she cared for him before she knew it, and he had discerned it from her behavior with him. She'd complained that he kissed her cheek, but he knew himself. He wasn't a pimply teenager who could kiss and fondle women, tell them good night and go whistling on his way. If he ever kissed Leticia Langley the way he longed to, he'd want to bury himself in her and love her till he spent himself, and she ought to have sense enough to know that.

He couldn't understand her thin reason for not having dinner with him on Christmas Eve and for preferring instead to be alone. He ran his fingers through his hair. Maybe she wouldn't be alone, and he'd been a sucker.

"How many are we having for dinner Christmas Eve, Mr. B?" Ella, his housekeeper, called to him from the kitchen.

"Just the three of us. I'm not having a guest this year."

"Then what'll I do with that big turkey I ordered?"

"Exchange it for a smaller one. I'm going out." He headed out Thirty-eighth Street toward McLean Gardens, walking at a fast clip until he reached a red light, stopped and remembered that he hadn't put on a topcoat and that the wind was sending freezing air straight through his body. If he didn't know better, he would think he was entirely alone on earth. The brilliance of the moonlight and the silver coldness of the stars added to his loneliness. Right then, he would have been happy to meet a dog on the street, but the barren limbs of the trees were the only moving things he saw. He turned back, walking at a slower pace.

How had he let himself do what he'd sworn never to do again? He was vulnerable to her. They had so much in common, and he felt so comfortable with her that she'd sunk into him before he got his defenses up. If he knew why she'd rather spend Christmas alone than with him, or if she had another man, he could deal with it, but he believed she cared for him, so this didn't make sense. But he wasn't going to ask her why. Not now or ever.

"Oh, my Lord, I've hurt him, and he'll never forgive me. What on earth was I thinking? He wasn't being nice. He cares about me," she said in a loud voice.

She dialed his number, and when she got his answering machine, she hung up and dialed his cell number. He didn't answer that either. It seemed as if her heart hit the bottom of her belly.

What had she done? She knew Max's level of sensitivity and that, in spite of his sometimes tough manner, he hurt easily. Pain, almost physical in its intensity, wracked her. How had she been so thoughtless? And why didn't she accept his invitation when she knew she wanted to be with him?

By his actions, Max had shown her that he was her friend and that he cherished her friendship. And what had she done but behave like a foolish schoolgirl, too stupid to realize that the man cared for her and that, with his looks, status and prestige, he could have any of a number of women as his Christmas Eve dinner partner.

As days passed, it became evident that he was avoiding her at work. Her column on women politicians in Washington was quoted widely by the television pundits and congressional leaders, and every reporter at *The Journal* congratulated her, except Max.

She had to find a way to make amends, to tell him that she was godly sorry. With Willa spending Christmas in South Carolina with her children and grandchildren, Leticia ordered Christmas Eve dinner from a caterer and ate at home, more miserable than she could remember being since her father's death. She pushed the food around on her plate, unaware of her actions. She could have been with him, but instead she'd hurt him terribly and herself as well. Salty water rolled down beside her nose and on to the food that she held at her lips. What if he, too, were miserable? Sobs wracked her until she no longer had the strength to cry. Why couldn't she relate to people as she wanted them to relate to her? She covered her face with her hands. She had to talk to him.

Christmas morning, she answered the telephone and heard Kenyetta's voice. Two weeks earlier, she would have sworn that she would never welcome that sound. "Hi, Ken. Merry Christmas."

"Merry Christmas to you, too," her cousin said. "Except this is no merry time for me. Girl, would you believe that SOB Reggie Parrish got a divorce and is marrying some gal in Hyattsville after screwing me around for almost five years? The SOB sent me an invitation to the wedding, and it's addressed in his own handwriting. If I ever see him again, his ass gon' be mine. When I finish with him, his new bride will have a eunuch on her hands. Not that it will make a difference to her. When he had all of his important parts, he didn't hack it."

"Slow down, Kenyetta, and get a hold of yourself. If you commit a crime, you'll go to jail, and then you'll really be miserable. Besides, you're not in love with him, so just forget about him."

"He used me."

"You told me you were using each other."

Kenyetta ignored that bit of truth. "I didn't get a damned thing out of it. He couldn't take me anywhere, and he sure wasn't shit in bed. Wilson put down more in one hour than Reggie came close to doing in almost five years, but, hell, Wilson ain't shit either. That brother's like a stallion. He won't hang around a minute longer than he gets what he wants. The jerk."

Leticia didn't want to talk about Reggie what's-his-name and especially not about Wilson. "They're out of your life," she told her cousin, "so be thankful. Now you're free to find a nice guy who will really care for you."

"Hmph! What's with you and that number ten you had at the Kappa dance? That's one fine brother. Snooty, but a real knockout."

"Don't ask me. I messed up."

"Girl, get on your knees. Crawl. Whatever. He wouldn't get away from me."

She wished Kenyetta would listen to herself. That philosophy probably accounted for her short reign as queen of Wilson Gallagher's world. "I said I messed up, Ken. I did not say I owed him every shred of my pride."

"Okay. You know it all. How about going to a movie?"

"Fine. But not today. I have to work things out. Thanks for calling."

Leticia hung up, got the telephone book and looked for Max's home address, but he was not listed, and the telephone operator wouldn't give it to her. She knew that if he wouldn't answer her phone calls he would ignore her e-mails. She hadn't seen him in the office that Friday, the day after Christmas, although she heard his voice twice in the corridor. In any case, she didn't consider the office the proper place for what she needed to say to him.

Late Friday afternoon, she passed Max's office on her way to see Joel, saw the light beneath his door and shivered from the pain of their separation.

"Come in," Joel said when she knocked. She opened the door and walked in. Leticia didn't pay much attention to the deep tan-colored walls, yellow drapes, walnut furniture and the high-back tufted leather chair in which Joel sat, comfortable in his masculine environment and with his status as editor in chief. "Hey, what's with you? Did you lose your best friend?" he asked her.

She nearly choked. "Did I . . . maybe. I don't know. Joel, do you know Max's home address?"

His frown didn't surprise her. After all, Max was less than ten feet from Joel's office. "Sure, I know it, but he's right down there in his office. Can't you ask him for it?"

"I could, but I don't think he'd give it to me. Please, Joel. I won't do anything bad. I swear."

"Sit down. You're miserable, and so is Max. I've seen him in all kinds of moods, but not like this. I turned that corner by Rube's office, and he bumped into me and nearly knocked me speechless. He muttered something and didn't even stop walking."

"Joel, please. It's my fault."

Joel fingered his chin as if in deep thought and then appeared to have reached a decision. "I'll give it to you, and I think you ought to patch it up with him. I've known Max for years, and I know he's straight. I also know that he cares a lot for you. I wish my daughter would bring me a man like Max."

"Sometimes I don't use my head, Joel."

"Oh, you use your head, all right, and I suspect that's the problem. If you try following your heart, he'll create a whole new world for you. The Max I saw with you at the Kappa dance was a different Max—happy, proud and very possessive of you. By now, you ought to have him eating out of your hand."

Maybe that was true, but maybe it wasn't. She had to go on what she knew, and she knew she'd hurt Max. "I don't want him to be unhappy because of me."

"Then you know what to do. Be honest with him, and

forget about pride. The people who have the most pride live the loneliest lives." He wrote the address on a small yellow pad and handed it to her. "Monday morning, you'd better be grinning when you come in here."

She thanked him and, when retracing her steps, passed Max's door with a heavy heart, and for the first time in her memory, she had a feeling of hopelessness.

Leticia rose early the next morning, Saturday, so agitated that she'd been unable to sleep. But during her tempestuous night, she had at least come to an important decision. She would visit Max at his home, before she slept again, and she would go to him late in the afternoon, before it was time for him to keep a date, if he had one. She didn't believe he would be rude to her in his home. It was her only chance.

She dressed with great care in an avocado-colored, sheer woolen dress that flattered her, and at twenty minutes to six, she rang his doorbell. Her heart seemed to have stopped beating as she held her breath and waited. The door opened, and Max stared down at her. His lower lip dropped, and his eyes seemed twice their size.

"Leticia! What are you . . . ? What's going on?"

She steeled herself against the effect of his aura, something that hadn't bothered her in the past. "Hi, Max. May I come in?"

He stepped aside. "Yes. Of course you may. Excuse me for a minute. I'll . . . get presentable. Have a seat in the living room." He pointed to what she supposed was the direction.

Her glance traveled down to his feet, and she couldn't help smiling. So he didn't like to wear shoes. She strolled in the direction to which he'd pointed.

"Who's that? Ella? Max? Did someone come in? My throat feels parched."

Leticia followed the sound of the voice to the back of the house and what seemed to be a sunporch. "Oh. Hello," she said to the woman who she knew at once was Max Baldwin's mother.

Sitting in a wheelchair and wearing a burgundy velour robe, the woman smiled at her. "I hope you came to see Max. He needs a lift, and I hope you're it."

"My name's Leticia, Mrs. Baldwin, and yes, I came to see Max." She shook the woman's proffered hand and hunkered in front of her. "Did you say you had a dry throat? I can get you some water. Would you like some?"

"Oh, thank you. I would. My medicine makes me feel like somebody put a hot poker in my throat, but it's making me well, so I'm not complaining. I'm so glad you're Max's friend. You know, I don't need a nurse, but he insists that I have one, and she's in addition to Ella, his housekeeper. I know I'm blessed. Lots of men would put their mother in a nursing home, but he wouldn't even consider it.

"He gives up a lot because of me. I know he does, but I'm getting better, and I'm walking a little more every day. He's—"

Leticia interrupted her, because she didn't think it fair to learn about Max's private life from his mother. "I'll go get you some water."

"You come back now," the woman said, clinging to Leticia's hand.

"Don't worry. I will," Leticia told her, stood and kissed the woman's forehead. Figuring that the house's structure had some logic, she found the kitchen at once.

"Hi. I'm Leticia. Where are the glasses? I want to give Max's mother some water."

"I'm Ella, Miss Leticia. I'll take Mrs. Baldwin the water."

"Thanks, but I told her I'd bring it, so I'd better do it." She filled the glass and headed back to the sunporch. But as she reached the stairs, Max bounded down to the bottom step.

"Where are you going with that glass of water?"

She didn't pause. "Your mother wants some water."

"Here you are, Mrs. Baldwin." She noticed that the woman's hand shook as she reached for the glass. Leticia slipped her left arm around Jean Baldwin's shoulder and held the glass to her lips.

"Thank you. I'm nervous thinking I'll drop it. Beryl—she's my nurse—won't let me use any energy. I know she loves me, but if I don't do things, I'll never get strong."

Leticia sympathized with the woman. Being dependent somehow deprived a person of dignity. She patted the woman's hand. "You'll be as good as new, Mrs. Baldwin. It's hard, I know, but have faith and try to be patient. Next Christmas, you'll be the one who roasts the turkey."

"Lord, I hope you're right. You're a sweet girl. I want you to come see me again."

"Thank you, ma'am. I'm going to take this glass back to the kitchen." When she reached the staircase, Max stood where she'd left him.

A case of lightheadedness made him unsteady, and he leaned against the dining room doorjamb. Shaken. What he'd seen minutes earlier didn't seem real. Leticia Langley was in his house, talking with his mother as if they'd been friends for years, giving her water and kissing her cheek. And it had not been for his benefit, because Leticia couldn't see him.

Max knew why Leticia had come to his home, so he didn't ask that question. "Have a seat over there," he said to her, and pointed to a big leather chair near the fireplace. She sat down, and he pushed a leather pouf in front of the chair in which she sat and took a seat on it.

"How did you find my address?"

"I begged Joel for it. Max, I know I hurt you." She held up a hand to ward off his intended interruption. "You wouldn't take my calls, and you avoided me in the office. I was miserable Christmas Eve and Christmas Day, because I wanted to be with you. I spent Christmas Eve alone. Yes, I felt sorry for myself, but I faced some realities. No one on earth means as much to me as you do. Can you and will you forgive me? If you can't, I'll have to accept that, but I don't think I'll forgive myself."

The pain etched in her face touched him deeply, and he wanted to forgive her and let bygones be bygones. "It wasn't exactly hallelujah time for me. At first, I couldn't believe that you'd refused to spend Christmas Eve with me."

She looked straight into his eyes, and he knew how important it was to her that he believe her. "Apart from my belief in my intellectual ability, I don't have a surplus of self-confidence, Max. You could have Christmas dinner with any single woman in this town, so why me? I thought you were being nice because you felt sorry for me."

He couldn't believe she'd said it. "*What? You're kidding, I hope.*"

"No, I'm not."

"I won't lie," he said. "It hurt terribly. I had planned a wonderful evening for us, but . . . I felt as if I could hardly make it through that night."

She reached out to him, then quickly withdrew her

hand. But when she spoke, she looked into his eyes. He could almost feel *her* pain, but empathy for her did not lessen *his*.

She got to him as he had known she would. "I'll try to stop thinking about it, Leticia. Time heals all wounds."

She stood. "Thanks. I know I can't expect more. I'll tell your mother good-bye and then . . . Would you please call a taxi for me?"

She walked toward the sunporch, and he had about a minute to make up his mind. When she got back to him, he said, "I'll drive you home."

She hadn't told him that she cared for him in precisely those words, but what she'd said amounted to that. He felt a lot better; he'd lie if he said he didn't. But could he take the chance?

Max parked a few doors from the white brick building in which Leticia lived, got on the elevator and walked with her to her apartment. Holding out his hand for her key, he felt the tension in her as she fumbled in her purse. She found the key ring, looked up as she handed it to him, and the pain reflected in her eyes gripped him the way a wrench tightens around a bolt.

He opened the door, stared down at her, and his heart began to race. His hands itched to roam over her body, to bring her so close to him that air couldn't flow between them. He sucked in his breath, caressed her right cheek with the back of his left hand, turned and walked away.

It was then or never, and she knew it, but she couldn't make herself call him back. As he walked, his strides seemed less purposeful than his usual gait. She stood in the doorway and watched the man who always held his head high look down as he moved with wooden steps. Shudders plowed through her when he pushed the button for the elevator.

He half turned, glanced her way, and her head said call him. Zombielike, she took a step forward, and he turned fully toward her. The tone announcing the arrival of the elevator sounded to her like the knell of death and, of its own volition, her right hand extended toward Max. The elevator went unheeded, and the door closed. He took a step toward her, and she opened her arms. Slowly, he started to her. She moved with arms wide, and then they raced to each other. There in the hallway, she leapt into his arms and, neither moving nor speaking, they held each other.

With an arm tight around her waist, he walked with her back to her door, but he didn't seem inclined to go further. She turned into him and, as tremors possessed her body, she held him without shame while tears bathed her face.

"It's all right, sweetheart," he whispered. "Don't be unhappy. There's no reason. We're together now, and that's what matters."

She braced her hands against his chest and looked into his eyes. "But nothing has changed, Max. Nothing."

She had a feeling that at that moment, he stopped resisting, for the touch of his hands seemed sweeter and more loving.

"You're wrong, sweetheart. Everything has changed."

"But you . . . you left me."

For the first time, he smiled, and its warmth flooded his face. "You don't want me to kiss your cheek, so what was I supposed to do?"

"I will not dignify that question with an answer."

"Okay, but will you bring me scones and cookies?"

"I'll think about it."

His arms tightened around her in a fierce hug. "You're precious to me, Leticia. So precious. Don't forget that. Good night."

She told herself not to second-guess him, that he probably needed time to come to terms with their relationship. She wasn't satisfied, but for now, she was content.

Max left Leticia walking on a cloud, high from the happiness he felt. She knew enough about him to understand him and to know whether she could accept him for himself. Seeing her at his front door had been a severe shock, but if she registered that fact, she didn't show it. He marveled that in the midst of her distress, Leticia could forget about herself and show his mother consideration and kindness. He got into his Town Car and headed for Georgetown and home.

"I see you've been keeping that one to yourself," Ella said when he walked in. "I gave your mama her dinner, Mr. B, but I waited for you. Tell me about this young lady."

After washing his hands, he joined Ella at the breakfast-room table. "Leticia is . . . Look, I'm not sure I want to talk about her, Ella. I'm still working it out."

Ella cleared her throat with unnecessary vigor. "Okay, you can tell me that, but your mama will never accept it. She's ready to welcome her new daughter-in-law."

"I can't blame her; Leticia gets to you in a hurry. But tell Mother to slow down, will you?"

Ella placed her fork on the side of her plate and looked at him. "You telling me she doesn't mean anything to you?"

"No. I'm not, and for now, that's as far as I'm going with it."

"Well, at least you're eating, and that's more than you've done for the past two weeks. Whatever she did while she was here, I sure hope she keeps on doing it."

"I hope it gets well beyond that," he murmured under his breath, and he didn't doubt that it would. But when?

Chapter Twelve

Max had hardly reached his home in Georgetown before Leticia's feeling of contentment deserted her. What was wrong with her? Or more aptly, what was wrong with him? He wanted her, so why didn't he do something about it? After being in his home and seeing how he lived—with an invalid mother, a housekeeper and nurse—she understood him much better. His seeming reticence about reaching out and what appeared to be standoffishness made sense. By his own choices, his life was circumscribed in a way that most men would find unpleasant and unacceptable, but he did what he knew to be right and didn't resent doing so. Still, that didn't mean she shouldn't go after what she wanted, and since the togetherness she experienced with Max on the Covington boat, he'd had his own place in her heart, and she knew she wanted him.

She heated a frozen pizza in the microwave oven, opened a bottle of pilsner beer and ate her supper in front of the television, its dull images reminding her of her intention to get a new high-definition TV. Joel had challenged her to come to work Monday morning with a grin on her face, but at the moment, she couldn't force the semblance of one.

The telephone rang, and after debating the possible rewards of answering it, she lifted the receiver. "Hello."

"This is Max. Hi. If you're not busy tomorrow, could we spend the day together?"

She didn't hesitate. "That would be wonderful. Would you like to start with brunch at my place at about eleven? I'm reliable in the kitchen. What should I put on?"

For a minute, she thought their connection might have been severed. The blatant silence baffled her, and she considered hanging up. Then, his laughter reached her through the wire, a happy, uninhibited sound.

"Don't ask me questions like that, Leticia. Wear something comfortable," he said, his voice laden with merriment. After reflecting on it, she had to laugh, for he had let himself imagine her undressed. "I'll be there at eleven, and I'm really looking forward to our day together."

"So am I, Max."

After hanging up, she looked at her watch. Twenty minutes past nine, just time to get to the liquor store and to Dean & DeLuca's at Thirty-third and M streets. She phoned a taxi and stopped first at the liquor store, where she purchased two bottles of Moët and Chandon champagne. "If we drink all that and still need more," she said to herself, "we can drink the wine I have at home and not know the difference." At the famous gourmet shop, she bought assorted fruit, expensive because it wasn't in season; Stilton, St. André, pipo crème and imported cheddar cheeses; slices of fresh-baked Polish ham; German summer sausage; sturgeon; and black pumpernickel bread. Next door, she bought some red and yellow long stem roses and then got into a taxi singing "Yesterday," a Beatles hit of the 1960s.

She fairly skipped into her apartment. "I'm through waiting for what I want to come to me," she reminded herself. "I'm grown, and I'm going after what I want. There's no mommie or daddy to tell me I can't have him. So move over, Red Rover!"

It was well after midnight when she decided that she'd set the dining room table to her satisfaction. If she were lucky, Max Baldwin would know a lot more about her when he left her apartment that Sunday than he did when he arrived, and she'd go to work the next morning grinning from ear to ear. She took a long, leisurely bubble bath, dried off and, feeling deliciously wicked, applied Fendi body lotion from her chin to her toes and, for the first time in her life, crawled into bed nude.

After wrestling with sleeplessness and with intermittent dreams that she would have been ashamed to divulge, she tumbled out of bed at sunrise, unconsciously hoping to accelerate the arrival of eleven o'clock. She put on a pair of sneakers, blue jeans and a tight-fitting red T-shirt, looked in the mirror at a sexy siren, shrugged her shoulders, decided that she looked great and left her hair as it was, half wild. Thank God for hair extensions. She cooled the champagne, set out the cheeses to allow them to come to room temperature, looked at the kitchen clock and saw that she still had a three-hour wait.

With nothing to do, she mixed a batter for popovers, prepared a muffin ring to bake them in and set that aside. The telephone rang at a quarter of ten. "Hello," she said, and marveled that the breathless sound came from her lips.

"Hi, Leticia. This is Allison. Bill and I decided a few minutes ago to have a barbecue, and we'd love your company. If you aren't busy, we could send the car for you."

Such was life. If she'd had nothing to do, no one would have called her. "I'd love to come, Allison, but I have a brunch date, and I don't know where it will go from here. May I have a rain check?"

"Of course you may. I'm glad you have something exciting to do. Bye for now."

With nothing else to do and unable to sit still, she walked from the kitchen to the dining room and back again. At a quarter of eleven, she preheated the oven so that the popovers would bake quickly. Then she remembered that she wasn't wearing perfume and applied some Fendi in strategic places. Exhausted from rushing around doing nothing, she finally sat down and told herself to be calm. Immediately, the doorbell rang, and she thought she jumped out of her skin.

She opened the door, looked up at him and said, "Hi," with all the cool of mountain spring water. But his smile knocked her off balance, flustering her.

"May I come in?" he asked her, and they both laughed, for she had asked him that question the previous afternoon when she stood at his door. "You look good enough to eat," he said, surprising her. "I wouldn't have dreamed I'd see you in this get up."

"Thanks. I think."

He handed her a pot of lavender orchids. "They're not the color of your lovely evening dress, but as close as I could find." The earthenware pot sat in a flowered porcelain cachepot.

"They're beautiful. You deserve a kiss for this. Thanks." She put them on the table in the foyer.

"Why did you decide to invite me for brunch?" he asked as they walked toward the living room holding hands.

"Probably for the same reason you wanted us to spend the day together," she said, realized that she'd sounded smart-alecky and quickly changed the subject. "Allison called a few minutes ago and asked if I'd like to go to their barbecue, but I told her I had a brunch date."

A half smile formed around his lips. "Hmm. I imagine what she's thinking. I gave her the same excuse when she invited me to brunch as I was leaving home. They're famous for their spur of the moment invitations. You can bet she added two and two and got four."

"You don't mind?" she asked, aware that her face had a worried look.

"Why should I mind? I'm proud that you like my company well enough to spend a Sunday with me."

That sounded too formal to her. She had to get them on a deeper level of intimacy. Hmm. He'd given up plenty in order to provide for his mother, and didn't consider it a sacrifice. She'd liked his mother, and the woman was a topic with which she could deal honestly and without affectation.

"How's your mother?"

His facial expression mirrored his surprise at the question. "Very well. Thank you for asking. She told me she'd like to go to a movie, that she's tired of the house, but I don't know how to take her there."

Leticia thought for a few minutes. "If the doctor agrees that she can go, look for some movie theaters that are wheelchair accessible and hire an ambulette. They're especially for wheelchair transportation. It will take her there and come back for her at the time you specify. Buy her a big bag of popcorn, and she'll be happy."

He stared at her so intensely that she'd have sworn he wasn't listening. But he was. "I hadn't thought of that. You're amazing. My mother loves popcorn. She's getting better almost daily. I'm going to take her to a movie before it gets too cold."

Leticia patted Max's hand. She couldn't resist touching him. Her thoughts dwelled on her belief that he would take care of her precisely as he cared for his mother.

"Your mother is very sweet, Max, and she's blessed to have you."

"Thanks, but I'm the one who's blessed."

She stood and reached for his hand. "If you're ready, we can eat now." In the dining room, she handed him a bottle of champagne and a white tea towel. "Would you open this, please?"

His gaze traveled over the table. "When did you do all this? It's an elegant feast."

"Right after you called me last night."

He opened the champagne and poured some in their glasses. "You've got many sides, Leticia, and all of them appeal to me."

"Thanks. I figured if we were going to drink anything, it ought to be good. The liquor store clerk recommended it when I told him what I was planning. I wanted to share something really nice with you. I'm not going to lead you to believe I'm sophisticated and that I have a taste for champagne, sturgeon and things like that, Max. The food I was raised on didn't even go with beer. But I love nice things, and I'm learning how to choose what suits me and my pocketbook."

She noticed that he didn't eat while she spoke and that he seemed to focus on her words. He spread some pipo crème on his bread, savored it, and smiled. "This is heavenly. I listened to what you just said, and I repeat, all of your sides appeal to me. I'm not used to that level of honesty in women with whom I've had an intimate relationship. That you trust me enough to tell me that about you makes you even more precious to me."

After the meal, he helped her carry the dishes and leftovers to the kitchen, rinsed the plates and utensils before putting them in the dishwasher. He pointed to the remaining fruit, cheese and ham and sturgeon. "What do we do with this?"

"We'll eat it when we come back." She looked at the long, tapered fingers of his left hand resting against the dishwasher, and her gaze traveled to his wrist and the watch nestled among the hairs growing there. The notion that she'd love to feel his hands moving over her body took her aback. Almost absentmindedly, she lifted his hand.

"You have such beautiful hands. Your fingers look like works of art. Long, perfectly tapered, strong."

She looked up at him and couldn't control the gasp that escaped her. She had always thought his hazel brown eyes beautiful. Now, they darkened to obsidian, yet a fire blazed in them. Shaken by what she saw in them, she looked downward, but his finger at her chin urged her to look at him.

"What is it?"

"Be careful, Leticia. Unless you know what you're doing, you're standing too close to the flame."

She bristled. "From my limited experience with you, I'm sure I have nothing to worry about." He was obviously taken aback by her remark but, emboldened, she caressed his right cheek with her left hand, staring into his eyes as she did so.

He grabbed her wrist, but she didn't give quarter and flattened out her palm in a loving exploration of his face.

"What's wrong with me, Max?" she asked him, abandoning caution. "Why won't you kiss me?"

His breath quickened, and he clasped both of her shoulders and stared into her eyes, his own unsheltered and ablaze with desire. "If I kiss you, I won't want to stop. Not now. Not ever. I don't feel casual about you."

It was then or never, and she might not get another chance. "I won't want you to stop. I need you. *Max, I need you.*"

She felt her feet leave the floor, and his groan of capitulation shook her as the wind shakes a bough. She waited. And then for the first time, his mouth was on her. Giddy with happiness, she parted her lips and sucked his tongue into her mouth. His hands roamed over her, caressing, fondling and squeezing. She couldn't get enough of him. She held him tight, unable to get enough of him. Her breasts ached, and the walls of her vagina contracted.

Frustrated, she grabbed his hand and rubbed it across her breast. She didn't know what ailed it, only that it needed some kind of relief.

"What do you want, sweetheart? Tell me."

"My breasts ache."

He released one, sucked the nipple into his mouth and a scream tore out of her. Suddenly he stepped back. "I want to make love with you badly, Leticia, and I've wanted it for months, but I'm not going to start this with you unless you're willing to commit to me. We have a lot in common, but I come with baggage, and I'll have it for as long as my mother and Ella are alive."

She was ready to promise him anything if he'd get into her body, but if he wanted a commitment, so did she. She had vowed to go after what she wanted, and she wanted Max Baldwin as badly as she'd wanted a university degree. Yet, though she had only limited knowledge of male-female relations, she knew that any solid relationship had to be founded on trust and truthfulness. So she let him know her reaction to his comment.

"Those two women are not baggage, at least not in my estimation. They're the people who have loved you and cared for you and who deserve your loving care and support. A commitment? I want everything with you. Everything that you know how to give me, and I don't mean material things."

But in spite of her declaration, he didn't move. "Is there another man in your life here in Washington or anywhere else?"

She was becoming agitated, fearful that he was slipping away from her. But she remembered his thoroughness as a journalist and as a private person and told herself that he had a right to ask.

She answered truthfully. "There is no one, and there hasn't been since I was eighteen and got a poisonous lesson."

His arms enfolded her. He stroked her back and soothed her with the whispered words, "I'll never knowingly hurt you."

She snuggled as close as possible. "I love the way you hold me and the way your hands feel on my body."

His kiss was neither gentle nor tentative, and she reeled beneath the thrill of it, not caring if he knew how he made her feel. He carried her to bed. An hour later, still locked inside of her, he smiled down at her. "I love you. You fit me like my glove fits my fingers. Oh, Leticia, I love you. I don't have to ask if you're okay, because I felt it."

He loved her? This tough loner, this man who had the envy and admiration of his peers, male and female, loved her? She tightened her arms around his shoulders, hooked her legs over his thighs and cradled him to her body. "I'm fine. I feel fantastic. Thank you. Would you believe I've wasted thirteen good years when I could have been having this?"

"Hey, wait a minute. It's different with different people. Remember your first experience."

She tightened her arms around him. "I wasn't thinking about that. Will it always be like this with us?"

"The more deeply we love each other and the more we learn of each other's needs and preferences, the better it will be."

"Gosh. I can see myself becoming a sex maniac. Can we do that again? Now?"

Her question must have pleased him, for he smiled with his eyes, lips and every muscle in his face. "Give me a couple of minutes. Do you love me, Leticia?"

"Yes. Yes. I've been telling you that ever since you walked into this apartment. I told you yesterday, too. I love you, Max." His lips settled on hers, and they went on a fast trip to ecstasy.

Later, they watched the Redskins football game, read the *Washington Post* to each other, ate the remainder of the brunch, drank the second bottle of champagne, went back to bed and made love again.

"I'll never forget this day," he said when he was about to leave her at nine that night. "It's been one of my life's happiest days."

"What will I do, I mean how should I act when I see you in the morning?"

His grin seemed to her more infectious than ever. "You'd better not kiss me. There's no telling how I'd react."

"I think I'd better stay away from you," she said, kissed him and opened the door.

He gazed down at her with such seriousness that she said, "I'm for real, honey. I'm not an apparition." He held her close for a second, stroked the side of her face, and left.

Max hadn't had time to drive home before the telephone rang. Leticia answered it, although she didn't feel like sharing any part of herself with anyone other than Max. "Hello."

"I'm sure you're surprised to hear from me, but I can't get you out of my system. There should be a law against what you do to me without trying. I'll never rest till I know you're mine."

"Who is this?" she asked, although she recognized Wilson's voice at once.

"You've wounded me. You don't even recognize my voice."

"No, I don't, and I'm about to hang up. One . . . "

"It's Wilson. I need to see you."

"What's the matter? Your ego's getting a beating because you met a woman you can't take to bed? Wilson, I'm too mature to ruin my life by getting involved with a philanderer like you. If you call me again, I'll get a warrant for harassment. Good night."

She blew out a long breath and told herself to be grateful that Wilson hadn't called while Max was with her. She understood the difference between them now. Wilson's concerns centered on his own needs and satisfying them and, consequently, he had only a shallow, ephemeral interest in her. But Max had communicated a deep and enduring love to her, a strong and tenacious need of her.

"I don't know much, but enough to avoid a fast-talking

schemer," she told herself. She changed the bed linen, showered, dried off, bathed her body in lotion, put on a long green gown and got into bed. If she slept nude, she'd be out of her mind before daybreak.

When Max got home, he avoided Ella. He knew his mother would be in bed, and he didn't want to share the events of his day with anyone other than Leticia, nor did he care to lie about where he'd been and what he'd done. After all, he rarely spent an entire Sunday away from home unless he was on business. In the kitchen, he got a red apple, polished it and grabbed a handful of the shelled pecans that Ella kept on the lower shelf of the refrigerator. Feeling contented because his house was quiet and peaceful and his world was right, he loped up the stairs to his room, humming the chorus of the hit song "If" as he went.

After a long, soothing shower, he dried off and got into bed. With his hands locked behind his head, he lay on his back staring at the ceiling. Shadows created by a streetlight played on the wall, altering color from beige to gray to beige. If he had known what he knew now, would he have waited with such patience to make love with her? And how could he have held himself back? He'd made love with a few women, but he'd never touched one like Leticia. She'd had no experience past her first time, an event that was, for her, almost dehumanizing, and she hadn't felt an urgent need to try it again. Not until she loved him and wanted him.

Although he had committed to her in his heart, he hadn't dreamed that a woman could make him feel as she did. As honest and forthright in bed with him as she was in her daily life, she went wild the minute he entered her, asked for what she wanted and needed and, so important to him, she enjoyed him and was eager for him to know it.

He loved working for *The Journal*, but he didn't think it healthy for both of them to remain there as competitors. He had options, and if she agreed to marry him, he'd take one of those options.

He reached over for the mobile phone that sat on his night table and dialed her number. "Hi, sweetheart," he said when she answered. "It seems like ages since I touched you."

He loved her laughter, and she treated him to a good sprinkling of it. "It's been longer than that since I felt those wonderful, magic fingers of yours."

"Is that all you remember?"

"How short do you think my memory is, Max?" she asked him. "Even if I was senile, I wouldn't forget anything that happened to us this day."

"Thanks. Are you in bed?" She told him she was, and when he asked what she was wearing, she described the green gown, adding that she hadn't dared sleep in her usual skimpy night wear. He couldn't fathom it. "Sweetheart, you must have a reason that gets by me. Kiss me. I'd better try and sleep."

"Me, too. Good night, love."

"Good night, sweetheart," he said, hung up, turned out the light and told himself to sleep. But the way she'd moved beneath him preyed upon his mind and his libido until daylight flickered between the window blinds. He rolled out of bed, put on a robe and went down to the kitchen. After a second cup of coffee, he felt human.

"What you doing down here so early?" Ella asked him when she walked into the kitchen.

"I have a lot to do today. Here, have a cup." He went back to his room, dressed, grabbed his briefcase and got into his car. He had once before thought he was in love, but he didn't recall having lost five minutes of sleep because of it. This was certainly different, and he had to find a way to keep it between the lines.

Five minutes after Leticia got to work that morning, Joel tapped on the door and walked into her cubicle. When she heard his steps in the hall, she thought it might be Max, but doing things tentatively was hardly Max's style.

"Joel. For goodness sake, come on in," Leticia said, wondering at his manner. Suddenly laughter poured out of her. The man thought he was giving her and Max an opportunity to break apart if they'd been in a clinch. "What's the matter with you?" she asked.

He rubbed his jaw with his thumb and forefinger. "How the hell would I know what to expect? Max was in here by seven-thirty this morning. Walked in singing that song Bridget and I made out with during the seventies."

She couldn't help grinning, and she finally stopped trying. "What song was that?"

He looked hard at her. 'If a face could launch a thousand ships . . .' A real love song. I see you two had a great weekend. Right on." He gave a thumbs-up sign. "Say, Layne Barton died. I need a front page story on him for tomorrow's edition."

Here it comes, she thought. "Isn't that closer to Max's area than mine?"

"Max is busy trying to write one of the senators out of a job. Look, Leticia, you and Max are going to have to compete and not kill each other. I'm not going to worry about whose area it is, just who I think can do the best job on it. If you're really in love, you'll work it out."

She glared at her boss. "I'm going to tell him you said that. Anyway, you're merely surmising, so please don't mention it to anyone else here."

"If I was stupid, I wouldn't have had this job for fourteen years. I'm glad it's going well, kid. You're better looking when you're smiling."

"Thanks, Joel."

At four o'clock, the office messenger delivered to her a note in the interoffice mail. "I've gotten through the day, sweetheart, but I'm certain I can't make it through the night without seeing you. Love, M."

She took out her cell phone and dialed his cell number. "Want to meet somewhere? I didn't tell Willa not to prepare dinner for me, so I have to go home."

"So do I. Let's have a glass of wine."

"Great. How about the Spy Lounge?"

"Works for me. I'll meet you there at a quarter of five. Why not call a taxi now, and it will be outside when you get downstairs."

"Will do. Bye for now."

"Bye. Love me?"

"Does the sun set in the west?" She hung up, took the obituary she'd written to Joel and went to the women's room to freshen up. In the six months that she'd worked at *The Journal*, she hadn't once combed her hair or applied lipstick in the ladies room. Nor had she worried about the tidiness of her clothing.

"I refuse to believe I'm doing this because I'm frivolous," she told herself. "But he'll show up looking like it's eight o'clock in the morning, and every woman he passes will be ready to fall down and ask him what he wants. So I'm combing my damned hair."

Her cell phone buzzed and she saw Kenyetta's number in the caller ID screen. This was not the time to start a conversation with her cousin, so she ignored the call.

When she stepped into Spy Lounge, Max stood immediately and came to meet her.

"I've waited all day for this," he said, kissed her quickly on the lips and led her back to their table.

She reached for his hand. "I hope you sleep well tonight."

"Why do you think I didn't sleep well last night?"

"Because Joel said you were here at seven-thirty, and he seemed to think I had something to do with it. If he only knew, he'd blow a gasket."

"Not so," Max said. "I'm positive that he'd be extremely happy. I may leave *The Journal*."

"What did you say? Don't make jokes, Max."

"If things between us go the way I hope, I'll leave. I have options, but I stay at *The Journal* because of Joel; he doesn't bother me, and anybody there with a smidgen of authority knows not to exercise it with me."

"Then why leave?"

"For you and me, it may be for the best. I'm a lousy actor, and I don't like pretense. Understand?"

Indeed she did. She made a note to return Kenyetta's call after she got home.

"This takes some serious discipline," Max said to Leticia when he left her at her apartment door a little more than an hour later.

"What happens if discipline doesn't work?" she asked him, mostly to understand his attitude about the intimate aspect of their relationship.

Both of his eyebrows shot up, his eyes widened as if he was surprised, and then he grinned. "Hell, in that case, I expect we'd give in to it and enjoy each other." He kissed her quickly and turned to leave.

She stopped him with a hand on his right arm. "That didn't quite do it for me."

His smile barely comforted her, because he laid his shoulders back as he did so. "I know my limits. Good night, love."

"And I guess I'd better learn mine," she said, sniffed the odor of food coming from the kitchen and smiled. Life was good. She went to her room, hung up her coat, kicked off her shoes and dialed Kenyetta's number. After about a dozen rings, she hung up.

However, Kenyetta was at home. Instead of answering the phone, she opened her door and saw Reggie standing there. "Well, what do you know, the dead are walking again. What do you want?"

He walked past her into the apartment. "For heaven's sake, cut the drama. You know I can stay away from you only so long." He said it as if he were her victim. "I need you. Come here to me, babe?"

How sweet it was. Send her an invitation to his wedding, addressed in his own handwriting, would he? "What you need me for? Your fiancée don't know how to put it down, or she ain't got nothing to put down? Which is it?"

"Aw, lighten up, babe. There isn't a woman out there who can equal you."

She narrowed her eyes, fastened her knuckles to her hips and looked him up and down. "I see, so you need a piece, huh?"

"I'm going crazy for you, babe." He started toward her, but she stepped back. "What the hell is this? You my woman, and you know you want me."

Her head began to pound, perspiration wet her

undergarments and it seemed as if a fog had descended between them. She could almost feel her nostrils flare. She found her breath and her voice. "You saying I want you? Man, in the five years you been coming here to dump your junk, I haven't once wanted you. I put up with you because you said you were going to divorce Veronica so we could get married, and I wanted that big house you live in. But, buster, you ain't shit in bed.

"You don't know a woman from a pregnant cat. I cheated on you and went to bed with a man who rocked me clear out of my senses. He screwed me so good that I didn't even know my name. In five years, you didn't come close to that. I don't need you, and I want you to get your useless ass out of my apartment and don't come back here. You the biggest mistake ever walked this earth. Go on, get out of here."

"Who's gonna make me?"

She whirled around, rushed to the foyer and pressed the intercom, and since he didn't know it was there, he didn't follow her. "Send the guard up here and hurry," she said in a low voice to the doorman, and unlocked the door.

"Were you talking to someone?"

"Yeah. I was talking to the building guard. I think he can make you leave. How'd you get past the doorman?"

"He was talking to a woman. You didn't call a guard to put me out."

"When did you ever know me to lie?"

The doorbell rang. "Come in," she said as loudly as she could.

A man wearing a guard's uniform, badge and cap, and looking like a linebacker for the New York Giants football team, walked in, stopped, spread his legs and put his hands on his hips. "What's the problem here?"

"I told this man to leave. He asked me who was gonna make him leave, so I called for you."

"You want him arrested?" She shook her head. "Let's go, buddy, and be sure I don't see your face on this city block again. Good night, miss."

Kenyetta dropped down on the sofa in her living room, the very spot where Reggie had taken her more times than she could count and always without thought or consideration of her sexual needs. She spread her arms wide, kicked up her heels and laughed at the top of her voice. She'd given Reginald Parrish his comeuppance, and she'd brought Mister Macho down in the presence of another macho man.

How sweet it was! Reggie was history, and if she'd learned anything from the debacle she'd made of her life, it was that Reggie and Wilson were cut from the same cloth. Users, both of them. One paid his way, and the other didn't, but both left you holding the bag. Good riddance to them!

Within minutes, her euphoria dissipated. What was she going to do now? She'd messed up with Leticia, and her cousin no longer turned to her for things. She hadn't bothered to make friends with the women teachers at school. Maybe she'd go back to New Orleans, where she had lots of relatives. She started to the kitchen for a soft drink, but stopped before she got there. New Orleans seemed like a good idea, and she could easily get a job teaching there, but she remembered the weather. She'd left there because she hated the interminable heat and humidity. But it didn't make sense to stay in Washington, which had the highest ratio of women to men in the entire country.

She went to her computer, accessed the Internet and began looking for towns that had an unusually high ratio of men to women. She was already over thirty, she reasoned, and her chances for marriage and starting a family were slim at best, but in Washington, they were practically nil. By midnight, she'd listed six towns from which to choose.

After mulling it over, she sat back, tired but happy. "Amarillo, Texas, here I come." She would discover that most of the men would be transients, waiting for the next rodeo.

Chapter Thirteen

Leticia couldn't have been more surprised when Max phoned her from his office to say that he'd engaged an ambulette to take his mother to see an old and very funny movie, "The Russians Are Coming, the Russians Are Coming."

"She was so excited when I told her that I felt guilty for not having taken her earlier. We're going to the five-thirty showing today, and I wanted you to know that I'll be leaving early."

"Thanks for letting me know. Next time you take her, uh . . . never mind."

"What were you going to say? I want to know."

"I was . . . maybe I could go, too."

"Would you like to go with us this afternoon? You can meet us at the theater, and you wouldn't have to leave work early."

"I'd love that. You don't think I'm intruding? I mean, you don't mind my coming along?"

"Mind? Knowing that you want to gives me a really good feeling, Leticia. I . . . I sense that you're there for me, and that's . . . important to me." He gave her the name and address of the theater.

"I'll be there at five-thirty." She hung up with a sense of wonder. Max was the most private person she knew. Even when they talked about their lives as they sat alone on Bill Covington's boat, he hadn't mentioned his mother, her illness and its influence upon the way he lived. Yet, he agreed that she could go to the movies with him when he took his mother on an outing that had to be very special to both of them. Could she let herself believe that Max saw her as a fixture in his life then and in the future?

She reached the theater minutes before the ambulette arrived bringing Max and Jean Baldwin. The ambulette driver pushed Jean's wheelchair down a temporary ramp where Max waited. "I'll be back here at eight o'clock," the driver said. "If I don't see you, I'll call you on your cell phone."

With one hand on the wheelchair and the other arm around her, Max greeted Leticia with a kiss on her mouth. "Mother, I'm sure you remember Leticia."

"I sure do," Jean replied, and opened both arms to Leticia, who bent and kissed her cheek.

"You look wonderful," Leticia said. "Didn't I tell you that next Christmas you would roast the turkey?"

"Yes, you did, and I'm working toward that."

Max bought two bags of popcorn. "Who's going to eat all that?" Leticia asked him.

"I'll eat one, and you and Max can eat the other one," Jean replied. They sat in the section for wheelchair families, but Jean insisted on sitting in a regular seat. The movie began, and Leticia immersed herself in it. The story was of a Russian submarine and its crew grounded off Cape Cod during the height of the cold war. The hilarious reaction of some of the local citizens brought loud and prolonged laughter from the audience. Leticia and Jean laughed until tears streamed down their faces, and by the movie's end, Jean had no popcorn left. On the way out, Max bought another bag for her to carry home.

"We have time for a drink or something before the ambulette arrives," he told them, and to Leticia, he said, "You ride back with us, and I'll drive you home."

She looked at Jean. "Looks like he can be a little bossy."

"I don't agree," Jean said. "In my experience, he can be very bossy. But I couldn't ask for a better son."

"I'm not here," Max said, clearly unperturbed about the gist of the conversation. "Talk about me all you want."

Two doors from the theater, he stopped at a coffee shop. "Would you like a soft drink or coffee? If we'd had dinner, I'd suggest a dessert, but—"

"Whatever your mom likes," Leticia said.

"Lemonade's fine with me. Max isn't going to let me have any more popcorn before dinner, and I know I shouldn't eat more, but that was such a treat. Last week after I met you, Leticia, I started reading your column and your reports. You're very good."

Leticia had a feeling that Jean Baldwin was seeking ways to let her know that she approved of her friendship with Max and to let Max know it without seeming to meddle. And it made sense, because anyone who knew Max at all would realize that he wouldn't tolerate interference in his private affairs. They spent half an hour in the dainty little shop while Jean enjoyed a glass of lemonade and Max and Leticia drank coffee.

"I don't know when I enjoyed anything so much. A

change of scenery has done me a lot of good. I'd almost forgotten what the world looked like away from the house and the back deck." She patted Max's hand. "And thank you for bringing Leticia. You two take me out again when you have time."

Leticia glanced at Max, hoping to discern his reaction to his mother's having included her in his future and letting him know that she wanted to see Leticia again. But he didn't react. Not that his cool and impassive expression was proof that he hadn't reacted. She'd learned that Max excelled at protecting his thoughts and ideas, and that he guarded his feelings even more zealously.

They left Jean at home bubbling over with her report to Ella on her first outing in eighteen months. Leticia was soon deep in thought as to whether she would invite Max to spend the evening with her. She knew where it would lead, and she wasn't sure it was the right thing to do if she was to have a permanent relationship with him. He spared her the torture of a decision. At her door, he opened it with her key and walked in with her.

"This excursion did wonders for my mother. She enjoys talking about politics and current events, but has to spend the day talking with Beryl and Ella, whose conversations always center on food and health. Ever since she met you, she discusses with me what you write as well as what I write. She's very proud that I know you. I'm glad you wanted to come with us."

"Gee. I didn't imagine anything like that. I just thought I'd like to see her again, and I didn't want to invite myself to your home lest you decide that was a habit of mine."

"She asked me if you were going with us, and I wanted to ask you, but I didn't know how you'd take it." He glanced at his watch. "I expect Ella has given her sup-

per, and I'd like to get back before she goes to bed, because she'll have a lot to say to me, and she'll be frustrated
if she can't say it."

With his arms around her, he looked into her eyes.
"Do you still love me?"

She closed one eye slowly and opened it in a long, seductive wink. "Did you do anything bad since I last told
you that you occupy a spot deep in my heart? Huh?"

His lips seared hers until tremors raced through her.
Then, his smile, warm and wicked, lit up her world.
"I'm always good, at least by my definition. Stay sweet."
He opened the door, winked at her and left.

She recalled his having said that he knew his limit,
and that was a good thing, because she had no idea
what her limit was. She did know that she was happy,
but as she thought of it and the fact that this happiness
derived from one person, fear pervaded her.

She told herself to have faith, but having faith in people hadn't netted her much. Her father was the only
person she'd been able to count on. She would never
trust or care much for Kenyetta again. Mark was true,
but he hadn't been tried, and the same went for Max.
She loved him, and she trusted him, but he was human.

Willa had gone home, and Leticia almost enjoyed
eating dinner alone. After tidying the kitchen, she
spent an hour reworking her column and then got
ready for bed. It had been a long time since she'd felt
physically tired, but she was, and she knew it stemmed
from another rare condition. Stress. She shook it off,
berating herself for having so little faith in Max and
what she meant to him.

"It's me, and what I think about me," she said aloud.
"When will I ever feel secure in my relationships with
people? I thought I'd made progress when I told Max
that I wanted him and needed him, but in spite of the

way he treats me, I doubt him . . . or maybe I doubt myself."

She answered the phone after its first ring, eager for the assurance that the sound of his voice would bring her. "Was your mother still up?" she asked after they greeted each other.

"She was, and she had plenty to say. Strangely, she didn't ask me one question about you, and when I commented on that, she had me know that she's a good judge of people, she's not interested in class and status, that she's seen enough and doesn't need me to make up her mind for her. She said she wants to put the wheelchair away, except when she has to go someplace that's too far to walk. She also wants to start going to church. I'm glad, Leticia, and I have you to thank for this change in her."

"She's got all of her mental faculties. Does she know how to use a computer?"

"Yes, she does. She used one before she got sick."

"Then why not get her another one with access to the Internet, so that she can get back into the environment of active people?"

"You're a blessing to me, Leticia, and not just for this reason. I'll get a computer tomorrow. That's precisely what she needs. She'll be less dependent on Beryl and Ella. What will we do this weekend?"

"I hadn't thought of anything," she said, and wondered why she hadn't. She loved him, so why was she being so casual about him?

"Hmm. I would have thought you were looking forward to our being together. I had some plans for last Sunday that—"

"Hold on. We spent most of last Sunday in bed. I wouldn't suggest that as a regular routine."

"Why the hell not? It beat any Sunday I'd ever spent."

"Same here, but if we do that every Sunday, won't it become commonplace?"

"For you, maybe. You telling me you might get tired of making love with me?"

"If you're going to put words in my mouth, put some in there that make sense."

"Okay. What can we do Sunday? You want to start with brunch at your place?" he asked in a droll attempt at humor. It would serve him right if she said yes.

"Unless you can think of something better," she replied, and waited for his reaction. Any man worth his salt would take that comment and run with it. In that respect, Max proved unexceptional.

"You're kidding," he said. "If I could think of anything better, I'd be doing it right now. Sunday brunch, and I'll bring the food and drink. I love you, woman."

"I love you, too," she said. After they hung up, she wondered why, minutes before he called her, she'd been so wary of their relationship.

At work the next morning, she found in her mailbox letters from Allison and from Margo Overstreet, president of Windmills, the service club she'd joined. Both asked if she would chair a committee to raise funds for the care of children whose mothers were incarcerated. She agreed, and after days of mulling it over, she remembered Max's dream of playing in a jazz combo. For the first time since the two had become lovers, she went to his office, entered and left the door ajar.

"Hi. What's up?" he asked her, pointing to a chair.

"I have a proposition for you." She told him about Windmills, and its fund-raising project. "It occurred to me that you could help us out and, at the same time, realize one of your dreams."

He dropped the pen he'd been tapping on the desk and sat forward. "Which dream?"

"You have friends who love to play jazz. Form a combo and play on the weekends. If you play for charity, there won't be any implication with regard to income tax, and you'll help some needy children. One of our members is a booking agent. She'd set up your dates. Since you'd be doing it for charity, there'd be no reflection on your status as a journalist. What do you say?"

"When do I start? I can get three guys who'll do it without charge to your club, just because they're longing for the opportunity to play to an audience. I'll have to put up with Wilson, but I can handle him. He's a first-class bass fiddle player."

"Don't worry about Wilson," she said. "He won't get out of line. I've seen to that." Both of his eyebrows shot up, but she pretended not to notice. "What will we call the band?"

"How does the Capitol Jazz Quartet sound?"

"Okay," she said, "But I like Baldwin's Jazz Quartet."

He ran his fingers over his hair, and she could see that he didn't much like the idea. "Tell you what. I'll ask the guys what they think and let you know later." She rose to leave. "You're an angel. This is really a dream come true. Ella's going to do her hallelujah thing when I tell her about this. Want to meet for coffee before going home? I feel like suggesting a drink, but I have to drive."

"Okay. Same place. Love ya." She blew him a kiss.

"Sunday can't come fast enough," she heard him say as she left.

Max very rarely let anything get between him and his work, but with a deadline facing him, he made three phone calls. An hour later, he phoned Bill Covington, told him about Leticia's idea and asked him if he'd sit in with his jazz combo occasionally. "It's for charity, man. Allison can tell you about it. We're raising money for her club."

"All right," Bill said. "I've got some Sunday nights free, and I can join you then. I'm sorry this didn't come up before the holidays. We could have earned a ton of money for those kids," Bill added. "Uh . . . by the way, how was brunch last Sunday, if you don't mind my asking?"

"Brunch? You mean . . . We're getting along fine, thanks. Give my regards to Allison." So the Covingtons had put two and two together and added it up correctly. All right. He had nothing to hide, but at the same time, he didn't intend to discuss Leticia and their relationship with any person other than Leticia. He hadn't meant to dust Bill off, but he had, and he didn't much care. Since the Kappa dance, he'd felt proprietary about Leticia. He knew he didn't own her, but he wouldn't care if other men thought he did, and if Wilson failed to recognize whatever bounds Leticia had established, the man would hear it from him.

By the time he got home that evening, he had Wilson for bass fiddle, Jack Barns for piano and Jack's brother, Timothy, for bass guitar. He himself would play lead guitar, except when Bill Covington sat in with them, and then he would play the Dobro. Two weeks later, he looked over the dates and locales that Nina Hill had set for the combo, from mid-January through February, and said to himself, "Damn! I could make a living doing this." But journalism was his first love and he was in it to stay.

"I'd better let Joel in on this jazz venture," he told Leticia when they met for lunch at the S & W Café a couple of days later. "Not that I'm planning to ask his permission. What I do any day before eight-thirty and after four-thirty and on weekends is none of his business. But Joel can be difficult when he gets a surprise that isn't to his liking."

"Besides," Leticia said, "we can use the publicity, and I plan to do a column on the tour and its benefit for Windmills. What do you think?"

"I can't wait to see what you'll say about my prowess as a musician, and I tell you right now, your praise had better equal what you say about my writing," he joked.

"You can't compare musical notes with words and phrases."

"If you're writing about your man, you damn sure can."

"You are not my man."

"The hell you say. Tell me that when I take you home." He'd see how long she held out.

She felt like baiting him, but she wasn't sure about the extent of his seriousness. Was he her man? What she was certain of was his tendency to hurt easily and to draw a curtain between them when that happened. He hadn't done that since they became intimate, but she had been careful not to precipitate it.

"If I say it, what'll you do?"

"I'll put you in your bed and make love to you until you scream uncle."

"Big deal! In my estimation and, especially in my experience, that is definitely not punishment. Anyway, you'd have to bribe Willa to leave work early."

"And you think I wouldn't do that?"

"She's loyal to me."

"But she likes me, and she wants me to have you for myself."

That made Leticia smile. "I guess you got in the last

word on that subject," she said. "When you play at places like the Rooftop and Blues Alley, we could take your mother. Do you think she'd like it? It would be nice if she saw you perform at least once."

"She'd be ecstatic, and so would Ella. That's a great idea. I'll see if I can arrange it." His gaze darkened as he fixed it on her. What she saw in his eyes was not desire, and she wished, not for the first time, that she could read his thoughts.

It was time she returned some invitations, but she didn't want to serve an ordinary sit-down dinner. She mentioned it to Willa. "It's not too cold for me to roast a couple of young pigs on spits out there in the barbecue pit, and we could have a great indoor barbecue," Willa said. "You never used that fireplace, but we could build a fire, and have a great buffet. It wouldn't be too much work, because I'd roast the pigs the day before and heat 'em in the oven. You give me carte blanche, ma'am, and I'll make you proud. For something like this, ten or twelve is a good number." She looked at Leticia with slightly sheltered eyes. "I sure hope you planning to invite Mr. Baldwin."

"Not to worry, Willa. He's at the top of my list." She went to the computer and checked the weather forecast, decided that a week's notice would have to suffice, since Max would be touring on subsequent weekends, and made out her list of invitees.

"I've got twelve with myself and Max Baldwin, Willa, and I have to tell you that not even in my dreams did I imagine I'd ever invite Broderick Nettleson to my home. To me he's like Walter Cronkite."

"Well, if he invited you, you can sure ask him back. You have nice things, and don't you worry a bit. It'll be flawless."

The day arrived for the first party she'd ever given. Willa had planned it so that they served themselves and then sat at the table, where she'd put proper place settings and name plates. Max arrived at a quarter of seven for the seven-thirty affair, and she couldn't have been happier to see him. He had a dozen red and yellow roses, six red and eight bottles of chilled white wine, and a bottle each of aged scotch whiskey, bourbon, vodka and VSOP cognac.

She stared at his burden. "You mean twelve people will drink this? I'm only good for one glass of wine."

"Willa's serving a substantial meal, so they'll drink a lot. The table is beautiful, and the aroma when I walked into this apartment is making me very hungry. Come in here." He pointed to the living room. "I want to tell you something. You're queen of this castle, and nobody who comes in here outranks you socially or professionally. Do you understand?"

"I know, but—"

"No *buts*. You're as fine a writer as Nettleson, and a better one than Allison Wade Covington, and I don't want you to forget it." His arms enveloped her, and his lips were sweet and gentle on hers. "You're also far more beautiful than either of them."

She laughed because he made her happy, and because she realized that he understood her. "You're precisely the tonic I've needed all my life."

His smile disappeared as quickly as light vanishes when one switches off a light bulb, and she knew he'd never been more serious. "I don't want you to say such things to me unless you mean them with all your heart."

"I meant that with all my heart."

He looked down at the Royal Bokara carpet that she'd bought a few days earlier and asked her, "Do I have the right to open the wine bottles and to serve the wine and liquor to your guests? If I do that, we're making a statement. You understand?"

"You have the right, and I'm happy that you want to do it, because I'm proud that you love me and I don't care who knows it."

He looked hard at her then. "You'll also be telling them that we're intimate, and that I'm special to you."

"I don't know why you love me, of all the women you meet and know, but I thank God that he brought us together, and I want everybody to know it."

"All right. I just wanted to be sure," he said, and it seemed to her that he'd just released a heavy burden.

Joel and his wife, Bridget, arrived first. "Thank goodness," Leticia said to herself when she opened the door. To her guests, she said, "Welcome and come on in. With the threat of a blizzard, I wouldn't have been surprised if no one came."

"My, what a cozy place," Beverly said. "Joel raves so much about your talents as a writer and your professionalism that I guess I didn't expect such a feminine setting."

"I'm learning," she said, and turned to Max. "I'd better see if Willa needs any help. I'll be right back."

"What would you like to drink?" she heard Max ask them.

"Scotch over ice," Joel said. "I want to see how the kitchen looks." Leticia heard him and knew that he had something to say to her.

Joel caught her at the kitchen door. "You're a smart woman. No man wants to be kept in the closet, so to speak. If you're proud of him, let him and everybody else know it."

She couldn't help smiling at Joel, who'd assumed

the role of her surrogate father. "You said he was special, and he is, at least to me."

"Right on, Leticia. This is a very attractive apartment. It's nice to know this other side of you."

"Thanks, Joel, and thanks for helping me out when I thought I'd lost everything."

"Is that the doorbell?" Joel asked her.

"Max can answer it. If they raise an eyebrow, he can always tell them that he doesn't live here."

"Yeah? I can just see Max explaining his private business to somebody. He'd get his back up if it was the angel Gabriel asking him why he opened your door."

"He's not that tough, Joel."

"Not to you, maybe, but that brother takes no tea for the fever. Trust me. I'd better go back there and get my drink before he dumps it out."

If Joel's statements were a warning that Max didn't tolerate foolishness, she didn't mind. With her, he was gentle and sweet, and that's what she needed from him. She went back to the living room as Max opened the door for Broderick and Carolyn Nettleson. Leticia greeted them and almost at once, her six other guests arrived.

Max embraced Bill Covington and kissed Allison's cheek, and that told her who, among the group present, he considered his real friends. "I presume that everyone here knows everyone," he said, and began serving them drinks of their choice.

The esteemed Broderick Nettleson asked for bourbon and water. When Max gave it to him, Leticia heard Broderick say, "Every piece Leticia writes is better than the last one, and she started out pretty high." He raised his glass to Max. "She's got good feminine taste, too. Way to go, man."

Leticia could hardly believe that Max put the bottle

he'd been holding on the buffet, picked up a glass, dribbled some wine in it and accepted Broderick's toast. "Thank you," Max said. "I appreciate your sentiments."

Willa and Leticia set the food on the buffet, except for one of the pigs, which Willa put in the center of the dining room table with an apple in its mouth and hot-spiced peaches and fluted mushrooms around it, on a bed of curly parsley. On the buffet she also put shredded pork from the other roasted pig with barbecue sauce, garlic roasted potatoes, steamed asparagus, green beans in almond butter sauce, a mesclun-raspberry salad, deviled shrimp, biscuits and jalapeño corn bread.

After they helped themselves and sat at the table according to their place cards, Willa came to the table and Leticia introduced her to the guests. They all toasted to her. "I don't know how many atheists we have here," Willa said, "but when you in Rome . . . " She let the thought hang. "Here, we say grace." She said it and went back to the kitchen.

Leticia looked at Max, facing her in his seat at the head of her table, and knew a moment of emotional turmoil, which she had to fight in order to control tears. She was happy, proud, and nervous all at once. As if he knew how she felt, he smiled and gave her the thumbs-up sign.

"It's not for nothing that I love him," she told herself, and settled down to enjoy the evening.

"Red wine or white?" Max asked as he served the wine. "Either is good with pork."

Leticia smiled inwardly. She had a party with interesting, accomplished guests, and she had a man who stood tall among them and who wanted it known that he was hers. *You've come a long way, baby. You still have a ways to go, but it's going to be all right. He's happy doing this, and I'm happy that he's mine.*

"I'm looking at this pig on the table," Paul Faison said, "and I can almost taste that crisp, cracking skin."

"He's meant to be eaten tonight," Leticia said. She looked at Max.

"I'll carve it," Max said, "but I'd better take it over to the sideboard. I don't mind being judged on my writing skills, but carving pigs, turkeys, geese, wood or marble isn't my forte." He took the platter and the carving knife and fork over to the sideboard, sliced the meat and returned with it neatly carved and mostly holding its shape.

"You were a butcher in your other life," Bill Covington said. "Right?"

"No, but I've worked at just about every other kind of job you can name."

They served themselves seconds, and some of the men filled their plate a third time. "This food is wonderful," Allison said to a chorus of amens. Max and Leticia helped Willa clear the table, and Willa served each of them a bowl of flaming peach cobbler.

"What kind of liquor did you put on this?" Lynn Weddington asked her.

"Cognac. For desserts, that's the only kind of liquor I use," Willa said.

"You must know something," Allison said, "because this is the best peach cobbler I ever tasted. Congratulations on a fabulous meal." Willa went back to the kitchen with applause sounding in her ears.

"If you'd like coffee and liqueurs, we'll have some in the living room," Leticia said, attempting without success to move her chair back. Immediately, Max was at her elbow and helped her up.

"I'm not used to having two glasses of wine," she whispered to him.

As if he'd been waiting for the chance, he slipped

an arm around her waist. "Sit in a comfortable chair. I'll serve the liqueurs and Willa can take care of the coffee."

"It's time she went home."

"Not to worry, sweetheart. I'll call a taxi for her."

They moved into the living room. Allison wanted to know if Willa had a sister who cooked as she did; Carolyn wanted the recipe for jalapeño corn bread; and Paul Faison asked if he and Darlene could take their dinner with Leticia on a daily basis. Carolyn got the recipe.

"It's beginning to snow," Willa told them, "and the weatherman said the wind's forty miles an hour."

"Get ready to leave," Max told her, and telephoned a limousine company of which he was co-owner. "It will be here in ten minutes, Willa, and the fare and tip are paid."

Max wanted to phone Ella and put her at ease, but he suspected that she was in bed, and he didn't want to disturb her. He wanted to spend some time with Leticia, but he couldn't risk being away from Ella and his mother during a blizzard when they could lose power or a pipe could burst, or some other unpleasant thing could happen.

Leticia walked up to him and placed a hand on his arm. "Are all of your windows closed? What about your garage door? I mean do you think your house is okay? A forty-mile-an-hour wind can do a lot of damage."

"I think the house is fine, but I don't know how strong this storm will be or how long it will last. You have the protection of a doorman and the men who work in this building, but if my house loses power, Ella and my mother won't know what to do. I had wanted very badly to be here with you for a while longer, but my gut feeling is that I'd better go home."

"Excuse me, but the taxi is here, Mr. Baldwin," Willa said.

Leticia hugged her housekeeper. "Thank you for a wonderful evening, Willa," Leticia said.

"You're welcome, ma'am. We can do this anytime you feel like it. I was in my element. Good night."

Max walked with her to the taxi, paid the driver and gave him Willa's address. "It was a great party. Good night."

When the guests had left, he put an arm around Leticia. "I was so proud of you. This party beat every one that I've attended at the home of any of your guests. It was perfect."

"You made it perfect, Max. I don't know a thing about drinks. You brought the wine, the liquor and the liqueurs, and served it so elegantly. I was surprised that you knew how to slice a suckling pig. When did you learn that?"

With his head back, he treated her to a hearty laugh. "I never saw one of those little rascals before tonight. I looked at it and said, 'What the hell? These other guys don't know how to carve it either,' and I happened to do it right." A serious look banished his laughing mood. "I wanted us to be together tonight, but the snow's very thick out there. I'd better go."

She wanted to tell him that he could spend the night, but she realized that she wasn't ready to take that step. "I'm sorry," she said. "It would have been wonderful."

His eyes twinkled with merriment. "Sunday? For the next six weeks, I'll be busy on weekends with the combo."

"Not all day, you won't." His kiss, warm and sweet, lacked the fire that she expected, but she remembered about his limit and didn't press. "Drive carefully, darling. You'll be carrying precious cargo."

* * *

Five minutes after she got to work Monday, Joel gave her a shock. "That was one helluva dinner party you pulled off Saturday night. I haven't enjoyed anything so much in ages, and we have a really good cook. The menu, wine, liquor, everything was perfect."

"Thanks, Joel. I'm so glad you enjoyed it." He didn't come to her office before he got coffee to tell her he enjoyed the food he ate at her house. "Are you about to drop a bomb?" she asked him, in case he needed the courage to say it.

"Well, I wouldn't say *that*. Max will be gigging for the next few weekends, so I want you to cover the prime minister's visit to the States, beginning with his stop at the White House and the state reception."

She jumped up from the desk. "Are you serious? That's any reporter's dream, and you know Max would ordinarily get that assignment. Are you trying to break us up? I don't want it. I don't want to be the reason why he's hurt."

"Don't be so noble, Leticia. He certainly wouldn't turn it down if I offered it and it normally belonged to you."

"How do you know, Joel, and how on earth can you be so cynical? One minute, I'm so happy I'm floating on air, and the next, you hand me this. You go tell him you're asking me to take this assignment, and come back and tell me what he said."

Joel stared at her, his expression decidedly less than friendly. "All right. I will."

When Leticia's cubicle door swung open, she didn't look up. "Good morning, Max. Who are you angry with? Joel or me?"

"The whole bloody world. What's he trying to do, drive a wedge between us? He led me to believe that he didn't have a problem with our relationship. Now—"

"He doesn't have a problem with it, Max. He's being Joel. There's a story, and he wants one of us to cover it. I declined."

He couldn't imagine a reporter declining a plum like that one. "Hell, you can't do that. Ever since I was in high school, I wanted to perform in a jazz band, and now I have the chance, so—"

"I turned it down, because it's not my job. You'd like to cover the prime minister while he's here, wouldn't you?"

"Of course I would. It's a job that ordinarily falls to me." He ran his fingers over his hair and then slammed his right fist into the palm of his left hand. "Look, I don't want to talk about this anymore."

"You can cancel the band's appointments."

"I don't want to cancel them. Dammit, I want to play those dates." He whirled around and left without saying another word. He was damned if he did and damned if he didn't. What a mess! He'd love to wring Joel's neck. Oh, what the heck! It was nobody's fault. He couldn't be in two places at once, and he wanted both jobs. He could accept it, but that wasn't what was really eating him. He'd broken one of his cardinal rules: he'd become intimately involved with a colleague, one who'd become his chief competitor.

He went back to his office and called Bob Weddington. "This is Max Baldwin," he said when Weddington's secretary put the call through.

"How's it going, Max? You didn't call to chat. What's up?"

"I may decide to make a move, and I'm checking my options. Did you fill that position of editor in chief?"

"Man, I'm flabbergasted. No, I haven't. I thought you were Joel's right-hand man."

"I don't know about that, but I don't have any complaints about Joel. This is about me. I am not comfortable competing with Leticia, and I want to give my relationship with her every chance. I hope you'll keep that in confidence."

"Of course. I certainly don't blame you for that. She's a gifted writer and a striking woman. I've liked what I've seen of her, and so has Lynn. If you decide to move, just call. It's here for you."

"Thanks." After he hung up, he sat with his head down and his hands covering his face. *The Journal* was home. He'd had numerous offers to join other papers, at least two of which were world renowned. But he hadn't moved, because he was happy where he was. Joel and the publisher appreciated him and his work, paid him very well and treated him as if he were a sacred cow. Neither Joel nor the copy editor touched his work, and if he moved, he'd demand those terms. Any first-rate paper in the country would give him a job and pay him well. But would he be happy if he left the place he'd loved and supported for the last nine years of his life? One thing was incontestable: he'd rather give up the job than lose Leticia, but he wasn't sure what he'd actually do. The decision might not be his. She had a temper and a strong will, and she wouldn't be a pushover for anybody.

Leticia knew she could interview the prime minister and report on his activities as well as any reporter extant, including Max, but she wanted to give her relationship with Max a chance. Nonetheless, she didn't feel comfortable turning down the best job her editor could have offered her. She had no intention of being a second banana of a reporter. She was good at what she did, and she deserved the credit for it. Still, she knew that readers of *The Journal* would wonder why Max didn't write that story. When it came to sensitive issues, politics and matters of national interest, they expected Max's byline. They trusted him, and he deserved it, but . . .

She got up from her desk, walked over to the window and looked down on Thomas Circle, something she did when frustrated, angry or sad. "This won't do," she said to herself. "I have to get my work done." She went back to her desk, telephoned Mark and talked with him about her dilemma.

"If you two break up over this, you didn't have enough going for you, Leticia. I'd be furious if my girl got a job that I wanted, and I'd probably take it out on her, although I'd later regret it. That man knows he's an ace, he knows the newspaper business, and he knows that if he can't or won't do a job, his editor will give it to another reporter. So why not you? If you turn it down, will you blame him or resent him?"

"Thanks, Mark. I said I wouldn't do it, but that was a stupid knee-jerk reaction. I love Max, but I'm a reporter. He's at the top, and I have yet to get there. I'll keep in touch."

"Right on. You'll upset him, but if he loves you, that won't keep him away from you."

She hung up and phoned Max. "Have you given Joel your decision? I mean, are you going to cover the PM?"

"No, I'm not, and I've told Joel as much. I gave my word to Windmills and to my buddies, and I do not renege on a promise. Besides, I can always follow a dignitary around recording his or her uttering and doings. I suggest you take it; you'll make the front page."

"I'm going to have a talk with Joel, because I have to

be certain why he offered me this assignment. He could have given it to Marie."

"You're out of your mind. I wouldn't let Marie cover a Tupperware party, and neither would Joel."

"I'm not out of my mind, and I'll see you soon, mister."

Minutes later, she knocked on Joel's door. "Come in, but don't stay. I'm busy." He looked up, saw her and said, "Have a seat. I don't know what the hell's going on here. Max just gave me notice that he's leaving."

"He what? What on earth are you talking about? Leaving where?"

"He said that as long as he's here, you'll never become a top flight journalist, that you'll always be considered his junior and that you deserve better."

She let out a long, tired breath. "He's crazy."

"No, he isn't. We've been very fortunate in keeping Max Baldwin here, because he can work for any paper in the country and make more than he makes here. He can freelance as a syndicated reporter and get rich. He loves you, and he's not going to stand in your way. As much as this unsettles things here, I admire him for it." With a vigorous shake of his head, he half smiled. "I've always admired the guy. He marches to the beat of his own drums."

"Yes," she mused, as her mind traveled over the many different facets of Max Baldwin that she had discovered in the seven months she'd known him. "He's as different and as complicated as he is exceptional."

"You'd be wise to take this assignment, Leticia. Don't hesitate because of Max; he's got it made, and he knows it. This isn't going to destroy your relationship with him. If it did, I'd say he was more shallow than I could have imagined."

"I'll let you know."

"Make it soon."

She didn't want to go to Max's office, but seeing him face to face would make it less likely that he would misjudge or misunderstand her. She knocked on his office door.

"Come in."

Standing by the door, which she left ajar, she said, "I've just left Joel. He said you're leaving *The Journal* of your own volition, so I decided to take the assignment on the PM." She wondered why he hadn't told her, but didn't consider asking him.

"I'm glad. I'd like to see you reach your potential, Leticia, and you won't do that by rejecting opportunities. Can we meet after work, same time and place?"

"I'd like that. See you then."

"I'm aware of your reason for leaving the door cracked open, sweetheart. I know that kissing you right where you're standing would make you go into hiding for a month. But it's all I can think about." His grin further unsettled her.

She left his office wondering if she'd ever be as self-assured as Max or Mark or even Kenyetta.

"But I'm not going to stop trying," she vowed. "Never!"

Chapter Fourteen

Max didn't waste time worrying about his departure from *The Journal*. He considered it a closed chapter in his life, and he was ready to go on to better things. But he hated leaving Leticia. Not that they weren't still together; they were. Knowing she was close by and that if she had a problem, he could intervene on her behalf had been more of a solace to him than he had realized. He reached for the phone to tell Bob that he was accepting the job as editor in chief of *The Maryland Tribune* when the phone rang.

He lifted the receiver. "Baldwin."

"Max, this is Sebastian Mills." Max nearly swallowed his tongue. Why would Mills, publisher of *The Tribune*, call him? "News gets around. I heard you might be thinking of leaving *The Journal*. My editor in chief is retiring. I need you. What about it? You get carte blanche, the only stipulation being that you maintain *The Tribune* at least at its current level and status. What about it?"

Stunned hardly described his feelings. Here was the opportunity of a lifetime, and he hadn't moved a finger to get it. "Give me a minute to catch my breath. When the phone rang, I was about to call Bob Weddington and accept his offer."

"You get a car and chauffeur, and I'll pay you twenty-five percent more than Weddington offered you. How about it?"

"I have to think about it. Bob's a friend, and I hate disappointing him."

"I won't fill the post till you give me a definite no."

"Thanks, man. I'll call you tomorrow."

He hung up and went to Joel's office. "Did you happen to mention to Sebastian Mills that I'm leaving *The Journal*?"

"Well, yeah. I knew he was looking to replace Mc-Knight, so . . . Look, Max. This is a great opportunity for you. Before you know it, you'll run the *Post* out of business. Have you talked with Leticia about this? She's in a dilemma about the assignment I gave her on the prime minister and your leaving here. And it doesn't make a bit of sense, because you're getting something far better."

"I hope none of us regrets this. Thanks for speaking to Sebastian. I appreciate it, and I'm going to take the job. I can write whatever and whenever I like, and I'll be my own man."

Joel rocked back in his chair and laughed aloud. "You've always been your own man. What about Leticia?"

He looked at Joel, older than his years, gray from the daily stress of competing with some of the best newsmen anywhere. "It's a wonder you aren't bald, Joel. You love this paper, you've set a high standard, and I hope I can do as well at *The Tribune*. It's been a pleasure working for you. I decided to leave because I don't like competing with Leticia, but I realize that once I take over *The Tribune*, we'll be more competitive with each other than ever. There doesn't seem to be a way to avoid it."

"Somehow that doesn't worry me. I want to be god-father to the first child she gives you."

Max cocked an eyebrow. "I've cleaned out my desk. Let's stay in touch."

Unaware of the changes taking place at *The Journal* and in Max's life, Leticia sat at her desk, checking the Internet for books on the prime minister and his private as well as his public life. She found one biography and numerous newspaper and magazine stories, but none that gave her a clue as to why the man took the political road for which he was famous. She wanted to link the man's past to his present, and she didn't want her story to read like gossip. She started down to Joel's office to tell him that she planned to spend the afternoon at the Library of Congress, and as she reached Joel's door, Max walked out of it.

"Hi. I need to talk with you," he said. "Would you please come with me to my office, and we'll close the door, because this is personal."

What now? she asked herself as she walked the few steps with him. With the desk empty of his presence, the room didn't seem so imposing. She walked in, and he followed her and closed the door behind him.

"There's no point in preliminaries, sweetheart. I just got an offer from Sebastian Mills at *The Tribune*, and I'm taking the job of editor in chief. I've cleaned out my desk. This has been my home, and I'll miss it terribly at first, but I'll miss having you near me so much more. Friday night's my first gig. Will you come?"

For a few seconds, she couldn't breathe, but merely stared at him. Wasn't it typical of him to gloss over the painful news? "I'm happy for you," she said when she caught her breath. "You deserve the recognition and the status. I'll miss you here, too." There was more, so much more that she wanted to say, but it wouldn't come out of her.

"We'll be real competitors now," he said, "but you do your job to the best of your ability as you've been doing; I'll do the same. And let's not allow our work to come between us."

"It won't be easy, Max."

"If you love me, nothing will come between us."

"How can both of us succeed? The minute you take over *The Tribune*, you'll start work on appointing a reporter to interview the PM or on plans to do it yourself."

"Of course, but our respective readers will stick with us."

He opened his arms, and she rushed into them, relishing his warmth and caring. "Go with my blessings, love." She had a feeling that her happiest times with him might be behind her. "Kiss me, and let me get back to my work."

Nothing, not even that Sunday when she'd spent most of the day in his arms, had prepared her for that moment. His lips brushed over her closed eyes, and from there, he savored every inch of her face with gentle touches of his lips, and when she thought she'd go mad waiting, he rimmed the seams of her lips with the tip of his tongue. She took him in, squeezed his body to hers with every ounce of energy that she possessed, and let him show her what he felt.

"I love you," she whispered, "and I guess I always will."

"I love you, too," he said, "and although I'll be a mile away, I'll be here for you. Don't ever forget that." She wouldn't forget it, but nonetheless, her faith in a future with him had vanished in a short thirty minutes.

* * *

Sunday, two days later, Leticia rose early, wary as to what the day would bring. Although she longed to be with Max, she was aware that she lacked some of the enthusiasm that she felt when anticipating that Sunday when they finally knew each other. She wouldn't describe it as wariness and certainly not as fear, but something was missing. She loved him, wanted him and needed him, but something didn't fit.

When the doorman rang to announce Max, she managed to say, "Ask him to come up." Then she rushed to the mirror, patted her hair, dusted her nose with the powder brush and hastened to the door. *What's wrong with me?* she asked herself. *I'm acting like he doesn't know me.* She opened the door, and when she saw his bright, hopeful smile, her doubts vanished. She opened her arms, and he dropped his packages and took her to him.

"What's the matter?" he asked her after he kissed her. "Did I sense a tinge of desperation in that kiss? Come with me." He walked with her to the dining room. "Sit over there while I put together our brunch."

She watched while he found the dishes, glasses and utensils, set the table and put out a dazzling array of food, poured wine into their glasses, bowed to her and said, "Madam, brunch is served."

Without any kind of warning, she began to cry. He rushed to her, put his arms around her and whispered, "What's wrong? Have I done anything to hurt you?"

She shook her head. "I have this awful feeling that it's never going to be right between us again."

"There's no basis for it. If we're true to each other, nothing will change. So, let's eat. I didn't have breakfast, and I'm starved. I have a wonderful day planned for us." He brushed his lips over hers. "Come on."

She looked at the crab cakes, smoked salmon, ham, cheeses, green salad, pumpernickel bread, rolls, cheesecake, pineapple nuggets and Snickers and laughed. "How'd you know I love Snickers?"

He reached for her hand and said grace, but afterward his face bore a puzzled expression. "You like Snickers? I didn't know that. I brought them because I love them, but I don't allow myself to eat them except on Sundays."

She reached across the table for the bowl of Snickers, put four of the candies on the table in front of him, and got up and put the remainder in the drawer behind her.

"More than four is not good for your perfect physique, so I'll just save these. Uh-huh." She cleared her throat and sipped some wine.

"You'd better eat first," he said. "Wine can sneak up on you."

She managed to eat some of everything and enjoy it. "I'll clean up," she told him.

"I'll do it," he said. "Say, would you look out that window. The sun was shining when I got here, and that's snow I'm seeing."

She looked out the dining room window, saw the snow and busied herself making a fire in the dining and living rooms. Maybe providence didn't plan for them to spend a Sunday browsing around Washington. He joined her in the living room, sat beside her on the sofa and pulled her onto his lap.

"I'm not going to ask you again why you were crying, because I suspect you aren't sure. But I want you to promise that if you need anything from anybody, come to me first. If it's possible, I'll get it for you. Your happiness is important to me."

She snuggled closer to him, locked her arms around his neck, and kissed him. She hadn't planned to start a fire, but she did and, within minutes the hands she

adored roamed over her body, caressing, searching, fondling and loving. When she could bear it no longer, she
begged him to put her in bed and finish it. A half hour
later, with their bodies still locked together, he stared
down at her, puzzled, his face the picture of unhappi-
ness.

"What happened, Leticia? Something went wrong.
You weren't with me. Tell me what the problem is. Tell
me."

"I know you're right, but I don't know what happened. It just . . . I couldn't let go."

His arms tightened around her. "Then try to tell me
how you feel." She turned her face to the side so that he
couldn't look into her eyes. "No. Look at me. If you
don't trust me and believe that I love you, we aren't
going anywhere."

She had no idea where the words or the thoughts
came from as she began to speak. "My mother died when
I was nine, and my father passed when I was twenty-six.
They loved me, and I knew it. From the time my dad
died until now, I wasn't sure anybody loved me and, in
fact, I had no one that I could count on. I didn't let it
bother me, or I thought I didn't. I finally let myself believe that you love me and got the courage to tell you
that I needed you, and now . . . " She paused, not wanting him to think her childish or immature.

"Now what?" His voice, soft and urgent, communicated tenderness and a willingness to understand.

"Now, you're leaving me, too. You were the main reason why I enjoyed coming to work every morning. Even
when I don't see you all day, I know you're here, close by."

"I'm not deserting you, Leticia. I'll always be there
for you. Get it into your head that you can depend on
me. If I stay at *The Journal*, you'll always be second banana. You deserve better, and Joel accepts that fact.

Promise me you'll be at the Rooftop for the group's first performance Friday night. I'm planning to bring my mother and Ella."

She knew he was trying to shift the subject from their unsuccessful coupling long enough to change her mood. "I'll be there. What time are you on?" He told her. "Where do you and I go from here, Max?"

"I'm going to do everything I can to tighten the bonds between you and me. It hurts that you are so unsure of me. I want you to know without a doubt, that you and I belong to each other, that you are the only woman in my life. But you have to believe it, Leticia. If you don't, we've nothing going for us. Not a thing."

He kissed her good-bye without his usual air of possessiveness, and without the self-assurance that she associated with him. What had she done? Hours later, she fought with herself, trying to banish her demon, for it threatened to destroy what was most precious to her. Max Baldwin had a will of iron. He could love her and at the same time stay away from her no matter how much it hurt him. And she couldn't make amends; if she didn't feel it inside, he'd know it. Besides, she didn't want to pretend with him; she wanted that honesty that they had shared from the beginning.

"Maybe I should see a shrink," she said to herself. "I don't want to go back to that lonely life. I'm thirty-one years old and I've never had a girlfriend who was a real buddy. Until Max, not one man had even claimed to love me, and I pretended I didn't care. I told myself I was smarter than most of the people I knew, that I was superior, and that that was enough.

"I got hair extensions, learned how to put on make-up, bought new and expensive clothes and taught myself how to dress, but . . . I thought I was making progress." She remembered the pain and shame she knew when she read the Valentine that Miss Harris, her ninth grade homeroom teacher, had placed on her desk: "Steam baths and loads of powder and paint will never make you something that you ain't." From then until she went for that interview at *The Journal*, she hadn't made a serious attempt to improve her appearance.

At daybreak, she was wide awake. She got up, got ready for work, went downstairs and sat at the table. If it had been possible, she would have gone for a long and solitary walk, but strolling in three inches of snow was not to her liking.

"What brought on that long face you got this morning?" Willa asked her. "You're living; you got your health and strength; you got a job and the sun's shining. Looks to me like you oughtta be smiling." She poured the coffee and sat down. "Let's say grace." She said it and looked at Leticia. "Anything wrong with you and Mr. Baldwin? I sure hope not."

"Not that I know of, Willa. You know, my mother died when I was nine, and I see in you what I missed by not having her as I grew up. I was going to scold you for asking me what's wrong, but . . . well, thanks for caring."

Leticia got through her first day at work in what her colleagues at *The Journal* already referred to as the AM era—*The Journal* after Max—and prided herself in her plans for her series on the prime minister. At the budget meeting that morning, Joel had warned the reporters not to start jockeying for Max's position, that it was not awarded but earned, ending the buzz as to who was next.

Around four o'clock that Friday, Leticia scampered home and prepared to see Max in a different role and setting. She managed to ingest a light dinner of broiled swordfish, sautéed spinach and a baked sweet potato. Afterward, she dressed in a burnt orange, scooped neck woolen dress that did justice to her legs, dabbed Fendi perfume in strategic places and looked for some earrings. She settled on a pair of gold ones that had coins hanging down for a little more than two inches. If Max was out of character that night, why shouldn't she be also? She arrived at the Rooftop a few minutes before the first set was to begin and asked for Max's table.

"Oh, here you are," Ella said when Leticia reached the table. "I was afraid you weren't coming."

"I wasn't," Jean Baldwin said, extending her arms to hug Leticia. "I knew you'd be here."

The four men came out with their instruments, and the manager announced them, told the audience that they were playing for an important charity, and invited them to put tips in a bank at the entrance. The band opened with a fast rendition of "When You're Smiling" and, to the obvious delight of a packed house, took off from there.

At intermission, Max came to their table and gave her a mild shock by kissing her on the mouth in the presence of his mother. "I had no idea you were so gifted, Max. This music was wonderful. You deserved an opportunity to display your talent."

"I don't think I've ever had so much fun," Max said. "Honest. And these people are acting like they're enjoying it. I saw one of the *Post*'s feature reporters sitting over there taking notes. I wonder what he'll write when he finds out I'm moving to *The Tribune*."

"If he's honest, it won't affect his review," Jean said. "Tell me why none of you does this for a living."

"Our decisions were based on the need to eat, at least mine was. That and the fact that I wanted to write as badly as I wanted to perform music. These few gigs will scratch my itch to perform jazz, at least for the present." He signaled for a waiter. "This table is on my tab." To Leticia he said, "Gotta get back. It wouldn't have been any fun if you weren't here."

She held his hand, detaining him. "I may not be able to get to all of them, but I'll always be with you in spirit." He gazed at her for a few seconds, kissed her cheek, and headed for the dressing room.

At the end of the performance, Max and Wilson Gallagher joined them at the table. Jean hugged Wilson and reprimanded him for not having visited her recently.

"It hasn't been easy, Mama Jean," Wilson said. "You know I'm always in trouble with Max. This time, I really stepped on his toes, but I learned a lesson." He looked at Leticia. "I'm sorry I behaved like a scoundrel. I hope you've forgiven me."

"What about Kenyetta? You did a real number on her."

"If I hadn't been smart, she'd have done one on me. Kenyetta and I are cut from the same cloth, and when I realized that, I got out of her way."

Leticia stared hard at him, seeing in him a different demeanor. "She learned a lesson. Seems like you did, too."

Something akin to gloom settled over Wilson. Leticia glanced up at Max, and the intensity with which he observed them surprised her.

"Yeah," Wilson said. "Every Napoleon has his Waterloo. Looks as if I've met mine."

So Wilson Gallagher had fallen for a woman who didn't find him interesting. He didn't have Leticia's sympathy but, to her mind, no one deserved unrequited love. "I hope you emerge from this experience a happier person," she told him, and meant it.

"I don't know about happier, but I'm certainly wiser, and you could say, more compassionate."

"You come see me," Jean said, "and Ella will make you some of that great cheesecake that you love. Don't you forget."

Wilson leaned down and hugged the woman. "I won't forget. You're still my best girl."

"The limousine should be out front, but I'd better check." Max left them to look for the car he'd hired, and Wilson went with him.

"What's wrong with y'all, Miss Langley?" Ella asked as if she had a right to the information. "Y'all should be more like lovers. Now I know why Max has been acting like somebody died. With his new job, he should be singing to the top of his voice. Whatever it is, you better make it right and soon."

"It's good with us, or so I thought. Why do you think I can improve it?"

"Because if he'd cooled off, he wouldn't be acting like it was the end of the world. He figures out what's gonna happen before he does or says a thing, decides to take his chances and never looks back. So if you want him, you'd better shape up." Leticia knew things had cooled somewhat between Max and her, and that it was good advice, but she bristled nonetheless. Yet she kept her reaction to herself.

Max arrived and helped his mother to stand. "The car is here. May I see you home, Leticia?"

She was about to tell him that, since he had to take his mother home, she could get a taxi, but a glance at Ella's stern and forbidding expression, and she said, "Thanks. I'd like that." But it evidently didn't satisfy Max, for as he opened her apartment door for her later, she could see that he'd wrapped himself tightly in his self-control.

"Your being there tonight meant more to me than you can imagine," he said.

"I wouldn't have missed it for anything, Max."

"I know." His lips seared hers in a quick kiss, and as if he'd reverted to the habit he had when their relationship had not been defined, he stroked her cheek and left.

She watched him leave. "I'm right back where I started with him, but it definitely will not kill me." She went inside, saw the red light flashing on her phone, checked and got a message from Mark.

"Our lawyer has sold Granddad's house and its contents, and you should shortly receive a set of photographs of our grandparents and a check for two hundred and seventy-three thousand dollars. Some of our relatives are not speaking to me about this, but I don't give a rat's tutu. Call me when you have time. Incidentally, your column on senior citizens and their pets was wonderful. See you."

"That money will buy me a house," she said aloud after she hung up. "Thank you, Granddad."

The prime minister's plane would arrive at Washington Dulles International Airport around noon the next day, Saturday, and she meant to be there. She wrote a note that she would give to one of his aides and put it in an envelope. If she was lucky, the ploy would gain her an interview.

She was at Dulles International Airport when the plane arrived, scanned the prime minister's entourage, chose the man walking closest to him and managed to press the letter into his hand. Wide-eyed and surprised, the man put the note into his pocket without looking at it, but she knew that his curiosity would compel him to examine it.

Two days later, after dinner, she sat down to watch the evening news, switched on the television and saw Max sitting with the anchorman. So this was an example of what one gained by being editor in chief of a major paper. Within minutes, she learned that Max had already obtained an interview with the prime minister, and that it would be reported in the next day's paper.

Anger furled up in her, but as he spoke, it dissipated. She rushed to her briefcase, got pen and paper and began to take notes. Ever the consummate journalist, Max reported not only the prime minister's reasons for coming to Washington, but interpreted them and gave his views on their validity. He didn't allow the anchorman to lead him or to confuse him.

The next morning, she dialed his cell phone number. "Congratulations on your interview last night. As always, you did a superior job. I was so proud of you. I took notes."

"Thanks, and thanks for calling me. I didn't get much notice. Are you going to let me see your notes?"

"Sure."

"How about lunch . . . No. That won't work. I'd ask you to have dinner with me, but that won't work either. Keep your cell phone handy, and I'll work something out. I love you."

"I love you, too, Max."

Max sat at his big wooden desk in his enormous office and stared unseeing out of the wall-to-wall windows facing him across the room. In spite of her obligation to follow the prime minister around the United States—from Boston to Oakland to New Orleans, New York, stops in between and back to Washington—Leticia had managed to attend each of his performances. And he knew she'd done so at considerable cost in energy and inconvenience, and in spite of the fact that he appeared to get more about the prime minister's visit for his paper than she got for hers. He got up and began walking from one end of the office to the other.

If Leticia were not a reporter for one of his major competitors, he would have alerted her to the telecast of his interview. He'd wanted to do it nonetheless, but it would have seemed like gloating. She'd been gracious about it and, for that, he was grateful. He'd wanted to invite her to accompany him to the embassy's dinner for the PM, but that would have been almost insulting to her, because it was not a purely social occasion. He was invited as a journalist, and she would want to be there as a professional in her own right. So, he had indicated in his reply that he wouldn't have a date. He didn't pray often, but he stopped pacing and, with his fists extended in front of him, he asked God to remember Leticia's needs and provide for her.

Could a marriage survive what he saw as their unsolvable conflict? If they married, could she banish her insecurity about his feelings for her? And where did these thoughts come from anyhow?

Leticia dragged herself to work that morning, three and a half weeks since traveling with the plane full of reporters covering the prime minister had taken over her life. She wasn't sure that tramping her way through the head-high bushes in Nigeria had been more of a challenge. As usual, she tackled her mail first. Near the bottom of the pile, she saw an envelope embossed with the insignia of the prime minister's embassy. Her fingers shook as she opened the letter, and a gasp escaped her when she saw the ambassador's invitation to a formal dinner honoring the prime minister.

"Oh, what the heck," she said aloud. "Every reporter got one of these." She was in the act of putting the envelope aside when she saw a gold-edged card. It read, "The prime minister would be pleased to grant you a private interview here at the embassy. Please call this number to confirm the date and time." She threw up her arms and sang out, "Whoopee!"

"I'm not telling Joel, Max or anybody else about this," she said to herself, laughing to express the joy she felt. "I want a different kind of scoop. I'm already following the PM around for my daily reports on his politics. This interview will produce something more." She telephoned the embassy, made the appointment for two days prior to the formal dinner, and determined that the PM had two daughters aged five and seven years. On the way home, she bought two Cabbage Patch dolls. And because she knew she shouldn't ask Max to accompany her to the embassy dinner, she phoned Mark, an elegant man and a date who wouldn't arouse Max's suspicions and cause him to walk out of her life . . . provided he remembered from their first meeting that Mark was her cousin.

After they greeted each other warmly, she explained to Mark that she needed a date and why. "I can't go to that formal dinner without a date, even though I'll be working. You and Max have met before but it would be nice if you could get to know each other."

"I wouldn't miss it."

"You can stay at my place. I have a guest room. I appreciate this, Mark."

"Any time you need me, just yell. And if that dude of yours gets his butt on his shoulder, I'll let him know who his equal is."

She couldn't help laughing. "Max is control personified. Thanks, cuz. See you in a couple of weeks."

Their meeting would be interesting. And it would happen. No one had to tell her that Max Baldwin's name wouldn't be high on the embassy's list of invitees. That evening when Max called her, she shoved aside the tinge of guilt. He hadn't told her he had an interview with the PM, so why should she feel disloyal?

"Before I forget it," he said after they greeted each other, "Ella and my mom are begging me to have a party after I complete the jazz tour. Will you be my date?"

"When is it?" she asked, wishing she hadn't when his pause confirmed that it was an ill-advised question. She quickly added, "Of course, I'll be happy to be your date, but I may need time to shop, so when is it?"

He told her and added, "You'll be perfect for me no matter what you wear. A dressy street dress will be more than adequate. Leticia, my mother walked alone and without any support today. From the time Beryl told me, I've been unable to concentrate on my work. I'm overjoyed."

"Oh, Max, I'm so happy. It's wonderful. I can't wait to see her walk. I wish I was with you right now."

"Would you love me? Really love me?"

"I *do* love you. More than you know. So much more."

"I'm listening to you." His voice darkened, and his tone had become heavier, rather like plodding feet. "What do you want for us, Leticia?"

Would she play chicken or would she bite the bullet and go after what she wanted and needed? To her mind, she had everything to gain. She thought of the women she interviewed in Nigeria and Kenya, some of whom fought all their lives against brutishness in their most intimate relationships. Against insurmountable odds, many of them fought every day for peace and respect in their home. Fought when neither the law nor the culture supported them.

Surely she had the guts to tell the man who represented what those women couldn't even dream of that she wanted him for herself alone. "What do I want for us? More than I have now. Much, much more." After saying it, she had an attack of dizziness, but she didn't care. She'd say it again.

"Did I hear you correctly?"

"I'm sure you did. I need more with you and from you than I get now. A lot more, and I don't want it piecemeal." She waited while the silence settled in her belly like lead in water.

"Would you say those words if we were together?"

In for a penny; in for a pound. "If I felt the way I'm feeling now, I would."

"How do you feel?"

"I am not happy with this almost, not quite relationship I have with you. After the PM goes home where he belongs, we have to fix this. You understand?

"What's funny?" she asked when he began to laugh.

"I've arrived at precisely the point where you are. Normally, after what you've just said to me, I'd be halfway to Woodley Road by now. But we'd only put a Band-Aid on the problem. I want to know where I'm headed with you."

"Me, too."

"All right, sweetheart. We have two more weeks of limbo. If we've stood it this long, two more weeks won't kill us."

"I guess not. Love you."

"And I love you. Good night, love."

She hung up and for a long time, she stared at the telephone receiver. *Would I have said those words if he and I were together and not talking over the phone? Maybe he's on to something, because I really can't see myself doing that. When I told him I needed him, I wanted him right then and right there so badly that I was on fire for him. The words I spoke today didn't come from my libido, but from my heart. Maybe a person shouldn't engage in self-analysis, but I think I have an inkling as to why I have such a hard time making real friends. I'm surprised that I am as close as I am to Max.*

She wanted people to like her and to be her friend, but she knew she wasn't as direct and as straight with people on a personal level as she should be. She didn't open up, but almost always wore her public persona, and that was probably the reason why a lot of people had cockeyed notions about her. She told herself that she wouldn't be happy unless she overcame the problem, whatever it was.

Ten days later on a Wednesday morning at eleven-thirty, she rang the bell at the embassy and presented her credentials. "Come in, madam," the uniformed serviceman said. "The prime minister is waiting for you in the drawing room. May I examine your packages, please?" He screened the packages several times, returned them to her and said, "Please come with me."

The big man rose when she walked into the room, took a few steps to meet her and extended his hand. "I've been looking forward to our talk, Miss Langley. Your note and the way you got it to me intrigued me, and you were right. I've talked about politics until the subjects are coming out of my ears. Let's have a seat."

"Thank you for agreeing to talk with me, sir. Do you mind if I tape our conversation?"

"No, I don't. That way, you won't misquote me. Now, you want to know what my position costs me and my family. The word is privacy. A guard even stands at my bedroom door, and it must be cracked open." She sympathized with him, and said as much.

He talked non-stop for half an hour. "Let's have some tea, or would you prefer coffee." She noticed that he moved his right foot and assumed that he pressed a bell or button beneath the carpet, for almost at once, a waiter pushed a serving cart into the drawing room. "You must be hungry." He asked her how she became a journalist and laughed when she told him how she got Max's assignment reviewing the chocolate fest.

"Honesty is a good thing, but it ought to stop short of cruelty," he said, passing the plate of canapés to her. When he spoke about his children, opened his wallet and showed her pictures of them, she handed him the packages.

"It's not much, but I wanted to give you something for your daughters."

To her astonishment, he opened the packages, gazed at the dolls and exclaimed, "Good gracious! These are Cabbage Patch dolls, and I forgot that my wife asked me to bring each of the girls one. She didn't travel with me, because she's expecting our first son. Well." He shook his head from side to side. "You've saved me from the wrath of my family when I get home. I want you to come to my country and meet my family and, of course, you will be a guest in our home." He stroked one of the dolls. "This is terrific."

About forty-five minutes later, she rose to leave, and with reluctance, for she had enjoyed the prime minister's company. He walked with her to the door where the guard waited. "Thank you so much for your time, sir, and for receiving me so graciously."

"It was my pleasure. I look forward to your being a guest in our home."

Giddy with happiness as she left the embassy and headed for her office at *The Journal,* she longed to tell Max about the experience, but she had to control the urge; you didn't show your hand to your competitor, not even if he was your lover. She'd barely sat down at her desk when Joel burst into her office.

"Did you see him?"

A grin spread over her face. "Did I ever? Max and the other reporters are writing about his position on every aspect of world politics, and my series covers that, too, but I know about his kids, his personal life, et cetera. I'm going to put the interview in a separate column. Good-bye, Joel. I have to get started on this."

Joel ran his hands over his hair. "Yeah? Well, you go to it. Uh . . . Is it gonna be front-page stuff?"

"That's what I'm gunning for."

His face bloomed into a broad smile. "Right on!"

She flipped on her recorder and began typing out the interview. After working half the night in order to finish it, the following morning, she handed Joel her column. "If this is as good as you think, you'll get a raise. Imagine one of my reporters getting a private interview with the prime minister." He shook his head and began to read.

Friday would be a day in which her life changed. Her telephone rang as she walked into her office. "Good morning. Langley speaking."

"What a hell of a coup you pulled off. I bow to you. Everybody's—"

"Hi, Max. Do you really like it?"

"Is that a serious question? Leticia, I'd give anything if I could have gotten even half of that information out of him. I tried, but he didn't budge."

She told him about the note. "He told me he appreciated that I didn't bring a photographer, that he was tired of worrying about whether his tie was straight or he was slumping in the chair and heaven knows what else. I was lucky. I forgot to ask Joel for a photographer. I'm happy that you liked it, Max. Your opinion means more to me than anyone else's, including Joel's."

"You're way ahead of the curve, Leticia, and I'm proud of you. My mother asked me to tell you that she loved the column. Are you aware that this is our last weekend apart?"

She bolted upright, calmed herself and sat down. "I hope it is."

"I have a gig Sunday night, and I want us to be together Monday evening."

"All right, Max. I'm already looking forward to it." She couldn't say more, because he called her on her office phone, and it wasn't secure. "Bye for now."

Her phone rang all morning, and she had more invitations to appear on television and radio than she could honor. "This is what happens when you do the unexpected and excel at it," Joel told her. "You and Max ought to have some brilliant kids."

"Probably," she said, shocking him. "That is, if he'll ever give me an opportunity to conceive them."

"Huh! Well, I'll shake him up." She had embarrassed him, but she didn't care. If he repeated it to Max, she'd be in Joel's debt.

Chapter Fifteen

"I didn't dream I could be so popular," Leticia said to herself when she answered her office phone shortly before noon.

"Hi, Leticia. This is Allison. Congratulations on this great column. It's all the buzz over here at my paper. None of us thought of getting a personal angle. People have stopped talking about the PM's politics; after reading your column, they're all talking about the man. I'm happy for you. This is a banner day. Leonia, Windmills' treasurer, just called to tell me that Max's jazz band has raised almost four hundred thousand dollars for us, and they still have two more nights to play. Our fundraisers have never cleared more than eleven thousand dollars. We're ecstatic."

"With Bill Covington joining them almost every weekend, it was a cinch."

"Nothing's a cinch in the music business, Leticia. Bill's a big name, but it was the music—some of the best jazz I've heard since the Modern Jazz Quartet. We have a deal with a recording studio that will give us a steady income from a CD. Could we have a drink somewhere this evening between work and going home?"

She almost hesitated. But if she didn't extend herself, she would never have friends. "Okay. Where?"

"Four-fifteen at Tequila Sunrise. Two blocks south of *The Journal.*"

"I'll be there." She didn't dare drink that time of day, because she wasn't used to it, and she didn't want to seem unsophisticated. Allison would have to understand.

They settled into the cozy lounge, and Allison got the waiter's attention. "I'm not much on alcoholic drinks, Allison." She felt like a fool confiding that to a woman like Allison. "I don't have anything against it. I . . . uh . . . guess I'm afraid that if I drink, I'll, uh . . . "

"You'll embarrass yourself? Let me give you a tip. Eat peanuts, potato chips or bread, cheese or anything that will line the stomach. Gin and tonic on lots of ice is a good drink, because the ice melts and weakens the mixture. Try that after you eat a snack. Wine on an empty stomach can rough you up."

"Are you and Bill going to the prime minister's dinner tomorrow night?"

"Try keeping us away. Everybody who's anybody will be there. I bought a new dress, and when Bill sees the décolletage, he's going to faint." She sipped her scotch mist and released a happy giggle.

"I was going to wear the dress I wore to the Kappa dance, but I guess I'd better not."

Allison's frown expressed strong disapproval. "I suppose you're going with Max. He'll look like a walking Adonis, so show him a new dress. You have the rest of today and tomorrow to find one."

"I'm not going with Max." At the sharp rise of Allison's eyebrows, she added, "My first cousin is escorting me. I'm going with my own invitation; if Max escorted me, it would seem that I was there as his date." She took a long sip of her drink, liked it, and sipped some more. "Allison, Max doesn't even know I'm going. I'm assuming that he hasn't asked me because it would almost be insulting to assume that I'm not invited."

Allison put her drink down. "Hey, wait a minute. Don't you two communicate? Bill and I thought you'd be lovers by now."

"Well . . . we were, but only a couple of times. Then, I loused up."

"But how was it? I mean . . . was it okay?"

"It was wonderful. I love that guy, and—"

"Does he love you?"

"That's the problem, Allison. He does, and I feel it, but how do you trust it to be real?"

"Hmm. Not good. You start by knowing that you are worth loving. I've known Max at least ten years, and I know there isn't a phony molecule in that man. He's tough, but I've long suspected that in some respects, he's frail. You let him know that he's your whole world."

"He is."

"I don't mean tell him. Show him, and he'll be a sweeter, more passionate lover and a stronger man in every aspect of his life." She raised her glass. "We're waiting for an invitation to your wedding."

Leticia raised her glass, took a long sip and said, "I'll work on it. Thanks." After hesitating, she added, "Friend." Allison didn't know why Leticia smiled. It was because Leticia was looking at the only person other than Max to whom she had ever confided intimate personal information. It felt good.

On the way home, she saw an avocado-green evening dress in Saks Fifth Avenue's window, went inside and tried it on. The color and style flattered her, so she bought it and prayed that Mark's accessories wouldn't clash with it. However, she needn't have worried. He phoned her around seven o'clock.

"Hey, cuz. What color's your dress? I don't want my accessories to clash with it."

"Avocado green. More green than yellow. Thanks for the thought."

"I always ask. I think I've got it covered with gray and pale-yellow paisley. Be there tomorrow at two, provided the plane comes in on time."

She left work early, went to the hairdresser and then met Mark in the baggage claim area at the airport. "You shouldn't have gone to all this trouble. I'm fairly familiar with Washington," he said, with a hug that belied his words.

"I always meet my guests."

They didn't have to wait long for a taxi. "Where's Woodley Road?" the driver asked after she gave him the address.

"I doubt he could find the market in Lagos, Nigeria," she said to Mark beneath her breath. "They come ostensibly to go to school and head straight to a taxi company to get a job." To the driver, she said, "Take the George Washington Memorial Parkway to the Fourteenth Street Bridge, cross it, exit left on to Massachusetts Avenue and drive awhile. I'll tell you when to turn off to get to Woodley."

Willa opened the door for them, looked at Mark, and gave him her best, hopeful smile. "Mrs. Evans, this is my first cousin and closest relative, Mark DuPree. Mark, Willa is my housekeeper and friend."

"If you look after Leticia, you're my friend, too," he

said, but Leticia noted the housekeeper's disappointment that the man was not a prospective husband. Mark radiated charm, and Willa blushed in appreciation.

"Your lunch is ready. It's light, 'cause you gon' have to eat dinner with those bigwigs, and I'll bet that will be at least seven courses."

Leticia showed Mark his room. "There's a pool in the basement if you want to swim. I can't go in with you, because I've had my hair done for tonight."

"And it looks great, too."

She left Mark to unpack and went downstairs to find Willa. "Is Mr. Baldwin taking you to this fancy dinner tonight?" Willa asked Leticia. She told her that he wasn't and why. "Hmph. Suppose he gets the wrong idea about you and your cousin. Mr. DuPree is a choice looking man, right up there on Mr. Baldwin's level. You sure he's a cousin?"

"Willa, his mother and my mother were sisters."

"Be sure Mr. Baldwin knows that, 'cause seeing you with your cousin gon' make him blow a fuse."

Willa's prediction of Max's attitude was on target. Leticia stood at the dining room door and watched Mark stride down the hall, elegant and supremely confident. "Gee whiz, Mark, you could make millions modeling tuxedos. You look super."

"Thanks. There're no flies on you, cuz. You're a beautiful woman, and you make that dress very special. Max Baldwin, eat your heart out."

She had selected the dress without the advice or suggestion of Kenyetta or the saleswoman, and because she knew she looked great in it. A sense of pride suffused her. "You're good for my ego. I'll call a taxi."

"That won't be necessary. I ordered a limousine for the evening."

Minutes after they entered the embassy and checked Leticia's wrap, Max arrived. Alone. And almost at once, his gaze landed on Leticia and Mark. First, he frowned as if verifying what his eyes told him he saw. Then, a scowl preceded the blaze of fury that flashed across his face.

Mark took Leticia's arm and propelled her toward Max. "You'd better greet him before he blows up."

"Why? He didn't invite me."

"You didn't invite him, either. Soften up, cuz. He came here solo."

The closer they got to Max, the madder he seemed to get. "How cozy! I didn't expect to have the pleasure," he said with a sneer.

Knowing that she should have expected his attitude, she ignored his comment, and put a possessive hand on his arm. "Max Baldwin, this is my first cousin, Mark DuPree. Our mothers were sisters."

"This is a pleasure, Max. I've been anxious to know you. I think we were introduced in passing at *The Journal* office several months back."

"Yes, I remember. I'm glad to see you again." After shaking Mark's hand, Max looked at her. "Why didn't you tell me you had an invitation?"

"Same reason why you didn't invite me," she said, miffed and not bothering to hide it.

"Look here, you two. If you'd communicate, you'd avoid friction and hurt feelings and, as much as I love my cousin, I'd be in New Orleans right now. Not that I mind enjoying an experience such as this one. I'll probably never step inside another foreign embassy." He looked at his watch. "Cuz, we'd better check in and get to our table. Max, let's meet right here in this spot after the dinner and the three of us go someplace."

"Good idea. See you back here later."

"If you hadn't taken control of that, I'd probably have baited him and loused up our relationship. Max doesn't tolerate foolishness."

"I got that much before we reached him. And you shape up. I told you when I saw him last summer that man thinks a lot of you."

They made their way through a seven-course meal, as Willa predicted, after which coffee, cognac and liqueurs were offered in the drawing room. As she stood sipping Tia Maria coffee liqueur with Mark and Max, the prime minister joined them and reminded Leticia of his invitation to visit him and his family. She introduced Mark to him and promised to visit him the following summer.

"My secretary will contact you and send you your tickets." She thanked him, but Max's expression of disinterest, or was it disapproval, told her that she might have to reconsider the offer.

"Very generous," Max said, "but I don't suppose you noticed how he looked at you."

"Actually, I didn't. I was too busy looking at you."

A grin spread over Mark's face. "I could tell you how to settle this, but I wouldn't be minding my business."

"Every woman here, married or single, envies me," Leticia heard herself say, effectively changing the subject. "I've got the cream of the crop right here." She raised her head and squared her shoulders in a haughty manner. Both men laughed. "This is one heck of a great feeling."

"Don't you think the men aren't envying us?" Max said.

"Yeah, and they're wondering which one of us you belong with," Mark added.

Max glanced at his left wrist. "It's a quarter of ten. Let's go to my house. My folks will be asleep, but we won't disturb them."

At his home, they played jazz records, sipped liqueurs, drank more coffee and talked until two-thirty. "I wouldn't have thought that a university professor would be such enjoyable, down to earth company," Max said to Mark. "Next time you're here, we'll plan something special."

"My home is always open to you, Max. Jazz is still alive and thriving in New Orleans. When you come, don't forget your guitar or Dobro, and I'll hook you up with some boss players. And bring cuz with you. We'll have a great time."

"Thanks. I will definitely plan to do that. I'm glad we had a chance to spend some time together, Mark, because it's clear that you're the equivalent of a brother to Leticia."

"I am that. See you soon." They told Max good night, and as they drove to Leticia's house, Mark said, "The next time you and I meet, I want to see Max Baldwin's ring on your finger. You'll meet many men before you top him."

She didn't answer, because it wasn't entirely up to her. Moreover, she probably had at least one strike against her, and unless she demonstrated to Max that she believed and trusted in his love for her, she could probably forget about him. She would show him if only she knew how. She said as much to Mark.

He unlocked the door of her apartment, walked in with her, removed his jacket, took her hand and led her to the living room. "Let's sit here for a minute. You

don't show him by doing what you did in regard to the
dinner at the embassy. You did the opposite." He held
his hands up, palms out. "I know you had a reason, but
you should have called him and at least told him your
plans. He would have understood. That's the way you
show him that you trust his love for you. Get it?"

"I get it."

The next morning, Leticia went with Mark to the airport, and when she returned home, Willa told her that
she had a call from Kenyetta. "She said it was important."

"Thanks. I'll call her, but that girl's full of drama." She
dialed Kenyetta's number. "Hi, Ken, you called me?"

"Girl, your picture's all over the paper. What was
Mark doing up here, and who was that number twenty
with you and Mark? That brother was saying something."

"Mark was my guest, and you met Max Baldwin at the
Kappa dance."

"You go on, girl. If I'd met that brother, I'd still be
salivating. How about introducing me to him?"

"You met him, flirted with him, and he didn't like
you. Period."

"Wh-what?"

"You heard me. It wasn't the first time. You knew Wilson was my date, but you went after him, and you
planned it before you met him. You even had an affair
with a married man named Reggie or something. Why
don't you go after a man who is unattached? Why are
you always after somebody else's man?"

"You telling me that the great Max Baldwin is *your*
man? Don't make me laugh."

"He's mine, and you're welcome to try your luck. It wouldn't net you a damned thing. When do you want to meet him?"

"Well, ain't you some shit! You practically threw Wilson at me. And, honey, don't deal me aces and think I won't play. As for your stuffed shirt Mr. Baldwin, I don't need him. Some teachers at school want to start an ice-skating club. You want to join? It's only forty-five dollars a month."

"No thanks, Ken. I've never had time to learn how to skate, and now I have other things on my plate. Nice talking to you." She hung up. If Kenyetta ever learned how to apologize for her nastiness, maybe they could be friends. Leticia started to the bathroom and stopped. She *did* trust Max's love for her, otherwise she wouldn't have given Kenyetta that dare. What a revelation! She dialed Max's cell phone number.

"You said you wanted us to be together Monday evening. Would you have dinner with me at my place?"

He didn't hesitate. "I can't think of anything that would please me more. Give my love to Willa."

Laughter, springing from the happiness she felt, poured out of her. "She'll fix a great meal for you even if I don't give her your message. I can hardly wait for Monday evening."

"I'm counting the minutes."

"You find something real pretty and sexy to wear," Willa said when told of Leticia's plans, "and I'll take care of the food."

After a day in which she reveled in more congratulations from her colleagues and friends, including Allison, Broderick Nettleson and Robert Weddington, journalistic giants, she rushed home to prepare for her evening with Max and what she hoped would be a resolution of their relationship.

Willa had set the table for two with a white linen cloth and napkins, silver-edged white porcelain, white candles and a centerpiece of white rose buds and baby's breath. A fire crackled in the dining and living rooms.

"You're not eating with us, Willa?"

Willa walked into the dining room, braced her hip bones with her knuckles and stared at Leticia. "Tell me you didn't ask me that. You musta learned by now that three's a crowd. I'm trying to get the man to propose. I don't flute mushrooms and go to the trouble to make lobster bisque for myself. I thought you invited Mr. Baldwin to dinner because you wanted to make some headway with him. Maybe I should just give you corn fritters and warmed up ham."

Leticia wrapped her arms around the little woman and hugged her. "You're precious. Just keep your fingers crossed."

"I'll do no such thing. I'll be in there praying. Now, you take care of business. You hear?"

Leticia greeted Max in a red silk jumpsuit, her gold coin drop earrings, and her hair hanging around her shoulders. He handed her a dozen long-stemmed red roses in a crystal vase. She put the vase on the table near the door and opened her arms to him. *May as well start it off right,* she figured. He held her close for a minute and then gazed down into her face.

"I've looked forward to this for a long time, and I can't ever remember being this nervous about anything."

"Don't be. I'm the one who's nervous. You're all I've thought about this day. Thanks for the flowers. They're beautiful."

He picked a yellow one from the bunch. "This one's for Willa."

"She'll freak out. How's your mom?"

"Walking. She hasn't gotten up the stairs, but she's told herself she'll do it next week, and I expect she will. She and Ella send love to you."

"Thanks. I'll call them tomorrow." She looked at him, resplendent in a gray pin-striped suit, light gray shirt, and maroon tie with a paisley handkerchief. What a man!

"Thank you for my flower, Mr. Baldwin," Willa said when she served the first course of cold sour-cherry soup. "You're a real gentleman."

"You're destroying my physique," Max said to her when he tasted the dessert, brandy Alexander pie, the seventh and last course.

"It'll take more than this to mess you up," Willa said. "I put the coffee in the living room."

"I'm practically in a stupor." He stretched his long legs out in front of him, put his hands behind his head and leaned back against the living room sofa. "Nothing like a perfect cup of espresso to top a great meal. Come closer and put your head on my shoulder. I don't dare risk more with Willa in the kitchen."

After a second cup of espresso, he asked Leticia, "Do you want any more?" She shook her head, and he took the tray to the kitchen. "I called a taxi for Willa," he said when he returned. "Be back in a minute."

"Good night, ma'am," Willa called.

"Good night, Willa, and thanks so much for a wonderful dinner." She put Mantovani's recording of

"Charmaine" on the CD player, dimmed the chandelier and said a silent prayer.

When he returned, she went to meet him, and at last she was in his arms. He plunged his tongue into her mouth, his hands caressed her naked back, and she thought she would die of happiness. He sat in one of her big chairs and put her in his lap.

"I'm not willing for things to continue as they've been. Have you decided that I love you and that you can depend on my love for you to outweigh everything and anything else?" he asked.

"Yes. I don't doubt it for a second." He asked why she was so sure, and she told him of her conversation with Kenyetta in which she knew he wouldn't be tempted by another woman. "You can't imagine how good it felt to have that assurance not only of my self-confidence, but especially of my faith in what I mean to you."

"You were right about her. She's definitely not to my taste. And I'm not interested in others now that I love you." His arms tightened around her. "Sweetheart, I have a home, but it isn't a real one. Until my mother and Ella came to live with me, it was too big. Now, it's too small."

He moved her from his lap and dropped to his knees. "I'm deeply in love with you. Will you be my wife? I'll love and care for you and our children for as long as I live."

She slid down beside him, wrapped her arms around him and said, "It's what I want more than anything. I'll be proud to be your wife."

He put a diamond solitaire on the third finger of her left hand and kissed the tears that streamed down from her eyes. They held each other for a time, and then he got up, helped her to her feet and said, "Now comes the hard part."

"What do you mean?"

"I want to build us a house, and the only place I've seen that I like is in Westmoreland Hills, Maryland, about twenty minutes by car from Dupont Circle. Ella wants to retire and live with her children in Louisiana, and Mom's raring to get back to work."

"But surely you're not suggesting that she go back to her house? She's had a stroke, and she's vulnerable to another one or even to a heart attack."

She felt him stiffen. "What are you suggesting?"

"She should live with us. Sell the house you have now. With what you get from it and the nearly three hundred thousand I got from my grandfather's estate, we can build a nice house without going too heavily into debt."

He stared at her, but she plowed on. "If your mother wants privacy, the house can have a sitting room off her bedroom, though I don't recommend that."

"Why not?"

"Because it will look as if she's not part of our family."

When he closed his eyes and faced the ceiling, she wondered if she'd said the wrong thing. Well, she was not going to take it back. "She's still young, and you shouldn't put her off someplace to herself."

"If I'd been praying, I'd say my prayers had been answered. You have no idea how happy you've made me. Your inheritance is yours. I provide food and shelter for my family, and there's no arguing that. We can add all of our other expenses together and split the payment sixty-five percent for me and thirty-five for you, while you work, that is. Is that okay?" She nodded. He seemed bemused. "I know you will work, but are we going to have some children?"

She looked at the big diamond on her finger, buffed

it against the side of her right breast and grinned. "Absolutely. And as far as I'm concerned, we can start on
one right now."

"Hold on, sweetheart. It'll be six or seven months before we can move into our home."

"And in the meantime, we can live in your present
house."

"I told you this was the hard part. We can't live in sin
around my mother. When do we get married?"

"A month. March sixteenth. I'd say the fifteenth, but
that's the Ides of March and as Julius Caesar discovered,
it's a real no-no."

Laughter poured out of him as he picked her up,
carried her to her bed and made love to her until they
drained themselves and lay limp in each other's arms
like a pile of discarded clothes.

"I love you," she said.

He gazed down at her. "You're my life, my whole
world. My Lord! I love you so much."

Leticia awakened the following morning to what
seemed to her an unreal world. She sniffed the scent of
the previous night's lovemaking, bounded upright in
the bed and forced herself to look at the third finger of
her left hand. Yes. She had a diamond on it, and Max
Baldwin had placed it there. She threw up both arms
and yelled, "Whoopee." As quickly as she could, she completed her ablutions, dressed, changed the bedding, and
hurried to the kitchen, where she knew Willa waited to
know the results of her efforts.

"Well?" Willa asked her. "What happened?" She thrust
the ring-bearing hand to within an inch of Willa's face.

"Glory be! If my name ain't Willa Evans!" She opened

her arms and hugged Leticia. "Thank the Lord. I just love that man. Imagine he brought me a yellow rose. When you gon' tie the knot?"

"March the sixteenth. You want to come work with us?"

"You know I do if it's all right with Mr. Baldwin."

"His housekeeper is retiring, so we'll definitely need you."

After breakfast, she went back to her room and telephoned Allison. "This is Leticia. I have something to tell you. Max and I are engaged, and I'm wearing his ring."

"Leticia, I'm so happy. This is wonderful. We knew it had to happen, because we're very close to Max, and we've watched the changes in him since the night we were all over at Brod Nettleson's place. Hold it while I tell Bill."

After a minute, Allison came back to the phone. "Would you believe Max already called Bill and asked him to be his best man, and that husband of mine didn't tell me? Bill said Max is ecstatically happy."

"I was planning to ask if you'd be my matron of honor."

"I'll be delighted. It will be an honor. I'll come over this afternoon, and we'll talk about our dresses and all that. Okay?"

"Super. And we'll have some sandwiches or something, and tea or wine or gin and tonic. Whatever. Allison, I'm so excited." After hanging up, she telephoned Mark.

"Mark, guess what? As of last night, I'm wearing Max Baldwin's diamond ring on the third finger of my left hand."

"Get outta here! Way to go, cuz. I'll have to call him and congratulate him. When's the big day?"

She told him. "And I'd like you to escort me. Will you?"

"I would have been hurt if you hadn't asked me. It's my job, and it will be my pleasure."

"My best friend, Allison Wade Covington, is going to be my maid of honor, and nobody will ever guess how good it makes me feel to say that. I'll be in touch."

She'd come a long way. It hadn't been easy, but she'd made it.

Epilogue

Five years later, Leticia Langley-Baldwin attended her Howard University graduation class's fifth anniversary reunion festivities, the highlight of which was a reception and dance at the Willard.

"You seem a bit unsettled," Max said for the second time. "What's the problem?"

"Nothing. I . . . uh . . . I'm looking for someone. I heard that she's here, but I haven't seen her yet. Oh, look." She stopped dancing, took Max's hand and said, "Come with me. I see somebody I want you to meet."

After weaving her way around several dancers, she stopped, pasted a smile on her face and said, "I don't know if you remember me, Geraldine. I'm Leticia Langley-Baldwin. This is my husband, Max Baldwin, editor in chief of *The Tribune*. I work at *The Journal* as a columnist and associate editor. Max, this is Geraldine Thomas. I told you about her right after we became friends."

"I remember it well. How are you, Miss Thomas?"

Geraldine Thomas looked hard at Leticia. Then, she said, "I'm fine, Mr. Baldwin. I used to read your columns when you were at *The Journal*, but you don't write regularly any more." She turned to Leticia. "You look different. What happed with your hair? It's so long."

Leticia couldn't help grinning. "I wear extensions, Geraldine. Short and unruly hair is no longer worth discussing. And when you think about what Barack Obama accomplished, neither is skin color. By the way, I owe you more than you will ever imagine. Thank you for helping me learn what is important in life."

"Are you serious? I'd like to know what *I* taught *you*."

Leticia looked at Max and took his hand. "That success as an intellectual can't bring complete happiness, that we need to love others and to accept and trust their love for us."

Geraldine appeared skeptical. "I didn't teach you that. I'm not even sure I knew it myself."

"Oh, yes you did, and I thank you." She opened her small purse and took out pictures of Joel, age four, and Allison, age two. "These are our children."

Geraldine looked at the pictures. "These are going to be two brainy as hell kids. Nice to see you again, Leticia. Keep up the good work."

As they walked away, Max said, "Something tells me you hadn't planned to be that gracious."

"You're right, but it occurred to me that it was she who motivated me to change my life, and change it, I did."

In this thrilling debut novel from Carrie H. Johnson,
one woman with a dangerous job and a volatile past is
feeling the heat from all sides . . .

HOT FLASH

Coming in June 2016

Chapter One

Our bodies arched, both of us reaching for that place of ultimate release we knew was coming. Yes! We screamed at the same time . . . except, I kept screaming long after his moment had passed.

You've got to be kidding me, a cramp in my groin? The second time in the three times we had made love. Achieving pretzel positions these days came at a price, but man, how sweet the reward.

"What's the matter, baby? You cramping again?" he asked, looking down at me with genuine concern.

I was pissed, embarrassed, and in pain all at the same time. "Yeah," I answered meekly, grimacing.

"It's okay. It's okay, sugar," he said, sliding off me. He reached out and pulled me into the curvature of his body, leaving the wet spot to its own demise. I settled in. Gently, he massaged my thigh. His hands soothed me. Little by little, the cramp went away. Just as I dozed off, my cell phone rang.

"Mph, mph, mph," I muttered, "Never a moment's peace."

Calvin stirred. "Huh?"

"Nothin' baby, shhhh," I whispered, easing from his grasp and reaching for the phone from the bedside table. As quietly as I could, I answered the phone the same way I always did.

"Muriel Mabley."

"Did I get you at a bad time, partner?" Laughton chuckled. He used the same line whenever he called. He never thought twice about waking me, no matter the hour. I worked to live and lived to work—at least that's been my story for twenty years, the last seventeen as a firearms forensics expert for the Philadelphia Police Department. I had the dubious distinction of being the first woman in the unit and one of two minorities. The other was my partner, Laughton McNair.

At forty-nine, I was beginning to think I was blocking the blessing God intended for me. I felt like I had blown past any hope of a true love in pursuit of a damn suspect.

"You there?" Laughton said, laughing louder.

"Hee hee, hell. I finally find someone and you runnin' my ass ragged, like you don't *even* want it to last. What now?" I said.

"Speak up. I can hardly hear you."

"I said . . . "

"I heard you." More chuckles from Laughton. "You might want to rethink a relationship. Word is we've got another dead wife and again the husband swears he didn't do it. Says she offed herself. That makes three dead wives in three weeks. Hell, must be the season or something in the water."

Not wanting to move much or turn the light on, I let my fingers search blindly through my bag on the nightstand until they landed on paper and a pen. Pulling my hand out of my bag with paper and pen was another story. I knocked over the half-filled champagne glass also on the nightstand. "Damn it!" I was like a freaking circus act, trying to save the paper, keep the bubbly from getting on the bed, stop the glass from breaking, and keep from dropping the phone.

"Sounds like you're fighting a war over there," Laughton said.

"Just give me the address."

"If you can't get away . . . "

"Laughton, just . . . "

"You don't have to yell."

He let a moment of silence pass before he said, "1391 Berkhoff. I'll meet you there."

"I'm coming," I said and clicked off.

"You okay?" Calvin reached out to recapture me. I let him and fell back into the warmth of his embrace. Then I caught myself, sat up, and clicked the light on—but not without a sigh of protest.

Calvin rose. He rested his head in his palm and flashed that gorgeous smile at me. "Can't blame a guy for trying," he said.

"It's a pity I can't do you any more lovin' right now. I can't sugar coat it. This is my life," I complained on my way to the bathroom.

"So you keep telling me."

I felt uptight about leaving Calvin in the house alone. My son, Travis, would be home from college in the morning, his first spring break from Lincoln University. He and Calvin had not met. In all the years before this night, I had not brought a man home, except Laughton, and at least a decade had passed since I had any form of a romantic relationship. The memory chip filled with that information had almost disintegrated. Then along came Calvin.

When I came out, Calvin was up and dressed. He was five foot ten, two hundred pounds of muscle, the kind

of muscle that flexed at his slightest move. Pure lovely.
He pulled me close and pressed his wet lips to mine.
His breath mixed with a hint of citrus from his cologne
made every nerve in my body pulsate.

"Next time we'll do my place. You can sing to me
while I make you dinner," he whispered. "Soft, slow
melodies." He crooned *You Must Be a Special Lady* as he
rocked me back and forth, slow and steady. His gooey
caramel voice touched my every nerve ending, head to
toe. Calvin is a singer and owns a nightclub, which is
how we met. I was at his club with friends and Calvin
and I—or rather, Calvin and my alter ego, spurred on
by my friends, of course—entertained the crowd with
duets all night.

He held me snugly against his chest and buried his
face in the hollow of my neck while brushing his finger-
tips down the length of my body.

"Mmm . . . sounds luscious," was all I could muster.

The Interstate was dark, unusual no matter what
time, day or night.

In the darkness, I could easily picture Calvin's face,
bright with a satisfied smile. I could still feel his hot
breath on my neck, the soft strumming of his fingers on
my back. I had it bad. Butterflies reached down to my
navel and made me shiver. I felt like I was nineteen
again, first love or some such foolishness.

Flashing lights from an oncoming police car brought
my thoughts around to what was ahead, a possible suicide. How anyone could think life was so bad that they
would kill themselves never settled with me. Life's stuff
enters pit territory sometimes, but then tomorrow comes
and anything is possible again. Of course, the idea that
the husband could be the killer could take one even

deeper into pit territory. The man you once loved, who made you scream during lovemaking, now not only wants you gone, moved out, but dead.

When I rounded the corner to Berkhoff Street, the scene was chaotic, like the trappings of a major crime. I pulled curbside and rolled to a stop behind a news truck. After I turned off Bertha, my 2000 SAAB grey convertible, she rattled in protest for a few moments before going quiet. As I got out, local news anchor Sheridan Meriwether hustled from the front of the news truck and shoved a microphone in my face before I could shut the car door.

"Back off, Sheridan. You'll know when we know," I told her.

"True it's a suicide?" Sheridan persisted.

"If you know that, then why the attack? You know we don't give information in suicides."

"Confirmation. Especially since two other wives have been killed in the past few weeks."

"Won't be for a while. Not tonight anyway."

"Thanks, Muriel." She nodded toward Bertha. "Time you gave the old grey lady a permanent rest, don't you think?"

"Hey, she's dependable."

She chuckled her way back to the front of the news truck. Sheridan was the only newsperson I would give the time of day. We went back two decades, to rookie days when my Mom and Dad were killed in a car crash. Sheridan and several other news people accompanied the police to inform me. She returned the next day too, after the buzz faded. A drunk driver sped through a red light and rammed my parents' car head on. That is the story the police told the papers. The driver of the other car cooked to a crisp when his car exploded after hitting my parents' car, then a brick wall. My parents were on their way home from an Earth, Wind and Fire concert at the Tower Theater.

Sheridan produced a series on drunk drivers in Philadelphia, how their indiscretions affect families and children on both sides of the equation, which led to a national broadcast. Philadelphia police cracked down on drunk drivers and legislation passed with compulsory loss of licenses. Several other cities and states followed suit.

I showed my badge to the young cop guarding the front door and entered the small foyer. In front of me was a white-carpeted staircase. To the left was the living room. Laughton, his expression stonier than I expected, stood next to the detective questioning who I supposed was the husband. He sat on the couch, leaned forward with his elbows resting on his thighs, his head hanging down. Two girls clad in Frozen pajamas huddled next to him on the couch, one on either side.

The detective glanced at me, then back at the man. "Where were you?"

"I just got here, man," the man said. "Went upstairs and found her on the floor."

"And the kids?"

"My daughter spent the night with me. She had a sleepover at my house. This is Jeanne, lives a few blocks over. She got homesick and wouldn't stop crying so I was bringing them back here. Marcy and I separated, but we're trying to work things out." He choked up unable to speak anymore.

"At 3 a.m."

"I told you, the child was having a fit. Wanted her mother."

A tank of a woman charged through the front door, "Oh my God. Baby, are you all right?" She pushed past the police officer there and clomped across the room, sending those close to look for cover. The red-striped flannel robe she wore and pink furry slippers, size thirteen at least, made her look like a giant candy cane with feet.

"Wade, what the hell is happenin' here?" She moved in and lifted the girl from the sofa by her arm. Without giving him a chance to answer, she continued, "C'mon, baby. You're coming with me."

An officer stepped sideways and blocked the way. "Ma'am, you can't take her . . . "

The woman's head snapped around like the devil possessed her, ready to spit out nasty words followed by green fluids. She never stopped stepping.

I expect she would have trampled the officer, but Laughton interceded. "It's all right, Jackson. Let her go," he said.

Jackson sidestepped out of the woman's way before Laughton's words settled.

Laughton nodded his head in my direction. "Body's upstairs."

The house was spotless. White was *the* color: white furniture, white walls, white drapes, white wall-to-wall carpet, white picture frames. The only real color came in the mass of throw pillows that adorned the couch and a wash of plants positioned around the room.

I went upstairs and headed to the right of the landing, into a bedroom where an officer I knew, Mark Hutchinson, was photographing the scene. Body funk permeated the air. I wrinkled my nose.

"Hey, M & M," Hutchinson said.

"That's Muriel to you." I hated when my colleagues took the liberty to call me that. Sometimes I wanted to nail Laughton with a front kick to the groin for starting the nickname.

He shook his head. "Ain't me or the victim. She

smells like a violet." He tilted his head back, sniffed and smiled.

Hutchinson waved his hand in another direction. "I'm about done here."

I stopped at the threshold of the bathroom and perused the scene. Marcy Taylor lay on the bathroom floor. A small hole in her temple still oozed blood. Her right arm was extended over her head and she had a twenty-two pistol in that hand. Her fingernails and toenails looked freshly painted. When I bent over her body, the sulfur-like smell of hair relaxer backed me up a bit. Her hair was bone-straight. The white silk gown she wore flowed around her body as though staged. Her cocoa brown complexion looked ashen with a pasty, white film.

"Shame," Laughton said to my back. "She was a beautiful woman." I jerked around to see him standing in the doorway.

"Check this out," I said, pointing to the lay of the nightgown over the floor.

"I already did the scene. We'll talk later," he said.

"Damn it, Laughton. Come here and check this out." But when I turned my head, he was gone.

I finished checking out the scene and went outside for fresh air. Laughton was on the front lawn talking to an officer. He bee-lined for his car when he saw me.

"What the hell is wrong with you?" I muttered, jogging to catch up with him. Louder. "Laughton, what the hell—"

He dropped anchor. Caught off guard, I plowed into him. He waited until I peeled myself off him and regained my footing then said, "Nothing. Wade says they separated a few months ago and were trying to get it together, so he came over for some making up. He used his key to enter and found her dead on the bathroom floor."

"No, he said he was bringing the little girl home because she was homesick."

"Yeah, well then you heard it all."

He about-faced.

I grabbed his arm and attempted to spin him around. "You act like you know this one or something," I practically screeched at him.

"I do."

I cringed and softened my tone five octaves at least when I managed to speak again. "How?"

"I was married to her . . . a long time ago."

He might as well have backhanded me upside the head. "You never—"

"I have an errand to run. I'll see you back at the lab."

I stared after him long after he got in his car and sped off.

The sun was rising by the time the scene was secured: body and evidence bagged, husband and daughter gone back home. It spewed warm tropical hues over the city. By the time I reached the station, the hues had turned cold metallic grey. I pulled into a parking spot and answered the persistent ring of my cell phone. It was Nareece.

"Hey, Sis. My babies got you up this early?" I said, feigning a light mood. My babies are Nareece's eight-year-old twin daughters.

Nareece groaned. "No. Everyone's still sleeping."

"You should be too."

"Couldn't sleep."

"Oh, so you figured you'd wake me up at this ungodly hour in the morning. Sure, why not? We're talkin' sisterly love here, right?" I said. We chuckled. "I've been up since three anyway, working a case." I waited for her to say something, but she stayed silent. "Reece?" More silence. "C'mon, Reecey, we've been through this so many times. Please don't tell me you're trippin' again."

"A bell goes off in my head every time this date rolls around. I believe I'll die with it going off," Nareece confessed.

"Therapy isn't helping?"

"You mean the shrink? She ain't worth the paper she prints her bills on. I get more from talking to you every day. It's all you, Muriel. What would I do without you?"

"I'd say we've helped each other through, Reecey."

Silence filled the space again. Meanwhile, Laughton pulled his Audi Quattro in next to my Bertha and got out. I knocked on the window to get his attention. He glanced in my direction and moved on with his gangster swagger as though he didn't see me.

"I have to go to work, Reece. I just pulled into the parking lot after being at a scene."

"Okay."

"Reece, you've got a great husband, two beautiful daughters, and a gorgeous home, baby. Concentrate on all that and quit lookin' behind you."

Nareece and John had ten years of marriage. John is Vietnamese. The twins were striking, inheritors of almond-shaped eyes, "good" curly black hair, and amber skin. Rose and Helen, named after our mother and grandmother. John balked at their names because they did not reflect his heritage. But he was mush where Nareece was concerned.

"You're right. I'm good except for two days out of the year, today and on Travis's birthday. And you're probably tired of hearing me."

"I'll listen as long as you need me to. It's you and me,

Reecey. Always has been, always will be. I'll call you back later today. I promise."

I clicked off and stayed put for a few minutes, bogged down by the realization of Reece's growing obsession with my son, way more than in past years, which conjured up ugly scenes for me. I prayed for a quick passing, though a hint of guilt pierced my gut. Did I pray for her sake, my sake, or Travis's? What scared me anyway?

GREAT BOOKS,
GREAT SAVINGS!

When You Visit Our Website:
www.kensingtonbooks.com
You Can Save Money Off The Retail Price
Of Any Book You Purchase!

- **All Your Favorite Kensington Authors**
- **New Releases & Timeless Classics**
- **Overnight Shipping Available**
- **eBooks Available For Many Titles**
- **All Major Credit Cards Accepted**

Visit Us Today To Start Saving!
www.kensingtonbooks.com